Praise for *The Whites*

'This is high-octane literature . . . Richard Price gets to the heart of those stories that everyone else refuses to tell. *The Whites* manages to patrol New York and deepen our sense of the city and all its dark corners'
Colum McCann, author of *Let the Great World Spin*

'Richard Price is such a terrific writer – strong, fluent prose, and a gift for knowing who his characters are and how they work. *The Whites* is Richard Price at the top of his form and that means it is very good indeed'
Alan Furst, author of *Night Soldiers*

'A devastating depiction of crime and punishment'
Evening Standard

'*The Whites* is a fine book about the corrupted moral universe in which his all-too-believable New York cops have to work . . . Billy is confronted by one hard choice after another as matters build to a tense finale'
Mail on Sunday

'Price has constructed a maze of a novel that alternates between scenes of intense introspection and scenes driven by dialogue . . . Although *The Whites* is resolutely a crime novel, steeped in criminal activities of all kinds, including those of the officers who have sworn to combat crime, it is also a psychological thriller . . . Billy Graves might be a distant cousin of Michael Connelly's sharply etched Harry Bosch, of the LAPD, a man of brooding action, prone to doubt, errors, and guilt but (we can be assured) an exemplary individual'
Joyce Carol Oates, *New Y*

'Magnificent, hugely complex tale of criminality, revenge redemption *****'

'An engrossing tale of moral relativism and crude justice'
Iris

'Price is acknowledged as one of the great American writers, and this nuanced story of a rogue New York detective drawn back into the pa murder in the present amply proves it . . . This novel reveals Price's de skill at its finest . . . He is a legend, and deserves to be'
Daily

'Electrifying . . . rs and a strong narrat

xpress

A NOTE ON THE AUTHOR

RICHARD PRICE is an acclaimed fiction writer, his eight novels include *Clockers*, *Freedomland*, *Samaritan* and *Lush Life*. He is also an internationally renowned screenwriter for both film and television, having written among other works *Sea of Love*, *Ransom*, the Academy Award nominated *The Color of Money* and multiple episodes of *The Wire*. *The Whites* is his first straight-shot urban thriller. He lives in Harlem with his wife, the novelist Lorraine Adams.

BY THE SAME AUTHOR

The Wanderers
Blood Brothers
Clockers
Ladies' Man
The Breaks
Freedomland
Samaritan
Lush Life

THE
WHITES

RICHARD PRICE

BLOOMSBURY
LONDON · OXFORD · NEW YORK · NEW DELHI · SYDNEY

Bloomsbury Paperbacks
An imprint of Bloomsbury Publishing Plc

50 Bedford Square
London
WC1B 3DP
UK

1385 Broadway
New York
NY 10018
USA

www.bloomsbury.com

BLOOMSBURY and the Diana logo are trademarks of Bloomsbury Publishing Plc

First published in Great Britain 2015
This paperback edition first published in 2015

British Library Cataloguing-in-Publication Data
A catalogue record for this book is available from the British Library.

ISBN: HB: 9781408864579
       TPB: 9781408864586
       PB: 9781408864593
       ePub: 9781408864609

2 4 6 8 10 9 7 5 3 1

Printed and bound in Great Britain by CPI Group (UK) Ltd, Croydon CR0 4YY

To find out more about our authors and books visit www.bloomsbury.com.
Here you will find extracts, author interviews, details of forthcoming
events and the option to sign up for our newsletters.

To my astonishing wife, Lorraine Adams
On my block we still play . . .
On my block we still pray . . .

To my sublime daughters, Annie and Genevieve

To my mother, Harriet, and my brother, Randolph Scott

To the memory of Carl Brandt (1935–2013)

And to the memory of my father, Milton Price (1924–2008)

Who ever thought they would not hear the dead?
Who ever thought that they could quarantine
    Those who are not, who once had been?
                        —Stephan Edgar, "Nocturnal"

Death investigation constitutes a heavy responsibility, and as
such, let no person deter you from the truth and your own
personal commitment to see that justice is done. Not only for
the deceased, but for the surviving family as well.
                —Vernon Geberth, *Practical Homicide Investigation*
                                    (fourth edition)

As Billy Graves drove down Second Avenue to work, the crowds worried him: a quarter past one in the morning and there were still far more people piling into the bars than leaving them, everyone coming and going having to muscle their way through the swaying clumps of half-hammered smokers standing directly outside the entrances. He hated the no smoking laws. They created nothing but problems—late-night noise for the neighbors, elbow room enough for the bar-cramped beefers to finally start swinging, and a plague of off-duty limos and radio cabs all tapping their horns to hustle fares.

It was the night of St. Patrick's, worst of the year for NYPD's Night Watch, the handful of detectives under Billy's command responsible for covering all of felony-weight Manhattan from Washington Heights to Wall Street between one a.m. and eight a.m., when there were no active squads in any of the local precincts. There were other worst nights, Halloween and New Year's Eve for two, but St. Patrick's was the ugliest, the violence the most spontaneous and low-tech. Stompings, blunt objects, fists—more stitches than surgeries but some very malicious acting out.

One-fifteen in the a.m.: tonight, as always, the calls could come in at any time, but experience had taught him that the most fraught hours, especially on a drinking holiday, were between three a.m., when the bars and clubs started shutting down, everyone pouring out into the streets at once, and five a.m., when even the most hard-core animals were out of fuel and lurching off to oblivion. On the other hand, the city being the city, Billy never knew exactly when he'd see his pillow again. Eight a.m. could find him at a local precinct writing up bullets on an agg assault for the incoming day squad while the actor was either still in the wind or snoring in a holding cell; it could find him hanging around the ER at Harlem Hospital or Beth Israel or St. Luke's–Roosevelt interviewing family and/or witnesses while waiting for the victim to either go out of the picture or pull through; it could find him strolling around an outdoor crime scene, hands in pockets, toe-searching through detritus for shell casings; or, or, or, if the Prince of Peace was afoot and Yonkers-bound traffic was light, he could actually be home in time to take his kids to school.

There were gung ho detectives out there, even on the lobster shift, but Billy was not one of them. Mainly he hoped each night that most of Manhattan's nocturnal mayhem was not worthy of his squad's attention, just petty shit that could be kicked back to patrol.

"SEOUL MAN, HOW YOU BE," he drawled, stepping into the 24/7 Korean's across Third Avenue from the office. Joon, the night clerk with his gaffer-taped horn-rims, automatically began gathering up his regular customer's nightly ration: three sixteen-ounce Rockstar energy drinks, two Shaolin power gel squibs, and a pack of Camel Lights.

Billy cracked a can of Go before it could be bagged.

"Too much of that shit make you even more tired," the Korean delivering his standard lecture. "Like a boomerang."

"No doubt."

As he reached for his Visa card, the security monitor next to the register caught Billy in all his glory: football burly but slump-shouldered, his pale face with its exhaustion-starred eyes topped with half a pitchfork's worth of prematurely graying hair. He was only forty-two, but that crushed-cellophane gaze of his combined with a world-class insomniac's posture had once gotten him into a movie at a senior citizen's discount. Man was not meant to start work after midnight—end of story, pay differential be damned.

The Night Watch office, on the second floor of the Fifteenth Precinct and time-shared with Manhattan South Homicide, which occupied it during the day, looked like a cross between a fun house and a morgue. It was a drear, fluorescently lit scrum of gun-metal-gray desks, separated by plastic partitions brightened with autographed eight-by-tens of Derek Jeter, Samuel L. Jackson, Rex Ryan, and Harvey Keitel, along with mug shots, family snaps, and garish crime scene photos. An eight-foot glass tank filled with miniature sharklike catfish dominated one cinder-block wall, an embassy-sized American flag fronting the other.

None of his regular squad were in: Emmett Butter, a part-time actor, so fresh to the unit that Billy had yet to allow him to spearhead a run; Gene Feeley, who, back in the late '80s, was part of the team that broke up the Fat Cat Nichols crack empire, had thirty-two years on the Job, owned two bars in Queens, and was just there to max out his pension; Alice Stupak, who worked nights in order to be with her family during the day; and Roger Mayo, who worked nights in order to avoid being with his family during the day.

It wasn't unusual for the room to be deserted thirty minutes into the tour, given that Billy didn't care where his detectives spent the shift as long as they answered their phones when he needed them. He didn't see the point of making everyone sit at their desks all night like they were in detention. But in exchange for this freedom, if any one of them—with the exception of Feeley, who was so old-boy-wired into One PP that he could do or not do anything he wanted—if any one of them failed to pick up when he called, even once, they were gone from the squad, dead batteries, toilet drops, drop kicks, theft, Armageddon, the Rapture, or no.

Depositing the grocery bag in his minute windowless office, Billy walked out of the squad room and down a short hall to the dispatcher's desk, manned by Rollie Towers, a.k.a. the Wheel, a big Buddha boy in track pants and a John Jay college sweatshirt, ass ballooning off either side of his webbed Aeron chair as he fielded the incoming calls, taking all requests for Night Watch from the various crime sites and fending them off like a goalie.

"Well look, Sarge, my boss isn't in yet," Rollie nodding to Billy, "but my guess is here's what he's going to say. Nobody got hurt, guy can't even say for sure it was a gun. I'd just throw a good interview at him, wait for the Fifth Squad to come in tomorrow morning, see if it fits any kind of pattern they're working, all right? There's really not that much for us to do on this one. No problem . . . no problem . . . no problem."

Hanging up and swiveling to Billy: "No problem."

"Anything happening?" Billy reached for one of Rollie's Doritos, then changed his mind.

"Throwdown in the Three-two, both shooters female, one on the sidewalk, the other in the rear seat of a ghetto cab. They're like maybe a couple yards apart, six shots fired back and forth and get this: neither of them gets hit. How's that for sharpshootin'?"

"Was the cab moving?"

"It started out, one of the broads was chasing the other through the Eisenhowers, she jumps in the car, screams for the driver to haul ass, but the minute he sees the guns he jumps out and starts hoofing it back to Senegal, probably halfway there as we speak."

"Feets do yo' stuff."

"Butter and Mayo are up at the Three-two watching Annie Oakley and Calamity Jane sleep it off."

"And the driver? For real."

"They found him eight blocks away trying to climb a tree. They took him in for an interview, but he only speaks Wolof and French, so they're waiting on a translator."

"Anything else?"

"No sir."

"And who do I got." Billy dreaded the voluntary sign-ups, the ever-changing collection of overtime-hungry day-tour detectives who nightly padded out his paltry crew, the majority of them no good for anything after two a.m.

"There's three, supposedly, but one guy's kid got sick, another was last seen at a retirement racket down in the Ninth, so maybe you should find out if he's in any shape to come in at all, and you better check out what Central Park sent us."

"He's in? I didn't see anybody."

"Check under the rug."

Back in the squad room, the sign-up, Theodore Moretti, was hiding in plain sight, hunched over, elbows on knees, at the desk farthest from the door.

"I'm in the air," he hissed into his cell, "you're breathing me in right now, Jesse. I'm all around you . . ."

Short and squat, Moretti had straight black hair parted precisely down the middle of his skull and raccooned eyes that made Billy's seem limpid and tight.

"How you doing?" Billy stood over him, his hands in his pockets. But before he could introduce himself as the boss, Moretti just up and walked out of the office, coming back a moment later, still on the phone.

"You really think you can get rid of me that easy?" Moretti said to the lucky-in-love Jesse, Billy right then recognizing him for what he was and writing him off accordingly. Although money was the prime motivation for those signing up for a one-off tour with Night Watch, occasionally a detective volunteered not so much for the overtime but simply because it facilitated his stalking.

ONE FORTY-FIVE A.M. . . . THE SOUND of tires rolling over a side street full of shattered light bulbs was like the sound of Jiffy Pop achieving climax, the aftermath of a set test between the Skrilla Hill Killaz from the Coolidge Houses and the Stack Money Goons from the Madisons, four kids sent to St. Luke's for stitches, one with a glass shard protruding from his cornea like a miniature sail. Where they got all the light bulbs was anyone's guess.

By the time Billy and Moretti stepped out of their sedan, the 2-9 Gang Unit, six young men in windbreakers and high tops, were already harvesting collars, plasti-cuffing belly-down bangers like bundling wheat. The battleground itself was lined with two layers of rubberneckers: on the sidewalk, dozens of locals, a few, despite the hour, with kids in tow; overhead, an equal number of people hanging out the windows of the exhausted-looking SROs that ran along both sides of the narrow street.

Sporting a shaved head and calf-length denim shorts like a super-annuated playground bully, Eddie Lopez, the unit FIO, stepped to Billy, a dozen as yet unused plasti-cuffs running up his forearms like bangles.

"These two crews been trading smack on Facebook all week. We should have been here before they were."

Billy turned to Moretti. "The kids in the ER, go over with somebody from the Gang Unit, start taking interviews."

"Are you serious? They won't say shit."

"Nonetheless . . ." Billy waving him onward, thinking, One asspain down.

From the opposite end of the block, emerging out of the tree-lined darkness like a charging carnivore, came a battered livery cab, hitting its brakes nearly on top of the arrestfest, a fortyish woman in a bathrobe popping out of the rear seat before the car had even come to a full stop.

"They say my son could lose his eye!"

"Seven dollars," the driver said, extending his hand from the side window.

"Here we go," Lopez muttered to Billy before leaving his side. "Miss Carter, all due respect, we didn't tell Jermaine to be out here two in the morning hunting for Skrillas."

"How do you know what he was doing out here!" The streetlight turned her rimless glasses into disks of pale fire.

"Because I know him," Lopez said. "I've had dealings with him."

"He's going on a financial scholarship to Sullivan County Community College next year!"

"That's great, but it don't throw a blanket over it."

"I'm sorry, Charlene," one of the women said, stepping off the sidewalk, "all due respect, but truth be known you're just as much to blame as the boy who threw that glass."

"*Excuse* me?" Miss Carter cocking her head like a pistol.

"Seven dollars?" the driver said again.

Billy slipped him five bucks, then told him to reverse out of the block.

"I hear you every community meeting," the woman said, "you keep saying, My boy's a good boy, he's not mobbing for real, it's the environment, it's the circumstances, but this here officer is right. Instead of confronting your child you keep making excuses for him, so what do you expect?"

The kid's mother became big-eyed and motionless; Billy, knowing what was coming, hooked her arm just as she threw a punch at the other woman's jaw.

The crowd rippled with clucks and murmurs. A spinning cigarette landed on Billy's shoulder, but in these close quarters no real telling who had been the intended target, so *c'est la guerre*.

As he stepped back to brush the ash off his sport jacket, his cell rang: Rollie the Wheel.

"Boss, you remember the '72 Olympics?"

"Not really."

"The Munich massacre?"

"OK . . ."

"We had a guy there, helped take the silver in the four-by-four relays, Horace Woody?"

"OK . . ."

"Lives in Terry Towers in Chelsea."

"OK . . ."

"Patrol just called in, somebody stole his medal. You want us to take it? Could wind up being a media thing, plus Mayo's just sitting at his desk talking to himself again."

"Then have him head over to the St. Luke's ER and babysit Moretti, make sure he isn't boosting scalpels or something."

"And the case of the purloined medallion?"

Lopez peered at him over the head of a thirteen-year-old manacled Money Stacker. "Hey, Sarge? No sweat, we can take it from here."

"Send Stupak to meet me," Billy said into the phone. "I'm heading over now."

It sounded like a whole lot of nothing, but he had never met an Olympian before.

TERRY TOWERS WAS A TWELVE-STORY Mitchell-Lama semi-dump in the West Twenties, one step up from a housing project, which meant a few less elevators chronically out of commission and hallway odors not quite as feral. Apartment 7G itself was small, stifling, and untidy, dinner dishes still on the dinette table at two forty-five in the morning. In the middle of the cramped living room, Horace Woody, deep into his sixties but DNA-blessed with the physique of a lanky teenager, stood hands on hips in his boxers, the taut skin across his flat chest the color of a good camel hair coat. But his eyes were maraschinos, and his liquored breath was sweet enough to curl Billy's teeth.

"It's not like I don't have my suspicions as to who took the damn thing," Woody slurred, glaring at his girlfriend, Carla Garrett, who leaned against an old TV console covered with esoterically molded liqueur bottles and dog-eared photos in Lucite frames. She was maybe half his age, on the heavy side, with steady, realistic eyes. The droll, resigned twist of her mouth confirmed Billy's hunch about this one being a dummy of a run, at worst a slow-motion domestic, but he didn't really mind, fascinated as he was by the older man's uncanny youthfulness.

"Some people," Woody said, "they just don't want you to have no life in your life."

There was a light rapping at the front door; then Alice Stupak, five-four but built like a bus, eased into the apartment, her chronic rosacea and brassy short bangs forever putting Billy in mind of a battle-scarred, alcoholic Peter Pan.

"How's everybody doing tonight?" she blared with cheery authority. Then, zeroing in on the problem child: "How about you, sir? You having a good evening?"

Woody reared back with narrow-eyed disapproval, a look Billy had seen Alice get before, mainly, but not exclusively, from their suddenly off-balance male customers. But as fearsome as she was for some to behold, Billy knew her to be chronically lovelorn, forever pining after this detective or fireman, that bartender or doorman, endlessly driven to despair that all these potential boyfriends automatically assumed she was a dyke.

"Ma'am?" Stupak said, nodding to Woody's girlfriend. "Why are we here?"

Carla Garrett pushed off the console and started camel-walking toward the back of the apartment, curling her finger for Billy to follow.

THE HALO-LIT BATHROOM WAS A little too close, uncapped bottles and tubes of skin- and hair-care products rimming both the sink and the tub, used towels drooping from every knob, rod, and rack, stray hairs in places that made Billy look away. As Woody's girlfriend began rooting around inside a full and ripe laundry hamper, Billy's cell rang: Stacey Taylor for the third time in two days, his stomach giving up a little whoop of alarm as he killed this call from her like all the others.

"You got it in there?" Woody barked from the hallway. "I know you got it in there."

"Just go back and watch your TV," Stupak's voice coming through the closed door.

When the girlfriend finally stood upright from the hamper, she held the silver medal in her hands, as big around as a coffee saucer.

"See, when he gets his drink on he wants to pawn it and start a new life. He did it already a few times, and how much you think he got for it?"

"A few grand?"

"A hundred and twenty-five dollars."

"Can I hold it?"

Billy was disappointed in how light it was, but he felt a little buzzed nonetheless.

"See, Horace's OK most of the time, I mean, I certainly been with worse, it's just when he gets his hands on that Cherry Heering, you know? The man has got a alcoholic sweet tooth like a infant. I mean, you could get a good bottle of fifty-dollar cognac or Johnnie Walker Black, leave it on the table, he won't even crack the seal. Something tastes like a purple candy bar? Watch out."

"I want my damn medal back!" Woody yelled from farther away in the apartment.

"Sir, what did I just say to you?" Stupak's voice flattening with anger.

"Start a new life . . ." the girlfriend muttered. "All the pawnshops around here got me on speed dial for when it comes in. Hell, he wants to take off? I'll loan him the money, but this here is a piece of American history."

Billy liked her, he just didn't understand why a woman this lucid didn't keep a cleaner house.

"So what do you want me to do?"

"Nothing. I'm sorry they sent you. Usually some uniform guys from the precinct come up, mainly just because he was a famous athlete, and we play Where'd she hide it this time, but you're a detective, and I'm embarrassed they bothered you."

When they opened the bathroom door, Woody was back in the living room, sprawled on the vinyl-covered couch watching MTV with the sound off, his jellied eyes dimming into slits.

Billy dropped the medal on his chest. "Case solved."

Walking with Stupak to the elevators he checked the time: three-thirty. Ninety more minutes and the odds were he'd have gotten away with murder.

"What do you say?"

"You're the boss, boss."

"Finnerty's?" Billy thinking, What the hell, you cannot not celebrate, thinking, Just a taste.

"I ALWAYS WANTED TO GO to Ireland," Stupak shouted over the music to the dead-handsome young bartender. "Last year we had reservations and everything but, like, two days before the flight my girlfriend came down with appendicitis."

"You can always get on a plane by yourself, you know," he said politely enough, looking over her shoulder to wave at two women just coming through the door. "It's a very friendly country."

And that was that, the guy leaning across the wood to buss the new arrivals and leaving Stupak to blush into her beer.

"I've never been to Ireland myself," Billy said. "I mean, what for, I'm around Micks all day as it is."

"I never should've said 'girlfriend,'" Stupak said.

His cell rang, not the Wheel, thank God, but his wife, Billy race-walking out onto the street so she wouldn't hear the racket and start asking questions.

"Hey . . ." his voice downshifting as it always did when she rang him this deep into the night. "Can't sleep?"

"Nope."

"Did you take your Traz?"

"I think I forgot but I can't now, I have to get up in three hours."

"How about you take a half?"

"I can't."

"All right, just, you know, you've been here before, worse comes to worse, you'll have a tough day tomorrow but it won't kill you."

"When are you coming home?"

"I'll try and duck out early."

"I hate this, Billy."

"I know you do." His cell began to vibrate again; Rollie Towers on line two. "Hang on a sec."

"I really hate it."

"Just hang on . . ." Then, switching over: "Hey, what's up."

"Just when you thought it was safe to go back in the water."

"Fuck you, what do you got."

"Happy St. Patrick's Day," said the Wheel.

BY THE TIME BILLY AND most of his squad made it to Penn Station and then to the long, greasy, lower-level arcade that connected the Long Island–bound commuter trains to the subway platforms at the opposite end, the cops who were on the scene first, both Transit and LIRR undercovers, had taken control of the situation better than he would have expected. Not sure what to preserve of the one-hundred-yard blood trail, they had cordoned it all off with tape and garbage cans like a slalom run. They had also miraculously managed to round up most of the sodden homebound revelers who had been standing under the track information board when the assault occurred, corralling them into a harshly lit three-sided waiting room off the main concourse. Taking a quick peek into the room, Billy saw the majority of his potential witnesses sitting on hard wooden benches gape-mouthed and snoring, chins tilted to the ceiling like hungry baby birds.

"Looks like the guy got slashed under the board here, took off running, and ran out of gas by the subway," Gene Feeley announced, his tie unknotted and dangling like Sinatra at last call.

Billy was surprised to see Feeley there at all, let alone first detective on the scene. But then again, this was Feeley's thing, the old-timer usually disdaining any run unless there were at least three dead or a shot cop, front-page stuff.

"Where's the body?" Billy thinking he'd be lucky to see his kids by dinnertime.

"Just follow the yellow brick road," Feeley said, pointing to the red-brown sneaker prints that marked the way like bloody dance-step instructions. "It's one for the scrapbooks, I'll tell you that."

They arrived at the subway turnstiles just as a southbound express pulled into the station, more pie-eyed revelers disembarking onto the platform, ho-shitting, laughing, stumbling, blowing *vuvuzelas*, everyone assuming the wide-eyed stiff was just drunk except for the two middle-aged detectives from the Crime Scene Unit who had opted to take the subway to work, their forensics kits making them look like down-at-the-heels salesmen.

Billy snagged a wandering Transit detective. "Listen, we can't have trains stopping here right now. Can you call your boss?"

"Sarge, it's Penn Station."

"I know where we are, but I don't want a fresh herd of drunks stomping all over my scene every five minutes."

The victim lay on his side, neck and torso compressed into a hunch, his left arm and leg thrust straight out before him as if he were trying to kick his own fingertips. It looked to Billy as if the guy had been trying to jump the turnstile, bled out mid-vault, then froze like that, dying in midair before dropping like a rock.

"Looks like a high hurdler just fell off the front of a Wheaties box," Feeley said, then wandered off.

As a CSU tech began teasing the wallet out of the victim's formerly sky-blue jeans, Billy stopped marveling at his live-action lava cast and took his first good look at his face. Mid-twenties, with wide open, startled blue eyes, arched pencil-thin eyebrows, milk-white skin, and jet-colored hair, femininely handsome to the point of perversity.

Billy stared and stared, thinking, Can't be. "Is his name Bannion?"

"Hold the phone," the tech said, pulling out the guy's driver's license. "Bannion it is, first name—"

"Jeffrey," Billy said, then: "Fuck me sideways."

"Why do I know that name?" the CSU tech asked, not really interested in an answer.

Jeffrey Bannion . . . Billy immediately thought of calling John Pavlicek, then considered the hour and decided to wait at least until daybreak, although Big John might not mind being woken up for this one.

EIGHT YEARS EARLIER, A TWELVE-YEAR-OLD BOY named Thomas Rivera had been found beneath a soiled mattress in the tree house of his City Island neighbors, the Bannions. He had been bludgeoned to death, the bedding atop his body spattered with semen. John Pavlicek, back in the late '90s Billy's partner in anti-crime but at the time of the murder a detective assigned to the Bronx Homicide Task Force, was called in when the body was found by a cadaver dog three days after the boy went missing.

Jeffrey Bannion's oversized, learning-disabled younger brother, Eugene, admitted to the jerking off—the tree house was where he always went for that—but said that when he discovered the boy, he was already dead. Nineteen-year-old Jeffrey told Pavlicek that he himself was sick in bed that day, said Eugene had already told him that he had done it. But when the cops turned the lights on the younger Bannion, Eugene not only stuck to his story but couldn't even begin to speculate on how Thomas Rivera had come to be in the tree house or talk about what kind of weapon had done the deed, no matter how much trickery or cajoling the Homicides employed, and it made no sense that a fifteen-year-old that dim could hold out on them.

Pavlicek liked the older Bannion for it from the jump, but they couldn't shake his sick-bed story, and so the younger brother went to the Robert N. Davoren juvenile center at Rikers, a Bloods, Ñetas, and MS-13 petri dish, where he was placed in Gen Pop without the requisite psych eval, a big oafy white kid who tended to throw indiscriminate punches when he was freaked, and his murder, only five days into his incarceration, racked up nearly as many headlines as that of the boy he had allegedly killed.

Within days, despite Pavlicek's full-bore campaigning, the Rivera homicide was marked "closed by arrest," formally shutting down any further investigative work. Shortly after that, Jeffrey Bannion packed his bags and moved in with various relatives out of state. At first, Pavlicek tried to swallow his frustration by burying himself in other jobs—although he never lost touch with Thomas Rivera's parents and he never lost track of Bannion's whereabouts—but when he learned, through connections, of two incidents of assault in which the vics were preadolescent males, one in each of the small towns Jeffrey was living in at the time, neither investigation leading to an arrest, his obsession with nailing this kid returned in raging full effect.

Eventually Bannion moved back to New York, sharing a house in Seaford, Long Island, with three friends. Pavlicek, still on him like Javert, reached out to both the Seventh Precinct in neighboring Wantagh and the Nassau County Detective Bureau, but either Jeffery had kept his nose clean or he had gotten even slicker with age. The last anyone had heard of him—and most galling of all—was that he had recently applied to the auxiliary PDs of a dozen Long Island townships and had been offered training by three.

"MY SUPERVISOR WANTS TO KNOW how long we have to be shut down for," the returning Transit detective said.

"We'll be as fast as we can be," Billy said.

"He says we got to mop that blood up out there by five-thirty, same for removing the body. That's when the commuters start coming in earnest."

Clean it up or preserve it . . . Clean it up or preserve it . . . Somebody will complain; somebody always complains.

As another mob staggered off the latest 2 train into Penn Station, a teenage girl stared goggle-eyed at Bannion for a second, looked up searchingly into her boyfriend's eyes, then wheeled and puked onto the platform, adding her DNA to the mix.

"It's a bad night for this," the Transit cop said.

Stepping back into the seamy arcade, Billy stared down the length of the tape. Other than the still-congealing blood, the killing floor—a debris field of candy wrappers, Styrofoam cups, the odd article of clothing, a shattered liquor bottle barely held together by the adhesive on its label—gave up too much and nothing at all.

As CSU continued to bag and photograph, as the LIRR and Transit detectives and his own crew began to work the waiting room, wandering among the semiconscious potential wits like a squadron of visiting nurses, Billy noticed that one of the commuters sleeping there had what appeared to be blood on his Rangers jersey.

He took a seat next to him on a wooden bench, the kid's head tilted back so far it looked as if someone had slit his throat.

"Hey you." Billy nudged him.

The kid came out of it, shaking his head like a cartoon animal just whacked with an anvil.

"What's your name."

"Mike."

"Mike what."

"What?"

"How'd you get the blood on you, Mike?"

"Me?" Still whipping his head from side to side.

"You."

"Where . . ." Looking at his jersey, then: "That's blood?"

"You know Jeffrey Bannion?"

"Do I know him?"

Billy waiting, One Mississippi, two . . .

"Where is he," the kid asked.

"So you know him? Jeffrey Bannion?"

"What if I do?"

"You see what happened?"

"What? What are you talking about, what happened?"

"He's been stabbed."

The kid shot to his feet. "What? I'll fucking kill them."

"Kill who."

"What?"

"Who do you want to kill."

"How the fuck should I know? Who did it. You leave them to me."

"Did you see it?"

"See what?"

"When was the last time you saw him? Where was he, who was he with."

"He's like a brother to me."

"Who was he with."

"How should I know. What am I, his bitch?"

"His what? Where do you live."

"Strong Island."

"More specifically."

"Seaford."

"Who else was with you, point out your posse."

"My posse?"

"Who, sitting here, in this waiting room, was with you tonight, everybody going home to Seaford."

"I'm no rat."

"I'm asking who are his friends."

Mike turned his head as if it were on a rusty turret, taking in half the dull-eyed commuters around him.

"*Ey,*" he blared. "You hear what happened?"

No one even turned his way.

"Anybody carrying anything tonight?" Billy asked.

"Like weed?"

"Like a weapon."

"Everything's a weapon."

"How'd you get that blood on you, again?"

"What blood," the kid said, touching his face.

"Was anybody in your pos . . . was anybody beefing with anybody tonight?"

"Tonight?" The kid blinked. "Tonight we're going into the city."

Billy decided to send him and everybody else to Midtown South in order to sleep it off, then be reinterviewed. His guess was that these interviews would yield nothing. He was also pretty sure that with half the eastern seaboard stomping through the crime scene like migrating wildebeests, the forensics would be useless as well. His money was on the surveillance tape.

HE CALLED IT IN TO his division captain, the guy instantly starting to quack like a duck as if Billy had killed Bannion himself, worked for a while with the Transit cops down by the subways and the LIRR detectives under the track information board, and then, praying for a money shot, climbed the stairs to the cramped room where the monitors were set up, only to be told by the tech on duty that the master hard drive that uploaded all the security footage had been damaged by a coffee spill a few hours before and the only way to salvage the film at this point was to send it out for file retrieval, a process that could take days, if not weeks.

Back down on the floor, needing one of his squad to supervise the witness transport, Billy started to approach Feeley but balked when he saw him yakking it up with a white-haired deputy inspector, the two of them probably swapping memories of their time together chasing Pancho Villa. He went looking for Stupak instead and found her standing in front of a riot-gated calzone shop interviewing a maintenance worker.

As soon as he told Stupak what he wanted done, her glance reflexively went to Feeley. "What," she muttered, "General Grant too busy prepping for Gettysburg?"

No one liked having Feeley on the squad, but no one liked him less than Alice, a hater of both the old boy network and shirkers in general. It was personal, too: despite her sixteen years on the Job, including seven in Emergency Services and three with the Violent Fugitive Apprehension Team, the old bastard took way too much pleasure in addressing her now and then as Babydoll.

Once Stupak was on her way, Billy fielded another overwrought call from his division cap, followed by one from the squad commander of Midtown South. Then, at seven a.m., with the scene secured and none of the possible witnesses in any shape to talk, Billy decided to sneak back to Yonkers just long enough to take his kids to school.

AT THIS HOUR THE TRAFFIC on the northbound Henry Hudson Parkway was mercifully light, and by seven forty-five he was turning onto his street. As he pulled up to the house, he saw Carmen standing on a six-foot ladder in front of the carport, trying to extract the deflated basketball jammed between the portable hoop and the backboard, the thing having been stuck like that since January, when it became too cold for the kids to play.

"Just poke it, Carm."

"I tried. It's in too tight."

Sitting behind the wheel in a half-trance of exhaustion, Billy watched her try to muscle the ball free, the morning sun turning her polyester nurse's whites the color of ice.

She was his second wife. His first, Diane, an African-American art therapist, had left him in the wake of the highly publicized protests over his accidental and near-fatal shooting of a ten-year-old Hispanic boy in the Bronx. In all fairness, the bullet that hit the kid had first passed through its intended target, a Dusted giant armed with an already bloodied lead pipe. At first, Diane, only twenty-three at the time to his twenty-five, tried to hang fire with him, but after the papers picked it up and a Bronx reverend with a fat press book set up a month-long protest vigil around their Staten Island home, she gradually came apart and then bailed.

Billy had met Carmen when he was in the Identification Squad posted to the ME's office, having been sent there from anti-crime as a form of internal exile after the shooting. She had come in that day to identify Damian Robles, until his OD, thirty-six hours earlier, her living husband.

Despite being a heroin addict, Robles had been a mixed martial arts professional with a ridiculously chiseled physique, and it embarrassed Billy to admit that two days after death the guy still looked better than Billy did on the best day of his own life.

Dead was dead, however, and twenty minutes after first laying eyes on her, as they stood side by side staring at the corpse through a long rectangular window, he just came out and said it: "What were you doing married to a lowlife like that?"

But instead of going for his face or screaming bloody murder, she calmly answered, "I thought he was what I deserved."

Within a month they were leaving clothes in each other's apartments.

Within a year they were sending out save-the-dates.

Her initial attraction to him, or so he thought at the time, was a no-brainer: sudden widow looking about and glomming onto the protective policeman standing by her side. Billy had always been a sucker for any kind of My Hero vibes when they occasionally came his way, but in truth he had fallen in love purely because of her looks and the way she sounded: her huge, smudge-rimmed eyes in a heart-shaped face, her skin the color of light toast, and that voice—lazy and smoky when she felt that way and backed by a deep and easy laugh that made him drowsy with pleasure. Lust was there from the beginning, but every other long-playing thing—trust, tenderness, companionability, et cetera—had only come about with time.

Not that living with her was any walk in the park. Her mood swings were fierce, and she was prone to savage dreams, often waking him up with her sleep talk, semicoherent tear-choked pleas to be left alone. And what he at first thought was a temporary desire for a protector in her life had over the years morphed into a river of visceral, mostly inarticulate need for him, a neediness he never quite understood but responded to with everything he had. She could never wear him out with her demands; there was something about her that made him want to be the best possible version of himself. He loved her, loved to come through for her, loved that what he had always thought of with embarrassment as his flatline personality, his bland stolidness, could become the rock in the raging sea of another soul's life.

Still, there was something inside her he could never quite get at. Sometimes he felt like a knight assigned to protect a maiden from a dragon that only she could see, and so he paid attention to the words when she cried out in her sleep, when her half-panicked rants became less coherent and maybe closer to the bone, but he was not a particularly analytical individual, so all his secret studying came to nothing. And given that he had been raised in a home in which he'd been taught to take people as they were, no questions asked, a home in which the character trait prized above all else was an Apache level of forbearance, he would die before straight up asking his wife of twelve years, the mother of his two sons, Who Are You.

"WHERE ARE THE SURVIVALISTS?" HE called from the car.

"You're taking them?" she asked.

"Yeah, but I left a body at Penn Station, so I got to go back right after."

"I can take them."

"No, just where are—"

"*Declan!*"

Billy's all-night eyelids butterflied in pain: Carmen's initial solution for finding anyone was to yell.

Stalling for a last heartbeat of inaction, he let his gaze stray to their front porch, where Carmen's green nylon St. Patrick's Day banner, all shamrocks and wee people, snapped in the wind, one day past its expiration date, although Billy knew that by dinnertime it would be replaced with the Easter banner, bunnies and parti-colored eggs on a backdrop of powder blue.

"I'll get them," he finally said, climbing out of the car like a man with prosthetic hips.

THE INTERIOR OF THE HOUSE was a rambling, amiable mess—a war chest's worth of boys' toys and sports gear strewn around the living room, smothering the worn brocade couch and matching easy chairs; a big yellow eat-in kitchen with its painted-wood "country" table perpetually covered with bills, circulars, condiments, and the odd hat or glove; three thin-walled bedrooms all crying out for a fresh coat of paint; and a sunken den that for some reason always smelled like mushrooms. And wherever one looked was evidence of Carmen's obsession with country cornball: real, ceramic, or papier-mâché Indian corn and pumpkins resting on every available surface, homely homilies inscribed on chain-hung plaques, farm-stand-purchased whirligigs, milkmaids painted on wooden ovals, and enough framed sketches of barnyards, thatched cottages, and lonely rural lanes to fill a Hallmark museum.

All of this occasionally set Billy's teeth on edge, but given his wife's childhood and early adolescence in the cracked-out Bronx of the late 1980s, her later teen years in the notorious East Metro section of Atlanta, and her current job as a triage nurse in the St. Ann's knife-and-gun-club ER, he didn't have the heart to question her taste in decor. In fact, he couldn't care less what the house looked like, as long as it made her happy. All he cared about was his books, the shelves in the den filled with crime novels written mainly by ex-cops, retirement for dummies self-help volumes, sports memoirs, and real estate study guides, these last foisted on him by John Pavlicek, who was hell-bent on hiring him to help run his empire of apartment buildings the moment Billy put in his papers.

Looking for the kids, Billy came upon his six-year-old, Carlos, sitting on the side of his bunk bed dressed in full camo, staring at his seventy-eight-year-old grandfather asleep under the kid's X-Men blanket. Billy's dad was a well-remembered city-wide Chief of Patrol who had first made his name as a foot soldier with the Tactical Patrol Force, a.k.a. Riot Squad, during the anti-war, let-it-burn days of the late '60s. These days, however, the old guy tended to go in and out of thinking that his grandsons were both Billy and that he was still living in his first home in Fordham Heights with his dead wife. Additionally, he often got up and crept into someone else's bed in the middle of the night, either one of the kids' or Billy and Carmen's, making pajamas mandatory sleep-wear for one and all.

"Let's go, buddy."

"Is Grandpa gonna die?" Carlos asked calmly.

"Not today."

Eight-year-old Declan, also wearing camo from boots to forage cap, was on his knees in the living room, trying to get the pet rabbit out from under a couch with a hockey stick, the huddled, personality-less thing hissing and sneezing like a Komodo dragon.

"Dec, just leave him there."

"What if he bites an electric cord?"

"Then we'll have rabbit for dinner. Let's go."

Just as they finally left the house, Billy's cell rang, the division captain again, and he locked himself in the car before the kids could get inside and screw his play.

"Hey, boss."

"Where are you at?"

"Midtown South doing the bullets and waiting for some of the witnesses to revive."

"Why'd you let them clean up the scene?"

"Because it's Penn Station, you have fifty thousand people walking through."

"It's a crime scene."

"Again, it's Penn Station. It's the crossroads of the Western world."

"What are you, Radio Free America? Since when does Transit call the shots?"

"This time they were right." Then adding: "In my opinion."

"How about the security tapes."

"Computer glitch."

"Computer glitch."

"They sent them over to TARU."

"Dad!" Declan belted out, slapping the car window.

"Billy!" Carmen came over with the frozen basketball. "What the hell are you doing? They're going to be late!"

"Who was that?" the division cap asked.

"Boss, one of the wits just gave up a name. I'll call you back."

AFTER DROPPING OFF THE BOYS at their school, Billy headed back into the city, wrote up his bullets for the day-tour detectives in Midtown South—it was their headache now—debriefed a few bosses, fended off a police shack reporter, ducked a TV camera, and got back in the car. When he finally re-returned to the house at one p.m., Millie Singh, the alleged housekeeper, was watching *Mob Wives Chicago* with his father in the living room, neither of them acknowledging his presence.

Millie barely knew her way around a mop, prepared spicy Indo-Caribbean dishes that would tear your throat out, and tended to take naps on the job. But back in the day she had been the only one in their moonscape of a precinct with guts enough to take the stand in a gang-related homicide, and as a result she'd had to sleep in her bathtub in order to protect herself from the nightly gunshots coming through her windows, until Billy and the others moved her into one of Pavlicek's newly renovated buildings. Ten years later, at roughly the same time that Billy's father had first been diagnosed with dementia, Millie's teenage daughter moved back to Trinidad to live with her father and she lost her job at Dunkin' Donuts. Hiring her as their housekeeper had seemed like a good idea at the time, and in all fairness to Millie, the kids loved her, she loved his dad, and she was in possession of a valid driver's license. Besides, Carmen liked to do her own housecleaning, if you could call it that.

Billy stepped into the kitchen, poured himself half a milk glass of vodka and cranberry juice—the only thing that could put him to sleep at this hour—and went into the bedroom. He stowed his Glock 9 on the top shelf of his closet behind a shoe box filled with old bank statements, and with a last burst of energy called Pavlicek to give him a heads-up about Bannion.

"Hey."

"I heard," Pavlicek said.

"What do you think," Billy said, crawling into the cool swan boat of a bed.

"That there's a God after all."

"It was a freaky scene."

"I heard that too."

"Heard from who?"

"The drums."

"Do the Riveras know?"

"I called them this morning."

"How'd they take it?"

"The mister was cool, Mom not so good. I'm going out to City Island to see them later."

"Good." Billy's eyes felt like sandpits.

"I want you to come with me."

"John, I'm sleeping."

"You saw the dead fuck. They might need to ask you things."

"Come on, this is private with you and them."

"Billy, I'm asking you."

He gargled the last of his drink, crunched on a sliver of ice. "Make it about six, I just got into bed."

"Thank you."

"You owe me."

"Afterwards we can pick up Whelan, then head downtown to the restaurant."

"The dinner's tonight?"

"Yes sir."

"OK, let me sleep."

"Hey," Pavlicek held on, "what's the most bullshit word in the English language."

"Closure."

"Give that man a cigar," Pavlicek said, then hung up.

. . .

HE HAD FORGOTTEN ALL ABOUT the dinner, the monthly steak house reunion of the self-christened Wild Geese, seven young cops averaging three years on the Job, fresh to anti-crime in the late '90s, a tight crew given a ticket to ride in one of the worst precincts of the East Bronx. Of the original seven, one had moved to Arizona after retirement, and one had died from a three-pack-a-day habit, leaving a hard-core five: Billy, Pavlicek, Jimmy Whelan, Yasmeen Assaf-Doyle, and Redman Brown.

They had been something else back then, preternaturally proactive, sometimes showing up at the trouble spots two steps ahead of the actors, and they were decathletes, chasing their prey through backyards and apartments, across rooftops, up and down fire escapes, and into bodies of water. Many cops administered beatdowns as a penalty for being made to run, but the WGs got high off the chase, often treating their collars post-arrest like members of a defeated softball team. They thought of themselves as a family, and family membership was extended automatically to those in the neighborhood they liked: the owners of bodegas, bars, barbershops, and take-out joints, but also the numbers runners— the numbers going back to the Bible as far as they were concerned—a few of the old school reefer men, and a handful of restaurateurs who had secret gaming rooms upstairs or in the basement where the WGs could throw some bones and drink for free.

As far as stolen goods went, fell-off-a-truck merchandisers oftentimes offered NYPD courtesy discounts on everything from kids' backpacks to designer pantsuits to power tools. A drink here, a standing hump there, a cut-rate cashmere pullover now and then—no one in the Wild Geese took money, demanded a sin tax, or even lost their civility. Although they were periodically called on to corral a few for the requisite trip to the Tombs, they generally tolerated whores who were reasonably discreet and, as an added bonus, funny. Nonviolent junkies were left on the street and used as informants. Their dealers, however, were fair game.

And if one of the family got hurt by a bad player—a street girl having her eye blackened or finger broken by her Slapaho Mac Daddy, a Wild Geeser catching a paintball or pellet-gun round in the back, a casino operator or bodega owner taken off by the local mokes—then they would all descend as one, and the beatdowns and banishments would commence. It was all about family; they would do the job as required, but they would really step to the fore for those they deemed "worthy," given that some people in the East Bronx, as elsewhere, as everywhere, would always try to get high to escape, want a little extracurricular loving, chase a money dream scribbled in numbers across a crumple of paper. Not all cops were as laissez-faire in their attitude toward the outriders of the precinct, but the Wild Geese, in the eyes of the people they protected and occasionally avenged, walked the streets like gods.

The good news and the bad news was that their kind of high-yield police work was a fast track to a gold shield. Within five years, all the original WGs had moved on, the irony being that Billy, who was the youngest and least experienced, had been the first one to get the nod. After the double shooting, which earned him both a citation for bravery and a civilian review board hearing, the department, in its slap/caress way, decided to promote him in order to bury him—in his case, to the basement of the morgue, since the Identification Squad, like any other, was composed primarily of detectives.

At the end of the day, some of the WGs became better detectives than street soldiers, others lesser cops behind their gold shields. Some discovered gifts never used before; others lost the opportunity to use the gifts they had had all along.

And it was also as detectives, dispersed to various squads across the boroughs, that, like Pavlicek coming up against a Jeffrey Bannion, they had all met their personal Whites, those who had committed criminal obscenities on their watch and then walked away untouched by justice, leaving their obsessed ex-WG hunters heading into retirement with pilfered case files to pore over in their offices and basements at night, still making the odd unsanctioned follow-up call: to the overlooked counterman in the deli where the killer had had a coffee the morning of the murder, to the cousin upstate who had never been properly interviewed about that last phone conversation he had with the victim, to the elderly next-door neighbor who left on a Greyhound to live with her grandchildren down in Virginia two days after the bloodbath on the other side of the shared living room wall—and always, always, calling the spouses, children, and parents of the murdered: on the anniversary of the crime, on the victims' birthdays, at Christmas, just to keep in touch, to remind those left behind that they had promised an arrest that bloody night so many years ago and were still on it.

No one asked for these crimes to set up house in their lives, no one asked for these murderers to constantly and arbitrarily lay siege to their psyches like bouts of malaria, no one asked to feel so helplessly in the grip of this nonstop black study that they had no choice but to pursue and pursue. But there they all were: Pavlicek forever stalking Jeffrey Bannion; Jimmy Whelan pursuing Brian Tomassi, the ringleader of a white street gang who, in the aftermath of 9/11, had chased a Pakistani kid into an oncoming car; Redman Brown stalking Sweetpea Harris, the murderer of a college-bound high school baller who had made him look bad in a playground pickup game; Yasmeen Assaf-Doyle forever tracking Eric Cortez, a twenty-eight-year-old small-time felon who had stabbed to death a reedy myopic ninth grader because the kid had talked to Cortez's fourteen-year-old girlfriend at their school.

And Billy himself, in his first year aboveground as a precinct detective after too many living below like a mushroom among the dead, shackled for all time to Curtis Taft, the killer of three females in one evening: Tonya Howard, a twenty-eight-year-old who had just dumped the man who would become her murderer; her fourteen-year-old niece, Memori Williams, who happened to be sleeping over the night Taft decided to get back at his ex; and Dreena Bailey, Tonya's four-year-old daughter by another man. Three shots, three dead, then right back to bed, Curtis Taft, as far as Billy was concerned, the most black-hearted of the Whites. But so were they all, if you asked each of their star-crossed hunters.

Twenty years after they had started out running the streets like high-topped commandos, almost all of them were living new lives. Redman got shot through the hips in a hostage situation, went out on a three-quarters medical, and took over his father's funeral parlor in Harlem. Fast-and-loose Jimmy Whelan put in his papers before he could be fired and became an itinerant building super, living from year to year in some of the finer basement apartments of the city. Yasmeen, who couldn't take the boss mentality, quit to become assistant head of crimes against students at a university in lower Manhattan and achieved a black belt in complaining about her new bosses over there. Pavlicek, already on the make while still in uniform, just got too busy being rich. Only Billy, the baby of the group, still hung in. He had no reason not to: as his father had declared over a raised glass on the night of Billy's graduation from the academy: "Here's to God, because the man had to be a natural-born genius to invent this job."

AN HOUR AFTER HIS PHONE call with Pavlicek, Billy was dreaming about Jeffrey Bannion—nude and adrift in an oversized bell jar filled with red punch—when one of the kids came home from school and slammed the front door as if he were being chased by wolves. A moment later he heard Carlos yelling at his brother, "You quit so I win!," followed by Carmen shouting, "What did I tell you about yelling in the house!"

Even so, Billy managed to fall back asleep for half an hour, until the sheets began to rustle and Carmen, naked, nuzzled into the small of his back, her left hand reaching around to burrow into his boxers. Billy was so tired he thought he would die, but her hand on his prick was her hand on his prick.

"We had three kids brought in with gunshot wounds three days in a row," she murmured in his ear. "Turns out the second kid shot the first for shooting someone in his crew, the third shot the second in retaliation, and the best friend of the second shot the third for the same reason. It was like the bonehead Olympics. Anything going on down there?"

"Give me a second, will you?"

After twelve years they were doing pretty good, he thought, hitting it twice a week more often than once, and they seemed to be putting on weight apace of each other, also not so bad, Carmen still able to pull off wearing a two-piece, although Billy kept his T-shirt on at the beach. In the beginning, there wasn't a physical position or a sexual fancy off-limits, but as they grew more comfortable with each other, it always seemed like straight-up missionary, after a little of this and a little of that, unfailingly ended with both of them afterward euphorically raiding the refrigerator in search of the next fun thing to do.

"So," she said.

And in a rush of bleary optimism Billy decided that maybe he didn't need to sleep this week after all.

MILTON RAMOS

The handcuffed drunk in the backseat had lost three thousand dollars betting on the NCAA Final Four and decided that it was the fault of his wife's face, which he promptly set to rearranging.

"March Madness. I was you, that would be my defense," Milton's partner said without turning around.

"Fuck her, and fuck you."

"You know what? Stick with that attitude, because judges hate sincere remorse."

"And what are you?" the drunk said, squinting at Milton sitting silently behind the wheel.

"Excuse me?" Seeking the guy's eyes via the rearview mirror.

"You know what *SPIC* stands for?" The drunk leaned forward, his alcohol-fueled malice expanding, searching. "Spanish Indian Colored. Otherwise known as Greaser, Savage, Nigger. Put them all together you get one big fucking unibrow Monkey. You."

Milton pulled the car over alongside Roberto Clemente Park, then turned off the ignition. He sat there for a moment with his hands palms up in his lap.

"Can we not do this?" his partner asked with an air of resignation.

"Ook, ook," from the rear seat.

Milton popped the trunk via the lever beneath the steering wheel, got out, and walked to the back of the car.

"The fuck's he doing?" the drunk asked.

"Shut up," the partner said, sounding both angry and a little depressed.

The rear door opened abruptly and Milton lifted the prisoner out of the car by his elbow. In his free hand he carried a telescoping baton and a grease-smudged towel.

"The fuck are you doing?"

Without answering, Milton frog-walked his prisoner into the maw of the park until he found what he considered a suitable spot. Not too open, not too constricted, and branches low enough to grip.

"What are you doing?"

"Down, please?"

"What?"

Milton popped him in the chest and the drunk was suddenly lying faceup in the grass, his shoulders on fire from the impact of landing with his hands cuffed behind his back.

"Jesus, man, what are you doing?" Near-pleading now, his voice suddenly much closer to sober than a few minutes earlier.

MILTON KNEW HE SHOULD NEVER have been given a gold shield. It was a misguided reward for being in the wrong place at the wrong time, a barbershop during a holdup in his own Bronx neighborhood when two assholes with .38s had come in while he was buried in aprons, towels, and shaving cream. The shop was a known numbers drop, easy pickings, and after they kneecapped one of the barbers, Milton kicked his chair around on its swivel and started shooting from beneath his polyester body bib, which promptly caught fire. By the time his barber whipped off the flaming sheet he had second-degree burns on his left arm and thigh.

Both perps, one shot in the throat, the other in the face, survived but went directly from Misericordia to the Tombs. The mayor and the police commissioner came to see Milton in the burn unit of that same hospital, the PC presenting him with his detective's shield in front of cameras.

The question put to him was "Where do you want to go."

Where. He wanted to go wherever he could hide.

Patrol had always been his thing, the street his wheelhouse—frontier justice, an eye for an eye, and the culling of information through extra-curricular beatdowns. He would be a terrible detective, and he knew it: not too bright with paper trails, not particularly subtle or patient in an interview room, and possessed of a freakishly violent yet icy temper when provoked.

Since the shootout at the barbershop he'd been transferred to seven different precincts in five years. Truculent and inept, he was a burden to each squad, until he landed at the 4-6 in the Bronx. Even before Milton arrived, the lieutenant there got the message that he was doing a great job with Detective Ramos, we all appreciate it, no more hot potato. Milton's new boss made the savvy decision to stash him in the bur-glary squad, which averaged thirty-five cases a month, all difficult to solve. But even in that Eeyore world of low expectation he managed to go three years without a single arrest, at which point he became the supervisor of night complaints, his job to come in at eight a.m. and farm out the complaints that had accumulated since the previous mid-night to the other incoming day-tour detectives—a housecat gig that reeked of dunce cap.

But after a long stretch in that purgatory, a new boss finally put him back in the regular squad, and six months after that there wasn't a known actor in the 4-6 who didn't come to dread hearing the phrase, usually spoken in a low-key, near-distracted monotone, "Get out of the car, please?"

MILTON TOOK THE DIRTY TOWEL and carefully folded it into a thick band. He then straddled the drunk and laid the towel across his throat. Snap-ping the telescoping baton out to its full length, he perched it length-wise along the center of the towel. Carefully stepping on the narrow end with his right foot, he pressed the steel rod into one side of the guy's throat. Then, holding on to a branch in order to keep his balance and modulate the pressure, he placed his other foot on the handle end so that now his full weight was coming down on the Adam's apple, that weight fluctuating between 180 and 190 pounds, depending on the time of the year and what holidays had just passed.

The drunk's suddenly bulging eyes turned a damp, golden red, and the only sound he was capable of making was a faint peeping like a newborn chick heard from one farm over.

After thirty seconds or so, Milton stepped off the baton one foot at a time, then squatted and lifted the thick towel beneath; the throat was unblemished. He replaced the towel on the guy's throat and once again balanced the baton across its center.

"One more time?"

The drunk shook his head, even the weak peeping sound gone.

"Come on . . ." Milton rose to his height, found his balance again at both ends of the rod, and started seesawing. "In case I never get to see you again."

CHAPTER

2

As they crossed the Triborough Bridge in Pavlicek's cream-colored elephant of a Lexus, Billy felt like he could stand up in the shotgun seat without grazing the ceiling. For its owner, though, the oversized SUV was a necessity. Pavlicek was nearly big enough to have his own zip code, six foot four, with a head as big around as a diving bell, the upper body of a power lifter, and hands that once, on a bet, had crushed a raw potato. Even with his face and frame somewhat softened by retirement and wealth, his presence still tended to make everyone around him, including Billy, behave. Big man, big car, big life.

In Billy's opinion, of all their original crew, Pavlicek had played the exit game most righteously. Any cop working a precinct could tell you where the money went, but Pavlicek's genius back in the '90s was to see where it wasn't: in the roofless brownstone shells that had become crack squats, the decimated walk-ups, the derelict working-class ghost palaces that had peaked in the 1940s, if they had ever peaked at all. He had bought them one at a time for a renegotiated accumulation of back taxes and liens, either from the city or the desperate owners themselves, paying an average of $7,500 in the beginning, never more than $50,000 later on, once other speculators started to get in the game. And after completing the purchase, Pavlicek was good at vacating buildings, offering first cash, then violence to the squatters and junkies still cooping after the sale.

In the early days, Pavlicek did all the dirty work himself, rarely needing to do more than show up unannounced at dawn and display his holstered service revolver or a baseball bat. As his holdings grew, he began contracting out these spontaneous evictions, as he called them, to others: mainly defrocked cops, guys who had gotten jammed up for taking money or beating a prisoner or worse, losing both their badges and their pensions in the aftermath and now desperate for even the shadiest of paydays.

Once the troublemakers and deadbeats were gone, he quickly rehabbed the properties and got decent people to move in—there were always decent people—Pavlicek specifically courting the elderly on Social Security or other kinds of fixed income, as well as those who could arrange for the city or their bank to make direct rent payments to his corporation, the bottom line being that five years after retirement Pavlicek owned twenty-eight mostly beat-up but relatively violation-free properties in Washington Heights and the Bronx, had a house in Pelham Manor the length of a tanker and a personal worth of $30 million if a dime.

But if he had been blessed with wealth, he had been cursed with loss: after three years of reasonably happy marriage, his wife, Angela, had attempted to drown their then six-month-old son in the backyard wading pool. Four months later, on her first leave from the Payne-Whitney Psychiatric Clinic, she tried it again. Nineteen years later she was still institutionalized, most recently at a residential treatment facility in Michigan, not far from her parents' home in Wisconsin. Pavlicek still grieved for her and still hated himself for being so oblivious to her pain and madness back then. As far as Billy knew, they were still married.

"You ever been out of the country?" Pavlicek asked as they cruised past the Forensic Psychiatric Center, a.k.a. the Hat Factory, on Wards Island.

"Nope," Billy said, trying to peer through the barred windows to the Thorazine-infused prisoners within. "My dad was in England a bunch of times, did a tour in Vietnam."

"That's him. Plus, war doesn't count."

"Been to Puerto Rico with Carmen to see her grandmother once."

"Puerto Rico is part of the U.S. Plus, visiting family doesn't count."

"Then I guess I've been living in my ass for forty-two years. What's your point, big shot?"

"Did I ever tell you about the time I went to Amsterdam with John Junior?"

"You went to Amsterdam?"

"Four years ago I was invited to talk at an urban renewal conference there, and I wanted to bring him. He was sixteen, it's a cool city, sort of, so he says, 'I'll let you take me to Amsterdam . . .'"

"Let you."

"'. . . let you take me if you get stoned with me there. Nick Perlmutter went with his dad last year and told me they got wasted together.' Says to me, 'Hey, at least you'll know who I'm getting high with.'"

"You did not do that."

"I'm sorry, you never got high?"

"With my kids?"

"Your kids are little, Billy. It's different later, it's like trying to hold back water with your hands. Trust me."

"You still don't have to smoke up with them."

Pavlicek shrugged.

Feeling a little scandalized, Billy shut up.

"In any event, we got there, made a beeline to the nearest coffee bar, sat outside facing this plaza, platz, or whatever, Junior's all showing off how he can read a pot menu like a wine list, orders us something supposedly mild, a few hits and we're both zotzed. It was fun at first—we couldn't figure out how to take our picture, holding the camera every whichaway, laughing, you know, stupid stoned. Finally this Dutch lady inside the bar takes pity on us, comes out and does the honors. Two American morons getting high in Amsterdam, never seen that before. We're laughing our balls off for about a half hour, then the paranoia just shuts us down like, blam. I mean like a solid hour of Can't Talk, sitting there wondering how do we find the fucking hotel, Prinzengracht, Schminzenstrasse, where's the Anne Frank House and are we bad half-Jews if we blow it off, how do we even just, like, stand up. Hours like that, then Johnnie finally turns to me, says, 'Well, this wasn't one of my better ideas, was it.' He flies home the next day, it's really a nothing city, but I'm stuck doing the panels. I felt horrible . . . I mean, OK, you're right, what kind of pandering asshole has to curry favor with his kid like that. But you know what? A week later I finally come home and I see that on his bedroom door Johnnie had taped blowups of all the photos of us that the Dutch lady took, and goddamn didn't it look like we had a blast. And now when we . . . It always plays for a laugh when it comes up in conversation, between the pictures and the way we tell it to people. It's like, after a while, the two of you are like a comedy team. And you forget, I forgot, how bad it felt, I just . . ."

Billy heard a sudden rasp of tears in Pavlicek's voice that he had no idea how to interpret and so he held his peace until they got where they were going, twenty strained minutes later.

THE RIVERAS, LIKE EVERYONE ELSE on City Island, lived on one of the short streets branching off the sole avenue that ran like a spine for two miles from the land bridge to the Long Island Sound. Their house, a run-down Victorian gingerbread, was at the tail end of Fordham Street, the lapping waves audible from every room. The family had two views: the Sound at a point where New York and Connecticut met underwater, and the ruins of the house directly across the way, not a hundred feet opposite, behind which the body of their son Thomas was found five years earlier, discarded and torn. The house was now in the midst of being demolished by the new owners, the walls collapsed in a violent heap, jagged spears of lumber shooting out in all directions like an abstract expression of its own notoriety.

Ray Rivera, now sixty pounds heavier than the night his son was discovered, stood on his lawn with Billy and Pavlicek, chain-smoking and staring at the wreckage across the way. His wife, Nora, was somewhere inside their house, undoubtedly aware of the visit but declining to come out. To Billy most of Rivera's new obesity seemed to be in his upper body and face rather than his gut, in the multi-tiered pouches under the eyes, the softening flesh of his broad chest, and the forward slump of his thick

shoulders. Billy had seen this transformation before in parents who strug-
gled daily with the violent death of a child. After a few years that emotional heaviness could visually de-sex a couple, leave them looking more
like each other than if they'd lived into their nineties together.

"You know, I have real mixed feelings about that shit pile coming
down." Rivera coughed wetly into the side of his hammy fist, took another
drag. "I keep thinking, Maybe they're destroying evidence, or maybe a
shred of his soul is still in there."

"He's not there anymore, Ray," Pavlicek said. "I know you know
that."

Billy saw movement behind a second-floor window in the Rivera
house: Nora up there, hours every day looking across the street.

"People asked us why we didn't move away, but it would have been
like abandoning him, you know?"

Suddenly the window opened and Nora Rivera leaned out, red-faced,
cawing: "Why didn't *they* move away!"

Pavlicek raised a hand in greeting. "Hey, Nora."

The window slammed like a gunshot.

"You know, I know people, and I could've made some calls, anytime
I wanted. Once a guy called me. But if I wanted that Jeffrey kid dead, I
would have done it myself."

"That's not you, Ray."

"I mean, do you have any idea how many times I sat on that porch
with a piece of steel in my hand? I always drank my way out of it."

"Is there anything you want to ask me about Jeffrey Bannion?" Billy
offered.

Rivera ignored the question. "Last year we went to the national Memory Keepers convention, Johnny here came with us," nodding to Pavlicek. "They had a bunch of workshops and seminars, and I sat in on a
support group for fathers with murdered kids." Rivera took another moist
drag on his cigarette. "And this guy, some old biker from Texas, he said
he sat in on the execution of his son's murderer in Huntsville. Said it didn't
make a difference. Called it a letdown. But I'm not so sure that would've
been the case with me."

"Ray," Pavlicek said gently, "we have to go."

"Our pastor says Jesus wants us to try and forgive, but I'll tell you, these last few years? I'm all about the God of the Jews."

THEY CAME UPON JIMMY WHELAN in the lobby of the apartment house where he lived and worked as the super, a run-down prewar with a deep H-block courtyard on Fort Washington Avenue. At this hour the food odors of three continents crept down the elevator shaft like fog.

Whelan looked good for forty-six, a lean, sometime weight lifter with a full head of brown hair, a big nose, and the exaggerated mustache of a gunslinger. Which wasn't too far off: by the time he'd retired he held the record for justifiable shots-fired incidents of any active police officer in the NYPD. Toward the end of his career, he was transferred to the Crime Scene Unit, one of the least likely places where a detective could find a reason to pull his weapon, but even with that squad he managed to get into a shootout, having wandered into a three a.m. bodega robbery while on a coffee run two blocks away from an indoor doubleheader being processed by his CSU team in the New Lots section of Brooklyn.

Dressed tonight in a dagger-collared cherry leather car coat and flare-bottom jeans, he was standing in front of the geriatric twin elevators, barking at a toffee-colored tenant with vaguely Asiatic eyes and a whippet mustache, the guy shoulder-toting a duffel bag as if on shore leave.

"What are you doing?" Whelan snapped.

"Spreading the joy!" His whiskey-hoarse voice just shy of a shout.

"The joy? Are you crazy? Get your ass back upstairs."

"How you doing, sirs!" the guy said, turning to Billy and Pavlicek and extending his free hand. "Esteban Appleyard."

Whelan abruptly walked away, shaking his head as if he had just about had it with this idiot.

"What you got in there?" Billy asked.

Appleyard opened his duffel to display mini-bottles of Rihanna Rebelle perfume, half-pints of Alizé VS cognac, and cellophane-wrapped packs of White Owl cigarillos.

"Have a cigar." Appleyard beamed.

"I don't smoke," Billy lied.

"I'll be in the car," Pavlicek muttered, wheeling so abruptly that he nearly collided with Whelan, who was steaming back for more Appleyard.

"Where's the money?"

"They gonna wire it to my bank."

"When."

"I don't know."

Whelan turned to Billy. "This guy just won ten million playing the lottery, can you believe that?"

"For real?"

Billy knew Whelan's irritation had nothing to do with envy. Taking his super's job to heart despite his run-and-gun résumé, Jimmy always projected this scolding vibe toward the more obliviously self-destructive members of what he considered his flock.

One of the elevators groaned open and a woman sporting an African head wrap stepped out, her arms filled with folded laundry.

Appleyard dug in his duffel and pulled out a bottle of perfume. "For you, *Chiqui*."

"I don't wear that," she said sharply, as angry at him as Whelan.

"Give me a kiss."

"You should move out of here," rearing back from his ninety-proof breath. "Everybody knows."

Looking to the lobby, now stripped of nearly all of its original 1920s furniture and mirrors, Billy was surprised to see Pavlicek still in the house, slumped over on the lone couch, his head sunk into his hands as if he were too exhausted to make it back out to the street.

"You got a car?" Whelan asked Appleyard.

"Buyin' one. I like that Maybach, like Diddy got. A nice chocolate brown."

"Can you even drive?"

"Drove a truck out of the poultry terminal for fourteen years before I got shot that one time," yanking down his sweater collar to show the skid-mark scar on his collarbone.

Whelan pulled out a set of keys, stuffed them in Appleyard's pocket. "You know my car?"

"The Elantra?" Appleyard sniffed. "I wouldn't be caught dead in that."

"You go upstairs and pack. You take my car and go up to my cabin in Monticello for a week. Figure out where you want to live, what you're gonna do with yourself, because around here, they're gonna eat you alive."

The woman nodded in agreement.

"Naw, man." Appleyard waved him off. "People know me."

"Exactly. Somebody comes to my door three days from now, says there's a smell from 5D? I don't want to find you, see some three-legged alligator tortured you for your ATM code, left you with a screwdriver in your ear."

"Yeah, well." Appleyard's duffel slipped from his grip, the perfume and cognac bottles clinking on the smooth stone floor. "I can't see that."

The African tenant finally took off, crossing the lobby on her way to the front door, Pavlicek not even raising his eyes to her as she glided past the couch, her voluminous housecoat brushing his knees.

"And stop handing that shit out or you won't even make it to two days. What's wrong with you?"

"How much you want for the cabin and the car," Appleyard asked, peeking into the duffel for spillage. "Because I know you want something."

"For a week?" Whelan said, squinting at the ceiling. "Fifteen hundred."

"And I'm supposed to worry about everybody else takin' me off, huh?"

"Make it two thousand and I'll come with you."

"Charge me for you to come to your own house? You got a TV up there?"

"Of course."

"They sell groceries up there?"

"No, everyone crawls around eating grass."

"Bars?"

"You stay out of bars."

"Naw, I'm gonna stay right here," handing Whelan back his keys. "This is my block."

"I tell you what," Whelan said. "I'll sell you the car for twelve grand."

"I don't think so." Appleyard laughed, then hauled the duffel back up on his shoulder and took off down the hall to knock on doors.

As they finally headed out to the street, Pavlicek falling in with them silently, Billy's cell rang, Stacey Taylor again, Billy killing this call from her too.

COLLIN'S STEAK HOUSE WAS SITUATED IN the financial district on a small cobblestoned lane lined with landmark nineteenth-century merchants' homes and low shebeens named after Irish poets, the whole plunked down like an antique snow globe dwarfed and surrounded by a futuristic ring of office towers. They were the first to arrive, and the publican Stephan Cunliffe, a Belfast transplant who by blood mandate loved cops and writers, brought over a tray of Midleton shots before they had even taken their seats.

"*Sláinte,*" Cunliffe said, hoisting his own.

Although Irish himself, Billy could live the rest of his life without hearing that particular toast again.

"Is Mr. Brown coming?"

"Redman's got a funeral service uptown," Billy said.

"And the lovely Ms. Assaf-Doyle?"

"As per usual, she'll be coming when she comes."

Which was twenty minutes later, swooping to the table like a rush breath, her enormous dark eyes beneath blue-black hair, wet and combed straight back as if she had just come from a workout, and wearing, as always, her trademark hippie coat, calfskin shearling trimmed with vaguely Tibetan embroidery and frogged buttons.

"Where's mine?" Yasmeen said, looking at the empty glasses.

Cunliffe snapped his fingers, and a fresh round appeared as if the waiter had it behind his back all along.

"My job this week?" Shrugging off her coat. "I had a girl in the dorms from India, lost her virginity to some douchebag in the Village, the guy made a tape and now he's threatening to send it to her parents if she stops putting out, so I had to go up to his skank-ass crib and scare the piss out of him, like, call out the dogs of war, right? Oh, and today? They had me investigating a missing sweater, anyways, *besahah*'," draining her shot. Then: "So, Billy, you caught the Bannion job?"

"Four in the morning."

"Penn Station, a real clusterfuck, right? Any leads?"

"At this point, ask Midtown South. I'm just the night porter."

"You ever see that movie? I almost asked for my money back."

"What movie," Whelan said.

"Anyways, here's to Bannion," hoisting her second glass. "When bad things happen to bad people."

"Hear, hear."

"First Tomassi, then Bannion," she said. "It's like justice started peeking under the blinds."

"When people say 'hear, hear' like that," Whelan said, "do they mean 'hear' like to hear something? Or like, 'Hey, over here.'"

"Whoa, wait." Billy held up his hand. "Brian Tomassi? What happened to him?"

"Are you serious?" Whelan said. "Do you not read the papers?"

"Just say."

"You know that stretch of Pelham Parkway by Bronx House where him and his crew chased Yusuf Khan in front of the cab?"

"Yeah, and . . ."

"Take two giant and one umbrella step south of there, Tomassi, two a.m. in the morning, tweakin' like a beacon, steps off the curb and becomes one with the 12 bus."

"When was this?"

"Last month."

"Just like that?"

"Just like that."

Laughing, Billy nodded to Whelan. "You push him?"

"I would've, you better believe that."

Billy remembered, the day after it happened, Whelan telling him that when the panic-stricken Khan, running blindly across the four-lane northbound parkway, had been struck by a muscle car doing sixty-five, the sound of the impact had been loud enough to set off car alarms for blocks around.

"Hey, what's the last thing that passed through Tomassi's mind after he got creamed by that bus?" Yasmeen asked.

"His ass," Pavlicek grunted, his first words since they had all sat down. "Christ, if you're going to tell stupid fucking jokes . . ."

Once again Billy noticed that he seemed on the verge of tears. "You OK, big guy?"

"Me?" Pavlicek brightened a shade too fast. "You know what I was doing today when I called you? Going through one of my buildings with an exorcist. I got a Chinese contractor to gut the place, his people go in, they come right back out fifteen minutes later saying it's haunted, no way they're going back in. So I went and hired an exorcist."

"The Chinese are the worst," Yasmeen said, "they're so superstitious."

"You ever see a Chinaman commit suicide?" Whelan added. "They don't believe in quick and painless."

"Where'd you get the exorcist?" Billy asked.

"This lady runs a smoke shop near my house. She's some kind of Wiccan with a sideline in ghostbusting."

"She's for real?"

"She knows what's expected of her, puts on a good show. Comes with flashlights, humidifiers, wind chimes, Enya tapes . . ."

"Who you gonna call . . ."

"Only thing is, they have their gods and we have ours."

"We have gods?"

They waited for Pavlicek to continue, but he seemed to have lost interest in his own story.

"So did it work or not?" Billy asked.

"What."

"The exorcism."

"It's ongoing," Pavlicek said, looking off.

"So, Billy, how's your family?" Yasmeen catching his eye—Let it be—then downing her third or maybe fourth shot.

"Good, you know, I mean my father's not getting any better, but . . ."

"My dad once tried to talk me into letting him come to live with us? I had his ass in a home before he got the first sentence out."

"You're all heart there, Yazzie," Whelan said.

"What do you mean, I'm all heart? The guy was a psycho. He used to get drunk and burn us with cigarettes. I got a heart. Why do you always want to make me feel so bad?"

"Yasmeen, I'm kidding."

"No, you're not," she slurred. Then, after a too-long beat: "Fucking Whelan. You always make me feel bad. What did I ever do to you?"

She then proceeded to descend into one of her legendary sulks, Billy knowing from experience that there was a good chance they wouldn't hear from her for the rest of the evening.

Yasmeen was the only woman Billy knew who could match his wife mood swing for mood swing. They even looked alike, although Yasmeen's coloration came from her Syrian father and Turkish mother, which had made being constantly addressed as *mami* and automatically spoken to in Spanish out on the street agitating enough for her to more than once ask for a transfer to a more upscale precinct. But she was a fierce friend, dressing down his first wife in the street directly in front of the demonstrators who had driven her to leave him after his shooting—well, that wasn't such a hot idea—then, years later, when Carmen was going through a particularly black spell, taking in their kids for an entire summer until his wife was back on her feet.

So Billy would put up with any kind of stormy behavior that came his way, but with Yasmeen now brooding in her tent and Pavlicek halfway to a morose coma of his own, the table suddenly had the energy of a brownout.

"Can I tell you something?" Billy began, trying to plug the gap. "You talk about exorcisms, I never told this to anybody before because it embarrassed me, but about six months into trying to nail Curtis Taft? Carmen convinced me to consult a psychic."

"Get out," Whelan stepping in like a straight man.

"Some old Italian lady up in Brewster, I mean, I was so desperate at that point . . . So I call her up, go to her house, I swear she looked just like Casey Stengel. Hey, how you doing, thanks for seeing me, and I walk into the living room, the walls are covered with appreciation letters from different police departments around the country, maybe a few from Canada, another from some town in Germany. It was pretty impressive until you go up close and read one: 'It has come to my attention that you might possibly have been of some assistance in the as yet unsolved homicide death of fill-in-the-blank. Thank you for your time and enthusiasm. Sincerely, Elmo Butkus, Chief of Police, French Kiss, Idaho.' But whatever, I'm there. I sit on the couch, she's in a rocking chair, I was told to bring some objects belonging to the vics, so I hand over a barrette belonging to the four-year-old, Dreena Bailey, Memori Williams's iPod, and Tonya Howard's Bible. I tell her what we think happened, Taft coming in there around sunrise, three shots and just walking out, going home, getting back in bed with his still-asleep girlfriend.

"She says to me, 'OK, here's how it works. I'm gonna sit here and think about what you just told me, and I'm gonna get a little worked up and I'll say things, a word, a phrase, and you write everything down. Whatever I say.' And then she says, 'Now, the things I'll be saying? I don't know what any of it means, they're like pieces of a puzzle that you got to put together, OK? You're the detective, not me, OK?'

"I say OK.

"'And oh, wait,' she says, 'by the way, I never charge cops for helping them, that's my civic duty, all I ask in return is a letter from you on your police department stationery thanking me for my assistance.' I say, 'Yeah sure no problem, let's go, let's go.' And then she starts rocking in the chair, rubbing Dreena's barrette, and lets it rip. 'Four years old, that poor little kid, she never had a chance, she'll never see her mother again, or play jump rope, that evil cocksucker, that fucking . . . BUTTER!'

"I almost jumped out the window she shouted it so loud, but I write down 'Butter,' then she's off again. 'What kind of cold-blooded scumbag would take the life of . . . RUNNING WATER!' OK, writing it down, 'Running water.' I mean, everything in the world is near running water, a river, a sink, a sewer, I mean, are you serious? Then she starts going on about Memori. 'Fourteen-year-old girl, her whole fucking life in front of her, this vicious pig, this miserable piece of shit, this . . . TIRES!'

"OK, 'Tires.'

"'He snuffs the life out of three young ladies and then what does he do? He goes home and crawls back in bed with his new girlfriend, like he just got up to take a piss, and can you imagine what a piece of work that stupid bitch . . . BROKEN TOILET!'

"And, I swear on my children, when she said that, 'Broken toilet,' I just about pissed myself."

"Yeah?" Whelan apparently his only listener.

"Listen to me," Billy said, leaning forward. "The bodies were discovered by Tonya Howard's new boyfriend when he came to the house about five, six hours later, and by the time we got there, rigor was going pretty good. We found Memori and Tonya in the living room and we thought that was it, but when I opened the bathroom door . . ." Billy wiped his dry mouth. "See, when Taft lived with Tonya, whenever he would discipline the little one he'd always take her into the bathroom, and that's where he took her to shoot her that morning, and after he shot her he stuck her head and shoulders in the toilet. Like I said, rigor had set in and we couldn't get her out, so we had to use a sledgehammer to shatter the porcelain. So, 'Broken toilet,' the lady said. Don't ask me how."

"Then what happened."

"I brought her back to the projects and let her into the apartment, see if she could maybe pick something up in the air."

"Did she?"

"Nope."

"What did she say when she saw the broken toilet?"

"Just nodded, like, 'I told you so.'"

"She got you on the running water, too," Whelan said, "if you want to be technical about it."

"That too, I guess."

"You write her that letter?"

"I'm working on it."

"The thing about the younger brother," Pavlicek suddenly said, addressing his clasped hands. "The one who went away for it? Truly stupid people are the toughest to interview because they can't tell when you've talked them into a corner. 'Forensics says he was killed with a golf club, Eugene. Is there a golf club in the house?'

"'I don't know.'

"'Well, we found one.'

"'OK.'

"'We found your fingerprints on it.'

" 'OK.'

" 'So how could you not know there was a golf club in the house?'

" 'I don't know.'

" 'Do you like to play golf?'

" 'No.'

" 'So then, once again, I have to ask, how'd your fingerprints come to be on the shaft?'

" 'I don't know . . .' "

Pavlicek took a breath, his gaze going from his hands to his untouched shot glass. "I remember, I tried to get Jeffrey's goat, so I ask him, 'It can't be easy living with a retard for a brother.' You know what he says to me? 'You should try it.' "

He reached for his Midleton's, threw it back.

"A real sweetheart," he muttered, then shut himself down, not once in his story having raised his eyes to his friends, leaving Billy to wonder whether maybe Bannion's murder had him deeply crashing, like a post-partum Ahab if the author had allowed him to kill the whale and go home to his family.

"Fuck you, with your 'I'm all heart,' " Yasmeen bawled, suddenly deeply drunk and in tears. "Why do you always have to make me feel so bad?"

Before Whelan could respond, she tilted into Billy, slurred in his ear, "Sometimes I can still taste you," then lowered her forehead to the table and went to sleep.

"I think for Jeffrey," Pavlicek said to no one, "Thomas Rivera, his brother Eugene, the whole thing was like snapping a tablecloth." Then, thickly, "If anybody had it coming, right?"

Billy and Whelan looked at each other blankly before raising their eyes to the waiter, who had finally come by to pass out menus and announce the specials.

BILLY'S FIRST RUN OF THE night didn't come in until just before dawn, an assault in a flower shop on a beat-up stretch of upper Broadway where

Harlem became Hamilton Heights, the roughness of the neighborhood offset by its heart-stoppingly abrupt view of the Hudson River, which seemed to leap up to meet the cresting avenue. Given the limbo hour, Billy's partner of choice was Roger Mayo, a hollow-eyed, scoop-chested chain-smoker in his eighth year on Night Watch, a borderline mute, a mystery, no one in the squad having any idea where he came from or where he went afterward. But Mayo was also a natural nocturnal, someone Billy could count on not to fall face-first into the lap of a suspect halfway through an interview at six in the morning, which was not nothing.

Wading to the sidewalk through double- and triple-parked cruisers, they passed the open back doors of an ambulance and saw a young chunky Latina sitting inside, a sepia necklace of fingerprints around her throat.

"How she doing?" Mayo asked an EMT.

"She's pissed."

Leaving Mayo to take her statement, Billy headed to the scene of the crime, the florist shop a cramped, ramshackle affair with wind-riddled, rotten wooden moldings around the door frame and the sole display window. The low-ceilinged selling floor was covered with cracked linoleum, and the near-empty flower refrigerator was overhung by a roughly built half-loft, the squeak and groan of shifting feet up there nearly drowning out the soft jazz playing somewhere behind a battery of poinsettias and greeting card spin racks down below.

Climbing a short flight of raw pine stairs, Billy found himself in a cell-like, three-walled bedroom, cops and medics obscuring his view of the perp, Wallice Oliver. The guy was a frail, bare-chested seventy-year-old with a pharaonic goatee, wheezing asthmatically as he sat slumped on the side of a narrow bed. The towel draped around his neck made him look like a geriatric boxer.

As an EMT inserted a spirometer in Oliver's mouth to gauge his lung capacity, Billy took inventory of his surroundings. In one corner a gold saxophone perched upright in its stand; in another stood a spindly desk, its blotter covered with a scatter of prescription bottles, a jar of olive oil, an ankh, a crucifix, and a Star of David. Scotch-taped to the walls were two photographs of Oliver as a younger man, one of him onstage with Rahsaan Roland Kirk, the other of him performing in Sun Ra's Arkestra.

Billy made his way through the milling uniforms to the bed.

"You want to tell me what happened?"

"I already said all that." Oliver reared back to peer up at him.

"Just one more time."

"She come in once, like around Valentine's Day," pausing to take a hit of Primatene Mist, "says she was looking to buy a plant for her mother, young girl, looked around, didn't buy nothing though, walked out, then came back a hour later, asked if I needed any help in here, and to tell you the truth I just barely support myself with this, you know? So she leaves again, then comes back a third time that night, knocks on the door right as I'm turning out the lights, steps inside, drops to her knees, puts me in her mouth, says, 'Daddy, you let me live up there, you can have me anytime you want.' Next thing I know I'm a man again, but she's Satan and everything in my life's all fucked up. I had a wife was a schoolteacher, a nice crib, moved out on them both to be up here under a seven-foot ceiling with her. I can't even straighten my back no more, and I tell you I will put up with a lot of meanness just to have a hard dick again, but the things she said to me tonight?" Oliver bowed his head, kneaded his waxy, amber fingers. "I have never been hurt by words like that in my life."

Leaving the scene an hour later, the rising sun accentuating the emptiness of the street, Billy heard his cell go off, Stacey Taylor again, this time a text:

i know u r screening my calls dont

MILTON RAMOS

I'm not even going to ask you who threw the shot, because I know you didn't see, right?"

Milton was talking to the head-bandaged Shakespeare Avenue banger, who was sitting up on his wheel-locked gurney in the trauma room of the St. Ann's ER.

"Where my clothes at," the victim ducking and weaving in an effort to look past Milton, standing less than a foot away from him in the curtained-off space. "Call the damn nurse."

Milton gave it a beat, watching dispassionately as the traumatized tissue around Carlos Hernandez's bullet-creased temple finally began to balloon in earnest, forcing the thick gauze dressing to slowly rise like a bloody soufflé.

"You know what?" he finally said. "Don't tell me. Take care of it yourself, or at least let him get another crack at you and finish what he started, because God's truth?" Milton shut his notepad. "I don't give a shit."

"Yeah, see? You going psychological on me."

"Really, I'm not. I mean this from the bottom of my heart, soldier boy, I don't give a shit. Just try not to let it go down near a playground or on a basketball court, that's all I ask."

Milton never saw the point of the detective squad getting involved ιn a gang shooting so early in the game like this, knowing that the 4-6 Street Intel Unit, on a first-name basis with every young Morlock out there, had probably already hauled in their informants. By this afternoon they would be not only smart-bombing the streets looking for the shooter but scarecrowing the two beefing crews—Shakespeare Over All and Creston On Top—from any planned retaliation and/or re-retaliation. The fact of the matter was, only two hours after getting creased, Carlos here was already old news, the only thing anybody cared about right now was minimizing the inevitable mayhem to come.

"I tell you what," Milton said, leaning in and putting a hand on Carlos's bare knee. "Give me a name and you get one free get-out-of-jail card, on me."

"I ain't in jail."

"Not today."

"You like putting your hand there?"

"I'd rather put it around your throat."

Milton turned to leave.

"You supposed to give me your card," Carlos said.

"I would, but I'm running kind of low."

Psychology, my balls.

COMING BACK OUT INTO THE main reception area, Milton walked past the Latina nurse manning the triage desk and up the center aisle of the waiting area, the benches eerily silent despite a full house. Reaching for the wall-mounted remote button that opened the door to the street, he hesitated, abruptly overcome with a powerful sense of having forgotten something important, the sensation like waking from an intense dream and trying to remember the fading details. He patted himself down—sidearm, notepad, wallet, keys, all there—then turned and started to retrace his steps, walking back past the triage station, getting as far as the door to the trauma room before stopping in his tracks and once again reversing his steps, this time coming back at an angle so that he could take a good look at that nurse without her noticing.

Standing in the near shadows, he stared at her, then stared some more, only snapping out of it when he felt her starting to sense his presence, at which point he put his head down and took off, not looking up until he was back out on the street, the sudden sunlight adding to his hyped sense of disorientation.

It wasn't until a few hours later, still in a daze as he typed up the Fives on Carlos Hernandez, that he belatedly registered the name tag that had been affixed to her whites, Milton reaching for a pad and writing it down in a chittery hand:

C GRAVES

Wanting to be alone with this, he slipped into the windowless bunk room. Ignoring the two detectives lying belly-up and near lifeless in opposite corners of the fetid cell, he perched himself on the edge of an unmade bed and tried to think it through.

C Graves. The *C* he got. The *Graves*, he assumed, was her husband.

"Carmen Graves," he said, trying it on for size.

So. Married, moved on, a few kids most likely, and a career.

Moved on.

It was enough to snatch your breath.

3

Stepping into the house at eight in the morning, Billy came across his father and his two sons seated at the dining table eating Eggos, Billy Senior in his pajamas, the boys, as usual, in full Enduring Freedom gear from dog tags to child-sized paratrooper boots.

"See, at the college, the students, they took over two buildings, one by the blacks, you know, the Afro-Americans, the other the white radicals, the Suburbans we called them," his father said. "I don't think they trusted each other, or at least the blacks didn't trust the whites. And Charley Weiss, my boss in the TPF, after two days standing around waiting for the go-ahead, he finally gets on the bullhorn, says, 'You have fifteen minutes to vacate the building or we're coming in after you.'"

"Dad," Billy said.

"Now, the, the Afro-Americans, they been around the block a little more, and they know we mean what we say, so after a little trash talk from the classroom windows, they pretty much come right out. But the Suburbans? They never had any dealings with the police before, so it's all a big adventure for them: 'Come and get us, pigs.'"

"Pigs?" Carlos looked up from his waffle.

"Dad."

"And whenever we had to go in someplace, Charley Weiss always put me in the first wave, 'Send in the Big Guy,' he used to say. Riots, black-outs, demonstrations—'Send in the Big Guy.'"

"The Big Guy," Declan whispered, his face shining.

"And so we went in, and we went in swinging. It was ugly, and some of us were sick about it after, but we cracked some heads that day . . ."

"Dad . . ."

"Some of those kids were crying and begging us to stop, but you get to this place in yourself, you're so pent up with all the damn waiting, your heart's pumping so hard . . ."

"Hey, guys . . ."

"I put one kid down who tried to snatch my radio, rammed him in the ribs with my baton like they taught us, it hurts like hell, let me tell you, he's laying on the ground, looks up at me, says, 'Mr. Graves, stop, please stop . . .' I take a good look at this kid, I'm . . . You got to be kidding me. Turns out he was the son of the people who we bought our house from when we moved out to the Island. Nice couple. Nice kid, too. Last time I'd seen him was about four years earlier, he must've been fourteen, fifteen, but we recognized each other that day, we surely did."

"Did you feel bad, Grandpa?" Declan again, the story a little over Carlos's head.

"Yeah, I did. I started yelling at him, 'What the hell did you grab my radio for?' He says, 'I don't know! I don't know!' I get him up, march him out of the building, take him around the corner to Amsterdam Avenue, and I tell him to go over to the St. Luke's ER, just get lost."

"My mom works at the ER," Carlos said brightly.

"I tried to tell myself that these kids had it coming, that they were trying to bring us down as a great nation, but yeah, I felt bad. That day I felt bad."

Knowing the worst was over, Billy finally retreated into his coffee, marveling, as always when he heard this story, that when his father finally retired, twenty years after those bloody sit-ins, his first job as a civilian was director of student safety at the same university.

"Anyways," Billy Senior rising, "I have to go pick up your grandmother at the bank."

Declan looked to Billy, then back to his grandfather. "Grandpa," he said not unkindly, "Gramma's dead."

Billy Senior stopped at the door, turned to the table. "That's not a very nice thing to say, Declan."

Billy watched his father go out to the driveway and get in the keyless sedan, knowing he'd sit there until he forgot why he was sitting there, then come back inside.

Up in the bedroom, Billy stashed his Glock, stripped down to his boxers, and fell into bed. Fighting off sleep, he stared at the ceiling until he could hear Millie's muffler-shot old beater coming down the street, signaling the start of her workday, which consisted of impersonating a housekeeper and, more importantly, watching daytime TV with his father. She would sit as close to Billy Senior as she could without jumping on his lap, while constantly touching his arm and commenting on the screen action, all in an effort to keep him in the here and now, which was becoming an increasingly demanding job.

In the way of these things, Billy's father had become his child, and he was determined to parent him in the manner in which he had been parented himself—with patience, amusement when he could manage it, and an infinite tolerance for the weakness of his mind. Growing up, Billy's mother had been just his mother, doing her duty as required, not exactly indifferent to him but more focused on raising and training his sisters, two out of three children, in her eyes, job enough. As a father, Billy Senior had been low-key but there, not much more demonstrative than his wife but a powerfully comforting presence in his son's life nonetheless. When he was home, he was home all the way—a skill Billy had yet to master with his own family—and no fool when it came to wading through his son's alibis regarding everything from flunking Spanish and Biology, to adolescent beer benders, to a brawl in a White Castle parking lot. He rarely punished and, in a neighborhood where half the parents seemed to treat their screw-up sons like piñatas, never with his hands. But most important to Billy, his father attended all his football games, from peewee and sandlot through varsity, without ever once shouting red-faced from the sidelines or criticizing his son's play. In the Nassau County Youth League, when Billy had quarterbacked his team to a 3–0 midseason mark only to have his coach replace him with his own athletically inferior son, he remembered his father that Saturday morning trying to reason with the guy, but when he realized that the conversation was futile, he just shrugged and walked away, his eyes shining, on the edge of tears.

At Hofstra, which Billy attended for two years on a football scholarship, his father continued to show up in the stands, making it to the majority of the Pride's away games, including overnight trips to Orono, Maine, and Burlington, Vermont, until it all came to an end in the spring of his sophomore year, when Billy was busted for selling weed in the dorms. His father used whatever connections he had with the Hempstead PD to prevent Billy from being formally arrested, but he made no effort to intervene when Hofstra booted him off the campus. And when Billy came home the day of his expulsion, crushed and too ashamed to ask for his parents' forgiveness, his father, deciding that his kid's self-laceration was punishment enough, simply asked him what he intended to do with his life. When Billy couldn't come up with an answer, either that first night or the next, then and only then did he suggest the police academy.

WHEN BILLY CAME BACK DOWNSTAIRS at three in the afternoon, he was surprised to find Carmen's younger brother, Victor Acosta, and Victor's husband, Richard Kubin, standing together in a corner of the kitchen. Only two years younger than his sister, Victor looked barely old enough to vote, an effect, Billy thought, that had less to do with his short stature or his absurdly buffed physique than with his permanent expression of readiness—wide, alert eyes beneath arched, nearly triangular brows, lips slightly parted—making him appear as if he were perpetually attempting to pick up a distant voice bearing important news.

"Hey, what's up," Billy mumbled, embarrassed to still be in his pajamas.

"Hey," Victor said flatly, shaking his hand without meeting his eyes.

"You all right?" Billy asked, his brother-in-law coming off uncharacteristically grim, a photo negative of himself.

"Fine."

"Hey, how are you?" Billy extending his hand now to Richard, older, less eager-eyed, an easygoing enough guy—no gym for him—who tended to fade into the background when it came to Victor's family.

"I'm good," Richard saying it like he wanted to leave but didn't want to offend anyone.

"Where's Carmen?"

"Here." A third flatliner heard from, his wife standing behind his back in the opposite corner of the room, her arms crossed over her chest, her eyes fixed on the floor.

"What happened?"

"Nothing," Carmen said without looking up.

"Nothing?" Victor said sharply.

"What happened," Billy addressing the men now.

"We're adopting," Victor said. "That's all."

Carmen exhaled through her nose, studied the tilework.

"We just came by to share the good news," Richard added, his voice so even-keeled that Billy couldn't tell if he was being sarcastic.

"No, I'm happy for you," Carmen said, her gaze shifting to the backyard. "I am."

Billy followed the men out to their ancient Range Rover in the driveway.

"So wow, adopting," he scrambled. "Where from?"

"Brazil," Victor said.

"Brazil, huh. Boy? Girl?"

"One of each."

"Twins?"

"Can't break up a set," Richard said, unlocking the driver's-side door.

My husband . . . Billy had never thought of himself as having a problem with gay marriage, but he still couldn't quite wrap his head around another man uttering those two words.

"Did you tell your sister it's two?"

"I would've," Victor said, "but I was afraid her heart couldn't handle the joy."

"Anyways, that's terrific, really great," Billy said, then added by way of apology: "You want us to throw you a baby shower or something?"

At least that got them smiling.

When he returned to the house, Carmen was still standing wedged into her corner of the kitchen.

"What the hell's wrong with you?"

"Heather has two daddies," she muttered, looking away.

"I don't get it, your brother comes over with such big news, you couldn't even give him a hug or something?"

"Guess not," she said defiantly but starting to tear up a little.

"Just tell me what's going on."

"Why does something always have to be going on with you?" she snapped, then walked out of the kitchen, up the stairs, and into the bedroom, closing the door behind her.

And that's where they left it. That's where they always left it when it came to Victor and, if he thought about it, so much else.

AT FIVE IN THE EVENING, Billy walked into Brown's Family Funeral Home, on Adam Clayton Powell Boulevard. The chapel, a glorified living room, fluorescently lit and lined with folding chairs, was standing room only and awaft in dope smoke. A twenty-two-year-old banger tagged Hi-Life, who had been shot dead in retaliation for an earlier retaliation, lay in his coffin in a front corner of the chapel facing his people, most of whom were wearing oversized rest-in-peace T-shirts silk-screened with a photo of Hi-Life sitting on a stoop. A second laminated RIP snapshot on a bead chain hung off their necks like a backstage pass.

Walking down the room-length particle-board partition that divided the chapel from a line of office cubicles, Billy passed Redman's elderly father in the first cubicle, Redman Senior leaning back in his chair playing computer poker. In the second cubicle, Redman's twenty-three-year-old fifth wife, Nola, was lying on a daybed reading a book in her Côte d'Ivoirian accent to Redman's seventh or eighth son, Rafer, a toddler with a gastrointestinal feeding tube inserted into his stomach. And then finally, in the last cubicle, was the man himself, all six foot five of him, hunched over his desk slurping lo mein from a take-out carton, the spindly wire bookcase behind his back filled with unclaimed cremains in cardboard urns going back to the 1990s.

"There he is," Redman said, extending an absurdly long-fingered hand but remaining in his chair due to the bullet that had drilled him through both hips five years earlier.

"Christ," Billy said, waving away the chronic in the air.

"They pay like everybody else."

"You ever hear of secondhand smoke?"

"That's just a story they tell you."

"A conspiracy, you mean."

"You said it, not me."

"Like seat belts?"

"Government can't tell me to buckle up. I break some bones, that's my problem."

"Don't tread on me."

A toddler wearing a Hi-Life T-shirt down to her sneakers wandered in, then wandered back out unattended.

"How was dinner last night?"

"Not to be funny," Billy said, "but it was like a funeral."

"Not over Bannion, I hope. You all should have been Riverdancing up and down the block."

"What can I say, the whole thing was just off."

"I heard he was exsanguinated?"

"Never seen anything like it. Apparently he just bled out in midflight, came down like a shop sign."

"Exsanguinated . . . Makes my job easier."

"Not mine. I had me a blood trail long as a Nantucket sleigh ride."

An elderly woman, also in a Hi-Life tee, wandered the hall while coughing up her lungs. They both watched as she pulled back a heavy curtain drawn across the end of the corridor and found herself staring at a legless body lying on a prep table like a three-hundred-pound mound of pancake batter, a nine-inch steel syringe jammed into the jawbone through the side of the gape-locked mouth.

"Oh."

"Bathroom's near the front," Redman said. "The other way."

"Oh." She turned and wandered off without looking at them.

"Got to get a door put up," Redman said, resuming his dinner.

Rafer, now in a wheeled Elmo activity baby walker, came flying into his father's cubicle and had to be intercepted before he crashed into the cremains stand.

"Slow your roll there, Little Man," Redman said, wincing from the sudden movement.

It pained Billy to see him so fragile; back in the early days, Redman had once saved his life by catching him one-handed after he fell from a corroded fifth-floor fire escape while they were trying to hit a dope apartment through a bedroom window. Redman, coming up behind him, had been one story below, and he had snagged one of Billy's arms on his way down and held him like that, Billy's feet pinwheeling forty feet above the sidewalk, until he could grab onto something with his other hand. The memory of that aborted plummet could still make him shoot up in bed at four in the morning.

"Is he getting any better?" Billy asked, nodding to Rafer and unconsciously touching his own gut.

"No."

Redman had never been one to countenance blather, so Billy was at a loss for something else to say on the subject.

"See that shine-head nigger in there?" Redman pointed out a trimly built middle-aged man seated in the chapel sporting a bow tie and an inexpensive but impeccable white suit, his shaved scalp gleaming under the cheap chandelier as if Turtle Waxed. "Antoine Davis-Bey. That's the eel that got Sweetpea Harris out from under the rock."

"I fought the law and the law lost," Billy said, bracing for another Sweetpea diatribe.

"You know, I saw him last week, Harris. Came right in here for a friend's funeral, had the gall to come up to me at my desk and ask me how I've been, you believe that? 'Detective Brown! That leg still hurting you?'" Redman rearing back from his dinner in disgust. "He's been locked up a few times since killing Salaam, but I heard the last time he was smart enough to claim he had a drug problem, avoided jail for rehab, although some people would say sitting in a group circle eight hours a day and getting yelled at by every idiot and their cousin is worse than six months on a prison barge."

In Billy's estimation, Redman, for all his unrelenting focus on bring-ing Sweetpea Harris to justice, was less obsessed with his homicidally peevish White than he was with the victim, Salaam Pridgen. Like Red-man himself way back when, Salaam had been a fifteen-year-old high school phenom already being courted by college scouts, a too-skinny kid with cheetah speed who, as Redman would tell anyone who would listen, owned the most explosive first step to the basket he'd ever seen. A detective in Harlem at the time of the murder eight years earlier, Redman had been watching the boy play since ninth grade, for Rice, for the Gauchos, and even, now and then, in pickup games, anywhere from Marcus Garvey Park to some random one-hoop half-court attached to the ass end of an elementary school.

Redman had no trouble talking about these things to one and all, including the mute bodies he daily prepped for Homecoming, but only Billy and a few others knew that in addition to his interest in the kid, he had been sweet on Salaam's mother. In between wives at that time of his life, Redman had struck up a casual friendship with her while going to her son's games. For a while it looked like the friendship would lead to something more, but then her son's death turned her from a smart and vigorous woman with an appetite for the world into a dead-eyed stut-terer who took forever to turn to the sound of her own name.

"You repped this piece of shit too?" Redman grunted to Antoine Davis-Bey, who had materialized in the doorway of the cubicle.

"Black and poor," Davis-Bey said, winking at Billy.

"Black and poor, huh? That's a eight-thousand-dollar casket, and his people paid in cash."

"You're up, you're down. See how they're doing six months from now," tossing Billy a second wink, as if getting Redman's goat was everyone's idea of fun.

"You know what they call four hundred lawyers chained up and thrown into a volcano?" Redman said.

"Hey, guys," Billy said.

"And let me just ask," the lawyer checking the time on his oversized watch, "that eight thousand dollars, whose pocket is it in now?"

"How about I take that bow tie, twist it around your neck a few times, let go, and see if you spin around the room."

"Oh, for Christ's sake," Billy said, "you're like my kids."

"He started," Bey winking at him one last time and then heading out.

Watching him go, Billy looked toward the chapel and saw one of the eulogizers take the pulpit, three gold teeth and a blue Giants cap.

"Hi-Life, one thing about Hi-Life, he had jokes, man, he always had jokes. Like, he was always complainin' how his teeth was cold, right?"

"Fucking Sweetpea," Redman said, offering a strand of lo mein to his g-tubed toddler. "I keep waiting for someone to cap his ass."

"He's still living in the neighborhood?"

"122 West 118th, third floor rear, but I hear he spends most of his time with his quote unquote fiancée up in the Bronx."

"Well, if the Bronx is good at one thing, it's hurting people," Billy said. "He'll get his."

BILLY'S CELL RANG HALFWAY BETWEEN the funeral home and his car.

"I got your shield here," Yasmeen's husband, Dennis Doyle, said. "It was under our bed, you must've dropped it last night when you brought her home. You want to come get it?"

Before answering, Billy took a second to minutely analyze every dip and rise in Dennis's voice, searching, as always, for the slightest hint of anger.

"Hello?" Dennis said.

There was no edge that Billy could detect. There never was, and it drove him crazy.

"I'll come right now."

Sometimes I can still taste you . . . Yasmeen's last words to him in the steak house, and then whispered again into his ear right before she passed out for good, her arms around his neck as he lowered her fully clothed into bed. She had been way too drunk to drive after last night's catastrophe of a reunion, and with Dennis stuck working four to midnights as a robbery sergeant in the 4-6, Billy took it upon himself to drive her home, half-carry her up to the apartment, and lay her out for the night—completely on the up-and-up, as if Dennis had been watching on a hidden monitor.

All three had known each other since their academy days when, unwittingly, both Dennis and Billy were going out with her. Dennis was in love, Billy was not. It went on for five months like that, both boys in the dark until New Year's Eve 1994, when Yasmeen had walked into Gordon's, a cop bar near the academy, and both he and Dennis simultaneously moved to her. Billy got it instantly, the whole picture, and quickly, quietly stepped back, letting Dennis obliviously go forward into her arms, Yasmeen's sad and knowing eyes staring into his over Dennis's shoulder. And that was the end of that: No hard feelings, it was fun, you deserve the best.

Dennis proposed to her at the bar that night when they were both blasted, the barmaids sailing unsteadily about the dim, damp room with plastic crates of free beer. At first she said no, said, Who the fuck proposes to any kind of respectable girl at some shit-face, after-hours cop bar at five in the morning? Dennis felt so bad about his terrible timing that he started to cry, and it was those idiotic tears, to Billy's astonishment, that did it. OK, Yasmeen finally said while stroking Dennis's hair. Sure, let's get married. Billy saw the whole thing from the short end of the bar, and he thought it was the most pathetic proposal he'd ever witnessed—Dennis never even got off his stool.

He thought it wouldn't last a year, but it was going on twenty and counting: two girls, a three-bedroom terraced co-op overlooking the Hudson in Riverdale, and a summer place upstate in Greenwood Lake.

"SO HOW'S SHE FEELING?" BILLY asked Dennis, sitting across from him in the living room.

"You're looking at it," Dennis answered, tilting his chin toward the closed bedroom door at the end of the hall, Yasmeen's shucked-off Tibetan hippie coat still lying in front of the door like a shaggy guard dog eighteen hours after Billy had carried her inside.

"So listen," Dennis said, tilting forward from the edge of his couch,

"I'm sorry about last night, and I thank you for bringing her home, but help me out here: what the hell happened?"

"Hey, all I can tell you was that she was two-fisted throwing them back from the door on in. I don't know, maybe the news about Bannion got her all agitated about Cortez again."

"Christ, I hope not. I swear to you, living with her when she's on a Cortez tear? It's like a reign of terror around here, yelling at the kids, at me, first she can't go to sleep, then she can't wake up, first she can't eat, then she can't stop. I try to get her to smoke a little weed, but even that doesn't help."

"And she's drinking like this now?"

"She's been going through a patch."

"What's a patch."

"Two months, maybe?"

"Every night?"

Dennis opened his hands and closed them.

"That's not a patch, that's forty acres and a mule."

"I'm talking to some people about it," he said.

"But she's off Cortez?"

Yasmeen's White, Eric Cortez, had been—and as far as Billy knew still was—a real honey, a fully grown man who, five years earlier, had plunged a knife into the heart of thirteen-year-old Raymond Del Pino, ostensibly for talking to Cortez's fourteen-year-old girlfriend in the junior high school cafeteria.

That alone would have been horrific enough, but Cortez had also called his young vic twenty-four hours before the deed, just to tell him what he was going to do. Yasmeen's squad quickly learned about the call and the caller from the victim's friends, and in order to start building their no-witness case against Cortez they needed to get their hands on his cell. But when they showed up at the murderer's apartment with a warrant for his phone, Cortez, sprawled on his couch with his half-wit girlfriend, glanced at the writ, laughed, and said, "That's not my number." And it wasn't: in her rush to get the judge to sign off on the warrant Yasmeen had accidentally transposed two of the digits. They were back in his apartment within two hours with the proper paper, but by then Cortez had ditched the object of their desire and that was the end of that, Cortez still out there doing his thing while Yasmeen, curdled with guilt, had spent the past five years banging her head against the wall searching for new ways to bring him in.

Dennis got up from the couch and pulled two legal boxes from under a small desk. The last time Billy had seen the Raymond Del Pino homicide cartons they were stuffed with case files, court docs, and note pads, just as they had been on the day she retired and finally snuck them out of the precinct, her overjoyed squad holding the doors for her all the way to the street. But now all they held were invoices, checkbooks, stationery, and stamps.

"Do you have any idea how elated I was when I saw her dump all that shit?"

"When was this?"

"A few months ago, I come out of the elevator and there she is, throwing everything down the incinerator chute. I couldn't believe my eyes." Dennis glanced toward the heaped coat by the door. "I was hoping that would be that."

"Look, if it's any consolation, she wasn't the only freak show last night."

"Billy, she's not a freak."

"No, hey, look, you know I didn't mean . . . But I have to tell you, Pavlicek? It was like somebody was walking around inside his head with a flashlight."

"Well, that's understandable, given the thing with Bannion."

"You think? Let me tell you something, if it was Curtis Taft who bought the farm instead? Are you kidding me?"

"Well, Pavlicek's a different animal."

"The hell he is. Did Yasmeen ever tell you about the day we came on three Ñeta Juniors tied up and head-shot in an apartment on Southern Boulevard? Scumbags, but still, they were kids. You know what Pavlicek did? He took us all out to Jimmy's Bronx River Cafe."

"People change."

"If you say so."

Behind the bedroom door, a broken-voiced Yasmeen called for her husband.

"So how's Night Watch?" Dennis asked, trying to ignore the softly cracked wails.

"You know, quiet, busy, quiet, busy. How's the kids?"

"Good, yours?"

"Everything's a weapon," Billy said as Yasmeen's cries became more full-throated.

"Got to have girls," Dennis grunted as he finally, reluctantly, rose for the bedroom. "The worst thing they do is exclude each other."

Alone now, staring out the window at New Jersey across the river, Billy afforded himself the luxury of remembering Yasmeen in the days before that night in Gordon's when Dennis had inadvertently pulled the plug on all their fun. They got along well enough over the months they were together, doing all the usual out-of-the-house dating stuff, but basically it was about the sex. They both swore to each other that they were the best fucks they'd ever been with, which wasn't saying much when you're both working-class Catholics in your early twenties, and Billy's entire erotic repertoire consisted of sticking it in as fast as he could, withdrawing partially as fast as he could, and repeating if necessary. At the time, Dennis was even more of a sexual bumpkin than either one of them; at his bachelor party he confessed to Billy, his best man, that he knew Yasmeen was no virgin when he proposed, but he loved her too much not to forgive her.

Dennis came out of the bedroom looking like a surgeon with bad news. For the thousandth time in the last twenty years, Billy wondered if he knew about them and just wasn't saying.

"Anyways . . ." Billy slowly rose and reached for his jacket.

"You sure you don't want some coffee, a shot of something?" Dennis stood there, tilting toward the kitchen.

"I'm good."

"You sure?"

"Seriously, I got to book."

Giving up, Dennis finally sat back on the couch. "I should have brought your shield down to you, you know?"

"No problem," Billy said, backing toward the front door.

"I just didn't want to leave her alone like this, you know?"

"Totally understood."

"I just hope she doesn't start getting crazy about Cortez all over again, you know what I'm saying?" Dennis staring right through Billy. "I just could not live with that."

THE NIGHT WAS NOTHING BUT softballs, the highlight being a report of two women hacking away at each other with hatchets or swords in front of an NYU dorm, which in the end turned out to be just a drunken fight between two Xenas coming out of a costume party and throwing down with their foam axes. By seven-thirty in the morning Billy was on his way home, making it nearly to his exit before he remembered the date and, with a dulling heart, dutifully hit the turnaround and headed back toward the city.

Carmen saw two therapists, one of them a stocky ex-nun who, sponsored by Local 1146 of the Home and Health Care Workers, bounced around from hospital to hospital in the Bronx like a circuit court judge. She had a makeshift office in the basement of St. Ann's that faintly reeked of the morgue at the opposite end of the hall, an all-too-familiar odor that seemed to underscore Billy's attitude toward his bimonthly shared sessions, especially when they were scheduled so early in the morning.

"You have to understand," Carmen said. "Victor, when he was a kid, he couldn't even keep his sea monkeys wet, and now he's going to have a child? It'll be dead in a month."

"Jesus," Billy said. "Are you hearing yourself? That doesn't even sound like you."

"Can you elaborate on that, Billy?" the therapist said, her tone mildly sedating.

"Yeah, Billy, can you elaborate on that?"

"Carm, he's your brother, why are you always so mad at him?"

"Why is he always so mad at me?"

Billy gave up.

"OK," the therapist said, "let's take your question first, Carmen. Why is your brother always so mad at you?"

"He isn't," Billy said.

"Let her talk now."

"We went over this a million times," Carmen said. "When he was twelve, I had to go live with my father in Atlanta and he felt like I abandoned him. One million times I have said this to you."

"'Had to' implies no choice."

"My father was *sick*."

"He was remarried. He had a wife," Billy said, expecting, then receiving, a warning finger from the therapist.

"His wife was borderline retarded," Carmen said, "just like him."

"So a fifteen-year-old girl 'had to' uproot her entire young life in the Bronx—mother, brother, school, friends . . ."

"I didn't *have* any friends."

Except Victor, Billy knew, Carmen always telling him that her younger brother back then was her only friend in the world, "like two nerds in a pod," she called them.

". . . and leave all those she loved in order to be with a man who walked out on her and her family so early in her childhood that she had no memory of what he even looked like?"

"There were other things going on," Carmen said. "I told you that, too."

"Yes, you did, but I think maybe the time has come to finally start exploring a few of those 'other things.'"

The room descended into a tense silence, Billy avoiding his wife's eyes, hoping that she would finally say something, anything, about what he had come to regard as the Flight to Atlanta.

"Would you feel more comfortable if your husband left the room?"

Carmen shrugged.

And so they all sat there, listening to the squeal of gurneys out in the hall for a full minute or more, until Carmen finally opened her mouth.

"I don't like the Cymbalta you have me on. It makes me too manic, plus I think it stops me from having orgasms."

"Jesus, Carmen." Billy blushed, not so much embarrassed for himself as pained for his wife.

Afterward, as they walked to the St. Ann's parking lot in silence, each to their own car, Billy remembered asking Carmen once why she hadn't spoken to her therapist about a serious issue involving their kids. Her answer—*"Because that's personal"*—had made him laugh so hard his eyes filled with tears.

MILTON RAMOS

Rose of Lima.

Daughters of Jacob.

Ten minutes in either institution made him feel like he was breathing air through a pinched straw. Visiting both in the same day left him feeling like a clubbed seal.

First that fucking school: some kind of parent/career-day event that had him standing there rocking from foot to foot like a beetle-browed dummy in front of two dozen third graders, the good-looking lay teacher in the back of the room nose-down in paperwork, not even listening or raising her eyes to him as he mumbled his way through the joys of the Job.

And those questions . . .

Did you ever kill anybody?

No.

(One, but he had it coming.)

Can I see your gun?

I'm not carrying one.

(No, you can't see my goddamn gun.)

Did you ever come to my *tío*'s house?

Who's your *tío*?

Reuben Matos. He lives on Sherman Avenue.

Yeah, once.

(At least.)

How much money do you make?

Enough to pay tuition here.

Do you ever get mad at Sofia?

Never.

(Never.)

How come she's so fat?

Milton looking to his daughter seated front and center, staring at him with resigned eyes, then back at the kid who asked the question.

How come you're so ugly?

Is her mommy really dead?

Yes.

How did she die?

Hello? This to the head-down half-a-nun in the rear of the room. What are you doing back there, smoking crack?

That's not a nice question, Anthony, she said, still not looking up.

What's your favorite team?

The Red Sox.

Boooo . . .

Do you like Big Papi?

I am Big Papi.

And again: Did you ever kill anybody?

I said no.

(Two, but they had it coming. Three.)

AND NOW THIS HERE, THE Daughters of Jacob Assisted Living Center, the air redolent of boiled hot dogs and Lysol, Mantovani strings drifting through the halls like musical Haldol, old folks sitting alone in the lobby just staring at air, filling him with anger at their AWOL kids. Before he could even make his way to the elevator banks, and not for the first time, one old lady, confusing him with some José from building services, asked him when he was coming to fix her radiator.

His aunt Pauline had her own small suite—at least he had been able to swing that for her—and as she went on and on about a gluey Hawaiian salad she had been served the week before, he sat on her living room couch and took in the art on display: a bowl of silver and gold papier-mâché fruit, a plaster pair of life-sized praying hands, two—count 'em—two ceramic menorahs, a glazed and mounted ram's horn, and a framed print of a fiddler floating sideways above an off-balance ghetto. Aunt, excuse, Tante Pauline had stayed in the faith, if only sentimentally, unlike her sister, Milton's mother, who married a PR to spite her parents. On the other hand, his father had married his mother to spite her parents, too. It was a match made in hell, and if his old man's this-time-for-good disappearance when Milton was ten was not exactly a cause for celebration, it wasn't nearly enough of a blow to throw anyone off their feed.

"So, you didn't bring Sofie?" Pauline asked.

"Sofia. She has school. I'll bring her on the weekend."

Seated across from him on an oversized throne chair, her hands clasped atop her kettle-drum midriff, his aunt tracked his gaze to the framed photos of his, and her, dead family members, the images scattered across the side tables and windowsills.

"I talk to them all the time," she said.

"Me too."

"In the middle of the night, sometimes I wake up and see my sister standing in a corner of the room."

"I see all of them."

"Your brother was such a sweetheart."

"Which one," although he knew. Little Man had been everybody's favorite.

"That day killed your mother."

"Killed my other brother too."

"Who, Edgar?"

"Yes," he said slowly, "your oldest nephew."

"Edgar was always so surly."

Milton stood up, took a little walk around the coffee table to settle himself.

"He took care of us, Aunt Pauline. My mom with her circulation, half the time she couldn't even make it out of the house."

"You were pretty surly back then, too. The both of you. But look at you now, a real man who doesn't forget his family."

"Family's everything."

"I can't even get my own children to visit me, but you come by like clockwork."

Of course he did. Pauline had taken him in for three years, right after the slow-motion massacre had come to an end, the move from the Bronx to her home in Brooklyn most likely saving his life.

He drew a breath before shifting gears. "Aunt Pauline, when you would come and visit us back then, do you remember a girl in our building, Carmen? Puerto Rican, about fifteen years old?"

"Carmen?"

"Maybe spent time with Little—with Rudy?"

"Carmen . . ."

"Skinny, big eyes, long hair."

"Wait, Carmen. From downstairs. Her mother was Dolores."

"Right. Did you ever see her with Rudy?"

"Dolores?"

"Carmen."

"What, like together?"

"Like anything, holding hands, making out, arguing maybe."

"Dolores had a son too, Willy? William?"

"Victor. But let's stick with Carmen."

"He was supposed to be a little, you know, that way, the boy, not that it bothered me."

"Aunt Pauline," Milton said, waving his hand. "Carmen. Did you ever see her with Rudy."

"I can't remember."

"Think hard."

"I wish I could."

"No problem." It was a long shot anyhow.

"Why are you asking about Carmen all of a sudden?"

"Nothing." Milton shrugged, trying to keep his voice as casual as he could. "I thought I maybe saw her. It was probably somebody else."

But was it really her? Oh yeah, you bet. How could he ever forget those

tea-stained big eyes, pulled down sad at the corners like the eyes of the
lost and burning girls on the *Anima Sola* postcards that used to turn him
on when he was a kid. He'd even had a crush on her for a hot minute
when her family had first moved into the building, a sense memory so
galling and torturous to him now that it made him want to rip out his
brain.

He glanced at the sunburst clock over Pauline's head: two-thirty, tea-
time. He went to the refrigerator and poured her a brimming glass from
the half gallon of Gallo Family Zinfandel she kept in there.

"Seventy-four years old, I'm finally an alkie," she said, her standard
line whenever he did the honors.

"You'll live."

"Why did you and your brother always call Rudy Little Man?"

"Because everybody else in the family topped out at five-eight, then
Rudy gets born and he's all of a sudden six-three."

"I don't get it."

His eyes turned dull as nickels.

"Whatever happened to Dolores?" Pauline asked.

"I heard she got cancer," Milton said, "about two years after the . . ."

After the what: tragedy? He hated that word, it reeked of, what . . .
Fate? Inevitability? Bullshit. Tears and a turn for home? Fuck you. Surrender to the mysteriousness of the Great Mysterian?

Surrender; what can ya do.

Plenty.

"And they never found those bastards who killed him," she said.

"No, they didn't, Tante Pauline." Milton rising, this time to leave. "And
they never will."

CHAPTER

4

By the time Billy arrived at the scene of a double shooting on the Lower East Side directly across the street from the Alfred E. Smith Houses, both victims, conscious and looking more pissed than traumatized, were being gurneyed into separate ambos as a mixed crowd of club kids and born-heres took snaps with their iPhones.

"Anybody looking to go out of the picture?" he asked Stupak.

"Doubt it. They were both howling pretty good before you got here."

"Anything on the shooter?"

"You're looking at them," Mayo said.

"Which?"

"Both."

"Yeah?"

"It looks like they were walking from opposite ends of Oliver," Stupak said, "and decided to jack each other at the same time. It's all on camera and we recovered the guns."

"Spy versus Spy, except they're both black," Mayo said, then, having filled his word quota for the night, stepping to the corner for a smoke.

"So my question to you, boss," Stupak said, "are they perps or victims?"

Billy thought about it a moment. "They're perptims."

"You think this is funny?" a young Hispanic woman snapped, her eyes shimmering with anger.

"Hey, how're you doing, did you know either of these guys?" Stupak asked easily, making her disappear into the Smiths. "Can you bring her back here please?" she asked a uniform.

Billy's cell thrummed inside his sport jacket, a fresh text from Stacey:

> can you please answer my calls please
> thats the only way to get me to stop

He knew her enough to know that this was true and it was time to get it over with. To brace himself he went into an all-night bodega and came out chugging a Turbo Tea.

"Hey, it's me."

"Jesus, he lives."

"Sorry, my phone's been . . ."

"Don't, don't, don't."

Was it the energy drink that made the cigarette taste so good or the other way around? "So what's up. You OK?"

As usual after building up a case against returning Stacey's calls, now that he was actually talking to her, he couldn't remember what the big deal was.

"Yeah, but I need to tell you something," she said.

"What's that."

"Have breakfast with me. It's a long story."

"Give me the headline."

"Just have breakfast with me."

"Stacey . . ."

"You'll be glad you did. Well, maybe 'glad' isn't the right word."

That right there was the big deal.

FIVE HOURS LATER, BILLY SAT in his parked car outside the tin can of a diner in Mount Vernon where he was to break bread with Stacey Taylor.

He smoked one cigarette, then another, delaying as long as possible the sit-down to come. Seeing her was always a wrenching experience, the psychic equivalent of returning to a battlefield with your former enemy years after the bloodbath that had scarred you both, eager to reach out but unable to rid yourself of the lingering acid that still bit at the back of the throat.

In 1997 Stacey had been a young reporter for the *New York Post,* an aggressive up-and-comer who glommed onto Billy's notorious double shooting in the Bronx, attempting to make her journalistic bones by investigating the rumor that he'd been high when he pulled the trigger. Backed by two independent eyewitnesses, both willing to go public, both claiming to have seen him doing blow in the rear of an Intervale Avenue bar an hour before the shooting, as well as two more witnesses who wouldn't go on record but corroborated the statements of the two who would, Stacey went in and made a hard pitch to her editors, touting the thoroughness of her background checks on her sources, then bombarding them with reports about police abuse in the area, anecdotal evidence that was as easy for her to gather out on the street as picking daisies.

In the end, she needn't have tried so hard. One week earlier, the *Post* had lost out to the *Daily News* on the suicide of a retired police lieutenant in a Queens dope motel, and her editors were hot to get back on top. The story was page one for two days running, so when it all fell apart shortly after, everyone involved got scorched, but no one as badly as Stacey. In the end it came down to those background checks: in her anxiety about losing her scoop to the time-sucking demands of a thorough vetting of her sources, she hadn't done them at all.

The real background checks—conducted, embarrassingly enough, by the *Daily News*—revealed that one of the on-record eyewits was the brother of a heroin dealer Billy had sent upstate, while the other had twice before born false witness against cops as payback for his own slew of arrests in that precinct. As for the two others who would only talk off the record, no one had seen them since the article hit the stands.

With Stacey caught flat-footed in her lie, and with no hard evidence to back up her account, the story was quickly buried, although never retracted. Within the week she was out the door, the story behind her story having become its own newsworthy story, the subject of self-examining op-ed pieces across the country and not a few panel discussions.

Excoriated for unhesitatingly scuttling a good cop's reputation to further her own, emotionally whittled to a nub by her disgrace, and unable to support herself even if she chose to make a stand, Stacey moved back in with her parents in Rochester. With her father's help, she became a part owner of a food truck christened My Hero, which was more or less permanently stationed across the street from the SUNY Brockport dormitory complex. After two years of full-time sandwich making in this drizzly exile, she endured another blow when both her parents died in a collision with an ambulance at an intersection three blocks from home. She spent the first two weeks after the funeral living alone in their house hoping for a visitation, then put it on the market. A few months later, temporarily flush with the proceeds of the sale, a small inheritance, and the buyout money she received from selling her share of My Hero, she quietly returned to the city.

Unable to find work as a reporter but banking on the skills she had developed as one, she reinvented herself as a private investigator, earning just enough to take a lease on a one-bedroom walk-up near Columbia University. For a while she held on to the hope of finding her way back into the newspaper business, but that pipe dream came to an end the day she accepted an invitation to address an Ethics and Ambition seminar in the university's J-school, the experience leaving her feeling like a still-sentient cadaver picked over by medical students in an anatomy class.

Rather than enjoying the poetic justice of Stacey's downfall, Billy felt torn—no, actually sorry for her, mostly ignoring the fact that she had tried to advance her career on his broken back. In fact, he had been the one to make the first move, reaching out to her with an e-mail a year after she returned to the city, and since then they had gradually, cautiously become friends. For her part, Stacey had been both astonished and humbled by his lack of vindictiveness, never once imagining that his gentle overture was motivated by anything other than old-time Christian compassion.

WHEN BILLY FINALLY GOT IT up to enter the diner, he spotted her at once, sitting at a booth in the back—north of forty now, too thin, too much wine, too much late-night TV—paradiddling an unlit cigarette against the Formica and reading the paper that had shit-canned her eighteen years ago for getting it all wrong about Billy and the shooting. She was wearing a ribbed turtleneck that made her look even bonier than she was and accentuated her slightly scoliotic posture. Her hair, a blond so ashy that it was impossible to tell how gray it might be turning, was pulled back in a short, rubber band–bound ponytail, and her watchful eyes were, as always, a little too quick, as if she were jonesing for something she couldn't have. She'd been a golden girl once, and she took her tumble hard.

"Hey, how's it going," Billy said as he took a seat.

"The meat's so tough that it got up off the plate and beat the shit out of the coffee, which was too weak to defend itself."

"No kidding."

"The PI business sucks. I hate the people who hire me, and I hate the people they want found."

"I hear you."

"Never serve a subpoena on a guy holding a pan of bacon. I put up my arm to protect my face and ruined a perfectly good North Face coat."

"Good thing it was a cold day," he said mildly, then, wanting her to get to it: "So . . ."

"I'm back to writing."

"For money?"

"Not much, but you bet."

"Good for you." This could take a while.

"I'm writing an online sex column."

"A what?"

"For this e-zine, *Matterhorn*."

"What's an e-zine?"

"Don't worry about it—my nom de plume is Lance Driver."

"A guy?"

"A guy advising other guys."

"Wow, that's . . ."

"Yesterday I advised some moke that if your girlfriend wants to stick a finger up your ass it doesn't mean she thinks you're a fag."

"No?"

"It means she's curious, she wants to know your body."

"OK," Billy said. "How far up?"

Stacey finally lit her cigarette, took a quick drag, and then put it out before they could arrest her.

"I draw the line at the first knuckle."

"OK," shifting in his seat. "So what did you want to talk to me about?"

"I have a new boyfriend."

"Oh yeah?"

"I'm forty-five and I have a boyfriend, he's fifty-seven and he has a girlfriend. I mean, what the fuck, right?"

Whatever it was that she had to share, it was making her very nervous, although calling Stacey nervous was like calling water wet. When she was in a state like this it was cruel to rush her.

"The boyfriend, what's he do?"

"He edits *Matterhorn*."

"He's good to you?"

"That's a very considerate question."

"Yes? No?"

Stacey looked off. "He's no stranger to the vine."

"How much?"

"Two bottles, maybe a little more. He's a sweet drunk, but it's like talking to a small child towards the end of the evening."

"Did you try AA?"

"I can't even get him to Triple A."

"He'll lose you."

"He'll die is what he'll do."

"Threaten to walk out."

"I don't want to."

"Threaten?"

"Walk out. I haven't had a boyfriend in eight years. I like caring about what I look like again. I like being spooned."

"Sounds like a problem there, Stace."

The waiter finally came over, the guy sporting a reddish-gray comb-over and an apron up to his sternum.

"Try the grape jelly omelet." Stacey coughed. "It's excellent."

"Just coffee." Then, turning back to her: "Not that I don't enjoy seeing you, but why am I here?"

"Are you ready for this?"

Billy waited.

"You remember Memori Williams had this twin sister?"

"Shakira, right?" Billy took one of Stacey's cigarettes; this couldn't be good.

"Shakira Barker. How twins can have different last names I'll never understand."

Billy envisioned that couch in the living room again, Memori's head in Tonya Howard's lap, the entry wound above her right eye like an erupted raspberry.

"Last I heard, Shakira was doing better," he said hopelessly, "taking one of those mothering classes from the Children's Initiative."

"Yeah, well." Stacey took a breath. "Not no more."

Billy just stared at her: This is why I screen your calls, this is why I . . .

"What happened."

At the end of Stacey's tale, Billy was staring at his ashy coffee, his jaw askew with fury.

"I need you to find someone for me," he said.

"I thought you would," Stacey sliding a single sheet of paper across the table. "Got the horse right here."

Billy speed-scanned the document and learned that Curtis Taft was still working for the same security outfit that had employed him at the time of the triple homicide and was now living in Co-op City in the Bronx, although the place to find him this week was neither work nor home but at Columbia Presbyterian, where he was recovering from surgery on a perforated ulcer.

"I thank you for this," holding up the sheet.

Stacey shrugged and then looked away, Billy sensing the mortification that still coursed through her veins over the long-ago debacle that had ended her career.

"Seriously," Billy said, his own mortification equal to hers, given that she'd been right about him all along: when he had fired the shot that killed a man and then entered the groin of the ten-year-old boy who had been standing behind him, he was coked to the gills. All the WGs were that night, a fact they would keep to themselves until the day they died.

"SO, MR. TAFT, HOW ARE we feeling today?" Billy's voice burbling with rage-induced pep as he whipped back the curtain that curved around the hospital bed. The sight of his White made Billy tingle with a rush of dazed energy, made his eyes brim with light.

"Aw, you again," Curtis Taft moaned, rolling his fleshy head away.

Billy couldn't believe it: the guy had nearly doubled in size since the murders, his torso so inflated that his arms looked like flippers.

Taft attempted to reach across himself in order to press his call button, but Billy grabbed his wrist.

"Perforated ulcer, huh? Goddamn, from what I hear you can get that from smoking, but you smoking? Shit, you don't even eat off plastic as far as I remember, right? Everything had to be in stone bowls, incense all over the place, a real my-body-is-my-temple-type individual. So, my theory is," poking the soft mound of dressing across Taft's belly, "this right here? I think it's just Tonya and those kids in there getting to work on you."

"I don't know what you're talking about, Graves, get the fuck out of here." He reached for the call button again, Billy this time yanking it out of the wall.

"What's going on over there," the old guy on the other side of the curtain called out.

Billy stepped over and raised the volume on his ceiling-suspended TV.

"So," flopping down on the side of Taft's bed, "you hear what happened to Memori Williams's twin sister, Shakira?"

"Who's Memori," Taft said, then, barking to his roommate: "Yo, call the nurse station."

"Oh c'mon, you got to remember Shakira, real wallflower type? Well, that wallflower just killed a sixteen-year-old girl last week, stabbed her through the lungs with a bread knife over in Jersey City, can you believe that? She's in Hudson County CC right now, but she'll wind up in Clinton Correctional Institute for Child-Eating Psycho Bitches—that is, if they aren't full up, in which case they'll put her in Bellehaven, that temporary women's wing they got out there in Sparta, but the ACLU is trying to get that shut down because of the rapes. We'll see."

"I don't know no Shakira nobody." Then, attempting to sit up, barking: "I told you call the fucking nurse."

Billy shoved him back down, Taft grimacing through his close-cropped beard. "Now, Memori was a handful, no doubt, fighting in the cafeteria, cutting school, running away from home, always with a boy, but Shakira, she was no trouble to anybody, fourteen years old and never been kissed, had all the answers in class but too shy to raise her hand. But soon as you killed her sister . . ."

"I din't kill nobody, and you know it."

". . . as soon as you killed her sister, all of a sudden she starts banging with the Black Barbies, gets caught with a razor in her mouth going through the metal detectors, threw a chair at a teacher, they finally sent her to a social worker, the lady says to her, 'Kira, what happened to you?' You know what she said back? 'Well, somebody's got to be my sister.'"

"Graves, you just pissed off because you ain't police enough to catch a fuckin' cold. Cops like you, you just grab the first nigger you see and hope for the best. Well, it didn't work out so well, did it."

"Anyways, Curtis, that was five years ago and now the kid's a nineteen-year-old murderer with two babies of her own, and she is as fucked as fucked gets. It would probably have been better if she was in the apartment that morning and you put a bullet in her head too, because this, this is gonna be one slow-motion death she's facing in there. So, as far as I'm concerned, they are *all* in there," poking his sutured gut again, "all those angry females chewing you up from the inside out. And when they finally cut you open to see what killed your ass, you know what they're going to find? Teeth marks, motherfucker, nothing but teeth marks."

"You stop that bullshit right now," Taft said more quietly, his eyes going a little bit wide.

"Tell me you don't feel them," Billy pressed. "Look at me and tell me you don't feel them."

Gingerly touching his gut as if something might pop out, he looked at Billy full-on, no resistance, after all these years, no resistance, Billy's heart slamming as he scrambled to seize the moment.

"You were raised in the church, right? I remember interviewing your sister, she said you all were."

"So," Taft said carefully.

"So you believe in God?"

"Who don't believe in God."

"Know your Bible?"

"Some," Taft said, still palming himself.

"Remember your Luke? Jesus coming on a man had so many demons inside of him that when He asked for his name . . . You remember what the man answered?"

"Legion," Taft said, his eyes unblinking.

"Legion, that's right. Legion. A whole fuckin' battalion. And that's what you're dealing with too."

Taft removed his hand from his belly, placed it flat on the bed, then went still.

"Now, you know and I know that the only way to get those angry bitches out of you before they can finish what they started is for you to make a clean breast of it and say what happened that day. Say it right now, say it to me, and they will be gone before you know it."

Taft kept staring at him, his mouth slowly going as round as a doughnut, just staring and staring until he apparently saw what he wanted to see in Billy's eyes, that small quivering . . .

"Graves," his voice abruptly all the way back, "I got a better chance of cleaning you out in court for harassment than you got of giving me a motherfucking parking ticket. Where's the goddamn nurse."

Billy yanked the pillow from under Taft's head and held it an inch from his face. "You know how easy it would be to punch your ticket right now?"

"But they know you're here," he said, shoving the pillow away with surprising strength for a man fresh out of surgery. "So what are you gonna do, huh? This a public building, you gonna kill me? Kill that man in the other bed, too? What are you gonna do. *Fuck* you."

"Hi there, everything OK?" The nurse in the doorway sounded cheerful but in charge.

"Nah, he's just upset over me being like this," Taft said.

"You'll be fine," she said, no one's fool. "Are you just about done in here, sir? I think your friend—"

"Needs his rest," Billy finished for her, then, leaning over Taft as if to say goodbye, whispered, "You will never get rid of me," and walked out of the room.

UNABLE TO LEAVE THE HOSPITAL, Billy paced the main hall atrium, now and then charging halfway back to Taft's room, then reining himself in until a security guard finally approached him to see what was up. Flashing his ID, Billy muttered something about a sick cop, the square badge at first backing off leery, then quickly losing interest.

And then Billy saw her, Taft's wife, tall and gracefully obese, pushing a two-year-old in a stroller across the sun-dappled floor. He reflexively moved to her, then blocked her way.

"Hey, Patricia, right?"

She stopped and stared, not able to place him.

"Bill Graves, I was at your wedding."

She reared back, got taller, gave him a face like a fortress. "I remember you."

As well she should. When he had heard that Taft, less than a year after the murders, was getting married, Billy and Whelan, who was about to retire in any event, put on suits and crashed the wedding. Right after the minister asked if anyone objected, Billy sang out, "Right over here, because that bastard is a baby-killing triple murderer. He did it once, he'll do it again."

They got their asses good and kicked that day; half the wedding party, both male and female, were correction officers related by blood to Taft. But it was worth it just to ruin the ceremony—or maybe not, given that the incident led to his being transferred to Night Watch, his second banishment to the underworld, most bosses believing that working any kind of steady midnights was just this side of a firing squad.

"So," Billy said amiably, "I just want to know, how's it working out for you two, everybody happy?"

"You have no right to be accosting me," her voice as stiff as her posture.

"I just want to ask you, does he ever wake up in the middle of the night all covered in sweat and screaming his head off? You know what I'm talking about, right?"

She waved to the same security guard across the floor, but Billy retinned him without even looking in his direction, the man once again backstepping to his post.

Billy felt light as a feather, out-of-his-mind spontaneous. "How's he as a dad?" nodding to the stroller, kid number three from what he'd heard. "A real disciplinarian I'll bet."

She attempted to walk away, but Billy, astonishing himself, blocked her escape.

"One last bed question: does he ever get up, say, about six in the morning, come back about an hour later, a little winded, maybe a little bloody? I'm just curious."

"I work for Christian Outreach," her voice suddenly a hoarse, teary mess, "I *help* people, and you have no right to talk to me like this."

No, he didn't; suddenly red-faced, Billy turned from her without another word and walked away.

FINALLY STRIDING ACROSS THE CENTRAL atrium toward the exit, Billy was startled to see Pavlicek coming in through the revolving doors, moving like a sleepwalker, his eyes off-center and shining as he made his way through the slanting beams of captured sunlight to the elevator banks.

"John!"

"Hey," Pavlicek said flatly, turning to Billy as if they had just seen each other an hour ago.

"What are you doing here?" Billy's voice still burbling with adrenaline.

"My doctor's here."

"You OK?"

"Yeah, just some tests."

"Tests for what?"

"Cholesterol's through the roof."

"Yeah? What's he got you on, Lipitor? Crestor?"

"Vytorin."

"Jimmy Daly takes that. He says it's a lifesaver."

"Tell me about it."

"You're not here to see Curtis Taft by any chance," Billy asked, his voice sly-dog low.

"Curtis Taft works here?" Pavlicek blinked.

Billy took a moment, then: "He's a patient. I just about put my hands around his throat."

"Still fucking with him, huh?" Pavlicek sounded elsewhere, his eyes over Billy's shoulder as if there was bigger game to be had.

"You all right?"

"I just told you."

"I mean otherwise."

"It's a funny day. I'm late for a meeting."

"A meeting here?" Billy not sure whether he was still too jacked to keep track of the conversation or it was just careening off point on its own.

The elevator arrived, Pavlicek silently giving him his back as he stepped inside.

"Hey, what's your doctor's name?"

"What for?" Pavlicek towering over everyone else in the car.

Billy tapped his own heart. "You're not the only one."

"Go to someone up by you," Pavlicek said as the door began to close. "My guy's not all that."

THE SIXTEEN-YEAR-OLD YEMENI kid lay flat on his back, arms flung wide, staring up with his one unexploded eye at a cardboard placard taped to the ceiling: "SCREW THE DOG—BEWARE OF OWNER." Above the words was a caricature of a stubble-jawed bruiser aiming a hand cannon at the viewer, the circumference of the muzzle almost as big around as the guy's head. The real shooter—who had accidentally killed his best friend while showing off his father's gun, which had been hidden beneath the cash register—was on the floor too, sitting at the end of a food aisle. Glaze-faced and weeping, he was being interviewed by Alice Stupak, squatting on her hams as she attempted to gently tweeze out his version of events.

As Billy stood by the front window debriefing the first uniform on the scene, Gene Feeley came into the store with a young man, not a cop, the kid involuntarily inhaling when he first saw the body.

"Back in the day the homicide rate around here was so high, Jackie, that the precinct had to split in two just to keep pace with the bodies," Feeley explained. "But those days are dead and gone, so they say, although I would no sooner walk down the street unarmed around here than I would if I was living in Iraq."

"What's going on, Gene?" As far as Billy knew, Feeley had the night off.

"My sister's kid, he's doing a paper for his journalism class, I thought I'd help out."

"No kidding," Billy said, thinking, The guy never shows up when he's supposed to, now he starts showing up when he isn't.

"Uncle Gene," the kid said, taking in the gun cartoon directly over the body. "Look at that."

"Go on over there," Feeley said, taking his nephew's iPad. "I'll take your picture, you can tweet it on Facebook."

"Maybe you should wait until they finish," Billy said.

"No problem, Billy," one of the CSUs said, raising up from the body and taking the iPad from Feeley. "Go ahead, Gene, get in with the kid."

A moment later, the store owner, the hem of his pajama bottoms

peeking out from beneath his trouser cuffs, finally stumbled into the
store, his gun permit held out before him like a magic charm. Avoiding
looking at either the dead kid or his son, he walked right past Billy to
Feeley, the most senior-looking cop on the set.

"Talk to her," Feeley said, chucking a thumb at Stupak, who was coming back up to the front.

"Talk to me? What's wrong with you?" she snapped. "Your hearing
aid on the fritz?"

"Watch your mouth," Feeley said, heading for the door.

"Where are you going?" she squawked, her arms outstretched in mock
bewilderment.

"I got to be somewhere."

"Somewhere *where*," she blew. "You're *here, here's* where you got to
be, so how about you stun the shit out of everybody and do your fucking job for a change."

"Alice," Billy pulling her back.

"You better talk to her," Feeley said to Billy.

"Talk to me?" The front door shut with a jingle.

"Alice . . ."

"Talk to *me*?"

"Take it easy, he's off tonight."

"Oh yeah?" she said, grabbing the store owner by the arm and steering him off to a neutral corner. "How can you tell?"

MILTON RAMOS

He sat in his den. He had a den now, damp-smelling in a way he couldn't eradicate but a den nonetheless. He didn't even know what a den was when he was a kid. And not just a den: he had a house, a goddamn house, was the unencumbered owner of a two-story, three-bedroom, mock mock-Tudor. Of course, the neighborhood was so shitty that he had to enclose the entire exterior in decorative iron security grilles, which made it look like a birdcage for a pterodactyl, but it was his, earned and paid for. And he had Sofia, sitting next to him now, watching, for the second evening in a row, *Pocahontas*. He must have seen that thing seventy-five times, *Snow White, Little Mermaid, Sleeping Beauty, Mulan*, and all the others at least as many times as that. But he never grew bored, because what he was really doing was watching her watch the movie.

She was built like him, like her late mother, and she came in for her share of schoolyard torture. When he had been the porker back then, the teasing had quickly ended after the ringleader lost two of his brand-new front teeth to a cross pipe on the monkey bars. But she was a girl, and he had no idea how girls were supposed to deal with that kind of cruelty and so he let her watch slim pretty young females being rescued from their tormentors by handsome boys, night after night after night. A real father of the year.

Big, fast, and devoid of mercy—ever since he was a kid, that had been the rap on him. Everyone outside his family had always been afraid of him—in school, then later on the street, then later on the Job, even though he had never provoked a fight in his life. Devoid of mercy, devoid of humor, devoid of personality. But he loved deep if not demonstrably: his mother, his two brothers, and his wife, all gone now. And this kid right here, who—fortunately, he guessed—had been an infant when her mother passed.

"Give me a sip," she said, nodding to the glass of Yellow Chartreuse in his hand.

"Cut it out."

"I want some," she wheedled in a high teasing voice, the same ritual every night.

"It's medicine, I told you that."

"I'm sick," dropping her forehead to his arm. "Please?"

He dipped a finger in the glass and touched it to her tongue. "It's bedtime, go upstairs."

"Carry me."

"I can't, my back hurts," he said, wincing.

"Maybe you had too much medicine."

Milton winced again, this time for real. "Go ahead, Marilys is waiting, I'll come up later."

Moving like Creeping Jesus, Sofia reluctantly headed for the stairs, placing one foot then the other on each riser, groaning like an old lady before stepping up to the next. One foot then the other, her nightly protest march.

"Go ahead now."

Milton switched to ESPN, then reached for the lined sheet of yellow paper on the coffee table, so obsessively handled today that it was starting to blacken along the folds. He left it unopened in his lap.

He tried to concentrate on the last five minutes of the Nets-Thunder game, but his thoughts drifted, as they often did after a few shots, to Sofia's mother, Sylvia, seven years earlier the victim of a hit-and-run driver on Bronx Park East, directly in front of the geriatric hospital where she had worked for a radiologist.

If he had to describe their eight-year marriage in two words, if he was allowed to go back in time and rescript their wedding cake, he would choose, in sky-blue icing, *Good Enough,* as in good enough companions, good enough lovers, good enough parents. *Good Enough,* as in if God or some fortune-teller had told him, early on in their relationship, that Sylvia was to be his mate until the end of his days, he wouldn't have complained. Except the end of her days came first.

MARILYS IRRIZARY, MILTON'S HOUSEKEEPER AND Sofia's five-days-a-week stand-in mother, had a distinct tread: halting and striving for cat-burglar light, as if just leaving the bedroom of a colicky baby. But she was a short, solid, broad-foot Guatemalan, and he could always hear her on the move from anywhere in the house.

She came into the den and stood directly behind where he sat on the couch.

"She's waiting for you."

"I'll be up," draining his 'Treuse without turning to look at her.

"I finished everything I could, but there's still stuff in the dryer."

"You're going home?"

She leaned over his shoulder for the empty glass on the coffee table, the sweetish tang still hanging in the air.

"I could stay."

Most witnesses at the scene of the accident, the vehicular homicide, disagreed on the make and model, let alone the color, of the car. One old guy was able to come up with a description of the plate, which he said was out of state, had a tree splitting the numbers against a blue-orange sunset.

"Or I could go."

Visiting that half-cocked witness on the sly two days later, Milton asked him how he could possibly remember the tree splitting the digits against a blue-orange sunset yet not recall any numbers or letters off the same.

3-T-R, left side of the tree, the old man said. It had come back to him that very morning on the toilet.

Make and model?

Black maybe gray Accord or Camry, those cars to him like two peas in a pod.

The case wasn't Milton's, of course, the visit enough to get him suspended for hindering the investigation of the local squad, although probably not really, given the mitigating circumstances, emotional duress, extreme grief, et cetera. Nonetheless, he kept the news of the partial plate to himself.

From one flight above, the front door opened, then closed, followed by the jingle of keys in the lock, Marilys heading for home.

Three weeks after Milton's talk with the eyewitness, a middle-aged male with a suspended driver's license lay on his deathbed in Cherokee County Memorial Hospital after suffering grievous wounds in a car accident. Aaron Artest, an individual who lived in Queens but had unexpectedly returned to his hometown of Union, South Carolina, about the same time as Sylvia's funeral, told investigators that an old rust-bodied sedan with heavily tinted side windows had pulled up next to his gray Accord—plate 3TR-AM7—as he was driving alone on Highway 150. The unseen driver kept apace for a minute or so, as if to make sure he had Artest's attention, before poking a shotgun out of the passenger window, which, naturally, inspired Artest to haul ass. Then his brakes, which had been serviced not even a month before, on the day he left New York, must've somehow given out.

"No, he didn't fire at me," Artest said to the cops. Then: "It looked to be a Nova, no wait, a Caprice, hang on, hold on." Then his dying words: "Just give me a minute."

Milton clicked off the TV without registering the outcome, retrieved his glass, poured himself another Chartreuse, then finally unfolded the paper in his lap, the names and addresses written there writhing like eels.

> Carmen Graves. RN, St. Ann's Hospital.
> Det. Sgt. William Graves, Manhattan Night Watch.
> 684 Tuckahoe Road, Yonkers.
> Declan Ramon, 8. Carlos Eammon, 6.
> Immaculate Conception Day, 24 Van der Donck Street, Yonkers.

Big, fast, and devoid of mercy.

All he could say in his defense was that his older brother had been worse.

From two floors above he finally began to hear his daughter plaintively calling out for him. He had no idea how long she'd been at it, the sleepy but insistent oscillations of her voice coming down on his ears like the offbeat siren of some alien ambulance.

5

It was one of those fortuitous early mornings when Billy was able to crawl into bed a half hour before Carmen had to get up, the bakery warmth of her body coming at him as he raised the quilt, making him both alert and drowsy. Still asleep, she rolled into him, a heat-radiant breast fanning flat against his ribs, an equally hotted-up thigh carelessly flung over the front of his suddenly ridiculous boxers. But she was still lightly snoring, and with the kids about to overrun the base camp it was better for him to concentrate on the stray curls of her hair that had managed to find their way up into his nose. It was all he could do not to sneeze.

"So you're calmed down about Taft now?" she asked him thirty minutes later.

"Yeah, but I think I want to do this thing," Billy watching her from the bed as she slipped into her whites.

"You should," turning away from him to brush her hair.

He could hear both boys flying out of their bedroom as if someone had shouted, "Incoming."

"But why should I?"

She took a breath. "Because you want to. Because it would make you feel better. Because it's good karma."

"It's not like we're rolling in dough."

"Well," applying mascara now, which as far as he was concerned was like applying black paint to coal, "we're not exactly on the street either."

Something containing liquid shattered in the kitchen, neither of them reacting.

"So you really think I should?"

"I think you want my permission or something."

"I don't need your permission."

"I agree."

"So I should do it, right?"

"*WHO*."

"Billy Graves, looking for Miss Worthy."

Hearing his flat Irish municipal accent from the other side of her door, and most likely assuming he was just another Hudson County homicide detective, Edna Worthy—the grandmother of Martha Timberwolf, the girl murdered by Memori Williams's twin sister, but really by Curtis Taft, if you wanted Billy's opinion—called out, "It's open," letting him into her Jersey City apartment without so much as looking away from the TV.

She apparently made ends meet as a baby farmer, three subsidized foster kids roaming her overheated living room like cats, although as old and heavy as she was, she could barely rise off the couch.

"Can I sit?" Billy asked.

She gestured vaguely to the left side of the room, nothing there like a chair.

At first glance, Miss Worthy, a TV remote in one hand, a cell phone in the other, seemed unaffected by the catastrophic loss that had been visited on her only two days earlier, Billy chalking up her indifferent demeanor to a long, tragedy-packed life; it wasn't as if he hadn't witnessed this kind of non-reaction in people before. But then he noticed the carefully arranged semicircle of plastic-framed photos on the Cheerios-littered coffee table in front of her, the murdered girl staring back at her grandmother from all of her ages, toddler to confirmation to junior high school cap and gown, the face consistently heavy and glum, as if she had known her fate from the day she was born.

"Martha was the only blood to me left," Miss Worthy eventually said, reaching across herself to pick up a toddler who came close enough for her to grab. "Now she's gone, too."

"I'm sorry about that," Billy said.

"She helped me take care of these kids, and so how am I supposed to do that now. This ain't a hotel, but you should have seen where they was before."

"I'm sorry," he said again, glancing at a card table strewn with the silver-foiled leftovers of a half dozen condolence casseroles.

"Well, they all going back now. Except maybe this one here," lifting up the kid in her lap like a kitten. "She looks like Martha a little, maybe she can grow up to be some kind of conversation to me, but it's gonna be a race between her growing up and me growing down."

"I hear you."

"So what do you want to know I ain't already said ten times to the other detectives?" Miss Worthy asked, palming crumbs off the girl.

"Nothing, really. I just came by to offer to help you with the burial, you know, if you need it."

Miss Worthy finally looked at him straight on, her cat's-eye glasses catching the light. "You police or not? 'Cause if you're not, I'm calling them right now," holding up the business card of the last sport-jacketed individual before Billy to come into her home.

WHEN BILLY ENTERED BROWN'S FAMILY Funeral Home, Redman, draped in his work apron, was displaying, from the breastbone up, a man in his fifties to two of his younger relations in the middle of his living-room-turned-chapel. Not ten feet away, Redman's son, velcroed into his activity walker, watched SpongeBob on a fifty-four-inch flat-screen, the volume insanely high, although no one seemed to be bothered by it.

"That don't look like him," the male of the two said.

"Did you see him when they brought him in here?" Redman asked.

"I'm just saying . . ."

"If you want, I can try to put him back the way he was," winking at Billy.

Billy sidled up to the TV and turned down the volume. A few minutes later, unhappy but not sure what to do about it, the relations left the building without saying goodbye.

"So what's up?" Redman asked, whipping the sheet off the lower half of the body, revealing a makeshift diaper fashioned from a tall kitchen Glad bag in order to capture any post-embalming leakage.

"I want you to bury someone for me."

"Who."

"A murder vic, sixteen years old, her people don't have dime one."

Redman's wife, Nola, came in with a shopping bag of clothes: brown suit, white shirt, a tie, socks, and shoes, the suit and socks still bearing their price tags from Theo's Discount House of Men.

"Where is she now?"

"Well, she lived in Jersey City."

"So, Essex County morgue?" Redman began muscling the pants up over the Glad-bag diaper, the effort making his face bead with sweat.

"I assume."

"That's out of state."

"So?"

"That's extra."

"You want my E-ZPass?"

Redman propped the body into a sitting position so that Nola could get its arms into the shirt, their son now rolling across the room while chewing on a take-out menu.

"How much do you want to spend?"

"How do I know?" Billy said. "How much does it cost?"

"Depends on the casket, the wood, the lining, the vault, the service, I assume you want a minister, some kind of celebrant, pallbearers, limo and a hearse out to the cemetery, do you have a cemetery lined up?" waiting on his wife to finish the buttoning. "Then there's the pickup, the body prep, burial clothes if you need them, flowers, printed programs, you want those memorial T-shirts? I have a guy for that, then there's the grave marker, the plot, the opening, the closing, the death certificate . . ."

"Just help me out here, OK?"

Redman wrestled the shirt tails into the pants, lifting the body off the gurney with one hand in order to do it, then stepped away to mop his brow while his wife threaded and then knotted the tie.

"Who's this kid to you?" he asked.

"Collateral damage from Curtis Taft. It's a long story."

Redman looked at his wife for a nonverbal business discussion, which ended when she abruptly took off to corral her son as he threatened to topple the cosmetics cart, a rolling jungle of wigs, makeup jars, brushes, palette knives, and cotton swabs.

"I can put something together for seven K," he finally said.

"Seven. Are you high?"

"You want to take your business up the street? There's four parlors in the next two blocks, anyone offers you under that they're going to put her in a cereal box, take her out to the cemetery on the bus."

"I don't have seven K."

"I'll ask you again, who is she to you."

While Redman and Nola began dealing with the dead man's socks and shoes, Billy told them the whole story, from the death of Shakira Barker's twin sister five years earlier through her long slow nightmare transformation into a murderer herself, the victim, Martha Timberwolf, lying on a slab across the Hudson with no one to send her Home.

"I'll do it for six," Redman said, "and that's costing me."

Nola stiffened a little but said nothing.

"Thank you, I appreciate it."

"Can you pay up front?"

"No problem."

"Can you do cash?" Redman rolling his prep cart close and pulling a chair up to the body.

"If that's how you want it."

"Because that would help me."

"Help me help you," Billy said, watching as Redman slipped on a pair of rubber gloves, then reached into the chaos of the cosmetics cart and extracted a tube of Krazy Glue. After squeezing out thin lines of the gunk on the lacerated palms of the dead man, he used his finger to carefully coat the skin.

"What are you doing?" Billy asked.

"What, this? If I don't put some kind of adhesive on these defensive wounds here and people start stroking this guy's hands at the service? They could walk away with a souvenir."

Billy took a moment, then shifted gears. "You see Pavlicek recently?"

"He came in here a few weeks ago to see how my son was doing."

"How was he?"

"My son?"

"Pavlicek."

"What do you mean?"

"I'm not sure, I ran into him at Columbia Pres today."

"Oh yeah? What was he doing there?"

"He said he was seeing someone for his cholesterol."

"I'm not surprised, are you?"

"He looked like a zombie. I swear to God, every time I see him these days, it's like he's on a different drug. Tell me that's high cholesterol."

"All I know is," Redman carefully recapping the Krazy Glue, "men that big can't just eat whatever they want."

"SO, THIS WITNESS, SO-CALLED WITNESS, Michael Reidy, that you interviewed—remember him?"

Sitting across the desk from Elvis Perez, a tall, vulture-necked detective working the Bannion homicide in Midtown South, Billy tried to recall the face of the blood- or ketchup-stained drunk in the Penn Station waiting room. "Sort of," he said.

"Well, we lost him."

"Lost him."

"We have his address from your Fives, but he's not there, and he's not answering his cell, so I was wondering if you remember anything he might of said to you or you overheard that maybe didn't make it into your notes."

"Do you know how many people we interviewed that night?"

Perez tossed a pencil on his desk and stifled a yawn. He had the kind of droopy eyes that suggested he had never recovered from the exhausting experience of being born.

"So where are you at on this?" Billy asked.

"Nowhere, really."

Billy gestured to the manila folder on Perez's desk next to a small plaster statue of San Lazaro.

"May I?"

Even in the bloodiest CSU photos, Bannion retained his startling Black Irish handsomeness, the best-looking corpse Billy had seen since Carmen's first husband.

"The ME said the wound was jagged," Perez said, rolling his chair away from the desk and then running the flat of his hand along the inside of his thigh. "The actor was no surgeon but he knew where to cut."

"And nothing on the perp?"

"Plenty. He was short tall black white heavy slim, came flying in on a skateboard, rolled away in a wheelchair. Are you kidding me? The guy could've been seven feet tall with a turban, a beard, and an AK, screaming, 'Death to America,' and everybody there would've chalked it up to the DTs."

"How about the tapes?"

"We finally got the south plaza footage back, but all it shows is Bannion running to the subways after the fact. The tape we really need, from over by the LIRR information board, we're still waiting on. TARU says it could take a few days, a few weeks, or never. All that state-of-the-art equipment and some asshole spills a cup of coffee. How's that for bang versus whimper."

"For what?"

"Forget it. You want to see what we got?"

Perez slid the disc into his desk monitor, Billy standing behind him, ignoring the buzzing of his cell.

The captured stretch of arcade between the Long Island commuter trains and the subway entrance at first appeared deserted, all the action having taken place out of the camera's range, the grainy footage of nothing and no one evoking the bleariness of the hour. But then here came

Bannion running loopily into the picture, his light blue jeans turning purple with blood, his dripping shoes leaving those dark liquid footprints until he came to a baffled stop in front of the turnstiles and started fishing through his wallet for what—his MetroCard?—fishing and fumbling, and then, just as Billy had speculated at the scene, abruptly attempting to hurdle the low barrier but suddenly locking up in midair as if flash-frozen and dropping directly on top of the turnstile before falling to the ground.

"It's not like it's without entertainment value," Perez said, "but it all happened on the other end."

"And how long for that tape again?"

Perez shrugged.

Night Watch was strictly one and done; set up the morning man and move on to the next post-midnight felony. There were simply too many runs in a night, a week, a month to keep tabs, or even remain curious, about past crimes and still have the wherewithal to focus on the next one coming down the pike. Night Watch jobs, an old boss once told Billy, were like individual tears in a crying jag.

Still . . .

"Do me a favor?" Billy asked. "Can you let me know when it comes in?"

THAT NIGHT HE WAS SADDLED with another strange player doing a Night Watch one-off, Stanley Treester from the DNA Liaison Unit, and when Billy entered the Metropolitan Hospital's trauma ER to oversee a run-of-the-mill stabbing, he found him sitting on the edge of a gurney staring intently at a damp-eyed elderly man under a blanket. The old guy, oblivious to Treester's presence, stared off into the middle distance as if into the void.

"I messed up," the patient said to no one.

"Who's this?"

"I thought I knew him from when I was a kid," Treester said, his eyes never leaving the other man's face.

"Do you?"

"No."

"I messed up," the man said again.

"Does he have anything to do with the run?"

"No."

"Then . . ." Billy about to tell him to get in the game, then thought better of it.

"And I'm going to hell."

"I'll sell you my ticket," Billy said, before walking off to find the crime.

The actual investigation into the stabbing took about five minutes, the Samaritan who had brought the victim to the hospital confessing the moment Mayo flashed his ID, the story behind the story being two brothers, a fifth of Herradura, dominoes, and a knife.

Stacey Taylor's call came through while the doer was being cuffed. Billy, grateful that it wasn't the Wheel with another run, answered right away.

"It's four in the morning, you know that, right?"

"I'm sorry, did I wake you?" she said.

"What's up?"

"Nothing. I just wanted to see how it went today with Taft."

"I messed up, just went in there with no game plan and messed up."

"Yeah, well, you're only human."

"But I want to thank you for your help."

"Hey, that's how we do."

Still on the phone, Billy momentarily went south, thinking about the last few days: Bannion, Taft, Miss Worthy, but mostly John Pavlicek, wandering into Columbia Pres like someone had hit him on the back of the head with a bag of nickels.

"Hello?" she said.

"Hey. Sorry," Billy coming all the way back, then: "Let me just ask, how good are you with hospital records?"

"Which hospital?"

"Columbia Pres."

"I know a guy there."

"Yeah? Who?"

"Then you'd know him too."

"I need you to look up an outpatient for me."

"Who."

He hesitated. "John Pavlicek."

"Your guy from the Geese? What's wrong with him?"

"That's what I'd like to know."

"Do you know who he sees there?"

"Somebody for his cholesterol. Or so he says."

He heard her light up, then expel that first buzzy lungful. "All right."

"What do you charge for something like this?"

"When have I ever taken your money?"

Billy's guilt made him wince.

"Maybe you should start."

THIRTY MINUTES LATER, AS HE was leaving the hospital, his cell rang again: Yasmeen on the downside of a wee-hours drunk, her voice like wet flannel.

"I'm just calling you to say I'm really sorry."

"About . . ."

"The other night, I got so drunk, you know? I didn't even know you drove me home until Dennis told me in the morning."

"Oh c'mon, how many times . . ."

"Denny's a good guy, you know? He really is."

"Well, being he's your husband and all . . ."

The silence on the other end reeked of wrong answer.

"Anyways, it's four-thirty in the morning, don't you think you should . . ."

"You want to hear something?" she cut in. "Raymond Del Pino's older sister just had her second kid, you know what she called her? Yasmeen Rose. She told me it's because I was the only one who never gave up trying to get Eric Cortez."

"Well good for her," Billy said, fishing for his car keys. "And good for you."

"Good for me," she slurred. "I'm telling you, that baby is cursed."

MILTON RAMOS

2130 Longfellow Avenue, a six-story walk-up in the still semi-shitty East Bronx, was over a hundred years old but it had been built by fresh-off-the-boat artisans, and despite the fact that by the time Milton came to be born here it was a dump—its gappy mosaic tile floor like a piss-bum's smile, its walls festooned with wilting poker chips of plaster, and its glassed-in apartment directory listing long-dead Jewish and Puerto Rican tenants like a roll call of ghosts—it still had its touches of old-world flair. But now, as he stood in the vestibule more than twenty years after he had fled for the safety of his aunt Pauline's apartment in Brooklyn, he was shocked by what had become of his earliest home on earth, gutted and rehabbed in the cheapest possible way, the old crowned lathe-and-plaster brown-coat walls replaced by featureless plywood, the multicolored stone floors by prefab squares of ceramic, the ancient swaybacked marble risers by painted pine, and the amber-glassed hall-way sconces by overhead halos of sputtering fluorescence.

"It stinks in here," Sofia said, standing alongside him beneath the dented aluminum mailboxes.

"Don't say stinks, say smells," he said, then, gesturing to the stairs with the head of his 34-inch Rawlings Pro Maple (because you never knew): "Beauty before age."

. . .

A BASEBALL BAT IS A versatile thing. As Milton learned while still a teen-ager, a moderate swing across the shins will get a piece-of-shit dope slinger to share with you his strategy for keeping financially afloat, which basically comes down to stiffing Peter in order to pay Paul, then stiffing Paul and finding new suppliers. Another rap will get the slinger to tell you who the most recent Peter is, who the most recent Paul. And if, a day later, you bring the butt of the bat down reasonably hard on the splayed knuckles of either Peter or Paul, both of whom wanted to kill that little rip-off artist, you will find out the names of the hitters who were sent out to consummate the deed. Now, once you get the actual hitters in an unoccupied apartment, bound hand and foot with gaffer's tape—you won't put another piece of tape across their mouths until they try to talk their way out of dying by telling you everything, including the truth—you can just go ahead and play home-run derby until the walls, the ceiling, and your clothes are streaked with red.

Sofia had a hard time climbing—"I like to go as high as I can," she had once explained to him, "because then all I have left is to go down"—and by the third floor she was struggling. But he was as patient with her as he had been when climbing these same steps all through childhood with his morbidly obese mother, her trudge-mantra back then, "What a world Milton, what a world," thrilling him with terror.

4B, Sofia announced. Who lived here?

Mrs. Sanchez, she was a very nice lady.

She was nice?

Yes.

4C. Who lived here.

The Kleins.

Were they nice?

They were old.

The apartment doors, once oak, were now all single slabs of siege-mentality sheet metal, their numbers, in his time screwed-in brass, nothing more than hardware-store decals. But he couldn't care less about these particular outrages against memory, because in the end the information they provided was the same information as twenty years ago, and any way you cut it the doors and their numbers would always tell the same story.

4D. Who lived here?

If he let her, she would announce every apartment in the building. But in a way, that was what they were here for, Milton taking his daughter on this stations-of-the-cross pilgrimage as an inoculation against the worst parts of himself, as a living, breathing reminder of what he had to lose if he allowed himself, at this moment in time, to follow his nature.

4D. Who . . .

The Carters.

Were they nice?

They were OK. They had a son who was retarded.

What's retarded?

Not right in the head.

What?

Stupid but not his fault.

Sofia rolled that around for a bit, then: What was his name?

Michael.

Did the kids make fun of him?

Some.

Did you?

No.

How about Uncle Edgar?

No.

How about Uncle Rudy?

He could be kind of mean, but he was a kid.

Did you and Uncle Edgar get mad at him when he did that?

He was just a kid.

Did Grandma Rose get mad at him?

She didn't get mad at anybody.

Were there other retarded kids in the building?

No, but one boy was gay.

He kissed other boys?

I guess.

What was his name?

Victor.

Did the kids make fun of him?

Oh yeah.

Did you?

No. Actually, one time when some older guys were pushing him around outside on the street, I made sure they never did that again.

How did you do that?

Don't worry about it.

4E. Who lived here?

Some girl, Inez. I can't remember her last name.

Was she nice?

I guess.

Did you like her?

I didn't hate her.

Did you want to marry her?

No.

4F. Who lived here?

Guess.

You.

And Grandma Rose and Edgar and Rudy.

Can we go inside?

There's other people in there now.

NO MATTER HOW MANY FAMILIES had lived behind that door since the Ramos family ceased to be, no matter how often the rooms and walls had been torn up and rebuilt in the name of affordable housing, 4F would always be haunted, and he could easily imagine some of those that moved in here afterward waking up and weeping in the middle of the night for no reason they could understand.

Little Man's death, if you wanted to look at it that way, was nothing more than a gruesome case of mistaken identity. The targeted dealer, as anyone in the building could have told the men sent to lay him out, lived in 5C.

So why, Milton just had to ask his killers that day in the empty apartment, did you go to 4F?

That's when they talked about the sulky girl on the stoop, Miss Information.

Describe her, Edgar said.

And they did, after which the Ramos brothers stared at each other in astonishment.

That girl on three? Milton said to Edgar. Then, turning to their prisoners, hog-tied and belly-down on the floor, She said your guy lived in 4F? You're sure?

Arching up to offer their gleaming faces, backs bowed, they swore to all the angels in heaven. How were they to know? They were sent out without the apartment.

And you told her the dealer's name? He still couldn't believe it.

We swear on our mothers' eyes . . .

And she said 4F . . .

Yes. Yes. Yes.

Now they're crying, Edgar grunted, tapping his bat against his calf.

Well, you know who else lives in 4F? Milton asked, lifting his own bat from behind his ear, the tip making small, not quite lazy circles. Us. His brothers.

SOFIA WALKED DOWN TO THE third-floor landing, Milton behind her, absently rapping the walls on his way down.

3D. Who lived here.

I don't know.

3E. Who lived here.

I don't know.

3F. Who lived here.

Breathe . . .
The gay kid.
Victor? Who else.
His mother.
What was her name.
Dolores.
Who else.
Breathe . . .
His sister.
What was her name.
I can't remember.
Did you like her?

LATER, AFTER LONG SHOWERS, HE and Edgar knocked on 3F and came
face-to-face with Carmen's mother.

Where's she at.

The answer—Atlanta—put Milton off his game for twenty-three years.
The same might have been true for Edgar, but the dead hitters had friends
and his big brother lived only another week.

His mother, heart-stunned, only a week after that.

DID YOU WANT TO MARRY her?

Unconsciously humming, Milton rested the knob of the bat against
the 3F peephole: Guess who.

Dad!

What.

Did you want to marry her.

Marry who. Then: I don't remember. Then: You know what? You're
right, it stinks in here, let's go home.

As they started back down to the vestibule, Milton imagined his
immense, huffing mother passing Carmen on the stairs at some point
back then, the skinny girl with the martyred eyes most likely having to
backtrack to the nearest landing in order for Mrs. Ramos to have enough

room to pass, the two of them with self-conscious smiles, his mother's tinged with humiliation.

"WHAT'S WITH CALLING ME 'DAD,'" Milton asked as he unlocked the car door. "What happened to 'Daddy'?"

"It's a baby word. The kids make fun of you if you say it."

"You got to learn to stand up for yourself, Sofia," he snapped, "otherwise those kids are never going to stop, and that kick-me kind of mentality of yours is going to make you miserable until the day you die, you understand me?"

No response—well, what the hell was she supposed to say?

"I'm sorry, I didn't mean to yell."

"It's OK," Sofia saying it in that resigned way of hers that made him feel like tearing out his heart and feeding it to the birds.

AN HOUR LATER, AFTER DROPPING his kid off at her school, he sat in his car halfway down the block from the house in Yonkers, far enough away not to draw anyone's attention but close enough to observe.

They had a house; he had a house. They had kids; he had a kid. Graves had a gold shield; well, so did he.

He was a widower, but no one here had any hand in that. So why on top of everything else, everything he had a right to feel, did he also feel, in this moment, envious? Where the hell did she get off having a normal life. What kind of ice-cold freak was she to just sail on like this, to make a go of it like anyone else.

Even before he and his brother had beaten two men to death at an age when all they should have been thinking about was sports, music, and ass, his sense of being "normal" was a tough sell in the mirror. He had always felt himself to be something of a miracle beast, trained to walk upright and mimic human speech. But after that day, a day launched by her, he never gave a moment's thought about belonging to any species but his own.

He saw the old man come out and slowly bend to retrieve a rolled-up newspaper from the lawn, Milton gut-reading him, despite his frailty, as an old school boss, still carrying an air of sober authority. Then, an hour later, a middle-aged Indian woman, most likely his caregiver, stepped out on the porch to have a smoke. There was no sign of Carmen (probably at work), the kids (probably at school), or her husband. Knowing Graves to be in Night Watch, Milton assumed he was either in the house catching up on his sleep or—more likely, given that the sole car in the driveway was a piece-of-shit Civic definitely belonging to the caregiver—he'd gotten stuck with an early morning run.

The thing was, now that he'd finally found her after all these years, found her as sure as he'd found that Palmetto State cracker that snatched away his wife, where did he, where did they, go from here. In the past, no matter what actions he had taken on behalf of his dead, the suffering he had inflicted in return had always been of limited duration, whereas his suffering only intensified, leaving him afterward feeling more alone, more heartbroken, more subhuman than ever. For him, balancing the books had always been like bare-handedly punching to death a man whose face and body were studded with nails. And right now, at this point in his life, the thought of going through that again was unbearable, the cost, mentally if not physically, unsurvivable.

So let it go.

Can't.

Then find another way.

Find another way.

It should have been funny, Billy thought, but it wasn't. Anytime you get called in to see the school therapist about your child, funny is the last thing on your mind. But still . . .

The day before, Declan had apparently pushed a kid who had been taunting him, knocking him face-first into the edge of an open locker door. The injury was minimal—they were eight-year-olds, after all—but there was a little blood and a broken pair of glasses. And so now, he and Carmen were seated in an empty classroom talking to a young man who couldn't have been more than a year or two out of school himself, asking whether Declan's birth had been a difficult one, whether they "employed" any physical form of discipline at home, whether there was any history, on either side of the family, of . . .

"How about we just get Declan to apologize to the kid and we pay for the glasses?" Billy amiably cutting him off.

"Those would be appropriate gestures, no doubt, but I think . . ."

"*No!*" the word flying out of Carmen's mouth like a command to a wolf as she thrust herself forward in her chair. "Where the hell do you get off asking me about giving birth to him, and how dare you ask us if we smack our kids around, if we have crazies in our family. I am a nurse, I am a *healer;* my husband is a New York City detective, he *protects* people.

This is who we are and this is what we can't *do* today, because were stuck having this time suck of a talk with *you*."

"Carm," Billy said uselessly.

"And no, my son isn't going to apologize to that little shit, and no, we're not going pay for those glasses. But you know who should? You and this whole goddamn school, because what happened yesterday is all your fault. You put on this stupid, boring show about the planets, all these poor kids dressed up like silver-foil meatballs, 'Hello! I am Mercury! Hello! I am Saturn!' And you know, *you know,* one poor kid has to come out and say, 'Hello! I am Uranus!' Jesus Christ, you're a shrink, do you know how humiliating that is? And of *course* he's going to get teased and teased, and if he's got any heart to him, like my son has, at some point he is going to push back."

The therapist, more bemused than intimidated, looked down at his notepad, reached for his pen, then thought better of it.

"And if you people try to suspend him? Or even so much as lift a finger to discipline him? We're going to go first to our lawyer and then to the papers. And how stupid will your science teachers look when the story gets out. Don't they watch the news? Uranus isn't even a planet anymore."

With that she got up and walked out, leaving Billy to placate.

"I didn't actually see the play?" he said mildly. "But she's kind of got a point."

When Billy caught up to her in the school lot, he expected her to still be steaming, but instead she was close to tears.

"Tell me I didn't just fuck up," she pleaded, grabbing his hand. "I just get so scared for them, you know? Tell me I didn't fuck up."

WHEN BILLY WOKE UP AT four, the backyard was a beehive, Declan and Carlos dueling with Wiffle bats, Millie smoking up a storm behind their one tree, and his father, oblivious to the action around him, reading a book while lounging in one of their vinyl-weave lawn chairs. After returning to his bedroom for his slippers, Billy called Carmen at the hospital to see how she was holding up, made himself coffee, threw on last night's dress shirt against the chill, and stepped outside.

In the time it took him to prep, the boys had switched from fencing to tossing a football, each Mighty Mouse sidearm heave ending with the passer collapsed on the ground, and each reception, no matter how high the ball, willed into a diving catch, Dec and Carlos apparently more interested in flinging themselves into the earth than making it to the NFL. And although his own young quarterbacking chops had not only afforded him a halfway decent adolescence but a free ride to a Division I school, Billy couldn't care less if his kids became all-stars or ballerinas or computer geeks, as long as they learned the importance of never panicking when they got punched in the face.

Setting his mug on the backyard steps, he pulled up the waist of his pajama bottoms, dragged over one of the other aluminum-framed chairs, and took a seat by his father. The old man was half-dozing now, a creased paperback of *The War Poems of Thomas Hardy* sliding off his lap. A number of other well-worn paperbacks were piled in the grass at his feet, Billy not even having to look at them to know what some of them were: the collected poems of Rupert Brooke, of Wilfred Owen, of W. B. Yeats, Alan Seeger, Robert Graves, and Siegfried Sassoon. Maybe Walter de la Mare.

Billy Senior's grandfather, a Marine, had been fatally gassed in the Battle of the Argonne Forest in 1918; for his daughter, Billy Senior's mother, who had been nine at the time, her father's martyred absence became a permanent, supernatural presence. As a result, for as long as Billy could remember, his own father, brought up haunted by a man he never knew, had been obsessed with the Great War, especially the literature that it produced.

When he became head of student safety at Columbia University at the age of fifty-eight, Billy Senior, exploiting one of his job perks, immediately began to audit classes. He took basic 101s his first year, intermediate-level courses his second, advanced his third. He never participated in discussions or took exams, but he did all the required reading on his own, keeping a low profile year in, year out. Then, wanting to test himself in his fourth year, he wrote a paper on the work of soldier-poet Isaac Rosenberg and handed it in, never expecting the teacher to read it, let alone to raise it above his head in the auditorium the following week and ask, "Who's William Graves?"

The same professor, using his connections abroad, secured a scholarship for him to the annual three-week summer seminar on Literature and the Great War, in either Oxford or Cambridge, Billy could never remember which. That July, Billy Senior attended classes while Billy's mother either tooled around town or took day trips to the south of England, the only time his parents had ever traveled together outside of the U.S. The summer after his mother died, his father went back to England on his own, the first of eleven solo summer pilgrimages until the time came when he was no longer able to travel by himself.

Of all his father had accomplished after retirement from the NYPD— heading up campus security for a major university, doing the same work for Mount Sinai Hospital and for the New-York Historical Society— nothing had impressed Billy as much as watching this high-school-educated man in his fifties slip into those high-wire Ivy League classes to shadow-educate himself, Billy Senior taking to scholarship the same way many other men his age and station in life took to grandparenting and TV.

Tossing the remainder of his coffee onto the grass, Billy leaned over and picked up the collected Yeats, slowly flipped through the book, and saw his father's exquisite but strangely unreadable handwriting on nearly every page.

"What you got there?" Billy Senior asked, rising up from the tar pit.

"You used to read to me from this when I was a kid, you remember? 'The Second Coming,' it scared the crap out of me."

"How about returning the favor."

"Read to you?" Billy looked around the yard. "With my delivery? You might as well ask me to break-dance."

Billy Senior sat up a little, opened his eyes. "I remember working the Bronx for a while back in the late seventies when they started having those block parties with turntables and the disc jockeys scratching up the records, everybody spinning around on cardboard flats, spouting out these bragging rhymes . . ."

"You should hear some of your grandson's stylings," Billy said.

". . . next thing you know every kid with a portable tape recorder's marching up and down the streets belting out bad poetry."

"It's still kind of like that out there."

"Look, I don't mean to sound like some cranky old white guy and it's not like I didn't appreciate what that stuff was doing on the positive side in those neighborhoods, it was just, aesthetically? I hated it."

"Well, they can't all be Sam Cooke."

"Nothing wrong with rhythm and blues, my friend. Some of those singers were true bards."

Billy had to smile. The designation "bard" had always been his father's highest form of praise, synonymous with "sublime" and just a shade under "godlike."

"Dad, do you remember my friend Jerry Hart? After his freshman year at Fordham he came home and told his father that he wanted to be a poet. You know what Mr. Hart said to him? 'Anybody'd write a poem would suck a dick.' Excuse my French."

"Cocksucker," Senior said without heat.

"What?" Billy had never heard his father say anything worse than "shit," and rarely that.

"Cunt licker."

The boys stopped playing.

"Cocksucking motherfucking kike-faced little nigger boy." Another bland delivery.

Billy signaled for Millie to bring the kids into the house.

"Dad, what's happening."

"Are you going to read to me?" his father said.

"What?"

"You said you'd read me something," gesturing to the Yeats still in Billy's hands.

"What just happened."

"Happened with what?" Senior's eyes remained clear and untroubled.

Billy took a moment. "All right," he finally said. "Hold on."

Flipping through the Yeats, nervously rejecting poem after poem as being either too long, too beyond his understanding, or having too much unpronounceable Gaelic, he defaulted to the horror poem of his youth. But after quickly scanning the first few lines—the wildly spiraling falcon, the blood-dimmed tide, each image troubling him more than they ever had before, and then returning to "things fall apart, the centre cannot hold"—he closed the book.

"I tell you what," he said, rising to his feet. "How about I recite 'The Face on the Barroom Floor.' That one I can do from memory."

SOMEBODY HAD ANGRILY SCRAWLED "DOPE house" with a broad Sharpie above the apartment 6G peephole in the Truman Houses.

"The quality goes in before the name goes on," the CSU tech standing next to Billy said before entering the scene.

The living room was devoid of furniture, empty save for a few scattered, overfull ashtrays and some still-burning candles set in juice glasses here and there. An emaciated blond woman, looking sixty but most likely around thirty, lay star-fished face-up on the linoleum, a welt of gunpowder-stippled flesh beneath her left collarbone the only sign of violence done to her that was not self-inflicted. Another CSU tech, squatting by the body, gripped her by the jaw and rolled her head from side to side, ran his rubber-gloved fingers roughly through her lank hair, and then unbuttoned her blouse, all in search of other entry wounds.

Before anyone thought to stop her, another young mummy, her eyes looking awl-punched into her head, wandered in through the partly open front door, said, "I forgot my purse," laid eyes on the dead girl, "Oh, April, you still here? I thought . . ." then swirled to the floor.

"WE WAS JUST SITTING AROUND passing the peace pipe, that's all, nobody hurting nobody," the revived woman, Patricia Jenkins, said through a billow of exhaled smoke to Billy and Alice Stupak as they all sat in a stairwell down the hall from the dead girl in 6G.

"All of a sudden this boy comes in with a rifle, says for everybody to give it up, but we're all skyin' so nobody wanted to do that. Donna asked him if he maybe just wants to party with us instead, and he says, 'You disease-drippin' bitches?' He takes all the rock we got left, then goes through everybody's shit for money, cell phones, and whatnot."

She paused for another lungful of smoke, ran a shaky finger across her brow. "He already turned to go, got a hand on the damn doorknob, April says, 'Shit, I bet that ain't even loaded,' and I'm like, 'Oh God . . .'"

Billy glanced at Stupak, neither of them wanting to distract her yet by taking notes.

"That boy, he hears that, he just turns around slow, sticks out that rifle like stickin' out a arm, got the bullet end almost right on her, and bang. Then he leaves like he should of done if April had kept her mouth shut. Then we all like froze until he's gone, then we go too."

Still smoking, she lowered her forehead onto the heel of her palm, closed her eyes, and wept a little.

"All right, Patricia," Stupak began, easing out her pad, "I know you want to get this guy as badly as we do, so help us out here. The shooter, was he white, black, Hispanic . . ."

"Lightish Dominican."

"Dominican. Not, say, Puerto Rican, or . . ."

"Dominican."

"And when you say a kid . . ."

"Like, high-school-dropout age."

The fire door to the stairwell opened, all three turning to see Gene Feeley, the elusive war horse, size up the party and then, hands in pockets, lean against a cinder-block wall directly behind Stupak's back.

Alice took a moment, her temples pulsing with anger. "This guy, do you remember what he was wearing?"

"A orange sweat suit, tops and bottoms."

"Any words or images?"

"Said 'Syracuse' up the leg and across the chest."

Feeley coughed, shifted his feet, Billy watching him like a hawk.

"How about hair? Long, short . . ."

"Had, like, a short crop brushed forward like a Caesar cut, and those devil sideburns, you know, like a pencil line going down his jaw from each side then meet up under his chin, and he had a little mascara on his eyebrows like the boys now do to make them darker."

"Beautiful. And, other than what you told us already, can you think of anything else he said?"

"Not really."

"OK, Patricia," Stupak's eyes bright with the hunt. "How about you come with us to the precinct so we can show you some photo arrays?"

"Can I smoke there?" she asked. "Last time I couldn't smoke."

"No problem," Alice said, rising and reaching out to help the woman to her feet.

"Hey, Patricia," Feeley said, still leaning against his wall. "Before you go, you don't happen to know this kid's name, do you?"

"Oh yeah," she said. "Eric Cienfuegos, he lives upstairs in apartment 11C."

"There you go," he said to Stupak, then sauntered back out to the hall-way.

"I want a transfer," she announced to Billy the moment Feeley was gone.

"I'll handle it," Billy said, wondering how.

"That's what you always say."

"Just let me make some calls."

"You always say that, too."

Burning with embarrassment, he jerked his head toward Patricia Jenkins, standing there like a scarecrow draped in laundry. "Just take her to the house."

HE FOUND FEELEY AS HE was getting into his car, a restored '73 Dodge Polara, double-parked across from the scene.

"What," Feeley looking up at him through the rolled-down driver's window.

Billy, hunched over to be on eye level, just stared.

"She had some goddamn mouth on her the other night," Feeley said. "Embarrassing me in front of my nephew like that."

"Gene," Billy began, his back killing him already, "I asked the Chief of D's last week to take you off my hands, I told him how unreliable you are, how you undermine me and everybody else in the squad. You know what he said? He said, Just do me a favor and keep him with you, I'll throw you another detective to pick up the slack."

"Where the hell do you get off . . . Do you know what I've done on this job?"

Billy stood up to stretch, then stooped to the window again. "Actually, I do. In fact, when I first came up, my loo once pointed you out to me, said if he ever got murdered he hoped they'd throw you the case, this way, the actor'd be on death row by the end of the year."

"Who was the loo."

"Mike Kelley, retired from the Five-two about three years ago."

"Kelley," Feeley grunted. "He put in some good work there."

Billy stood up again, took a breath, came back down. "Look, Gene, I can't do anything about you, we both know that, but here's what I propose. Don't show up anymore. I'll cover for you, sign you in, sign you out, this way you can max out your pension without wasting your time going through the motions and I can get my squad back to the way I want. What do you say."

Feeley sat flustered for a moment, then looked at Billy with a face like a fist. "Nobody tells me what to do."

MILTON RAMOS

The sisters—they had to be sisters, check out the mouths—came into the 4-6 precinct house just as Milton walked out of the vending machine room with a bag of Fritos and a can of Hawaiian Punch.

"My fiancé's missing," the less-big woman announced to Maldonado, the desk sergeant.

"How long," he asked without raising his eyes from his paperwork.

"Yesterday, day before."

"What's his name," still not looking up.

"Cornell Harris."

Thinking about where he was headed shortly and what he planned to do when he got there, Milton lost his appetite and tossed the chips without opening the bag.

"Got a picture?" Maldonado blindly put out his hand.

"No," the girlfriend said.

"Here," her sister said, digging into her bag and taking out a snap. The girlfriend looked at her. "Why'd you take his picture?"

"'Cause I did. So what."

"So what?"

"This guy?" Maldonado finally looked at them. "That's Sweetpea Harris."

"I know."

Milton checked the time, then took a sip of punch.

"He's missing?" Maldonado said. "Like that's a bad thing?"

"He ain't like that no more," the girlfriend said.

"He turned himself around," her sister said.

"Like this?" Maldonado stood up, curled a hand over his head like an umbrella handle, and pirouetted.

"See, that's why people hate on you around here."

"Actually, they don't," Maldonado said, returning to his reports.

"You should ask harder about that."

"In any event, it's got to be forty-eight hours before someone can be considered missing."

"That's what it is, forty-eight hours," the girlfriend said.

"You said yesterday," he said.

"She meant the yesterday before yesterday," her sister said. "That's forty-eight hours."

"Oh. OK."

"Yeah, he was, we were fighting on the phone, then I heard some other guy say, 'Hey Sweetpea, come over here.'"

"Oh yeah? Then what happened."

"Sweetpea said, 'Oh shit,' and hung up."

"This is getting to be a real mystery," Maldonado said, again without looking at them. "Where was this?"

"I don't know. Concord Avenue maybe?"

"Maybe?"

"I was on the phone, how do I know."

"When."

"Around three."

"Last night?"

"Yeah."

"Gotcha!" Maldonado lightly slapping his desk. "See? That's not forty-eight hours."

"Fuck him," the girlfriend said. "Let's go to Missing Persons direct."

"They'll tell you the same."

As they turned to leave, raised middle fingers over their heads like pennants, Maldonado called out to them, the snapshot of Sweetpea Harris in his extended hand. "Keep it," he said. "We already have one."

Once the two women finally made it out the door, the desk sergeant looked over to Milton. "Thoughts? Comments? Suggestions?"

Milton glanced at the wall clock again and drew a deep, shaky breath. "I got to be somewheres."

HE SAT ALONGSIDE HER DESK as she listened to his heart, a stray fingertip brushing his chest.

He thought just the boom of it would knock her off her chair.

All she had to do was recognize him and it was game over.

What could he possibly do after that?

"Turn, please?" The cold disk now pressing into his lower back.

"Sounds pretty clear," she murmured, making a notation on his emergency room form.

"Maybe now they do."

"Any history of bronchitis, asthma . . ."

"No."

"Any recent injuries?"

"No."

"Been under any stress?"

"Everybody's under stress."

"I'm asking about you," finally looking up from her notes, her Pietà eyes blind in her head.

"Tell the truth, I'm feeling a little stressed right now."

"Well sure, you're in a hospital," she said, looking over his shoulder to a small ruckus in the waiting room.

How about you on that front? Milton thought. *Any stress on your end?*

"How about allergies, any allergies?"

"Could be."

"What's 'could be,'" looking at him again.

"I just got back from visiting my brother in Atlanta." He almost said "my brother Rudy," but that would make it too easy. "He bought his kid a cat since the last time and I got a little cloudy in the chest."

"That's no good," writing again.

"You ever been to Atlanta?" he asked.

Since taking a seat next to her, the tension he felt had him speaking in a near mumble, and either she didn't hear the question or she was just off somewhere in her head. Either way he didn't want to ask again, didn't want to lead her any more than that. It would be too much like begging.

Just recognize me. Stop me in my tracks by saying my name, then drop to your knees to ask my forgiveness and explain to me through your tears why you did it. Then maybe, just maybe, we can both survive this.

Last chance for us both.

When he next looked at her, she was staring back at him as if he had spoken aloud, her eyes fixed with a look of unguarded intensity.

His shortness-of-breath gambit was no longer a joke.

"Are you on the Job?" she finally said.

"I work for FedEx, it's right on the form there."

"Huh. My husband's a cop and I could have sworn . . ."

"I get that a lot."

Recognize me, just let me see you tremble with memory, I'll settle for that . . .

But the moment passed. She went into her desk, brought out a blood pressure cuff, and gestured for his arm.

Seated as close as they were, he could reach out and grip her by the throat so fast she couldn't make a sound, couldn't signal or even move. He could choke the life out of her before anyone even knew what had happened.

"Your BP's through the roof."

"Must be the cats," he said hoarsely, Milton near livid with despair.

When Billy got home the next morning, he was relieved to discover that Carmen was at work and the boys at school. He went directly to the refrigerator, made himself his double usual, and was asleep within the hour.

He awoke at three-thirty to find himself back-to-back in bed with his father, who was chatting up a storm with his dead wife. The boys were somewhere in the house killing each other.

Billy got out of bed, put on his bathrobe, and went back into the kitchen. As he shambled to the coffeemaker, he nearly tripped over Carlos's camo jacket, which lay in a heap on the floor. When he picked it up, the jacket was tacky to the touch and smelled of paint. Holding it in front of himself by the epaulets, he discovered what he at first took to be a red five-pointed star, still in the process of drying, planted between the shoulders.

No, not a star. The bulk of the image was more fan-shaped than round, and the five points were actually all emanating in a curved line from the top of that fan, the thing now looking more like a handprint—was a handprint, a big one.

"Carlos!"

The kid came up from the basement wearing nothing but his under-pants.

"What happened to your jacket?" Showing him the damage.

"I don't know."

The outline of the hand was crudely precise. Not casual. Not acci-dental.

"Did anyone touch you today?"

"Touch?"

"Put their hand on you." Then: "A grown-up?"

"I don't know."

"You don't know," Billy starting to pace a little. "How about did any-body talk to you today. Other than your teachers."

"My friends?"

"Not your friends, grown-ups."

"No."

"Are you sure?"

"I don't know." Carlos shrugged, bored by the whole thing.

Billy took a breath; was he making something out of nothing?

As if reading his father's mind, Carlos wheeled toward the basement, Billy half-relieved to see him go. But then he stopped at the head of the stairs and turned back around.

"Oh, wait. A man came up to me and said, 'Say hello to your par-ents.'"

"What? Whoa, whoa . . ." Billy felt a sprung dampness on the back of his neck. "What man?"

"By my school, he came up to me."

"And said what."

"I said already."

Once again, Carlos tried to make a run for the basement, this time Billy having to grab his arm.

"Carlos!" his older brother shouted from down in the dark.

"What do you mean 'by' the school," Billy said. "In the school? Out-side? Before school, after . . ."

"When I was going to the bus home, he came up to me and said say hello to your parents but I didn't talk to him, I swear."

"What else did he say."

"Nothing, he just left."

"Did he say . . . Did anybody else see him?"

"I don't know."

"What did he look like?"

"I don't know."

Billy's bathrobe felt like an oven.

Declan, bored with waiting for his brother to return to the basement, came upstairs. He, too, was stripped to his underpants.

"Did you see the man who talked to your brother?"

"Yeah."

"Did he talk to you?"

"No."

"What did he look like?"

Declan extended his arms sideways and puffed up his cheeks.

"Fat?"

"Biggish."

"What else."

"He was, he had a mustache."

"What else."

"He had a big head, bigger than yours. But less hair in the front of it."

"Good. What color was he?" Billy couldn't imagine anything in the refrigerator that wouldn't make him vomit.

"Kind of brown."

"Brown like Mommy or brown like Uncle Redman?"

"White-brown, like Mom. I don't call her Mommy anymore, it's babyish."

"No it's not," Carlos said.

"OK, OK, what was he wearing?"

"A jacket."

"And a tie," Carlos added, pulling on his balls.

"A jacket and a tie. What else."

"Pants," Carlos said.

"And he had a lump," Declan said.

"What do you mean?"

"A lump," Declan touching his left hip where Billy carried his gun. "Like yours."

WHEN CARMEN CAME HOME FROM the hospital at eight that evening, Billy was still in his bathrobe. An hour earlier it had been all he could do to feed the boys and his father their cut cantaloupe and Stouffer's microwaved dinners.

"Are you kidding me?" she shouted from the living room, then marched into the kitchen. "This is a hundred-and-twenty-dollar jacket. Carlos!"

"Easy, it's not his fault," Billy said. Going on three hours of sleep, his head was a boiled egg. "Some guy came up to him in the school parking lot, said, 'Say hello to your parents,' and, I'm guessing, did this to the jacket."

"What do you mean, some guy. What guy?"

"That's what I'd like to know."

"Nobody knew him?"

"I'll have to ask tomorrow."

"Why tomorrow?"

"The kids don't know. It's better to go back there at the same time, see who's around."

"What did he look like?"

"From what I could get out of them, he sounds some kind of Latin, heavyset, maybe a cop."

"A cop?"

Billy hesitated, then: "He could have been carrying," wincing the second it came out of his mouth.

"A gun?" Her eyes as big as dishes.

"Possibly, but maybe I'm just . . ."

"Jesus God," putting her fingertips to her mouth. "You sure he was a cop?"

"I'm not sure of anything. Like I just said . . ."

"Well, how old was he?"

He couldn't believe he hadn't asked that earlier, though it probably wouldn't tell him anything about the guy's profession.

"Hey, Carlos!" he shouted up the stairs.

The kid came down wearing a Knicks jersey over pajama bottoms.

"The man who talked to you, was he older than me, younger than me, the same age . . ."

"I don't know."

"Declan!"

Carlos's older brother came down wearing a *Scream* mask, just what Billy needed.

"How old was the man you saw."

"I don't know."

"Guess."

"Your age? Mommy's, Mom's age?"

Billy turned to his wife. "Anything else?"

Carmen didn't answer.

"All right, guys, go back upstairs," he said, not wanting them to get infected.

He moved to the sink and ran some water over his face. When he turned back around Carmen was robotically setting the table for breakfast.

"What are you thinking?" he asked.

"Look," she said, straightening up, a stack of plates tucked into her ribs like a football. "He said, 'your parents,' he didn't say our names."

"So?"

"So maybe he doesn't even know us. Maybe he's just some random whack who wandered into the parking lot. Or a parent the kids don't know. Or it wasn't him."

"Wasn't who."

"The guy who put the paint there. Maybe it was an accident. Maybe Carlos just backed up . . ."

"Into what, a wide-open adult hand covered in red paint?"

"How about the father of that kid Declan punched?"

"The guy's in a wheelchair."

"How do you know?"

He knew because he had gone over to their house on the sly to pay for a new pair of glasses. "I just heard."

"Then how about you?" she asked, dealing out the plates.

"How about me what?"

"Is there anybody on the Job . . ."

"I thought about it. There's nobody."

Carmen dropped a juice glass with her right hand, caught it six inches from the floor with her left.

"And you?" he said as lightly as he could. "Anyone giving you a hard time? Maybe at work?"

"Everybody gives me a hard time at work."

"How about a cop. They're in and out of that ER all day. Any of them hit on you?"

"Constantly." Then, clutching her stomach: "Should we call the police?"

Billy took a breath. "I am the police."

"MAY I WAKE THEE?" THE Wheel inquired, darkening Billy's doorway at two in the morning.

"This better be good," Billy said, a pillow over his head as he lay in a fetal curl on his joke of an office couch. He had never been this tired so early in the tour.

"We got a guy just brought his kid into Metropolitan, says he accidentally dropped her."

"What's a kid," still not moving.

"Four months."

THE YOUNG, DISHEVELED-LOOKING FATHER OF the injured infant, still in his bedclothes, was slim and tall, six-three, four, maybe more, although the anxious crook of his neck on this night seemed to shave a few inches off him as he paced the littered floor of the Metropolitan Hospital ER.

"He said the wife had a family emergency in Buffalo," the patrol sergeant told Billy. "Left him with the kid for a few days."

Billy's jacket buzzed, a text from Carmen at two-thirty in the morning:

can i burn the coat

"You know who that is, right?" the sergeant said, gesturing to the agitated pacer as Billy texted back.

absolutely not

"What? No, why?"

"You follow high school hoops?"

"It's all I can do to follow the pros."

"Aaron Jeter, played power forward for DeWitt Clinton about four years ago, took them to two state AA championships. You couldn't open the sports pages back then without there's a picture of him banging under the boards."

Billy took another look at the guy, this time noticing the outsized shoulder caps that topped his lean frame.

"Huh. And so where's he at now?"

"Now?" the sergeant shrugged. "Now he's here."

Alice Stupak, who put out a sympathetic, feminine vibe that she could turn on and off like a faucet, was usually the go-to detective for interviews of this kind, and she waited for the high sign to start working the guy. But Billy, after all that had happened today, wanted this one for himself.

"How are you doing, I'm Detective Graves," Billy having to look up as he introduced himself. The hand that enveloped his was as big as a first baseman's mitt. "You're Aaron Jeter, right?"

"What? Yeah," he said, staring anxiously over Billy's head to the closed-off rooms beyond the nurses' station.

"See, I'd be lying to you," Billy said, "if I pretended like I didn't know it already."

Jeter seemed deaf to the flattery, still riveted by whatever was happening beyond the screens.

"And your daughter?" Billy asked, as he gripped him lightly by a long, fluttering bicep.

"My daughter what," Jeter said, as Billy began walking him across the floor.

"Her name."

"Nuance."

His cell began to tremble again, Billy quick-checking Carmen's latest:

why not

Well, there was no answering her now.

"Nuance," he repeated automatically, then, reengaging: "That's a beautiful name."

BILLY STEERED JETER INTO A small, claustrophobic examination room that most detectives favored when responding to calls here—even the hospital staff referred to it as the Box—then took a seat on a backless rolling chair, the only place to park other than the examination table.

"So how are you holding up?" Billy asked, sliding his chair to the center of the room, effectively cutting it in half.

"Holding up?" Jeter's eyes moist and wandering. "I'm holding up bad."

"Of course you are," Billy said. "You're her dad."

"Is she going to be OK?" Staring at the shut door. "I mean, what are they saying?"

Billy had no idea. The CAT scan machine was down, and the radiologist hadn't gotten around to looking at the X-rays yet.

"All I can tell you is they're going to do everything they can."

"Good, that's good."

As Jeter tried to figure out where to situate himself, Billy gave him the once-over again, taking in the wrinkled pajama bottoms and T-shirt, the slippers, his uncombed hair sticking up like a frozen splash of tar.

"Look, I know this isn't the greatest of circumstances," Billy said easily, "but I just have to tell you, you had to be the best high school forward I have ever seen."

"That was a long time ago," Jeter perching tentatively on the edge of the table, then popping right up. "Can we go back outside?" Nearly begging him. "They're supposed to tell me how she's doing."

Billy's jacket buzzed with another text.

"Hey, listen, do you by any chance remember a kid played for Truman, Gerry Reagan?" Truman, Reagan, Billy's imagination leaning toward the presidential tonight. "He was my nephew. I mean, he still is."

"Who?" Jeter spinning like a top. "Can they find me in here? I have to know what's happening."

"He hated covering you, said it was the most humiliating experience of his life."

"Jimmy who?"

"So did you get to play after Clinton?"

"Huh? Yeah, just a year in Belgium."

"Still, better than most, right?"

"Hey, look . . ."

"So what are you doing with yourself these days. You working?"

"Working?"

"Are you employed."

Jeter stared at him like he thought he was nuts. "I'm a warehouse man at Trumbo Storage." Then: "Why are you asking . . ."

"Trumbo Storage, the big red brick building with the clock tower, right? Where's that, Bushwick?"

"Sunset Park. Listen . . ."

"Sunset Park, I remember when that area was nothing but gangs and strip clubs. But not so much now, right?"

"I don't . . ."

"Can I ask you what time you usually punch in?"

"Do I what? I don't know, seven, look I'm worried about my daughter, could we please . . ."

"Yeah, no, of course," Billy easing out his notepad. "So tell me what happened tonight."

Jeter exhaled. "Like I told already, we were playing, you know, like I was tossing her up a little, just a tiny bit, catch her, toss her. She loves that, makes her laugh every time."

"And . . ."

"And my cell rang and so I turned my head for a second, you know, thinking it was my wife . . . and she just slipped through my hands. I just turned for a second, not even that."

"And when was this, timewise . . ."

"I don't know, about an hour, hour and a half ago? Nobody's telling me nothing in here, is that bad?"

"They're just busy. So an hour and a half ago, say about one a.m.?"

"I brought her right in, I mean, look at me," grabbing the thighs of his pajama bottoms.

"No, you did the right thing, absolutely."

Again his phone began to tremble with a text, Billy afraid to look at it, afraid to turn it off.

"So I take it you live in the neighborhood?"

"Hundred and Fourteenth and Madison, the Tubman Houses."

"And you punch in at seven, so, East Harlem to Sunset Park, you need to wake up around, what, five? Five-thirty?"

Jeter hesitated, then quietly said, "I don't need that much sleep."

"But still, what were you doing up with her at one in the morning?"

"She's a little colicky, you know?"

"Yeah, no, I had that with both my kids, it's like a nightmare, right?"

"It's not their fault," he said, the corners of his eyes starting to bead.

"Of course, it's heartbreaking, those little things suffering like that."

As Jeter's tears continued to collect, Billy gave him a moment to live with his thoughts, to go to town on himself.

"You know what my nephew always said about you?" Billy asked softly. "He said you were the best natural ball handler he ever saw. Said it was like you had that rock on a string."

"Made all-city three years running," Jeter's tears coming freely now.

"I can believe it. But then, Aaron," Billy rising from his chair, putting his hand on Jeter's shoulder, "I just have to ask . . . How can an elite athlete like you, a master baller good enough to play pro in Europe, how the fuck can a guy with hands like yours drop his own four-month-old baby . . ."

"I told you, the phone rang . . ."

"And she's colicky, crying all night."

"She's colicky."

"One in the morning, you have to get up, what time did we say? Five? Five-thirty?"

"Is she gonna be OK?"

Billy moved in close. "Aaron, look at me."

Can't.

"Aaron, if I were to scroll down the incoming calls on your cell right now, am I going to find your wife or anybody else trying to ring you at one in the morning?"

"I don't know it was one exactly," his voice broken and hushed.

"Aaron. Can't you look at me?"

Jeter dropped his chin to his chest, then covered his eyes.

"Aaron . . ."

Again, Billy let a silence come down, the room a tomb.

"This is not me," Jeter finally whispered. "This is definitely not me."

"I know," Billy said softly, the next step to somehow get Jeter's statement on record before he could pull his head out of his ass and start wondering out loud about his rights.

As Jeter turned away and wept into the wall, Billy, unable to help himself, quickly glanced at Carmen's last three texts:

> can i wash it
> can i wash it or is it evidence
> wtf answer me

MILTON RAMOS

Milton rolled off Marilys, sat up, grabbed a washcloth and attended to himself, averting his eyes as she rose from the towel-draped couch and walked to the bathroom in order to do her thing.

Widow and widower, both on the north side of forty with three kids between them, over the last year they had become occasional humps of convenience, a casual pressure-relieving arrangement without the mess of a real relationship. Sometimes she wasn't in the mood and sometimes he wasn't, but nobody ever got their noses out of joint about it one way or the other. Besides, he was never much for kissing.

As he heard the shower begin to run behind the bathroom door, he lay back down and thought of Carmen's boys in the school parking lot today, bright-eyed and wild as chimpanzees, seemingly happy in their world and, as an added bonus, respectful to adults. Nice kids most likely, but when he was sizing up any child he came across for the first time there was only one question on the assessment test and one question only: were they the type who would get off on taunting Sofia?

All he had known this morning was that he wanted Carmen to feel things, to experience things, give her a taste of what it feels like to have the most precious people in your life snatched away from you, to feel without any warning the ground buckle and split beneath your feet. But now that he had set things in motion, he realized that today was nothing, an unnerving incident that would be forgotten in a week or two. What was required here was evidence of a pattern, of an intelligent presence, an unseen wolf lurking just outside the perimeter of her life until . . . Until what?

He had no idea how or when it should end. But he did know this: if his campaign went on long enough, he would eventually get caught and that would be the end of him. And the end of them.

He would lose her.

So let it go.

Can't.

You will lose her.

And then an exhilaratingly anarchic notion:

She'll go to better people.

He had a half-a-half-sister in Pennsylvania who was pretty decent, and a childless cousin in Staten Island, Anita, who he liked and liked him in return. Better that Sofia go to her, but what the hell was he thinking . . .

MARILYS CAME BACK INTO THE den, squat and stone-faced, her torso un-indented from shoulder to hip. When the two of them stood side by side they looked like matching salt and pepper shakers.

As she slipped into her jeans, he dug four hundred dollars out of his heaped pants and passed it along to her in a tight roll. He knew four hundred was shit pay for the days and hours she put in, but she needed to be off the books, and that was all he could afford if he couldn't deduct her come April 15.

"The toilet's backed up on the top floor, you need to call a plumber."

"All right," shrugging into his own pants. "So what did she eat today?"

"Carrots, like you said," stooping to pick up his discarded washcloth.

"Oh yeah? What else."

"A turkey burger without the bread."

"Uh-huh. What else."

Marilys peeled the bath towel from the couch and replaced the pillows.

"What else."

"She was crying for a treat."

"What's a treat."

"A couple of Mint Milanos."

"What did I tell you about that?"

"Let me ask you," she said, "what did *you* eat today?"

AND THERE WAS MARILYS, WHO knew Sofia better than anyone, maybe even himself. But she was an employee with a family and problems of her own. Sofia was just her job.

Nothing you did so far was even illegal.

Milton watched Marilys stuff her pay in her purse, then get down on her knees to retrieve her sneakers from under the coffee table.

Housekeeper, stand-in mother, semi-girlfriend. If he went then she went away, and Sofia would be up for grabs.

Nothing you did so far was even illegal.

The next day Billy made sure he was back home in time to drive the kids to school, then sat in the parking lot to survey the terrain as they charged toward the building.

Nothing but the same teachers, parents, and nannies he saw every morning on the days when he dropped them off. No one even vaguely resembling the rough description given to him by the boys.

Once the lot was empty of all souls, he continued to sit for another hour before taking off for a meeting with Stacey Taylor in the city.

Release time would be better.

THEY MET IN A BEER-DAMP neighborhood joint around the corner from Stacey's walk-up a few blocks south of Columbia University. At nine in the morning she was sitting at the not-quite-deserted bar reading the *Post* and eating a hamburger.

"Hey," Billy said, taking the neighboring stool and gesturing for a coffee. "How's it going."

"How's what going."

"I don't know, life, the boyfriend."

"The boyfriend's asleep," she said. "He gets up at three in the morning, has a cocktail or two, works on the magazine, and crawls back into bed at five. I could throw a flash grenade in there now, all it would do is scare the cats."

Billy took one look at the coffee set before him and knew it would taste like muddled cigarette butts.

"So, Pavlicek . . ." sliding the cup to the side.

"Pavlicek sees a doctor there, Jacob Wells, but he's not a cholesterol man, he's a hematologist. Been seeing him since August."

"Seeing him for what?"

"That I couldn't find out," she said. "Can't be anything good."

A too-tall, gaunt, middle-aged man sporting an old but expensive raincoat over pajamas came sauntering into the bar as if into the day-room of a nuthouse. He had a long narrow face, nose big and sharp as a tomahawk, one eye brighter than the other. He could have run a brush through his tangled gray-brown hair a few times, Billy thought; that wouldn't have hurt.

He kissed Stacey's hair without looking at her and signaled for a beer.

"What are you doing up?" she asked.

"I have no idea." He extended a hand to Billy, again without making eye contact. "Phil Lasker."

"Billy Graves."

"What would someone see a hematologist for?" Stacey asked her boy-friend.

"A million things."

"Besides sickle-cell anemia."

"All kinds of vitamin deficiency, B12, folic acid, iron, et cetera, throm-bocytosis, that's excess platelets, thrombocytopenia, that's low platelets, polycythemia, excess red blood cells, anemia, pernicious or otherwise, which is low red blood cells, leukocytosis, excess white blood cells, neu-tropenia, low white blood cells, all kinds of coagulation disorders, blood vessel abnormalities, hemophilia, scurvy, leukemia, acute and chronic, an encyclopedia of various syndromes, genetic or otherwise . . ."

Billy stared at him, then looked to Stacey.

"He's just a really good hypochondriac," she said.

"That means I'll live into my nineties," he said, sipping his nine a.m. Heineken.

Stacey looked away.

Billy left a few minutes later, drove home, and called Immaculate Conception. He left a message for the school security officer, asking for a meeting to review yesterday's footage of the parking lot, then fixed himself his usual Cape Codder, got into bed, and stared at the ceiling, his head a blender.

EARLY AFTERNOON FOUND HIM IN a small physical therapy clinic on the banks of the Cross County Parkway, thumbing through a two-month-old *People* magazine as his father worked on his core strength with a young Serbian physical therapist on the other side of the mirrored room. Ferrying the old man here twice weekly for his sessions was the most stultifying chore in the world, but Billy insisted on doing it himself.

"Milan, are you old enough to remember Marshal Tito?" Billy Senior asked the therapist.

"He died when I was very young," the kid said. "Try not to tense your neck."

"His real name was Josip Broz."

"Really."

Billy stopped reading.

"I was assigned to his security detail in sixty-three when he came to the United Nations."

"You're still straining, Mr. Graves."

"He was a very short guy, you know."

"Better. Keep your shoulders back."

"Loved the ladies, that was the biggest headache with him."

"Dad, are you kidding me?"

"I had dealings with Khrushchev back then, too. I was on the Manhattan Bridge surveillance detail in sixty-one when he came up the East River on the SS *Baltika*, into, I believe, Pier 71."

Dates names numbers, Billy's heart rising.

"They had a floating high school docked next door at Pier 73, Food and Maritime Trades, and I had to go over and tell the principal that with the big Commie coming, he had to shut down classes for a few days and, brother, he was not too happy to hear that, but the students took it like Christmas in July."

"Keep your shoulder blades back, imagine they're trying to shake hands across your spine."

"Do you remember the name of that principal?" Billy just testing.

"Frank Stevenson, a real no-nonsense guy, but you had to be, with some of those kids he had."

"How about the boat."

"What boat?"

"That housed the school."

"It was a ship, not a boat. A mothballed Liberty, the *John W. Brown*. The navy donated it to the city in 1946."

"Dad, you never told me any of this," Billy grinning and grinning. "This is history."

"You want history? How about Fidel Castro staying at the Hotel Theresa up on a Hundred and Twenty-fifth Street? Do you know those Cubans were smuggling live poultry into the top-floor suites? Did you ever try to catch a chicken with your bare hands? It can't be done. Your mother had to give me rubdowns for a week."

"You're killing me," Billy still grinning like a mule.

"Don't forget to breathe, Mr. Graves."

"So, Charlie, how's my little sister doing these days?" he asked Milan.

"Your sister?"

"She says you're off the sauce for good. Is that true?"

"Sauce?" Milan looking to Billy.

"Just roll with it," Billy muttered, going back to his mindless magazine.

"Yes, I'm off the sauce."

"Well, you better be, because if I have to come up there and get her again, this time there's going to be some laying on of the hands, my friend, that I can promise you."

■ ■ ■

AS HE WAS ADJUSTING HIS father's seat belt in the parking lot behind the rehab center, Jimmy Whelan called, Billy stepping away from the car to talk.

"What are you doing right now."

"Driving my father."

"Oh yeah? How's he doing?"

"The same."

"Same is better than worse. Listen." Whelan's voice dropped. "I need to talk to you about something."

"About Pavlicek?" the question just popping out of Billy without cerebral clearance.

"Pavlicek?" Jimmy sounding caught up short. "What about him?"

"Nothing," Billy said, burning to bring up the blood specialist but afraid of being asked how he had come across the information. "What did you want to talk about."

"Remember that movie *Fort Apache*?"

"With John Wayne, right?"

"What John Wayne. *Fort Apache, The Bronx*. They're doing a remake. Billy Heffernan's got an in with the people involved, and he asked me if I was interested in working on it."

"As what?"

"Some kind of consultant. You know, because of what we were doing around there back then."

"Sounds good to me."

"Money for nothing and chicks for free, right?"

"Could be."

"Why'd you mention Pavlicek?" Whelan asked, but Immaculate Conception was trying to ring through and Billy had to end the call.

After arranging a time to review the parking lot tapes with the head of school security, then taking a few minutes to calm himself down, Billy called Whelan back from a traffic jam on the Saw Mill River Parkway.

"Something going on with Pavlicek?" the first thing out of Jimmy's mouth. "I need to know."

"Forget it," Billy said, Pavlicek now the last thing on his mind.

"You all right? You sound off."

"I'm trying to drive here."

"Don't bullshit me."

"Something happened with my kid," this too coming out of him without any mental vetting.

"What happened with your kid?"

Billy didn't want to talk about it in front of his father, but the old man was down for the count.

"Jimmy," Billy keeping his voice low, "I'm freaking six ways to Sunday."

ALTHOUGH HIS MEETING WITH SECURITY wasn't until four, Billy was back at Immaculate Conception at two-thirty, the first of the parents to arrive for the pickups. For the next forty-five minutes, he studied every car coming into the lot until a side door of the building opened and the students began to exit, the youngest first, those not bus-bound lined up against the side of the building until each was retrieved by a minder.

Billy hadn't told his kids he was coming, and he watched as Carlos ran to his designated bus unaccosted, no one taking the slightest interest in him, least of all some wide-bodied, red-handed possible cop. The person who did catch his eye, though, was the teacher with a clipboard posted by the bus's folding yellow doors, the guy chanting, "No pushing, no pushing," as the kids scrambled up the short stairs to their seats.

THE BUS MONITOR TURNED OUT to be the school's remedial reading specialist, Albert Lazar, a short, erectly trim middle-aged man who projected an air of constant alertness, although that just could have been his slightly hyperthyroidic eyes.

"Like I said, I wasn't on bus detail yesterday, we're on a rotating schedule for that."

"I understand," Billy said, "but were you in the parking lot at all?"

"We all are at release time, it's required."

"OK, how about this: just looking around yesterday, did you happen to notice anyone that struck you as unusual?"

"Unusual meaning . . ."

"Maybe someone who looked a little out of place."

"Like what, a homeless person?"

"Like anybody," Billy not wanting to lead with a more specific description.

"Well, there were some nuns from the Poor Clares down from Poughkeepsie."

"Who else."

"A boy's divorced parents apparently got their signals crossed and showed up for him at the same time. They started arguing in the lot, then they both left without him. That turned a few heads."

"Who else."

"That's about it."

"Any men?"

"Men?"

"Man. Maybe some guy, walking around, you're thinking . . ."

"You know . . ." Lazar hesitated.

"Just say."

"There was someone I hadn't seen before, could've been some kid's father, but I don't think so."

Billy took a breath and asked for a description.

"I'd say a little taller than me, but not much, heavyset, dark, Hispanic, Italian maybe."

Billy felt a surge, his exhausted body having trouble handling it. "What was he wearing?"

"A dark suit, nothing fancy, shirt and tie."

"How about his hair? Curly, straight, dark . . ."

"Dark, I guess," then: "He could've had a mustache, but he looked so Mediterranean I might be putting it on him."

"Did he speak to anyone?"

"Not that I noticed."

"Why don't you think he was a parent coming to pick up his kid?"

"There's not that many fathers doing the afternoon pickups and I pretty much know them all, at least by sight."

"All right," Billy winding down, pulling his card out of his wallet. "Anything else you can tell me about him? Just off the top of your head. Anything . . ."

"Yeah, actually, there is," Lazar said, taking the offered card but not looking at it. "He struck me like someone in the security business."

"Meaning?"

"You know, the way he carried himself, very alert and no-nonsense. It's hard to explain."

"You just did," Billy said woodenly. He tapped his card. "Anything else you can remember, night or day."

He hadn't identified himself as an NYPD detective, just as a concerned parent whose son might have been approached by a stranger on school grounds, and he saw the teacher's face darken as he read the new information.

For an instant Lazar looked at Billy searchingly, then shut himself down.

"Something else?" Billy asked mildly.

"No," his eyes reading, Yes.

Billy lingered, giving Lazar a moment to say what was suddenly so troubling to him, but the teacher stepped into the bus to handle some rowdiness and that was that.

And then the older boys came charging out of the building like their hair was on fire. He refrained from calling out to Declan, allowing him to board with his brother. Not that he didn't want to take them home, want to keep them close right now, but he was desperate to see the tape, the security officer waiting for Billy in his office.

THE SYSTEM WAS BADLY IN need of an upgrade, the retrieved footage from the parking lot as grainy as an evaporating dream. Billy was unable to make out anyone's face, although he could track the progress of bodies across the lot.

"Are you kidding me?" Billy turned to the security man, Wayne Connors, a retired Westchester County state trooper.

"Hey, I tell them every week, I know Chinese take-outs with better surveillance equipment than us. You know what they say to me? We don't have the money. I say, What if something was to happen out there."

"Something did happen out there," Billy said.

On the third viewing he found who he was looking for, the guy built square and low to the ground, his back to the camera as he walked in front of the buses before stopping and bending briefly next to a kid—was it Carlos? who could tell?—so briefly that he could have simply been picking something off the asphalt or tightening a shoelace. Then, as he began to rise, he casually reached out to that kid's back or shoulder as if for support and calmly walked out of the frame.

"Look," Connors said after Billy had filled him in, "with the description you gave me plus what I saw just now, I think I have pretty good eyes on this guy. I'll post one of my people out there starting tomorrow."

"Great," Billy said, turning to leave.

Connors could post an army out there, this guy wasn't coming back. He'd done what he'd done knowing that Carlos's parents would see it and react, so no way he'd risk a return visit.

The question was, Where would he show up next.

AT TEN IN THE EVENING, Billy entered Whelan's apartment building and went down to the endless basement, its roughly plastered walls painted the color of dried blood. He walked past the pungent laundry room, past the caged storage bins filled with broken furniture and bust-ass suitcases, past the chained-up snow blowers and shovels and swapped-out radiators, until he reached the super's apartment, the peephole on its scuffed door dangling by one screw like a gouged eye.

"Who."

"It's me, don't shoot."

Whelan opened up wearing a towel around his waist and holding a Walther PPK.

His apartment, if you could call it that, was a converted utility room infused with that down-the-hall detergent smell and consisting, at the moment, of a single unmade bed, a mini-fridge, and a two-burner stove. The only other article of furniture was a padded workout bench, the floor around it littered with free weights and a pair of work boots. A clothesline ran on a diagonal from one corner of the room to the sole window, and the walls were bare of decoration except for a framed certificate announcing Whelan's induction into the NYPD Honor Legion. For a fully functional middle-aged adult, the place was utterly devoid of dignity, yet Jimmy Whelan was the most unconflicted, reasonably happy individual Billy had ever known.

"So what's going on?" Whelan asked, stuffing the Walther under his mattress and taking a pair of jeans from the clothesline.

"What I told you on the phone," Billy said, offering him Carlos's coat, the painted handprint now starting to flake.

"The mark of the Beast," Whelan said.

The toilet flushed, and a moment later one of the women from the upper apartments came out of the bathroom in her underwear.

On seeing Billy she yipped and retreated, but not before he caught an eyeful of caramel-tinted mommy fat and a generous behind.

"I'll come back."

Whelan waved him off, fished her clothes out of the rumple of sheets, and passed them to her through the bathroom door.

"So did you talk to the cops up there?"

"And tell them what, a guy came up to my kid, said, 'Say hello to your parents,' and maybe, I can't swear to it, maybe did this to his jacket?"

"Guy with a gun."

"I don't know that for sure."

"Or better yet, reach out to the Chief of D's, let him bring in a Threat Assessment Team."

"Again, based on what."

"Then I don't know what to tell you."

"I know."

Whelan lit a cigarette and halfheartedly attempted to make the bed with his free hand. "I mean, obviously, if there's anything I can do personally . . ."

"I appreciate it."

"If you ever need me to, I can stay with your family," he said, giving up on the bed.

"Let's hope it never comes to that, but thank you."

"Be like old times," Jimmy said, opening the window and flicking his cigarette upward onto the sidewalk.

Back in '97, when the news of the double shooting hit the papers and Reverend Hustle from two boroughs to the north took the ferry and set up his camp of demonstrators around Billy's Staten Island home, Whelan, like all the other WGs, volunteered on a rotating basis to stay with him and his soon-to-be ex-wife every night, until negotiations with the mayor's office brought the protests to an end, a full month after they had begun.

"So what do you think?" Whelan asked.

"About the guy?"

"About *Fort Apache*."

Billy paused, a beat behind the shift in topic. "When Brian Roe was the consultant on *Missing Persons NYC* they threw him four hundred dollars."

"A day?"

"That's what he said."

"I could live with that."

"He also said as long as you keep your thoughts to yourself and don't talk to the actors, they'll keep you on forever."

"As a consultant."

"I'm just telling you what he told me."

The tenant in the bathroom came out wearing tinted cat's-eye glasses, jeans, and a blouse, her hair swirled up in a damp white towel like a Mister Softee cone. Whelan walked her the fifteen feet to his door, then kissed her hard on the mouth, her knee reflexively coming up like a quarterback waiting for the snap. She left still wearing the towel.

"I have to be careful," Jimmy said. "Her husband just got out of Comstock, but I'm pretty sure he's staying with his other wife."

Gearing up to leave, Billy took back his son's jacket. "So how's your millionaire?"

"Who, Appleyard? All of a sudden he's got three new girlfriends, two crack hos and a trannie. I'm starting a dead pool: five dollars wins you a hundred if you pick the exact day, fifty if you pick the week."

"How about the month?"

"He won't make it a month."

"Do they even make crack hos anymore?"

"You should get out more."

"All right, brother," Billy said, stepping to the door himself.

"Why'd you mention Pavlicek today," Whelan asked abruptly.

"I told you, it was nothing," Billy said, turning back to the room. "Why are you so worried about Pavlicek?"

"I'm not." Whelan lit another cigarette.

Billy took a breath, then: "You said to me, 'Is there something going on with Pavlicek.' You said, 'I need to know.'"

"I said that? I never said that. You were the one that brought him up."

Billy pondered mentioning Pavlicek's lying about the hematologist again, then decided against it.

"So everything's good with him?" he settled for asking.

"Why wouldn't it be?"

When he was once again passing the laundry room on his way up to the ground floor, Whelan threw open his apartment door. "Hey, I forgot to tell you . . ."

Billy turned.

"This *Fort Apache* remake? It's in three-D."

MILTON RAMOS

His aunt Pauline, eight hours after an obliterating cerebral hemor-
rhage, lay on life support in the Jacobi Hospital ICU, flanked by her two
speechless sons, Herbert and Stan. Out of blood deference, Milton stood
at the foot of the bed, his hands resting on the guard rail. She was now
a machine-breathing vegetable, and over the past few hours three separate nurses had dropped by to gently campaign for pulling the plug so
that they could commence the harvesting, but neither of his guilt-ridden
cousins could even bring themselves to hold their mother's hand, let alone
respond to the request.

So when a fourth nurse came by to make the pitch, Milton cut her
off before word one.

"She's ready," he said.

Neither son protested or even looked his way.

So fucking like them . . .

After his mother and brothers died and Pauline had brought him into
her home, he had shared a bedroom with these two for years, but despite
his status as a first cousin, they couldn't get past the tragedy he brought
into the house with him, or maybe it was just his mixed-race jungle face,
or maybe like most everyone else he knew they were intuitively scared
of him. Whatever the reason, they had never accepted him as anything

but a nerve-racking boarder, as welcome into their lives as an unteth-
ered bear.

At least Pauline had taken him in with an open heart; her only bone
of contention, then and always, was his sullen demeanor. Not that she
didn't understand.

After the nurse left, a volunteer grief counselor came by and touched
his arm. "It's so hard to let a loved one go. But you have to take comfort
in the fact that even though she might be leaving you physically . . ."

"Talk to them," chucking a thumb toward his cousins, then leaving
for the street.

He wouldn't attend or even help with the funeral; they could at least
handle that. He had pulled the plug, and that was enough.

Herbert and Stan: if they weren't dead to him before, they sure as hell
were now, letting him call down the Reaper on their own mother like
that . . .

Loss and loss and loss, each one unasked for, each one, come the end
of the story, concluding with his hands gripping a scythe.

"HEY, STRANGER!" HIS COUSIN ANITA, like his aunt, one of the decent ones,
instantly recognizing his voice on the horn after a year without contact.
"What's going on?"

"Nothing," he said. "I haven't talked to you in a while."

"I know! How's Sofia?"

"You should see her."

"I'd love to."

"How about we come visit sometime."

"Say when."

She'll go to better people.

"Soon."

Loss and loss and loss, Milton seeing that house in Yonkers again,
that smooth-sailing home.

Why should they be happy.

Billy didn't find out about Sweetpea Harris having gone missing until a two a.m. playground shooting of a sixteen-year-old in Fort Tryon Park took him and Mayo over the Macombs Dam Bridge to Lincoln Hospital in the Bronx.

The victim's brothers were sitting in a small, dreary waiting room, three of them, mute and seething, visions of payback already playing in their eyes. They knew everything there was to know about what had gone down but he would have had better luck interviewing statues, and after twenty minutes of listening to himself talk, Billy got up from a coffee-stained couch with a blank notepad, just hoping that the aforementioned payback would occur after eight in the morning when he was heading up to Yonkers.

It was on his way back to the nurses' station that he first caught sight of the two homemade Missing posters push-pinned into the community announcements board, each featuring a low-resolution photo of Sweetpea Harris on purple printer paper that was bottom-fringed with tearaway phone number tabs, as if announcing the availability of a dog walker. Billy took one of the posters, stuffed it into his coat pocket, and moved on down the line.

An hour later, after one of the doctors came out of the OR and told

Billy that the vic would pull through, he returned to the visitors' room to see if the good news would maybe, just maybe, get the brothers talking. But they were already gone, Billy once again praying that the drama to come wouldn't play out until he was safely back in his own bed.

As he was leaving the hospital, intending to head back to Manhattan and monitor the canvass around the crime scene, he nearly ran into an army of the victim's other relatives bursting through the front door, those in front half-carrying the overcome grandmother as if she were their flagship. Billy was there for three additional hours, none of these further interviews yielding anything more than vaguely ominous variations on "They know who they are" and "I warned him" type pronouncements. Finally, the vic's fourteen-year-old stone-faced sister chin-signaled for him to follow her into the ladies' room, where she locked herself in a stall for a few minutes, flushed, and then left without ever saying word one.

The folded Post-it was perched on top of the toilet paper dispenser, the name and address of the shooter written in strawberry-scented neon pink with a swannish hand. Two hours later, armed with a search warrant, Billy followed six Bronx ESU cops into a Valentine Avenue apartment, catching the fifteen-year-old actor already dressed for school, his mouth filled with Franken Berries, his gun in an Angry Birds book bag.

Taking the kid to the nearest precinct, the 4-6, Billy handed him over for processing, then dragged himself upstairs to the empty predawn squad room in order to start banging out the requisite blizzard of paper. And when the day tour started rolling in at eight, he was still at it, blinking violently into the computer screen, his fingertips fluttering with the hour.

"What are you doing here?"

Billy looked up from his commandeered desk to see Dennis Doyle, a take-out coffee in one hand, a folded *Daily News* tucked up next to his ribs.

"What's it look like," he said, flicking a finger against the screen.

"Come take a break," Dennis said, walking to his office.

Billy followed him inside, planting himself next to a stack of manila folders on the lone couch.

"So how's she doing?"

"Not great," Dennis said, opening his paper.

"The drinking?"

"Everything."

A burly, expressionless detective came into the office without knocking, dropped a new folder on Dennis's desk, and left the room.

"You know, she called me the other day, told me Raymond Del Pino's sister named her baby after her," Billy said.

"I know, Rose Yasmeen."

"She told me Yasmeen Rose."

"I'm sure she did," Dennis said, glancing at the fresh reports.

"Still, no one ever middle-named a kid after me, you know?"

"It's the least they could do, after all she's been through."

"Listen, while I'm here . . ." Billy took Sweetpea's Missing poster out of the side pocket of his sport jacket and handed it over. "You know anything about this?"

Dennis read it and shrugged.

"Look at the guy," Billy said.

"Cornell Harris?"

"Sweetpea Harris."

"Redman's Sweetpea?"

"He told me Harris was half-living with his girlfriend on Concord Avenue. That's you, so I'm thinking maybe she came in here to file a report."

"Hey, Milton," Dennis called out.

The detective came back in the room.

"Can you check the 494s for this guy?"

"Nothing there."

"Don't you want to check?"

"I was here when his sisters or whoever came in to file on him, but it was only twenty-four hours and they never came back, so . . ."

"His sisters?" Billy asked.

"Sisters, girlfriends," the detective said. "You should ask Maldonado, he's the one sent them away."

"Just do me a favor and check the 494s," Dennis said. "Maybe they snuck back in when you were off. If there's something there, don't be a stranger. Otherwise . . ."

When the detective left the room again, Dennis opened his newspaper and spoke in a low voice. "'Sisters, girlfriends,'" shaking his head, "a real bloodhound."

"Maybe you shouldn't tell Yasmeen about this," Billy said, reaching for the poster. "It could jack her up about Cortez again."

"Are you kidding me?" Dennis said. "In fact, take it the fuck out of here when you go."

After a few minutes of small talk, Billy went back out into the general squad room to finish his reports, then thought about checking to see if Sweetpea Harris was in the system somewhere. At first he balked, not wanting to leave an electronic trail and risk having to answer anyone's questions, but then he did it anyway, masking his search with a half dozen other names, including Eric Cortez, only to discover that neither were incarcerated or had any warrants hanging over their heads. Which told him, after all was said and done, nothing.

Realizing that he was in no shape to drive, Billy turned off his phone and crashed in the 4-6 bunk room, as fetid and rank as any he had ever known.

WHEN HE FINALLY MADE IT home a few hours later, the TV was off. Eleven a.m. on a Saturday morning and no one was watching cartoons, the house as quiet as a monastery. Given that Carmen's car wasn't in the driveway, he assumed that she had taken the boys somewhere, which was A-OK with him.

Then Declan, still in his pajamas, came out of the kitchen.

"Dad?" His voice high and tentative. "We lost Grandpa."

"What do you mean?"

"He's not here."

"What do you mean he's not here. Did you check all the beds?"

"He's not here."

"The basement?"

"He's not here," the kid's voice starting to quiver.

Millie walked into the room, Declan turning to her for help.

"What's he talking about?" Billy said.

"He's not here," she said.

"Explain that."

"I come in this morning, the front door was open and he's . . ."

"Why didn't you call me?"

"We did," Millie said. "Your phone was off."

Carlos joined them in the hallway, the anxiety in the air inspiring him to hit his brother, who was too freaked by now to hit him back.

"Where's Carmen?"

"She's out looking for him."

"All right," Billy said, the heel of his hand pressed into his forehead. "All right . . ."

His first call was to his wife, but she had left without her phone, her "Killing Me Softly" ringtone playing in the kitchen, which made Carlos cry out, "Is Mommy lost too?"

His second call was to the Yonkers PD, the desk sergeant on duty informing him that Carmen had already given them a heads-up over an hour ago.

"All right, why don't you get them dressed," Billy said automatically, already roaming the neighborhood in his head.

HE BEGAN BY DRIVING THE residential streets nearest to home, knocking on doors and asking his neighbors to take a peek into their backyards, many of them saying that Carmen had already been there, then branched farther out, hitting the nearest commercial strips, poking his head into every supermarket, bar, and pizza place within walking distance.

At the corner of Mohawk and Seneca he ran into a trolling squad car—the only one assigned to the search, which infuriated him—the cops having no luck either. Then, fifteen minutes later, on a street of imposing Tudors and haciendas, he passed Carmen driving the other way, both cars hitting the brakes and nearly rear-ending each other as they simultaneously backed up at speed.

"I was taking a shower, I came down, Millie's cooking breakfast, she asked me if he was still sleeping upstairs," Carmen blurted, her eyes wild in her head. "Nobody saw him leave."

"All right, just calm down, we'll find him."

"It's my fault," yanking on her hair and then taking off again.

"It's nobody's fault," he said to the air.

Forty-five minutes later, Billy pulled over alongside a junior high school ball field and forced himself to be still.

OK, you're him . . .

THERE WERE DOZENS OF MYSTERIES to be solved. For starters, how does a man who can barely find his way around a reasonably small house, who has neither access to a car nor the wherewithal to drive one, make it from Yonkers, land of zero subways, to Harlem USA on his own. But there he was, Billy's hunch playing out like a Powerball winner, his father, walking up and down Lenox Avenue between 118th and 116th Streets like he owned the sidewalk.

For late March, the weather was downright balmy, the people mellow, and he had his father in his sights, so Billy remained in the car and watched the old man do his thing. He stopped and jawed with some old-timers who were sitting on the stoop of an abandoned brownstone cheek by jowl to a latteria on 118th. He bummed a cigarette from one of them, thumb-flicking a bent match against the friction strip of the matchbook with a practiced hand, even though, to Billy's knowledge, his father hadn't had a smoke since 1988, the year his wife had been diagnosed with lung cancer. Then, taking his leave of this crew, he shook hands all around before moving on down the block.

On 117th, he helped a young Asian woman disentangle her Maclaren double stroller from a narrow doorway. On 116th, he told three kids racing scooters through a crowd in front of a ShopRite to put on the brakes. He made eye contact with everyone who crossed his path, but not in such a way as to give offense; he just wanted to let them know that he was back and that nothing escaped his notice. Lenox between 116th and 118th—in 1959, it had been his first foot post out of the academy.

Billy finally stepped out of the car.

"Hey, Officer," calling to his father over the roof, then coming around to open the passenger door.

"DAD, HOW'D YOU GET HERE?" he asked as casually as he could.

"My driver."

"What driver was that?"

"Frank Campbell."

Billy took a breath. "Frank Campbell is off today, Dad," afraid to remind him that his personal driver for his last three years on the Job had been dead for a decade.

"Well, then whoever was covering for him."

Breathe . . .

"Do you remember his name?"

"Didn't catch it."

"Was he in the bag or plainclothes."

"Plainclothes."

Another old-timer, this one a handball-gloved double amputee in a wheelchair, rolled past the passenger window at eye level, caught sight of Billy Senior, and reversed his ride until they were face-to-face. Then, winking against the smoke streaming up from his lip-locked cigarette, the guy crisply, sarcastically saluted, before resuming his journey.

His father was not amused. "How the hell did he make bail?"

"Dad," Billy tried again. "Your driver, what did he look like?"

"Beefy, Hispanic, on the quiet side."

Billy stared out his window until the numbness passed. "Did he say anything to you?"

"He said, 'Where to, boss?' I said, 'Where do you think?' But I had to tell him, so yeah, it couldn't have been Frank."

"And where did he pick you up?"

"Right in front of the house. Caught me by surprise when I went out to get the paper."

Think . . .

"What kind of car was he driving?"

"The usual."

"What's the usual, Dad?" The stress of keeping it light starting to make his voice climb.

The old man went off somewhere.

"A Crown Vic?" Billy leading the witness, but Frank Campbell always drove him around in a Crown Vic.

"A Crown Vic," Billy Senior laughed. "Boy, that takes me back."

"Dad," he begged.

"And by the way, somebody's got to tell that kid to make sure the paper lands on the porch. It goes on the grass and the dew just soaks right through."

BILLY'S FATHER WAS A BIG hit at the 2-8, two blocks west of Lenox, the commanding officer remembering him from 1985, when he was a rookie up here and Billy Senior was the West Harlem division captain, and happily giving him a house tour while Billy, waiting for the relevant street camera uploads, made his calls. First to home, Carmen crying with relief and maybe something a little edgier, then to the WGs, seeing if anyone could help him find a safe house for his family until this psycho was caught.

At one point or another over the past twenty years, they had all given temporary shelter to each other, Billy moving in with Pavlicek and his young wife when he lost the house in Staten Island to his ex, Yasmeen moving to Pelham to help Pavlicek take care of his young son after his wife's collapse and institutionalization, Pavlicek sending the adolescent John Junior to live with Billy and Carmen when he and the kid needed a time-out from each other. Later, Jimmy Whelan had stayed with Yasmeen and then Redman when one of his endless string of basement super's apartments had flooded, although no one ever wanted to move in with Whelan. Then there was Redman staying with Billy and Carmen after his second or third wife had caught him with his third or fourth wife and set the funeral parlor on fire, and Yasmeen again, taking Carlos and Declan in that long-ago black summer when Carmen was unable to leave the bedroom and Billy had his hands full simply coaxing her down the stairs.

And now, once again, every one of them coming through: Jimmy offering his cabin in Monticello, Yasmeen the summerhouse in Greenwood Lake, Redman a two-room apartment directly above the funeral parlor—although he advised Billy to "think before you say yes"—and Pavlicek, the grand prize winner, offering them their choice of twelve newly renovated flats in buildings spread out over the Bronx and upper Manhattan, as long as they didn't mind the constant racket made by his nonstop work crews.

The uploads from the street cameras, when they finally came in, just added to the mystery, the Lenox Avenue tape showing Billy Senior arriving there on foot after having turned the corner from West 115th, the tape trained on 115th showing him once again on foot after having turned the corner from Adam Clayton Powell, which he entered from 113th, and so on, the precinct tech tracking his progress in reverse until an out-of-commission camera on 111th and Frederick Douglass Boulevard ended the trail with no sign of the car that had dropped him off somewhere south and west of where Billy had found him.

"THE HELL WITH THAT AND the hell with that," Carmen clutching her head. "I'm supposed to take the kids and live where, upstate New York? On top of some dead bodies in Harlem?"

"Harlem's totally different now."

"I don't give a shit if it's the new Paris. I'm just not taking my kids to live in a funeral home. Where's your head at, Billy?"

They were standing face-to-face in the toy-strewn living room, each of them alternately crouching and then shooting upright to body-English their arguments, raising and then lowering their voices as the awareness of the two freaked-out kids in the house went in and out of their consciousness.

"Pavlicek has a dozen clean apartments all over the Bronx," Billy pleaded.

"Clean as in vacant, as in no furniture, no bedding, as in no anything."

She straightened up and took a breath. "The point is, Billy, I have a job, they have school, and we're not having our lives uprooted by some socio-path. But do you want to do something for me?"

"Carmen, you're here at night by yourself with the kids. What am I supposed to do, stay home from work and sit in a corner with a shotgun?"

"I asked," she said slowly, "do you want to *do* something for me." Then, lowering her voice: "Your father? Today? He needs to be somewheres else."

"Like where," Billy on full alert.

"I don't know, maybe it's time for him . . ."

"Don't even say it."

"Billy, he doesn't know where he is, he doesn't know *who* he is. This maniac comes along . . . You want to talk about who's vulnerable around here? You want to talk about the one person, the, the straw that's going to break the camel's back? Look, you said it yourself, you're either work-ing or you're sleeping. One way or another you're never here, and I can't worry about him day in and day out, and frankly, with everything that's going on?" again dropping into that heated whisper. "I can't bear him right now. I'm sorry to be so . . . to be like this."

"What happened today, it wasn't his fault."

"Exactly."

"You want to kill him?" Billy's turn to start tearing up. "I put him in a home he'll be dead in a week."

"It's called assisted living."

"No fucking way."

"Then let your sister take him."

"She hates him."

"Too bad."

"She's got her hands full with her own mother-in-law." Billy back to pleading.

"She's got her hands full, huh? Not us, though, we're sailing to Tahiti next week."

"Jesus Christ, what the hell's gotten into you?"

"Get it through your *head,* Billy, we're not going anywhere. You don't want to put him in a, a, a place? Then you call your sister. She's his child too."

"Sometimes you can be a stone bitch, you know that?" Billy instantly ashamed to have said it.

Carmen at first looked struck, then furious, then left the room without another word, leaving Billy standing there, thinking, Why is he doing this to us?

From the kitchen, Carlos started howling in fury, his older brother having just punched him in the stomach.

BRENDA SOUSA, BILLY'S OLDEST SISTER, showed up three hours later dressed in a snowflake-patterned ski sweater and stirrup pants, her face a moon of aggrievement. Her husband, Charley, a private investigator specializing in insurance fraud, a small quiet man who always seemed to be embarrassed about something, brought up the rear.

Brenda marched up to her father in the kitchen without saying hello to anyone else, wrapped him in a brusque hug. "Hi, Pa," kissing him hard on the cheek, then turning to Billy. "For how long is this."

"Jesus, Brenda, he's right here."

"For how long."

"He's your father, too."

"Did I say he's not?" His sister always so angry.

"Not long."

"How long is not long."

Carmen, having no belly for her sister-in-law, left the room.

"I don't know, Brenda, there was a guy out there who picked him up today, drove him into the city, and just dumped him on the street."

"What? Why?"

"I don't know, but he's not safe here."

"So how is he supposed to be safer by me?"

"Because," Billy took a breath, "whoever took him is after our family." There, he'd said it.

THE NYPD THREAT ASSESSMENT TEAM, two detectives named Amato and Lemon, arrived at the house two hours later. Carmen made coffee, then all four of them took seats in the living room, Billy and his wife on the brocade sofa, the detectives facing them in the matching chairs.

"Who should we be talking to here," Amato asked Billy. "You or your father?"

"In terms of what."

"In terms of who might be out there with some kind of personal hard-on," Lemon said.

"You're talking about previous collars?"

"That or anything."

"Well, my dad's retired twenty years, so whoever had a hard-on for him is mostly likely dead or bedridden."

The detectives stared at him, said nothing.

"As for me, I mean, I put away my share of actors, but except for a few years in the Four-nine, I've either been with the ID Squad or in Night Watch, so . . ."

"Any run-ins?"

"With other cops?" Billy shrugged. "There's guys I didn't get along with, but never anything heavy."

"Can you give us some names?"

"Honestly? I'd rather not. We all shook hands in the end."

"What's wrong with giving them names?" Carmen asked, her arms crossed tightly over her chest.

"Because there's not one of them I can't pick up the phone and call myself," he said. "Because there's no need to bring up dead and buried beefs from back in the stone age."

"Then what's the point of them being here?" she muttered.

"How about off the Job," Lemon asked.

"I have no idea," Billy still arguing with Carmen in his head.

"Curtis Taft?" Amato's turn.

"What about Curtis Taft."

"You assaulted him in his hospital bed," Amato said.

"I'd say assault is a little overdramatic."

They resorted to staring at him again.

"I don't think he's so stupid as to come after me or my family, but by all means, do what you have to do."

There was a pause as both cops went into their notes.

"How about that shooting back when you were in anti-crime?" Lemon asked, still looking down at his pad.

"What about it?"

"There was a lot of press, a lot of angry people."

"It's been over fifteen years, you'd think they'd have plenty to be angry about since."

Carmen, still looking away, shook her head in exasperation, Billy having to restrain himself from getting into another fight with her, this one in front of their Threat Assessment Team.

"All right," Amato said, rising. "We'll put in a request for TARU to come out, mount a few cameras, and ask for the Yonkers PD to start running directed patrols."

"How soon for the cameras?" Billy asked.

"Hopefully right away," Lemon said.

"What do you mean, 'hopefully'?"

"All we can do is put in the request."

AN HOUR LATER BILLY AND Carmen were sitting on the couch, each with their arms crossed tightly over their chests as they pretended to watch something or other on TV.

This was how the slow process of ending a fight always began for them, with a sullen agreement to tolerate each other's presence while engaged in a nonverbal activity, during which, at some point, one of them would make a not-quite-spontaneous comment about something unrelated to the argument, something safe, delivered in an offhand monotone, that didn't require a response but usually got one, also to be delivered in the same flatline tone. From there, the exchanges, always off the subject of the fight, would gradually begin to pick up speed until they were actually talking and that monotone was replaced by the natural oscilloscope of unself-conscious human speech. Formal apologies, if the situation really demanded it, usually came later in another room or, if they could get away with it, never, neither of them wanting to risk another potentially volatile encounter if it wasn't necessary. But at the moment they were still in Stage One, the accumulation of stressed silence such that when the phone rang they both nearly levitated off the couch.

It was Billy's sister calling to complain that Billy Senior had no change of underwear in his overnight bag. That call was followed a minute later by another, this one to announce that he had no toothpaste, then another to bitch that he had no pajama bottoms, each "had no" apparently deserving its own individual call.

"What the fuck is wrong with her all the time?" Carmen said when Billy returned to the couch.

"She thinks he didn't like her when she was a kid."

"Only him?"

The next time the phone rang Carmen leapt to pick it up. "I swear to Christ, Brenda, why do you always have to be such a pissed-off bitch . . ." Then: "Oh," her tone downshifting. "I'm so sorry, I thought . . . Sure, he's right here, right here."

Carmen extended the phone to Billy. "It's somebody from Immaculate, Albert Lazar?"

"LIKE I TOLD YOU WHEN I called, I would have been perfectly happy to come to you."

"No problem," Billy said.

Lazar had sounded like a wreck on the phone, like he needed to unburden himself, and Billy didn't want him coming to the house and being subjected to the double-team tension of two freaked-out parents. He needed this guy to feel free to talk, and so he found himself in Lazar's tiny home office in Sleepy Hollow, formerly the bedroom of his college-age daughter, the leftover floral-patterned wallpaper combining with the teacher's visceral anxiety to shrink the already claustrophobic space to the size and feel of a sweatbox.

"So," Billy willing himself to be cool, "now that I'm here . . ."

"Understand, I had no idea that you were a detective until you handed me your card yesterday."

"No reason you should have."

"This is kind of a long story."

"How about we start with the punch line and work backwards?"

"Please, I need to tell it the way I need to tell it." They were alone, Lazar's wife and son watching TV one floor below, but he still seemed to feel the need to whisper. "Otherwise you'll never understand."

"Any way you want."

Lazar stared at his hands, his kneecaps motoring.

"So," Billy said.

"All right," Lazar said, dropping his elbows to his knees. "All right . . . Last week?"

Lazar's wife came into the room with a bowl of freshly made kale chips, her husband smiling at her with get-lost eyes. He waited for the sound of her retreating footsteps to fade before starting again.

"Last week? I had a few work meetings in Beacon, and I'm not really familiar with the town, but I was stuck there overnight and so purely out of boredom I took a walk and wound up wandering into a bar. Believe me, I hardly indulge, but I had a gin and tonic, and . . ."

"And . . ."

"Well, call me blind as a bat but I didn't realize it was a gay bar until I ordered drink number two."

"OK . . ."

"And I was so embarrassed that I just tabbed out and left." Tabbed out, Billy thinking, not the expression of a fair-weather tippler.

"It's just that when I was going out the door, I ran into my neighbor, one of my neighbors, Eric, from right up the block here, and when I saw him I was so flustered about coming out of that kind of place all I said was 'Be careful in there, I think something fishy's going on.' And he said, 'Thanks for the warning, I'll stay on my toes.'"

"So this Eric . . ."

"Eric Salley. Understand, I'm a very tolerant individual. I have no problem with him or anyone else being gay."

"Understood. So, this Eric Salley . . ."

"Is trouble."

"What kind of trouble?" When Lazar had difficulty answering, Billy added, "Is he making trouble for you?"

"No, not yet."

"Maybe he's tolerant, too."

"There's nothing for him to be tolerant about."

"Understood."

"Look, I teach at a Catholic school in a working-class city."

"Right."

"A rumor gets started . . . Those kids are my life."

"You're very popular, I know. But you're having a hard time telling me what it is you want me to know, so let me just ask, is this Eric Salley the one I'm looking for?"

"Looking for?" Lazar blinking in confusion.

Billy looked off, trying to control his temper. The guy was in the closet and he was scared of being dragged out. And that was all that this was about.

"So why am I here," he said. "He's trying to blackmail you?"

"No, but to be honest I never felt comfortable around him, and now every time I see him he smiles at me like he knows me. From what I understand he's lost his job and he's this close to losing his condo. And I don't want to go to the local police here, it would only make matters worse. So, I was wondering . . . is there any way, in your capacity as a New York City detective and the parent of one of our students, could you maybe have a talk with him before he does anything we'll both regret?"

"So Eric Salley was not the guy who approached my son."

"No, believe me, I would have recognized him from a mile away."

"How about you, are you the one?"

"Am I the one, what . . ."

Billy got up to leave.

"So, can you help me?" Lazar asked.

"I'll make some calls," he muttered, Billy-speak for Go fuck yourself, and then he was gone.

Leaving everybody home alone like that . . .

AS BILLY MADE HIS WAY back to Yonkers his anger toward Lazar started to fade. The guy had been terrified, had been carrying the burden of being who he was all his life and just couldn't imagine surviving the exposure.

But gay, not gay, or whatever else, Billy couldn't imagine living his day-in, day-out life with a secret so heavy on his heart that the only viable alternative was some kind of oblivion.

Sometimes he worried about Carmen having that kind of weight on her, some specific interior thing that made her so anxiously alert during the days and such a tormented thrasher at night, that made every therapy session he had ever attended with her feel like a complete waste of time, filled with sulky bluster and air-ball bullshit, that periodically and without warning dropped a black-dog mantle over her so profound that it might be days before she could bring herself to open the bedroom door.

There were times when he wondered whether she had been sexually abused as a child and never told anyone or as a frightened teenager had abandoned an unwanted baby—that's where his worst-case imagination came to an end—but one thing he knew for sure: if she could ever find it in herself to finally speak the name of her demon, she would most definitely survive. Her husband would make sure of it.

PULLING INTO HIS DRIVEWAY, BILLY saw the silhouette of a stocky male prowling the lawn.

At first he was too startled to move, then moved without thinking, bolting from the car to bull-rush the intruder from behind. As soon as he brought him to ground, landing on top of the guy in a way that forced the air out of both of them, a second figure came running from around the back of the house and bellowed, "Freeze!" while simultaneously blinding Billy with a fierce beam of light. At which point the first cop got up, turned to Billy, and punched him in the head.

And so he was introduced to 24/7 direct patrol coverage, Billy talking as fast as he could to avoid being cuffed and thrown into the back of the Yonkers PD cruiser sent to protect his home and family.

AT THREE IN THE MORNING, when Billy entered the sickly bright all-night gas station mini-mart off Frederick Douglass Boulevard, the young kufied African cashier was standing behind the counter, a half-smile on his face as he posed with cops, the majority of whom were holding out beers or candy bars for him to ring up while their partners snapped away with iPhones. The Wheel had said robbery-homicide, body on the scene, but all Billy saw was the cashier, the clowning uniforms, and Stupak.

"Where's the body?"

"Are you blind?" Stupak answered.

Wading through the posing cops, he took a closer look at the cashier: the smiling kid was stone-dead on his feet, a dime-sized bloodstain barely discernible on the chest pocket of his thick burgundy shirt. On the counter to his right sat a half-eaten Hot Pocket, still steaming from the microwave; to his left was a coiled nest of wooden prayer beads and an accounting textbook.

"Are you fucking kidding me?" Billy bellowed at the uniforms. "Everybody out."

Once they were gone, Billy took an extra moment to contemplate his upright victim, then had to turn away; staring into those unblinking yet still expressive eyes felt almost rude.

"It's like Madame Tussauds," Stupak said.

"You pull the store cameras?"

"Of course."

"Did you . . ."

"Of course."

"Any wits?"

"Feeley's in the back room interviewing the cabbie that called it in."

"Feeley's here?" Billy surprised but not really, having figured that after their car talk, Gene would either start showing up like clockwork just to spite him, or he'd take to heart Billy's suggestion to become a full-time no-show and never be seen again, a winning outcome either way.

"Is Butter here?"

"Give him a break, he just blew a big audition today."

"Playing what?"

"Are you going to make me say it?' "

"A detective, right?"

Stupak walked away.

"Hey, Sarge?" a uniform called out from the open door. "There's a guy out here."

Billy stepped out to see a plainclothes detective in jeans and a hoodie leaning against the door of what he guessed was a dope-confiscated vintage Firebird. Behind the narc, two uniforms posted at the pumps were waving off all cars, at this hour mostly taxis pulling in to gas up.

"Sorry to pull you out. I didn't want to contaminate your scene in there."

"Too late for that."

"John MacCormack," offering his hand, "Brooklyn North Narcotics."

"Excuse me," Billy said, walking over to the uniforms at the pumps. "These cars pulling in?" he said. "They're probably habituals, so start taking their vitals before you cut them loose, especially the hacks."

Moving back to MacCormack, Billy finally shook his hand. "So, John, what can I do for you?"

"I need to know your interest in Eric Cortez."

"Come again?"

"You ran his name yesterday? It raised a flag."

"Yeah, I did, him and a few others."

"Can I ask why?"

Billy knew the worst thing he could do was lie. "I was over at the Four-six wrapping up my Fives on a shooting. I had some time to kill, so I looked up a few bad guys from back in the day."

MacCormack looked off, smiling in temporary retreat.

"Like Facebooking old girlfriends," Billy said. "Why do you want to know?"

MacCormack let the question hang in the air, Billy not liking that at all.

"OK," Billy said, suddenly too nervous to wait him out, "I'm guessing that since Cortez is too stupid to be running any kind of crew or moving enough weight to be worth your while otherwise, he's your CI, most likely in deep for you with some bigger fish, and right now you're coming up here to see if he's into some of kind of outside jackpot that he neglected to tell you about. But I'm just guessing."

"Hang on a sec," MacCormack said, then walked away to make a brief phone call.

The CSU van finally rolled up, the emerging detectives heading to the mini-mart with their kits and cameras, probably unaware that the tall young man visible through the plate-glass window and looking as if he were ready to ring up a beer was their body.

"Look," Billy said when MacCormack came back, "it was just curiosity on my part. I probably shouldn't have run him and I'm sorry I did, but number one, I'm not looking to fuck anybody's play here, and two, you're coming to me at three in the morning about this and not answering any of my questions, so maybe you can just tell me this . . . Am I in some kind of jam here?"

MacCormack hesitated, looking at Billy as if sizing him up. "He just needs to be protected right now."

Billy nodded, masking his relief, then became angry with himself for showing his ass like that.

"Protected," he said. "You know what this guy did, don't you?"

"You mean the Del Pino homicide?" MacCormack pulled out a pack of Winstons.

"All I can think, he must be one hell of a snitch."

MacCormack stared at Billy for a moment longer in that assessing way, then just shrugged, game over.

"I tell you, with CIs?" he said, offering Billy a cigarette. "I try to think of it like this: all those Nazi scientists working on the V-2 rocket, we snatched them up like draft picks, us or the Reds, freedom or world enslavement. That was the stakes, so all is forgiven, welcome to Texas. I mean, Christ, some of those krauts wound up on postage stamps."

"Eric Cortez as Wernher von Braun," Billy said. "That there's a keeper."

MacCormack semi-laughed, then slipped back into the Firebird.

Billy stared at the Phoenix decal on the trembling hood for a moment, then just said it: "He's not dead, is he?"

"Cortez? No," MacCormack said, giving Billy a look that made him wish he'd kept his mouth shut.

MILTON RAMOS

She was throwing him all night.

First she wanted to do something in bed that they never did before and that made him blow his top in about two minutes flat.

Then, still turned on by what they'd just done, they went at it again—they were strictly one-shot lovers, and so that was a second first—Marilys moaning all the way through. Normally they were so silent that you could be sleeping in the same room with them and not wake up, so that right there was a third first, all three groundbreakers coming to pass in about twenty-five minutes.

They were both by nature physically modest people, so even though they had just fucked like banshees, when she finally came out of the bathroom still naked, Milton had no idea where to rest his eyes. And instead of immediately getting dressed like she always did, Marilys just sat on the edge of the bed without making any move for her clothes.

"Hey, Milton."

He had never heard her say his name out loud; somehow they managed to live amicably under the same roof for forty to fifty hours a week without ever saying each other's names, and he'd be lying if he said her doing so now didn't make him feel uncomfortable.

"What's up," still looking away from her water-dappled skin.

"I'm pregnant."

His first reaction was that she had just become pregnant in the last half hour, which was maybe why she had taken so long in the bathroom.

"What do you mean?" The question sounded stupid, he knew, but still.

She didn't answer.

Even in his state of low shock, he would not insult her by asking if she was sure it was his.

"OK," he said carefully, then: "What are you thinking?"

Her blue-black Indio hair, instead of being brushed straight back from her face as usual, had been carefully combed into long wet bangs that made her look a few pounds lighter, a few years younger.

"Because whatever you're thinking, I'll help you out."

"Thanks," still making no move to cover herself.

"I mean, now is not a good time for me, but anything I can do."

Much to his relief, she finally began reaching for her clothes.

"But so just tell me, what are you thinking?"

"I'm thinking it's a boy."

"You can tell, huh?"

"I have two sons, seven brothers, and seven uncles. It's a boy."

"OK."

He felt stoned, but not so badly that he couldn't deal.

She stopped reaching for her clothes and looked at him full-on. "Look, I don't want nothing from you and I'm OK raising him on my own, but that means I got to go back to Guatemala to be with my family, so pretty soon I can't take care of Sofia anymore, and I can't take care of you, that's all I'm saying."

"That's too bad," he said, both saddened and relieved.

A FEW HOURS LATER, A thermos of iced Yellow Chartreuse nesting in his cup caddie, Milton sat in the rear parking lot of the Bryant Motor Lodge and watched as Carmen's brother, Victor, pulled up in an old Range Rover, stepped out, and walked across the lot to the rear entrance, just like dozens of junkies, crackistanis, and pross-escorted johns had done since he had set up camp ninety minutes earlier. Milton had nothing against Carmen's brother personally; in fact, in some detached way he was happy to see him, the sad undergrown gay kid he remembered from Longfellow Avenue having grown into a fairly squared-away-looking man with clear eyes and a forthright stride even at this ass-of-night hour.

Victor had been easy to find—Milton just hadn't ever thought of finding him before. A sociology instructor at City College, he had a website that described the paper he was working on, calling it a study of the "quasi-family dynamics" that developed over time among the drug dealers and sex workers whose base of operations was an unnamed hot-sheet motel in the Bronx. Which wasn't hard to find either, since there was a notorious cluster directly across the New England Thruway from Co-op City, and talking to a few of the regulars along that stretch yielded not only the Bryant but Victor's working hours, which made sense, he guessed, given what the guy was going after.

Propping his bat in the passenger-side foot well, he slid his seat back as far as it would go, reached for the thermos, and drifted off, thinking about having unexpectedly run into Billy Graves in Dennis Doyle's office first thing this morning. After the fight-or-flight thing passed, Milton had instinctively sized him up physically, in case it ever came to that, then calmed down enough to get a rush off Billy's cluelessness. And then seeing him again later in the afternoon, this time gray-faced and shaking when he finally found his father, still half in his pajamas, walking his old post on Lenox Avenue like a living time capsule.

But Milton knew that what he had committed by taking Bill Graves Sr. from the house in Yonkers, given the man's deteriorating mental state, was both a felony and an escalation.

And now he was here.

Another escalation.

IN THE PAST, HIS RAGE, his satisfaction, climaxed in one act, one deed. But because of his desire this time around to keep his own life intact, he had decided on a strategy of long-term indirect payback, and in a way this was much harder on him, leaving too much time for thinking, for agonizing, for mulling over worst-case outcomes, for justifying and then retreating, retreating and then reversing.

Even worse, Milton was coming to discover, each act of carefully doled-out chaos set up a craving in him to get to the next one. He felt a burning urge to keep jacking up the stakes, intensify the act itself, until he could achieve something akin to that sensation of finality he had always experienced, for better or worse, in the past. But he was losing faith in his ability to rein himself in before the tale told out—if he had ever had that faith in himself to begin with.

When he'd taken Sofia to Longfellow Avenue he had thought it was to immunize himself from himself. But now, sitting here in the parking lot of Motel Hell, he realized that it had been more of a farewell tour. If things went out of control—*when* things went out of control, as he had always known they would—she would at least have some sense memory of the haunted house that, after twenty-three years, had finally claimed her father.

A son. Or so she claims. Well, it was hers. And his, scientifically speaking, but mostly hers, and he wouldn't interfere with her plans.

As two of the motel guests came out into the parking lot to swap powder for head, he thought about how Marilys had sat on the edge of the bed tonight, her hair combed straight down like a squaw, then thought about that thing they did the first time, the noises she made that second time.

He took another sip of Chartreuse.

But even if he was otherwise inclined about the baby, the way things were going he wouldn't be around to enjoy him in any event, and the kid would just become another log on the bonfire of loss.

Somewhere near a shot went off, a car peeled out, and a man lay on his back by the dumpsters, his legs slow-peddling the air. After a long moment he managed to flip himself over, raise up on all fours, and crawl back inside the motel.

They had always understood each other, he and Marilys, their silences pretty companionable, neither one ever a trouble to the other, although he always felt bad about not paying her more money.

The next thought that came to Milton was so major that after reflex-ively grabbing for his bat, he had to step out of the car in order to clear his head.

To avenge his family, he would be destroying what was left of it. The Ramos family would go from two here to two gone, which is to say no one left. But what if instead of Ramos obliteration they—he—went the other way and doubled their number?

He couldn't imagine what Edgar would say about this new way of thinking—his older brother was the only person he'd ever known whose darkness was blacker than his own, the only person who Milton had ever come close to fearing—but he was pretty sure that his mother would be weeping with relief.

He was still standing outside his car, bat in hand, when Carmen's brother suddenly came out of the motel, trotted to the Range Rover, and opened the passenger door. Victor grabbed a mini-recorder from the glove box, then dropped his car keys and accidentally kicked them into the night. Using the light on his cell phone, he sank into a hunch and began duck-walking all over the lot in an effort to find them, Milton watching as Victor unwittingly came in his direction, his bowed head like an offering.

AFTER HE'D IDENTIFIED HIMSELF HALF a dozen times through the steel door of her East Harlem SRO, Marilys, wearing a polyester nightgown, cautiously opened up, the scent of her skin lotion pleasantly knocking him on his ass.

"I should have called," he said, eyeing the steak knife in her left hand.

"What's wrong?" she whispered, her eyes wide with alarm.

"Nothing, can I come in?"

He had never been here before, and he was surprised by the number of plants she kept, both hanging and potted, and not so surprised by the army of religious tokens: the medallions and silver icons that festooned her walls, the plaster saints that stood on her dresser and night table, Marilys's minuscule home like Guatemala in a box.

There was nowhere to sit but the bed.

He took the time he needed to compose what he wanted to say, but once he got good and going he doubted he had ever uttered so many continuous words in his life.

"So, after my, what happened to my family, I lived with my aunt Pauline for a few years, she got me to finish high school out by her, I can't hardly remember any of my classes or teachers but I played a little football and I enjoyed that . . . Then after graduation, I worked construction off and on, was a bouncer in a few titty bars in Williamsburg when it was still like that, got hired as a bodyguard for Fat Assassin, which was a good gig until he wanted me to start lining up girls for him this one night in some club like I was his fucking sex gofer . . . I mean, as I look back on it, me swinging on him in front of his people wasn't the smartest thing to do, but . . . And then so of course we wound up taking it out back, which turned out very bad for the both of us, you know, in our respective ways . . . After that I kind of lost myself for a year or two, the less said about that the better, until a girl in the neighborhood that I liked who was a police cadet started talking that up, and, at the time I figured, Well, that's one way to keep myself out of trouble, but they rejected my application because I didn't have any college. So I went to Medgar Evers in Brooklyn, but only for a year, reapplied, got in, graduated, got my shield, got married, had Sofia, as you know, lost my wife, as you know . . ." taking a breather, thinking, What else, what else . . .

"With women? There was a girl, Norma, in, I think, tenth grade, that was the first time, a few one-time things, some girlfriends, but nobody for long, my wife of course, plus I wasn't above paying for it now and then, especially at first after she died, then you, of course, you know, the way we do."

What else . . .

"I drink too much, as you know, and . . . I guess that's it."

Of course that wasn't it, but there would be time for telling the rest later.

"So," looking at her perched on the foot of her own bed, the hanging plants behind her head making him think of a jungle cat emerging into a clearing, "what do you think?"

When he left forty-five minutes later, she kissed him on the mouth, which made him jerk back with surprise, then avidly lean in for more.

All these firsts . . .

10

There's something terrible going on the bathroom, he can hear Carmen moaning from behind the half-open door, a low animal keen, and then he hears a frantic scrabbling on the tiles as if she's desperately trying to get away from someone. He needs to get out of bed but he's physically paralyzed, not even able to brush away the pillow that has slipped over his face and is preventing him from drawing breath. She calls out his name in a hopeless sob, more like a farewell than a cry for help, and it's only with the greatest effort that he can even make a responding noise, a kind of high-pitched strangled mooing that actually, finally wakes him up. But though he is wide awake now, he still can't move or draw breath, and Carmen is still in that small room with him, and he's killing her, and Billy just cannot breathe or move, until suddenly he can, wrenching himself free from the bedsheets and stumbling into the bathroom, but of course there's no one there.

Sitting slumped and shaken on the edge of the bathtub, Billy wished—for the first time in nearly two decades—he desperately wished for a fat line of coke, the only thing he could think of to speed-vacuum his muzzy, terror-stricken skull.

■ ■ ■

WHEN HE FINALLY MADE IT downstairs, the first person he saw was his father, reading the paper in the kitchen, which was as per usual until he remembered that the old guy was supposed to be at his daughter's house.

The slam of a car door drew Billy to the window, his sister about to back out of his driveway.

"What are you doing, Brenda?" Wearing a T-shirt, jeans, and sneakers, he stood by her car door in the early morning chill.

His sister, having no intention of getting out of the car, or even turning off the engine, rolled down the driver-side window.

"I wake up this morning, I think it's Charley laying next to me, but guess who."

"I should have warned you about that."

"Oh. And let me tell you about breakfast," she said, lighting a cigarette. "We're all sitting there, me, Dad, Charley, and my head-case mother-in-law, Rita, and all of a sudden Rita says to Dad, 'So, Jeff, are we going to have relations tonight?' You know what our father says? 'Depends what time I get off.' And Rita says back, 'Well, call me when you know so I can cancel my game.'"

Billy took a light off Brenda's cigarette. "OK, so he thought she was Mom."

"Actually, he called her Irena."

"Who's Irena?"

Brenda put her car in gear. "Do you really want to know?" Then, reversing out of the driveway, "I can't do it, Billy, I'm sorry."

On his way back up to the house, Dennis Doyle called, Billy listening to him for less than a minute before jumping into his own car and taking off for the Bronx.

THE FIRST THING HE NOTICED when he raced into the St. Ann's ER was Carmen's workstation chair upside down a good fifteen feet from her desk; the second was the bright red spatter of drops leading to the curtained cubicle.

At the sight of him Carmen started yelling at the Indo-Afro-Asian interns that ringed her gurney. "Jesus Christ! I specifically said do not call my husband, as in, *do not*."

From what he could see of her partially averted face, there was a two-inch cut beneath her eye and the beginnings of a nasty shiner.

"They didn't call him, Carm," Dennis said. "I did."

"What happened." Billy wasn't sure who he was addressing.

"I think this might require some stitches," one of the interns said.

"What happened," he repeated.

"Oh for Christ's sake, it's a goddamn black eye!" Carmen back to barking. "Ice the goddamn thing, then let me go pick up my chair and get back to work. Jesus!"

Despite her fireballing, Billy saw that she was trembling. As was he.

"You caught the guy?" he asked Dennis.

"I told you three times, yes."

"In fact, you know what?" Carmen again. "I don't want you to go near my face at all. Go page Kantor."

"Where is he," Billy asked Dennis.

"Forget it, Billy."

"Is he still here? Where is he?"

"You know what?" Carmen said. "Screw it. Hold up a mirror for me, I'll do it myself."

"You have no idea what this whack's been putting us through," Billy said.

"What whack?" Dennis losing track.

"Dennis, I just want to lay eyes on him, I won't even go in the room."

"I don't think so."

"How about this. You don't let me see him, I'll walk out of here and pistol-whip the first fat-assed, do-nothing hospital guard I see."

"Gentlemen," an older doctor murmured as he slid past them and into the cubicle. "So, Carmen," he said breezily, "when can we expect the lawsuit?"

"Pretend it's my collar," Billy pleaded, "and that's Yasmeen on that table getting worked on."

Dennis did a quick 360 around himself. "You are not to talk to him."

"You got it."

"Not a fucking word, you hear me?"

As they walked to the impromptu holding cell, an empty storage room down a long corridor, Dennis held firmly to Billy's arm, his tense mantra every few steps "Remember what you promised me."

"Did he say anything?"

"Who. This guy? Not that I know of."

"Really," Billy said lightly. "Not before, not during, not after?" Then, when Dennis tightened his grip: "I'm just curious."

"Just remember what you promised."

"YOU!" BILLY SHOUTED AS HE tried to leap over Dennis's back and get to Carmen's attacker, who, guarded by a uniform, was cuffed to a chair at the far end of the room. The grimy, blaze-eyed stick figure in scavenged clothing looked at Billy with calm eyes and total incomprehension.

"What do you want from us!" Billy railed, this time with less heat. The guy was obviously a homeless nutter off his meds, if he'd ever been prescribed them in the first place.

"You promised me," Dennis said, his arms spread wide as he began chest-bumping Billy backward toward the door.

"Forget it," Billy said, lightly pushing him off before turning to leave under his own steam.

"I am John," the cuffed man abruptly announced in a voice so deep and booming they both jumped. "And I bring news of he who is to come."

THE BEST OF PAVLICEK'S OFFERED apartments was, as Carmen had predicted, a furniture-free one-bedroom in a shittier-than-usual part of the Bronx, but Billy didn't care. This morning's assault had thrown him into a state of shameless hyperprotectiveness, and until their stalker was caught, they were leaving Yonkers, the hell with the goddamn designated patrols, which had done nothing last night but freak out his wife, the low voices and roving flashlight beams coming through the bedroom window at all hours making her feel like a hunted animal—which, if you thought about it, was what she felt like most of the time without any help from them.

"I was hoping so bad that was him, you know?" Billy said, perching himself on a living room windowsill that afforded him a partial view of the outfield in Yankee Stadium, one block west of the apartment. "At least it would all have been over."

"They'll catch him," Pavlicek said restlessly. "She's home now?"

"I had to drag her out of there, but yeah, she's home."

"Doctors and nurses, they always make the worst patients, right? They think they know everything, then when something happens to them they get all pissy and embarrassed. They're like two-year-olds, tell me I'm wrong."

For a man seeing a hematologist he seemed to be moving pretty good today, Billy thought, the guy roaming in a tight, repetitive circuit like a big cat in a small cage.

"All right, look, I'll get my guys to bring some furniture in from the warehouse, but it might take a day or two. Meanwhile, I'm having my security guy come up to the house and hook you up with a CCTV."

"John . . ."

"I can't believe you don't have one. In fact, it boggles my mind. First thing I did when I bought my pile was put in a system. I wouldn't have my family set foot in there until it was wired like the Pentagon, are you kidding me? Christ, Billy, you haven't seen enough shit in the last twenty years? You think you're immune? No one's immune. None of us."

"When you're right, you're right," Billy said, just trying to calm him down. "Thank you."

Pavlicek took a seat on one of the radiators, dropped his head, and ran his hands through his hair. When he looked up again it was like a sleight of hand, his expression having morphed from fiercely agitated to helplessly bewildered.

"How are you feeling these days?" Billy asked.

"What do you mean?"

"You know, your cholesterol."

"My what? I'm good."

"Good. Glad to hear it."

"So, how are the boys," Pavlicek said, just to say something.

"They're boys," Billy answered in kind.

"Kids. All we want in life is for them to be happy, right?"

"Sure."

"I mean, what are we asking."

"I know."

"John Junior, do you remember all the grief he put me through? With the rehabs, the dealing, the graffiti collars, dropping out of school . . . And that fucking room of his, I'd walk in, him and all his friends reeking of skunk, looking like red-eyed morons, 'Hey Mister P,' sitting there with the sideways hats over their ears. 'Hey, kids! Who knows what century it is? A hundred bucks to whoever can tell me what fucking century we're in or even just what planet we're on,' they're like, 'Uh, duh, uh . . .'"

"I remember," Billy said, recalling John Junior in his teens, an oversized bruiser like his father but in reality a sweet-tempered con artist who'd rather munch than punch.

"But I tell you, last year?" Pavlicek back to pacing. "I come home one day, he's there, says to me, Read this, and it's an acceptance letter from Westchester Community College. I didn't even know he applied. He says he wants to take some business classes, then get something going for himself. I tell him, Come work for me, you'll learn more about starting your own business than ten colleges, he says no, he wants to do it on his own. I say, If you work for me you'll earn enough money to hit the ground running, he says, Dad, all due respect? It's important for me to do this without help from you. Can you believe that? I was so proud of him I wanted to bust."

"Hey, it was his time and he recognized it," Billy said. "Many don't."

"What's that?" Pavlicek tilted his chin to the side pocket of Billy's sport jacket, Sweetpea's purple Missing poster still peeking out like gaudy origami.

Billy passed it over.

"Cornell Harris," Pavlicek read, then: "That's Sweetpea, right?"

"Looks like he pulled a Houdini," Billy said. "Or got Houdinied, more likely."

"What the hell do you care?"

"I'm not saying I do."

"Worry about your family."

"What do you think I'm doing here?"

"Worry about your kids." Pavlicek started to balloon again, his voice bouncing off the bare walls.

Billy stopped answering, refusing to engage.

"This fuck? Are you kidding me?" Pavlicek crumpled the poster, then tossed it backhand into a corner. "Piece of shit . . ."

Hoping he would storm himself out, Billy remained seated and watchfully silent until Pavlicek suddenly made his move, coming toward him so fast that he didn't even have time to raise his hands. But instead of throwing a punch, the big man blew right past him and without another word stormed out of the apartment, the flung-open door pockmarking the plaster of the tiny vestibule before slamming back into its frame on the rebound.

Trying to calm himself, Billy gazed out the window at the clean geometry of the distant stadium grass for a moment, then, turning away, picked Sweetpea's poster up off the floor and dialed the number that hung in multiples from the bottom.

DONNA BARKLEY WAS A SHORT, thick, snub-faced woman to begin with, and her company-issued maroon blazer did her no favors, her fingers barely peeking out of the too-long sleeves, the jacket's center back vent angling out over her high and wide butt like an awning.

"Hey, how are you," Billy said, rising from his white plastic chair in the cement pocket park alongside the office building where she worked as a security guard.

She took a seat, reached into her bag for a Newport, fired up, and then turned her head away to exhale, exposing the cursive *Sweetpea* inked across her left carotid.

"Arista," Billy said, reading the insignia on her jacket. "They take care of you over there?"

"It's a job for pay," still not looking at him. "I got two kids and a grandmother."

"I hear you," he said, removing the crumpled Missing poster from his jacket and flattening it against the tabletop.

"You were only supposed to tear off the phone number on the bottom," she said, "not take the whole damn thing."

Billy gave it a beat, vigorously scratching his up-tilted throat. "So, let me just start by asking you a few questions, see where that takes us."

"Who are you with again?"

"Like I said to you on the phone, I'm an independent investigator." She gave him a look. "You got an ID?"

He handed over his driver's license.

"Something with your business on it."

Digging into his wallet, he pulled out a card for Sousa Security, his brother-in-law's outfit, which listed him as the assistant head of investigations, even though he never did a thing or took a dime.

"And this is for free?"

"I said that."

"Why is it free."

"Because," Billy looking her in the eye, "like I also mentioned to you on the phone, we're opening an office near Lincoln Hospital and if I can find him for you, word'll get around and hopefully it'll bring us clients."

A pigeon landed on their table, Sweetpea's fiancée glaring at the filthy thing but making no move to shoo it away.

"Has he ever been gone this long before?"

Taking her cell phone out of her purse, she responded to one text, then another, Billy torn between repeating the question and just packing it in.

"Outside of incarceration?" she finally said, still texting. "Now and then."

"So what made you so concerned this time?"

"Because," she said, stuffing her cell back into her purse, "we were talking on the phone, then some white guy called his name, and all of a sudden Sweetpea hangs up and where is he."

"OK, this guy . . ." he said, opening a steno pad.

"White guy."

"This white guy who called his name, did he say anything else?"

"He just said, 'Hey Sweetpea, come over here.'"

"Then what."

"Then Sweetpea said, 'The fuck you want.' Then the guy said, 'Seriously, Pea, no kidding, come over here.'"

Billy looked up from his notes. "And you're sure the guy was white?"

"My phone doesn't come with eyes, but I know white when I hear it and that guy was white all day long."

"OK," Billy said. "Then what."

"What?"

"What did you hear next."

"Click."

"And roughly what time was this?"

"It was three-fifteen exact, you know how I know? Because he kept yelling at me. 'It's three-fifteen, bitch! Where the fuck are you?'"

"Good," Billy back to writing.

"Good?"

"Do you have any idea where he was when he called you?"

"I know that exact, too. He was just leaving my building to come get me, yelling, 'I'm walking out right now, I'm walking out right now.'"

"Walking out of . . ."

"502 Concord Avenue."

"502," writing, then: "This white guy, any ideas?"

"Not per se."

"What do you mean, 'not per se.'"

She shrugged as if the question wasn't worth answering.

Billy hesitated, then, chalking up her truculent vagueness to a general case of whitey hatin', moved on.

"Was he having any problems with anyone recently?"

"Well, he's a talent promoter, you know?" Her voice softened for the first time. "Trying to help the community, but these kids he takes under his wing, they expect miracles."

"Any kids in particular?"

"I'm just saying"—looking away—"in general."

"All right." He put down his pen. "I did a little research on your fiancé before I came here, it's a crucial part of a job like this, and I need to ask you . . ." Billy back in her eyes. "Is he still slinging?"

She stared at him as if he were too thick to live. "I don't want to talk out of my area of expertise."

"Do you want me to find him or not?"

She continued to stare, Billy once again ready to call it a day.

"One last . . . I asked you before if you had any idea who this white guy was and you said, 'Not per se.' I need for you to elaborate on that 'not per se.'"

"Not per se meaning, like, I don't know who he is, per se."

"But you know . . . what, his type?"

"Oh yeah."

"From what, his tone of voice?"

"Uh-huh."

"And what type would that be."

"Your type."

"My type . . ."

She fired up another Newport, took a drag, then exhaled in a slow steady stream.

"You know what Sweetpea always used to say NYPD stands for?" she said, tossing Billy's bullshit business card on the table as she rose to her feet. "'Not Your People, Dawg,'" having read him like a comic book from the door on in.

HE WAS STILL SITTING AT the table when he got a call from home, the unexpected sound of his younger son's plaintive voice making him knotty.

"Hey, buddy, what's up?"

"I didn't even do anything and Mom started yelling at me like I did," Carlos said.

Billy exhaled with relief. "Well, she had an upsetting experience this morning, so don't take it personal and just extra-behave today, all right? You and your brother both."

"But I didn't do anything."

"Carlos, just do me a favor, OK?"

"OK."

Another incoming call flashed Pavlicek's name across his screen, Billy ignoring it. "Everything else all right?"

"Yeah."

"You sure?"

"Yeah."

"What are you doing right now?"

"Talking to you."

"All right, I'll be home for dinner, OK?"

"OK."

"And everything's OK?"

"Yeah."

"Your brother's OK?"

"Yeah."

"Grandpa?"

"Yeah."

"All right, buddy," he said, as Pavlicek attempted to ring through again. "I'll see you at home, OK?"

"You didn't ask about Mom."

"I'll see her back home too."

"Do you want to talk to her?"

"I'll talk to her at home," Billy said, knowing all too well that when things were tense between them the phone was not their friend.

HE STARTED TO CALL PAVLICEK back, hesitated, and instead called Elvis Perez at Midtown South to see if there was any kind of progress on the Bannion homicide. Perez was out, so Billy settled for leaving a message.

He sat there for a moment, thinking about Pavlicek's afternoon flip-out over the Sweetpea poster, then looked over his interview notes, which yielded only two pieces of hard information: 502 Concord, three-fifteen a.m.

If he were so inclined he could do a canvass for possible witnesses. But it probably wouldn't be too smart: a detective from outside the local precinct, on his own, knocking on doors in the middle of the night to ask about Sweetpea Harris, especially if Sweetpea turned out to be dead, Billy imagining the barrage of questions that would then come his way, none of which, at this point, he would be prepared to answer, especially after having come so close to stepping in it simply by entering Eric Cortez's name into the system.

So, it had to be someone else, and not a cop. For a hot second he thought about hiring Sousa Security but then bagged the idea; there was something about his brother-in-law he didn't quite trust. It wasn't that he was a liar exactly—more like an omitter, as if the answers he gave you had to hold up in court.

So.

"Hey, it's me."

"Hey," Stacey's voice high and on the shaky side.

"I have some work for you this week if you're up for it."

"Yeah, sure, absolutely," once again sounding sunny but strained, as if someone was standing behind her with a knife.

"Are you OK?"

"Sure."

Billy hesitated, then: "Where do you want to meet?"

"Can you come to my place?"

In all the years they had known each other, she had never invited him to her home.

"Yeah, no problem, what's a good time?"

"Now."

HE BEGAN TO SMELL THE stale waft of old cigarette smoke coming from Stacey's apartment midway in his wheezing climb to her floor. When he finally reached her landing, Billy took a moment to catch his breath, then followed his nose down the long hallway to 6B, where she greeted him in the open doorway with a smile so tense he thought her face would crack.

With its dim corridors, greasy slit of a kitchen, and small living room filled with indifferent furniture and overflowing ashtrays, the apartment reeked of resignation, and it made Billy ache to think what life could have been like for her right now if she had only looked elsewhere to make her journalistic bones.

Her boyfriend's plaid bathrobe matched the fabric of the couch so well that Billy didn't even realize the guy was in the room until he reached for his beer.

"Hey, how are you." Billy couldn't remember his name.

Lying flat on his back, the boyfriend made no effort to sit up or even turn to face him. "Superb."

Stacey stood mutely between them, looking first at Billy, then her boyfriend, then back to Billy, her face still tense and expectant.

It was the collection of amber prescription bottles on the coffee table that first caught his eye. Then the edge of the butterfly bandage on the ridge above the boyfriend's averted brow. Then the face full-on, as lumpy as a thumbed hunk of clay, his skin the color of overripe bananas, the sclera of one eye hemorrhaged to a neon red.

"Did you call the cops?" he asked Stacey.

"Of course."

"And?"

"They came."

"And?"

"And nothing."

"What happened," he asked the boyfriend.

"Some gentleman must have come into the vestibule right behind me last night and . . ." He shrugged.

"What did he look like, this gentleman."

"He was behind me."

"Did he say anything?"

"Nothing."

"Race, hair, clothes . . ."

"Nothing." Then: "It's my own fault."

"Why do you say that?"

The boyfriend turned his face away again.

"Why do you say that?" Billy's voice sharper now.

Stacey touched Billy's arm.

"What time was this," asking both of them.

"About one in the morning," the boyfriend answered.

"And where were you coming from."

"The Jaunting Car."

"What's that."

"The bar where he first met you," she said.

"Were you there too?"

"I left about an hour and a half before he did," sounding embarrassed about it. No, not embarrassed, he thought, more like defeated.

"Did anybody in there talk to you? Either of you?"

"People in there tend to talk to themselves," the boyfriend said.

"Anybody giving you a hard time?"

"Not really."

"What's 'not really' mean?" Billy getting hot again.

"A seventy-five-year-old cirrhotic called me an asshole."

"Anybody else?"

"Call me an asshole?"

"I'm trying to *help* you here."

"I appreciate it," the boyfriend said carefully.

"All right, let me make a call," Billy said, this time by way of an apology. Gesturing to the opened beer, he said, "You have an extra one of those?"

As Stacey headed to the kitchen, Billy retreated to a corridor off the living room and worked to get a handle on his rage.

He tried to picture it: this guy stays to drink after Stacey—and not for the first time—is unable to coax him out of the bar and so just gives up and leaves. He continues to drink alone for another ninety minutes, waiting for happy, or bright, or successful to kick in, before finally giving up and herky-jerking his way home. And at one in the morning, he couldn't have been more of a staked lamb out there, a street-dumb, self-hating smart-ass reeking of death wish, probably not even caring, once he got his load on, whether he was heading home or straight off a cliff.

Fuck the mugger: what detective worth his salt wouldn't want to strangle a guy like that himself? Victims like Stacey's boyfriend made you feel like a nameless bit player in some narcissistic melodrama performed before an audience of one.

Made you feel demeaned.

Billy paced the short corridor, hating on the victim while trying not to give a thought to the person who had battered his face into a bloody stew.

It couldn't be him.

Coming back into the living room, he ignored Stacey's offered beer and went right at the boyfriend.

"The guy who beat you, what did he take?"

"My dignity."

Billy threw him a look.

"And my wallet," he quickly added.

Then not him—unless he took the wallet to throw Billy off. But that would defeat the purpose, would obscure the message, and the message was the point, unless, unless . . .

"All right, let me make a call," he repeated.

Before leaving, Billy looked around the apartment one last time; then, thinking once again how Stacey's life might have turned out if she'd been a little less reckless with him, he added, "I'm sorry."

"For what?" she asked brightly, but she knew.

HEADING TO HIS CAR, BILLY called home and got no answer, not even the answering machine. He called again and got the same, which made him break into a trot.

What was he up to.

Billy had been expecting him to keep moving in deeper on his family, but attacking Stacey's boyfriend—*if* he had attacked Stacey's

boyfriend—seemed to be about going outward, maybe going so far outward that he and everyone else would be going crazy wondering if it was
still him, and if that, in fact, who the fuck knew, was his game plan, then
who would be next? Millie Singh? His sister? Maybe one of Billy's friends,
or one of his friends' spouses or kids, then after that, maybe going in deep
again, and the next time he came after Carmen or the kids or his
father—Billy flashing on the boyfriend's bashed-in face—the outcome
would be a lot more catastrophic than a vandalized jacket or a free ride
to Harlem.

Was this guy a genius?

Or had Stacey's boyfriend just straight-up gotten mugged . . .

Either way he had Billy by the balls.

A third fruitless call home while driving north on the Henry Hudson had him pushing eighty-five.

Stacey called as he was flying past the Roosevelt Raceway. "Hey, you
walked out so fast you forgot to tell me about the job."

"Turns out it's not happening for a while," he said, wanting to keep
her and hers out of the line of fire.

PULLING ONTO HIS STREET IN the early dark of the evening, Billy saw a
figure sitting motionless on the front porch of his house. Knowing that
no cop patrolling the grounds would just take a breather like that, he
glided to a stop a few driveways down, got out of the car, and began to
cautiously make the rest of his way on foot. But apparently his tread
was heavier than he imagined; sensing Billy's approach, the figure slowly
rose and then eased into a shooter's stance. Pulling his own weapon, Billy
carefully stepped back into the shadowed shrubbery, the numbing notion
abruptly rising in him that it was too late, *he* was too late, and that everyone inside was gone. In sudden free fall, Billy mindlessly recited the roll
call of his dead as he sighted his Glock, center mass, center mass, and
was about to squeeze one off when Carmen opened the door behind the
shooter's back.

"Dad, come inside, you're going to get sick out here." Then: "What
the hell are you doing? Give me that."

"There's someone out there," Billy Senior said tentatively, allowing his daughter-in-law to bring him back into the house.

TWO HOURS LATER, JIMMY WHELAN, ACCOMPANIED by a small, nervous, near-mute woman, most likely another of his vertical harem of tenants, entered the house without knocking.

"Jimmy!" Carmen kissing him while shielding the shiner side of her face. "I'm sorry, this is a total waste of your time."

"Don't worry about it," Whelan said. "This is Mercedes."

The woman eyed the dinner dishes as if all she wanted in life was to clear the table.

"What's the matter with you," Billy nodding to the grip of the Walther sticking straight up from behind Whelan's belt buckle. "You never heard of a holster?"

"If you conceal it, then no one knows you're carrying and it defeats its own purpose. Hey! Chief Graves . . ." Whelan saluting as Billy Senior came into the living room. "Remember me?"

"You're that kid from Billy's street team."

"I am that kid."

"You make detective yet?"

"You bet."

"Where are you posted?"

"Fort Surrender," winking to Billy.

"I never liked that moniker, it's too cynical for my taste."

"Well, sir, we live in cynical times."

"What's a rook to think?" Senior said. " 'Congratulations, son, you've been assigned to Fort Surrender.' "

"You got a point there, boss."

"Well, keep up the good work," the old man said, turning to the TV.

Billy nodded toward the porch, and Whelan followed him out.

"THE GUN WAS HIS?" WHELAN asked after getting the update.

"It's his old service piece, I had it spiked the day he moved in."

Whelan briefly stepped over to the window. Peering into the house, he tried to catch the eye of his sleepover date, sitting on the couch next to Billy Senior.

"Not for nothing and thanks for coming, but did you really need to bring the girl?"

"She's never been out to the country."

"You're being funny, right?"

"About what?"

"All we have for you is a bunk bed."

"We'll make do. So what else is going on."

Billy thought about bringing up Sweetpea, bringing up Pavlicek, then let it pass.

"All right, my brother," Billy wrapping him in a brief hug. "Gotta go."

Halfway to his car he stopped and turned. "Hey, let me ask you, Tomassi . . . Are you sure he was hit by a bus?"

"Am I sure?"

Pulling out his wallet, Whelan gestured for Billy to come back to the porch. "The American Express card," he intoned, handing over a crime scene photo of his White, chest-crushed and staring up at the stars from beneath the front wheels of a Pelham Bay–bound number 12 bus. "Don't leave home without it."

"WELL, THE OTHER TAPE CAME in," Elvis Perez's voice in his ear, the Midtown South detective catching Billy on his cell as he was paying for his nightly speed bag at the Korean's. "From the LIRR end?"

"And?" Billy saluting Joon on the way out.

"And it doesn't really help us."

"Why not."

"There's too much of a mob under the track information board. It's like watching worms in a bucket. We can't even ID Bannion until he separates out from the crowd, and by then he's already spurting."

"You can't track him in reverse and blow up the frames?"

"Worms in a bucket."

Back at the office, the headline was that Feeley had reverted to being a no-show. Otherwise it was a next-to-nothing tour: a push-in robbery in Sugar Hill, a cabbie in the Meatpacking District getting beat on by two men after he had refused to take them to Brownsville. Neither required his personal attendance, so after sitting there in his office for a few hours listening to the Wheel effortlessly repel three more requests for the squad, Billy put Mayo in charge and headed up to the Bronx.

502 CONCORD AVENUE WAS AN eroding brick single-family Victorian chopped up into multiple SROs, and at three-fifteen in the morning there were no lights on in any of the six windows that overlooked the lifeless street. But 505, directly across the way, was a six-story walk-up, and Billy counted three lighted apartment windows on the second, third, and top floors, meaning three possible habitual night owls, three possible witnesses to the possible abduction of Sweetpea Harris.

Billy woke up the tenants on the second floor, an ashy-skinned middle-aged man, dumb with sleep, coming to the door in his boxers as a woman in the back of the apartment screamed like hell about having to get up for work in a few hours. On the third floor, the door was answered after five minutes of pounding by a moon-faced African in a wrinkled caftan, kufi, and busted slippers, this guy having no English to him, but the TV in his otherwise furniture-less living room was playing so loud that Billy couldn't imagine him hearing anything out on the street short of an explosion.

The sixth floor was the charm, the tenant, Ramlear Castro, a young, heavily inked Latino, his eyes pink with dope, coming to the door in sweatpants and a hairnet. Billy flashed his ID and Castro gave him his back, retreating into the apartment but leaving the door open for Billy to follow him inside.

"May I?" Castro held up a blunt.

Billy shrugged and a moment later the punky tang coming across the wobbly-legged kitchen table thrust him back into high school.

"Yeah, so yeah," Castro began, "I was up that night you said, and I was sitting right here, I like to write poetry here, and I heard like this *pop pop pop*, which around here don't mean firecrackers, and I thought it was Timpson GCG throwing down with Betances Crew again. But when I looked out the window all I saw was this guy getting out of his car and walking to the back like he was going to open the trunk, you know, but he was coming up on it sideways, you know, careful, then *pop pop pop* again, the driver like jumping to the side, but I didn't see no one shooting at him, I just heard the shots. And then after those shots went off, the driver just shoots his own damned trunk like he was putting down a horse, emptied the whole clip or whatever."

"Wait, this is after you first heard the *pop pop pop*?"

"Yeah."

"So the *pop pop pop* was someone else?"

"Which *pop pop pop*."

"The first. The one that made you go to the window."

"Yeah."

"Then the guy got out of his car and shot his trunk."

"No, then the second *pop pop pop*. I didn't see no one shooting, but the driver like jumped to the side of the trunk when the shots went off, and then the third *pop pop pop* was the driver shooting back."

"Into his trunk."

"Yeah."

"Like what, returning fire?"

"Returning fire, yeah."

"So like somebody was shooting at him from inside the trunk?"

"Could be," offering the blunt across the oilcloth-topped table, Billy demurely passing. "Then he shot back."

"So the driver came out of the car with a gun."

"Didn't I say that?"

"It was already in his hand?"

"I guess so."

"What did he look like?"

"Who, the driver?"

Billy waited.

"I couldn't say."

"First thing that comes to your mind."

Castro closed his eyes. "He had white hair."

"An old guy?"

"No, he had white hair, you know, straight hair."

"So a white guy?"

"Could have been."

"Not Latino."

"Could've been."

"Black?"

"I don't think so, but could've been."

"So you didn't get a look at his face?"

"Couldn't see it, because it's like a straight-down view from up here, that's how I know about the hair."

"Clothes?"

"Some kind of coat, I don't know. Shoes."

"How about the gun."

"From the sound of it, I'd say a single-action .38 'cause of the rhythm of the shots, you know, *pop pop pop*."

"You know your firearms?"

Castro inhaled again, blew out enough smoke to announce a pope.

"Not really."

"Tell me about the car."

"Had a trunk, that's all I remember."

"So . . ." Billy hesitated, then: "No chance it could have been an SUV?"

"Could have been."

"You know," Billy leaned forward across the small table, "I asked you maybe ten questions, all I'm getting back from you is 'could've been's."

"Hey, Officer," Castro leaning forward right back at him, "I'm looking down six stories, three in the morning, high as a fuckin' kite. I think I did pretty good here, wouldn't you say?"

MILTON RAMOS

Marilys, watch!" Sofia shouted, blow-darting the torn wrapper hanging from her straw across the small table into her father's chest.

"Don't call her Marilys anymore," Milton said.

"Why not?"

Marilys caught his eye: Go slow.

They had never gone out of the house as a threesome before, and this dinner at Applebee's was something of a test drive. The waitress arrived with their dinner orders, Double Barrel Whisky Sirloin for him, Double Crunch Shrimp for the lady, and a Fiesta-Chopped Chicken and Spinach Salad for Sofia, who immediately went into a jaw-quivering sulk.

"How would you like Marilys to come live with us?" he said.

"Yah! Yah! Yah!" His daughter shouting up a storm again.

"Easy, easy," he winced, although the din level of the room approached that of a machine shop.

"Can she sleep with me?"

Milton looked at his fiancée, a half-smile threatening to break across his face.

Scraping off the breading, Marilys put one of her deep-fried shrimps on Sofia's plate. "So this is it, I'm not working for you anymore?" she said.

"Of course not."

"But we're not getting married until next month, you said."

"So?"

"So I can work for you until then."

"Are you serious? I want you to go home and pack your stuff. I'll come by tomorrow with a van and move you in."

"I have a lease."

"Don't worry about your lease."

"So what do I do then?"

"What do you mean?"

"What do I do once I move in?"

"Nothing. You know, just be with me, take care of Sofia and the house."

"Sounds like my job but without pay."

Milton blushed. "If you want I'll get you a housekeeper, how's that."

"Don't be ridiculous."

"All I'm trying to say is, you'll never have to worry about money again."

"I don't want anybody working for me," she said. "That's crazy."

"It's up to you."

Marilys stopped eating, stared at her plate. "I got a better idea."

"What's that."

"Can I say?"

Milton waited.

"My mother."

"Your mother."

"If she comes to live with us, she can help me with Sofia and the baby. And she loves to clean."

"Your mother . . ."

"All I have to do is go back and get her."

"To Guatemala?"

"She's never been on a plane before."

Sofia quietly took a shrimp off Marilys's plate, dipped it in the ketchup atop her father's fries, neither of them reacting.

"You don't want her to?" Marilys said. "It's your house."

"Our house."

"Well, you're the man of it, so whatever you say goes."

Sofia took another shrimp, a handful of fries.

"Excuse me for a minute," Milton said, then rose from the table, Marilys tracking him with anxious eyes as he made his way to the front door.

A wife and two kids, OK, Milton mulling it over as he paced the empty parking lot.

But the mother-in-law . . .

Then: *Think of it like this: drop the "in-law" part and that leaves you with "mother."*

Which, given that he had just lost his aunt Pauline, the closest thing he'd had to one, was not so bad.

When he returned to the table, he found Marilys, apparently having lost her appetite, feeding the rest of her breaded dinner to Sofia piece by piece.

"She's good with kids?" Milton asked.

"She raised me. Raised my sons too."

"How about otherwise."

"Not great."

"Pain in the ass?"

"Kind of."

Sofia had become way too quiet, Milton wondering if it was ever possible to truly talk over a kid's head.

To repeat . . . New mother, new wife, new son, all in one swoop.

Then, studying his already-child, working her way through the rest of his untouched fries: *New grandmother, too.*

"All right," he said, lightly slapping the table, "go get her."

Marilys put a hand to her heart, huffed in relief. "When should I go?"

"How about tomorrow? I'll cover the airfare."

"I swear to God"—touching his hand—"if you don't like her she can go right back, it's not like she doesn't have family."

"Just go get her."

"I can save you money on the tickets," she said excitedly, "my cousin's a travel agent."

"Well, there you go," wishing she'd gone and come back already.

Marilys leaned across the table and kissed him on the mouth again, which this time made him tense up given that his daughter was right there.

"Oh, Milton," Marilys saying his name for the second time in his life.

"Oh, Milton," Sofia aped, her eyes as lightless as pebbles.

LATER THAT NIGHT IT TOOK him most of a bottle of Chartreuse to work up the resolve to quit drinking. He had never been anybody's idea of a light drinker, but since the day he first saw the adult Carmen in St. Ann's, he'd gone completely off the rails, each night worse than the last, waking up every morning on the couch wondering how the one a.m. sports recap had morphed into cartoons.

Well, no excuse for that now, Milton pouring what remained of the bottle into the sink.

Still drunk on the liquor that hadn't gone down the drain, he took to wandering the house in order to start reassigning rooms: his first wife's sewing nook now a nursery for his son, the sometime fuck-pad guest room—no need for that anymore—going to his mother-in-law, as well as the nearest of the three bathrooms, hers alone. What else. Divide the den and make a playroom. All the hallway closets going to all the ladies. Then, running out of steam, he finally headed off for his own bedroom, walking in and seeing it for the first time as the gray cell it had become.

A five a.m. after-hours bar shooting in Inwood kept Billy on the job until ten in the morning, and when he finally made it home at eleven, still pondering his interview with Ramlear Castro, he was startled to see TARU techs everywhere. To cover the block from intersection to intersection, they were mounting Argus cameras on telephone poles, as well as on the house itself, the buzz and whine of all this work chasing away any hope he had of immediate sleep.

Thirty minutes later, as he was standing at the kitchen counter flipping through the *New York Post* and sipping his morning Cape Codder, Pavlicek called. This time Billy picked up.

"You're screening my calls?"

"What?" Billy too tired to come up with any coherent excuse.

"Look, I was just trying to reach out to apologize for getting so crazed on you yesterday. It's just that I have so much shit raining down on my head right now I might wind up moving in there with you."

"In where with me." Looking out the kitchen window, Billy spotted Whelan and his sleepover date making out on the kids' trampoline.

"Are you serious?" Pavlicek said quietly.

Christ, Billy recalling that barren, echo chamber of an apartment with the stadium view.

"Speaking of which, I talked to my guys and I can have it ready for you day after tomorrow. All you'll need are towels and sheets."

"'My guys.' You're always talking about your guys," Billy stalled. "The only guys I have are my kids."

"Yeah well, you have your squad, too."

Billy put the phone to his chest. Just say it.

"Hey, John, I'm sorry to put you through all that trouble, but I talked it over with Carmen, and we're going to make a home stand."

Silence on the other end, then: "Are you sure?"

"Yeah, yeah, Intel sent over a Threat Assessment Team, TARU's out there right now putting up cameras, Yonkers PD is running directed patrols, it's like the fortress of solitude over here. It's nuts to pull up stakes."

Another bloated pause. "Are you OK?"

"Yeah," Billy said. "I mean, given the circumstances."

"Because you don't sound like you."

"Yeah? Who do I sound like?" Then telling himself, Don't strain for jokes.

"You're not ticked because I lost it over Sweetpea, are you?"

"Absolutely not."

"Is that why you weren't taking my calls?"

"I don't know what you're talking about," Billy said.

Whelan and his tenant, still in a kissing clinch, came into the kitchen through the rear door.

"I mean, how hung up are you over that skell?"

"John, I'm not hung up on him, I was just curious," Billy said carefully. "And now I'm not. Listen, I got to go feed the kids, I'll call you later."

"Just another Smirnoff morning," Whelan announced, nodding to the bottle.

"It's either that or chloroform," Billy said.

The tenant went silently to the refrigerator, took out the milk, and poured some into a saucepan that was already sitting on a back burner.

"Hung up on who," Whelan asked.

"What?" Billy stalling once again.

"You said, 'I'm not hung up on him.'"

"Sweetpea Harris," Billy said. "He's gone AWOL, and I think he bought the farm."

"No shit," Whelan pouring himself a coffee. "And John's giving you grief over that? What for?"

Billy took another sip of his drink.

"Do me a favor and tell me something," he said. "The other day, when I asked you why you were so hung up on Pavlicek . . ."

"Me?" Whelan reared back.

"You never answered my question."

"What question."

"Why you were all over me about Pavlicek."

"How was I all over you?"

Billy stared at him. "Jimmy, do you know something I don't?"

"Like what?"

"Jesus Christ, look out that window," Billy exploded, pointing to the TARUs crawling all over the front yard. "And that window, and that one," Billy spinning like a bottle. "I'm getting shredded here, I'm juggling chain saws, so if I ask you for a straight answer on something and you start playing me like I'm some idiot?"

Whelan held up a hand. "If I tell you this, you cannot tell anyone, you understand?"

"Is it his health?"

Whelan blinked at him. "What's wrong with his health?"

"Then just say."

Whelan took a long pull off his coffee. "He's trying to buy my building from the owner. But it's kind of very delicate right now, very touch and go, and I just thought maybe he said something to you about it."

Billy stared at him. "That's it?"

"What do you mean, 'That's it.' Are you kidding me? He swings this deal, I go from super to building manager at twice the pay. And if that works out, he's going to throw me more buildings. I mean, you know me, I don't need much, but I would like a little more than I got."

One of the security cameras fell out of a tree, nearly braining a passing TARU before smashing against a lawn chair.

"Anyways, this thing with Sweetpea going off the grid?" Whelan rinsed out his cup. "You should tell Redman when you see him today."

"Why am I seeing Redman today?"

"The funeral."

"What funeral?"

"For your kid."

Billy went white.

"I would go," Whelan said, reaching for his jacket, "but I have a guy coming for the boiler."

The tenant poured the heated milk into a glass and handed it to Billy. *"Para dormir,"* she said, laying her cheek on her palm and closing her eyes.

EDNA WORTHY WAS THE ONLY mourner to show up for her granddaughter Martha's funeral service that afternoon, so the folding chairs that lined Redman's living room–chapel were populated by a handful of last-minute stand-ins: Redman, his father, his wife, Nola, holding their son, Rafer, four of the old men who hung out every day in the windowless reception area of the parlor like it was their old-man clubhouse, two dragooned cops from the Twenty-eighth Precinct Community Affairs Unit, and Billy, who was paying for the whole thing.

"But Jesus said, 'Suffer the little children, and forbid them not, to come unto me: for of such is the kingdom of heaven,'" the four-hundred-pound minister intoned from the pulpit before pausing to take a hit of asthma spray.

"Suffer, you see, in the, the parlance of those times, did not mean to endure pain, it did not mean to put up with mistreatment. What it meant was to permit, to allow," pausing again, this time to reach for the diaper cloth draped over the shoulder of his three-piece box-plaid suit and swipe at his face. "You see, in those days children were not allowed to address adults directly, not allowed to speak up without the permission of another adult. Seen but not heard, I know you know that saying, and not just from olden times, I'm sure many of you heard it growing up—when Daddy is talking to Uncle at the dinner table, when Momma is talking to Auntie, you sat there, ate your peas, and maybe raised your hand for permission. But Jesus was saying, 'I don't want no middleman between me and these kids, I don't stand on manners, I don't need no hand raising, no permission slips, no velvet-rope doorman, just let them kids in, and today, today, Marrisa has come into the club direct . . ."

"Martha," her grandmother muttered, but loud enough.

"She has come into the club direct, has gone, in fact, straight to the VIP room, where He is waiting for her with two chilled magnums of Holy Ghost love."

"Are you kidding me?" Billy whispered.

"You said a hundred dollars for the celebrant," Redman whispered back. "That's what you get for a hundred dollars."

"So what's going on," Billy asked, as a prelude to bringing up Sweet-pea.

"Later," Redman said.

"'Blessed are the gentle,'" the celebrant crooned, "'they shall have the earth as their heritage. Blessed are those who mourn; they shall be comforted . . .'"

"Her name is *Martha*," the grandmother low-blared again, staring at the floor.

Nola passed her son to Redman, got up, and took a seat next to the old woman, putting an arm around her shoulders and staring without expression at the casket.

After a few minutes of fussing in his father's lap, Rafer started to cry, and Redman, needing both hands to rise from his chair so he could leave the room, briefly passed him on to Billy. Trying to stabilize the boy, Billy advertently pressed the feeding tube protruding from the kid's stomach, then jerked his hand away as if he had touched a snake. Embarrassed by his reaction, he reflexively looked to Redman, now waiting for them in the doorway, the grimly knowing look on his face burning Billy to the core.

"SO WHAT'S GOING ON?" BILLY repeated, once they were settled in Redman's cubicle.

"There's some big-foot kid going around the neighborhood," Redman said, dropping Rafer into his activity walker, then locking the wheels.

"Says he's working for a charity, selling boxes of candy bars to the store owners, fifty dollars a box, the implication being that if they say no they're gonna get their ass beat or something thrown through the window. Half the damn neighborhood's got those things by the cash register."

"For real?"

"Everybody say he's all soft-spoken about it, but it's like, Make no mistake."

"You want me to do something?"

"*I* want to do something," Redman said.

"Did he try it on you?"

"Hell no. People are too scared of this place. It's like, muscle an undertaker? Who's going to take on that kind of karma."

Enough.

"Can I tell you something?"

Redman waited.

"I think Sweetpea Harris was murdered."

"Did somebody tell you it was my birthday? Because it is."

"Well, many happy returns."

"Who did the honors?"

"I was hoping you could tell me."

"Me?"

"He was your guy."

"My guy, huh?" Redman said. "How'd you come to know about this."

Billy hesitated, then thinking, In for a penny, he began running down his interviews with Donna Barkley and Ramlear Castro, all the while bracing for another Pavlicek-style outburst about keeping his priorities straight.

"So the window witness tells me that this guy gets out of his car, walks to the back, ducks some shots, and then empties a clip into the trunk. Which to me sounds like maybe, probably, there was someone in there with a gun, like maybe the driver forgot to pat him down before he stuffed his ass inside."

"Did he give a description of the shooter?"

"Not really." Then: "He said he had straight hair, like a white guy, maybe a Latino."

"He saw that from the sixth floor but nothing else?"

"Apparently."

"Well then," Redman rubbed what was left of his receding corkscrew crop, "include me out."

"Done."

"So I hear you're moving into one of Pavlicek's apartments," Redman said.

"Actually, we're not."

"Just as well."

"Me and him, he and I, we're not getting on right now," Billy said, testing the waters to gauge how far he could take this. There would be no coming back from saying too much—that he knew for sure.

From the chapel they could hear Redman's father up on the podium singing "He's Prepared a Place for Me" in a high and furry voice.

How far . . .

"He's seeing a hematologist, did you know that?" Billy said.

"Who is, John?"

Billy didn't answer.

"Man, you're all full of news today."

"I'm just telling you."

"The hell he is," Redman said, sounding annoyed.

How far . . .

"I hired someone to find out."

Redman's stare could have stopped a train.

"I know," Billy said, "but I was worried about him. I *am* worried about him."

"I don't understand why you couldn't just straight out ask him yourself."

"I did," Billy said. "He lied to me."

A dapperly dressed funeral cosmetics salesman, pulling a sample case on rollers, poked his head into the cubicle.

"Let me ask you something," Redman said, gesturing for the salesman to step off for a minute. "And I'm not even talking about any shit in the past, but do you have anything going on in your life right now that you don't want anybody knowing about?"

Billy didn't answer.

"Exactly. So whatever the hell is going on with Pavlicek these days?" Redman reached down to lift his crying son out of the walker. "If he wants to tell people, he'll tell people. Meanwhile, why don't you just respect the man's privacy and leave him be."

Too far.

COMING HOME AT TWO IN the afternoon, Billy walked in on Carmen and her brother weeping up a storm on the living room couch.

"What happened," Billy said.

"Nothing," Victor said, wiping his eyes. "It's all good."

"He's freaking out about being a parent," Carmen announced with unnerving happiness. "And he didn't know where else to come."

"I feel like an ass," Victor said.

"You and Richard are going to be the best parents," she gushed.

"I kill aspidistras," Victor trying to laugh at himself.

"Hey, you have that dog, right?" Billy just wanting to keep this good thing going.

"It's Richard's dog."

"I was just telling him," Carmen said, "no one was more freaked about having children than me. The dreams I had before Dec was born?"

Billy nodded, thinking, You still have them.

"I swear, Victor, I'm going to help you every step of the way," Carmen tearing up again. "Those babies are going to love you."

"Thank you," Victor whispered huskily, holding her close.

"THINK OF IT LIKE THIS," Billy said to his brother-in-law out in the driveway. "Cavemen had kids, so can you."

"And the average life expectancy was what?"

"That's not the point."

"Billy, I'm playing with you," he said, waving to Carmen, who was watching them from the living room window.

"You know, Victor, your sister, she's a real high-wire act but she's got heart by the mile."

"I know."

Billy lit a cigarette, inhaled, then twisted his mouth to divert the smoke.

"So why is she always so tough on you?"

"She's ashamed."

"Of you?"

"Of herself, don't ask me why. Because she left me to take care of our so-called father down south? I was thirteen. And now I'm thirty-six, you know?" Shrugging the whole thing off. "But I do know this. Whenever she acts like she's trying to push me away? She's in a lot more pain than I am."

Billy felt like crying.

"I don't know," Victor said, taking his car keys out of his jacket, "with the twins on the way? I find myself thinking about family all the time, and I just want her to feel good about being my big sister. Even for a minute."

Billy nodded, then leaned in close as if Carmen could hear him through the living room glass. "Can I ask you something? How freaked are you really about these new kids of yours?"

"Not too," Victor said, waving goodbye to his sister in the window.

TOMIKA WASHINGTON, A TALL, SLENDER, light-skinned woman looking to be in her fifties, was stretched out in her bathrobe on the carpetless floor of her railroad-flat living room, the rawhide bootlace that had done the deed still around her neck. A rolled towel was propped under her head, as if to make her comfortable, and a washcloth was carefully draped like a veil over her face, as if to prevent her from staring at her killer—both gestures, Billy knew, textbook signatures of remorse.

With Butter and Mayo canvassing the neighbors and the Crime Scene Unit stuck in traffic, Billy was alone with the body when he heard a knock at the door. On the off chance that the actor had slipped the barricade in order to come back and apologize to his victim, Billy drew his gun

before opening up and was surprised to see Gene Feeley, his elusive butterfly of love, standing there in what had to be the last Botany 500 three-
piece suit in existence.

"You have Tomika Washington in there?" Feeley asked. Then, sliding past Billy: "I just want to see her."

"You know her?"

Ignoring the question, Feeley stood motionless over the body for a
moment as if paying his respects, then dropped into a squat and delicately parted the lower half of her bathrobe.

"You looking for something, Gene?"

"That right there," pointing to a fading tattoo of a bird high up on
her thigh. "You see that? That was his brand."

"Whose brand?"

"Frank Baltimore," he said, closing her robe as carefully as he had
opened it. "He was kind of a player around here for a few years in the
eighties, used to stamp his bags with a blackbird, same for a girl or two
like Tomika here."

"She was hooking for him?"

"Never. Well, not for him—I mean, yeah, on her own, later, but she
was strictly his girl before that. He found her down in Newport News
on one of his dope runs when she was seventeen, beautiful kid, brought
her back up and threw her a crib in Lenox Terrace. She told me she thought
she was living in a fairy tale."

"She told you."

"Before I was transferred to the Queens Task Force after Eddie Byrnes
got shot, I was in Narcotics up here and I had occasion to bring her in a
couple of times, see if there was any kind of conversation we could have
about Frank. She didn't know shit, but she never gave me grief about getting picked up, had these country manners, didn't know how not to be
friendly, just never really got the hang of this place, you know? And when
Frank finally went upstate she got tossed out on her ass, a down-home
kid ashamed to go home. Oh, it was a bad time for her, first she got dope
sick, which is when she started turning tricks, and then when rock came
on the scene? I would see her on the street, down to about ninety
pounds . . . But even then she always had that smile for me, always that

well-brought-up-southern-girl thing going on, and when she'd get picked up by the cops she had my number and I'd try to get her out of whatever jam she was in, but it was hopeless. Anyways," kneecaps popping, Feeley rose to his feet, his eyes still saying goodbye, "I heard she finally got herself clean a few years ago through some church program, so good for her."

"That blackbird tat?" Billy just had to say it. "It's kind of in a hard-to-know-about place, Gene."

At first Feeley threw him a hard look, then shrugged. "If I wasn't so afraid of catching the Package in those days? Me and her, we could of had a little something. We came pretty close once or twice, but . . . you know, what can I tell you, it wasn't to be."

"Any ideas about the actor?"

"With the towel, the washcloth, I'm thinking it's someone close, a relative maybe. She has a nephew in the halfway house on a Hundred and Tenth and Lenox, Doobie Carver, a real nutcase. If you'll allow me, I can take it from here."

"All yours," Billy said, happy to see him seize the initiative on any run, for any reason.

Feeley stepped to the door, hesitated for a beat, then turned back to the room.

"I have to tell you," gazing down at Tomika Washington so intently that Billy wasn't quite sure who he was addressing, "I know I can be a real hard-on, and you don't have the juice to tell me to do shit, but you're a good boss, you respect your people, you don't have a political bone in your body, and you don't ever pass the buck. So," finally meeting Billy's eye, "after tonight? If you want me gone, I'll put in the call myself."

"How about you stay," Billy heard himself say.

"I would appreciate that," Feeley said solemnly, offering his hand.

"Does this mean you're going to start showing up when you're supposed to?"

Feeley threw him another look—*Don't press your luck*—then bent down one last time to Tomika Washington. "Take care, honey," he said.

MILTON RAMOS

She was supposed to come over at nine the next morning for the money to cover her airfare, but instead Marilys showed up at seven-thirty, Milton opening his eyes to see her standing red-faced and trembling at the side of his bed.

"What's wrong?"

"I'm so stupid," she whispered, her voice clotted with tears. "She doesn't have a passport. She doesn't have anything."

"Who's she."

More drunk than hungover, Milton sat up, stood up, and then had to sit back down as the Chartreuse rebooted.

"My mother, why am I so stupid."

"OK, all right," grinding the heels of his palms into eyes. "What time is it?"

Marilys dropped down alongside him, her shoulders as slumped as his own. "This was a bad idea."

"OK, so you'll go get her when she gets one."

"No. I mean getting married."

"Getting married is a bad idea? Since when?"

"Last night I dreamed the priest was blessing us and my mother just crushed."

"Crushed?"

"Like a flower, when they speed up the movie and you see it bloom then dry up then crush down to nothing. To dust, because she wasn't there."

"Wasn't where," his skull like a soft-boiled egg.

"There when we got married. She died in her house because she wasn't with us."

He took a deep breath, and his back teeth tasted bile. "Listen to me"— taking her hand—"you had a dream. It's a dream."

"No."

"Everybody has bad dreams. You should see some of mine."

"Mine always come true. Always. When I was a girl, I dreamed one of my brothers was in the hospital, and the next day he broke his back. When I was married the first time, I dreamed my husband got cancer, and I buried him in a year."

"Then whatever you do, don't ever dream about me," Milton joking to smother his growing panic.

Leaning into him, Marilys broke down, her boiling tears searing his skin.

"OK. How about this: we work on getting your mother a green card, a passport, or whatever. Meanwhile you come live with me, have the baby, but we wait to get married until you can bring her over."

"No."

"Jesus Christ," Milton starting to sweat. "Why not."

"We live like a man and a woman, maybe the same thing happens to her."

"I feel like a prisoner of your brain right now, you know that?" Despite the sharpness of his tone, he meant it more as a plea than a rebuke, though she seemed not to have heard him at all.

"We can't do it." Then, looking up at him like Our Lady of Sorrows: "Maybe I should just go back to work for you, live by myself."

"You're killing me."

"Maybe I should just go back to live with her."

"In Guatemala? Are you crazy?"

"I don't know what to do."

Milton shot to his feet, then immediately sat back down. "What about the baby?"

"It's still our baby."

"I know that," he snapped, then, casting about for the next anchor: "What about Sofia?"

She put her head in his lap, her hand clutching his hip.

"Jesus Christ, what about *me*?"

She began to cry, her hot tears this time turning him on, which only increased his panic.

"OK," he said, not raising her head. "Let's think this through. Who do you know in Guatemala."

"My family," she said, then: "What do you mean?"

"All right, your cousin the travel agent, who does he know?"

"I don't know who he knows."

"You know what I mean by 'knows'?"

"I think so," she said, then: "Yeah, I do."

"How about you call him."

"He doesn't open up until ten."

"Then call him at ten."

But it was only eight, and they sat in coiled silence on the bed until nine. Then, without any preliminary communication, they began to go at it—and whether it was the overlay of doom in the air or just the emotional rawness of the last ninety minutes, when he finally rolled off her they were both crying like babies.

At ten, she went down into the den to make the call, leaving him damp-skinned in his bed. He loved the idea of making a family with her, yet until now he had never thought he actually loved her. But something had changed this morning. Milton Ramos was officially in love with Marilys Irrizary. If he had a pocket knife he would carve it into a tree.

FORTY-FIVE MINUTES PASSED BEFORE HE heard her coming back up to the bedroom door, forty-five minutes during which he had been afraid to so much as blink. But when she appeared in the doorway her relieved laughter came to his ears like a flock of butterflies.

"He said he has a friend."

"Dreams," Milton said. "You're crazy, you know that?"

"Maybe," she answered, her face near radioactive with joy.

Her travel agent cousin on Fordham Road in the Bronx had told her that he would be able to swing a round-trip ticket for her, Newark to Guatemala City and back, and a one-way ticket for her mother, all for fifteen hundred dollars, which was a good deal compared to the prices posted online. But in exchange for the deep discount, he wanted to be paid in cash.

Whatever.

The wincer came later in the day when Marilys called him at work to say that her cousin had made some calls to a law firm in Guatemala City with embassy connections and found out that the package price for getting her mother a passport and a U.S. work visa, both delivered within forty-eight hours of payment, would be eighty-five hundred American dollars.

Milton's first reaction was to balk altogether, his second to negotiate the fee. Unable to do that, and fearful of losing his crazy, superstitious *amorcita* forever over a few thousand bucks, he bit the bullet, went down to his union's pension loan unit, and withdrew the money.

Whatever whatever whatever.

AT SEVEN IN THE EVENING the line for the JFK express bus, which began across the street from Grand Central Station, was nearly two blocks long, the waiting travelers looking antsy and drawn in the early twilight gloom.

"It would have been easy for me to drive you," Milton said for the sixth time.

"I like the bus," Marilys said, leaning into him for warmth. "The bus always gives me good luck."

Fifteen minutes behind schedule, the sleek, oversized carrier appeared at the crest of Thirty-ninth Street and Park, and then just sat there through three green lights, torturing the people waiting two blocks below on Forty-first.

"Anyways"—handing her a gift-wrapped package—"it's for your mother, from me and Sofia."

Instead of stashing the present in her bag, which would have frustrated him, she opened it on the spot, flapping out the hemp-colored serape he had bought from a Guatemalan street vendor in the West Village.

"Milton, it's beautiful."

"I didn't know her size, but it's basically a bath towel with a neckhole so . . ."

Marilys put her hands to the sides of his face and kissed him in front of everybody, Milton still a little awkward with her new full-frontal affection but starting to get used to it just fine.

The bus began to roll downhill to the waiting crowd, but so slowly that it caught a red light while still a block away, some people around them audibly groaning in frustration.

When the doors sighed open a few moments later and the passengers began to get on, Marilys continued to linger with him, until, worried about her missing the flight, he hustled her onto the bus himself.

It wasn't until she was well on her way out to the airport and he was most of the way back to the Bronx that Milton realized what an idiot he'd been.

Who the hell sends a gift of Guatemalan clothing to a person already living in Guatemala?

Having caught yet another pain-in-the-ass, last-minute run, this one a nonfatal stabbing in an East Village halfway house, Billy finally walked through his front door at ten the next morning to find John MacCormack from Brooklyn Narcotics sitting across from Carmen in the living room, two untouched coffees between them.

"I thought I saw a Firebird up the street," Billy looking to his wife, who imperceptibly shook her head in warning, as if he needed any kind of high sign here.

"My supervisor says I should have pushed you harder the other night," MacCormack said.

"Pushed me harder about what."

"He was talking about collecting your guns, but I told him that was probably an overreaction."

"An overreaction to what."

MacCormack slowly got to his feet. "I need to ask you again," going into Billy's eyes. "What's your interest in finding Eric Cortez."

The only one seated now, Carmen repeatedly ran her palms down the thighs of her jeans, her face quizzical and tense.

"You know what?" Billy's all-night exhaustion helped keep him calm.

"I told you that the first time you asked me. What I also told you was that I had, I have, no intention to mess with anybody's play. So. You want to collect my guns? I don't know what the fuck for, but bring in your people and go at it."

"Is he dead?" MacCormack asked.

"What?"

"You asked me the other night if Cortez was dead. Why."

"Carm, let me talk to him in private."

"I'm not going anywhere," she said.

"Why," MacCormack said again.

"Because animals like him tend not to have long lives and I hoped he was. But if I thought asking you would put me in any kind of jackpot, I would've kept my mouth shut. I'm twenty years on the Job, how stupid do you think I am?"

MacCormack stood there scanning him for tells.

"So he is dead?" Billy asked, an honest question.

"No."

"Then I don't get it."

"Billy, what's going on."

"Carmen, just . . ."

"Hey, look who's here!" Billy Senior nearly shouted as he walked into the room and slapped MacCormack on the back. "Jackie MacCormack! I thought you were in Florida!"

Billy watched as MacCormack went into his internal face file for a moment, then shook his father's hand.

"Billy Graves, how the hell are you?"

"Never been worse," the old man said, then wandered into the kitchen, where Millie was making his breakfast.

"What was that about?" Billy asked.

"He's your father?" MacCormack seemed a little dazed.

"Yeah, how does he know you?"

"He doesn't. He was with my old man in the TPF for a few years back in the sixties. I wasn't even born yet. I just recognized him from pictures my mother keeps around."

Billy peered into the kitchen, his father sitting there now, eating dry cereal and watching a talk show on the miniature TV that sat next to the microwave.

"He's pretty much shot," Billy said.

"Are you sure about that?" MacCormack still coming off slightly stunned. "Because I have to tell you, I look nothing like my dad."

Billy experienced an all-too-familiar surge of optimism, then shut it down, the rhythm of his father's inexorable deterioration always spiked with these cruel upticks of startling keenness that raised his hopes for a moment before dashing them with the next time-warp slippage into dementia, Billy suddenly desperate to get away from his father before the next inevitable reminder came about of what a fool he was, is, always will be around the old man, until death took him away.

Snapping back into the here and now, Billy first looked to his wife, then to MacCormack, both staring at him as if they had been following his thoughts.

"You want to collect my guns?" he said, ejecting the clip, then handing MacCormack the grip end of his Glock. "I have a Ruger in a lockbox in the basement, and my father's old hand cannon is in his room. My wife can take you, have a blast."

Billy walked into the kitchen to fix himself a double double, praying that his father would just keep his mouth shut and not make him weep. He didn't return to the living room until he heard the front door close; when he did, the sight of his Glock sitting on the coffee table in front of Carmen pulled him up short.

"Where'd he go?"

"Outside."

"What do you mean, outside. He left?"

"He's waiting for you."

Billy looked out the window and saw the dope-confiscated Firebird gurgling at the foot of the driveway, MacCormack behind the wheel and the passenger door open.

"Are you going to tell me what's going on?" she asked.

"I have no idea," he said, walking out of the house.

. . .

THE STATE-RUN NURSING HOME IN Ozone Park smelled like cooking diapers. Eric Cortez was in the dayroom, Velcroed into a wheelchair, his face a soft balloon over his withering torso, his eyes, beneath a strapped-on hockey helmet, the popped silver of a gaffed fish.

"For the seizures," MacCormack said, nodding to the helmet.

"What happened?"

"He was shot in the head about three months ago and left for dead. A kid, actually the kid's dog, found him in a trash bag behind a housing project up in Dutchess County."

"When I ran him I didn't see anything about this."

"It's not our investigation, plus we weren't too eager to post it in case someone was interested in finishing the job."

"What kind of hitter's going to have access to the system?"

MacCormack stared at him.

"Are you serious?"

"The bullet was a 135 grain Speer Gold Dot from a Smith and Wesson .38, standard police issue."

"So what? We don't have a monopoly on that. Plus he was a snitch."

"What do you think, he was the only one we were running? And when he stopped showing up for our meets, none of the others knew shit. Then we got the call from Dutchess. So when you went online looking for him . . ."

"So you're looking at cops?"

Neither of them was looking at Cortez anymore.

"One of the people we interviewed said that he overheard our friend bragging on knowing about a protection-for-pay racket coming out of a Brooklyn precinct about two weeks before he caught a bullet. Maybe he wasn't just bragging."

"So you're looking at cops?" Billy having no memory of just saying this.

"We're vetting a few."

"Anybody looking good for it?"

MacCormack didn't answer.

"But that's where you're looking . . ."

MacCormack cocked his head. "Why, you think we should be looking somewheres else?"

"Do I? No, I'm just curious." Then: "I wish I could call this a tragedy."

Taking Billy by the elbow, MacCormack led him to the lobby. "It's most likely one of the crew he was ratting on, but if it wasn't, if there's something to this protection ring, I mean, that trumps anything else going and we want to cover our bases."

When they got back to Yonkers thirty minutes later, Billy's father was sitting on the porch reading the newspaper, his mouth hanging open in concentration.

From the driver's seat, MacCormack ducked his head to take in all the TARU cameras trained on the house and the street.

"Something tells me the worst thing I could've done today was take away your guns."

THE GIRL SAT ON HER narrow bed in the sour-smelling suite, grinding her knuckles into bonemeal. A shoe box filled with Saran Wrapped twists of coke and Ziplocs of pot sat on her desk, and a hollowed-out copy of *Gravity's Rainbow* packed with tens, twenties, and hundreds lay open on her dresser.

"*Gravity's Rainbow*, I never heard of that," Yasmeen said as she photographed the cash. "Is that a good book?"

"I never read it." The girl's numb gaze was locked onto the wedge of the Brooklyn Bridge visible from the dormitory window. "It's my dad's favorite."

Yasmeen silently hip-bumped Billy out of the way as she photographed the shoe box. He was there but not there, NYPD not allowed anywhere on campus without the permission of the university.

"Can I call my dad?"

"Absolutely."

Billy caught the eye of the roommate, who had started the ball rolling with a complaint to her therapist in the school's Wellness Center.

"Don't look at me," she said in a clipped Punjabi trill. "She's the drug dealer."

Two more school security officers, both retired detectives like Yasmeen, sauntered into the room, their faces immobile with boredom.

"SO REDMAN SAID YOU FOUND out Pavlicek's seeing a hematologist?" Yasmeen asked, shrugging her Tibetan hippie coat onto the back of her chair.

"I did," Billy said, unable to read her tone.

They were seated at the window table of a hummus café directly across the street from the dormitory.

"Is it serious?"

"I have no idea."

A waiter came out with their orders, a bottled beer for Billy, a mug of herbal tea for Yasmeen.

"I've been on the wagon all week," she said. "It's incredible how fast your body forgives you."

"So you don't know anything about this?"

"About what?"

"About John."

"I think somebody said he was having headaches."

"What do you mean headaches, like migraines?"

"That's all I know, and I don't even know if I know that."

They watched through the window as the girl was finally escorted out of the dorm by the two other school security officers and handed over to city detectives, the kid's college career at an end barely into the second semester of her freshman year.

"This job is such bullshit, I swear to God," Yasmeen said.

Billy took a sip of beer, brushed someone else's crumbs from the tabletop. "And what do you hear about Eric Cortez these days?" he asked.

"Cortez? I haven't checked on him since forever."

"No?" Looking out the window.

"But I still see Raymond Del Pino's family a few times a year. It's so hard for them to get over losing him, you know?"

"So you don't know he's in a nursing home out in Queens."

"Cortez is?" Yasmeen perked up. "Really? Why?"

"He was shot in the head and stuffed into a garbage bag upstate."

"That's . . . Are you shitting me? Wow."

"His brain's a bucket of mush, and the only time he can move is when he has a seizure."

"If I go visit him, can I bring my camera?"

"You know how I know? They investigated me to see if I was the actor. They wanted to collect my guns."

"You?" dumping a ton of Splenda in her mug. "Why you?"

"They thought the shooter might be a cop. So when I ran his name, they thought I might be trying to track him down to finish what I started."

"You ran his name? Why'd you run his name?"

"You know what they asked me? If I had any leads for them."

"And you said . . ."

"That I didn't."

"But why the fuck did you run his name to begin with?"

"Because this is freaking me out."

"What is?"

Billy took her napkin and wrote:

Tomassi Bannion SweetP Cortez

Yasmeen's phone rang. "Excuse me," she said, pulling it out of her coat pocket, then half-turning away.

Even with the cell pressed to her ear Billy could make out the tinny wail of her younger daughter's voice.

"What's wrong," Yasmeen asked wearily, massaging her temple. "OK, whoa, who's pinching you . . . Jacob. Fat Jacob or Black Jacob . . . Is he there? Put him on the phone . . . Just, Simone, if you don't put him on the phone right this second," rolling her eyes at Billy. "Is this Jacob? This is Simone's mommy. Listen to me, you know that monster that lives under your bed? Your parents tell you he's not real, but they're lying to you. Not only is he real but he's a friend of mine, and if you lay one more finger on my daughter I will make sure he comes out from under there when you're asleep tonight and sucks your eyes right out of your

head, you hear me? Yes? Good. Now give the phone back to Simone . . .
Stop crying and give the phone back to Simone."

Yasmeen hung up. "I hate bullies."

"Is he dying?" Billy asked.

"Is who dying."

"Pavlicek."

"Is Pavlicek dying? Is that what you just asked me?"

"He's my friend, if you know something I don't know just say."

"Huh," Yasmeen starting to flush as she snatched up Billy's list of
Whites. "So, what are you asking, do I know if he's got some kind of fatal
sickness that made him lose his rudder and go rogue on all these scumbags?"

"I didn't say that." Billy's turn to flush. "I just want to know how sick
he is."

"The guy's healthy as a horse, he's worth something like thirty million dollars, and he lives like a king."

"That's good," he said. "That's what I want to hear."

"So what else, you think he misses the good old action-packed days
of yesteryear? He's bored? The fuck is wrong with you, Billy."

"I don't know where you're going with this."

"Where *I'm* going with this?"

"I just asked about his health."

"And why the hell were you running Cortez to begin with. Who told
you to do that. And Sweetpea? Denny said you were walking around with
some fucking Missing poster for Sweetpea Harris. And yeah, I was being
nice about it before, but you hired some PI to investigate John's medical
records, didn't you."

Having fucked everything up now, elephant-stomped across every
line, Billy belatedly opted for silence.

"But you know what?" Yasmeen shrugged her coat back on as if about
to storm out. "Even if you're not a paranoid delusional and somebody
out there's taking these shitheads out, so what? Who cares? Animals like
these?" Jabbing at his list as she rose to her feet. "They tend to breed. And
so when they go young? It's called the trickle-down effect, our gift to the
future."

"Are you hearing yourself?" Billy sputtered.

"Are you hearing *your*self?"

The conversation was over.

"Fucking Billy." Yasmeen dropped back into the chair, her eyes suddenly shining like wet steel.

"What's wrong."

"Besides listening to you?"

"Besides listening to me."

A tremor set up house in the fingers of her right hand and Billy passed her the rest of his beer, which she drained like a Viking. He ordered her another.

"Yazzie, what's wrong."

"I'm sorry I'm just so tense all the time these days," swiping at her eyes with the dirty suede sleeve of her coat. "I think I'm going through menopause."

"What are you talking about, menopause, you're forty-three." Billy grateful for the change of subject.

"It could be early onset, you know? I lay in bed at night, I'm hot I'm cold I'm clammy I'm burning. I'm driving Dennis crazy."

"You always drive Dennis crazy."

"I have nightmares about my kids, all these bad things happening to them. I sit up in bed sometimes, I'm drenched, the whole bed. And my first thought is that it's blood, I'm covered in blood, but since about three months ago, I don't even get my period anymore. Don't get me wrong, I don't miss having it, but all this other shit that goes along with losing it? And I think animals can sense it. We went down to Florida right before New Year's to visit Dennis's parents? I took Dominique to feed these ducks and they went crazy, chased us, I swear to God it had to be a mile. If I had my gun we'd of had duck for dinner, the whole family. I just want it to be over."

"You should talk to somebody," he said.

"I am talking to somebody, you moron, I'm talking to you."

They sat there in silence for a long moment, ignoring the few students starting to wander in for lunch.

"I just want to stop having these dreams about my kids," she said, tagging the waiter for a third beer. "Sometimes I wish I never had kids, so many bad things can happen to them, but it never bothered me when I was in sex crimes, just now. This fucking menopause, maybe it's a good thing to have your period, a little blood loss every month, you know, like a pressure valve. How about Carmen, she's not menopausal yet, right? What is she, forty?"

"Thirty-eight."

"She's so lucky."

"Maybe it's not menopause," he said. "Maybe you're pregnant."

"Right. Do me a favor, ask your wife how long this thing lasts."

"She's a triage nurse."

"I don't know, Billy, you're all worried about Pavlicek? Maybe you should worry a little about me instead."

"You'll be all right," he said, running out of safe things to say.

MILTON RAMOS

Thirty minutes into packing up Marilys's one-and-a-half-room apartment, Milton more than got it: of course she was half a loon when it came to believing in her own bad dreams, the place was a virtual botanica, the high shelves above the two-burner stove and the cabinet beneath the bathroom sink housing a riot of spirit oils: Ogun, Pajaro Macua, 7 African Powers, Angel de Dinero, Angel de Amor, and Amarra Hombre, a.k.a. Hold Your Man, the last two also in mist form. And then there were the jars of spiritual floor wash in the back of the closet: Court Case, Steady Work, Money Shower, Chain Breaker, Do What I Say, Obey Me, Adore Me, and, once again, Hold Your Man, Milton wondering as he packed if she had been sneaking some of these concoctions into his house all along, washing the floors and walls but most important, he knew, the door frames, thresholds, and windowsills, in an effort to land him. He was fine with that, flattered in fact, but now that the potions had done their job, where the hell was she?

It was one in the afternoon on the day after she had boarded the bus to JFK and he was still waiting for her call from Guatemala City. At first he told himself, Third-world country, travel chaos, shitty to nonexistent cell service, there could be a million reasons. But after a few hours of thinking about all the cash she was carrying, *third-world country* began to morph into *abduction, chaos* into *rape,* and *bad cell reception* into *murder.*

Deciding that he didn't want any of her mojo collection in his house, he unpacked what he had just packed, then went to work emptying her medicine chest, another cabinet of curiosities, including a few unmarked jars that he wouldn't open on a bet. But he found no over-the-counter items and, more jarringly, no pharmacy-filled vials, no recognizable medications—every bathroom cabinet on earth held doctor-prescribed meds—which meant she either didn't take any and was as healthy as she looked or she was too poor to take proper care of herself and was medicating on the medieval plan, the mystery of the absent meds once again hammering home to him how little, after all these years, he actually knew about her.

His cell rang, not Marilys but Peter Gonzalez, a half friend of his from the TSA.

"She wasn't on United, American, or Delta. There were four other airlines flying out of the New York area with a connecting flight to Guatemala last night and this morning, but I figured those three were both direct and had the cheapest fares so . . ."

"So . . ." Milton sat on her bed.

"Aeromexico out of JFK last night had two Irrizarys on their manifest, a Carla and a Maria—are you sure Marilys is her legal name? It could be a nickname, a childhood name, or something."

"Hang on," he said, putting the phone down and quickly rustling through her garbage until he found a rent receipt and a Con Ed bill.

"Yeah, Marilys Irrizary, keep looking." Then: "Hello? You still there?"

"You're welcome," Gonzalez said.

"Sorry. Thank you."

Going back to packing, he returned to her closet and then went through her dresser, both of which were half empty, leaving Milton struck by how few actual possessions she had. Lastly he collected her crucifixes, icons, and religious statuary: Saints Michael, George, Lucy, and Lazarus, the Infant of Atocha and Our Lady of Guadalupe, all the usual suspects. Then, after surveying the rest of the apartment one last time and not finding anything else worth taking, he began to carry her stuff down to the street, needing only four trips to complete the job, six medium-sized boxes going into the back of a rented U-Haul with a capacity for ten times that amount.

Gonzalez called back a few hours later, while Milton was in the process of unpacking those same boxes in his house.

"Spirit, Avianca, Taca, Copa, no Irrizarys on any of them."

"All right," Milton said. "Thank you."

Fighting down panic, he busied himself with unwrapping her saints until he dropped and shattered the Black Madonna and Child, at which point he lost his shit in earnest.

Whatever happened to her, it had happened here.

She had never even made it out of the city.

"WE CAN'T START LOOKING UNTIL forty-eight hours," Turkel, the lone detective on duty in the Missing Persons Unit said. "You know the drill."

Milton had never been on the customer side of a squad room desk before, and he hated it.

"You can't jump the clock for me?" Redundantly flashing his tin.

"Last time I did someone a favor, they put me on desk duty for three months."

"What am I asking here," Milton said, thinking, You're behind a fucking desk right now.

"Look, how about you fill out the report, give it to me, if she's still missing tomorrow midnight, give me a call and I'll bump her to the top of the list."

TWENTY MINUTES LATER, WHILE STILL waiting for Turkel to find the right form, Milton left the office and returned to his squad in the 4-6.

"I understand where Missing Persons is coming from with the forty-eight-hours rule," Milton said, sitting between mountains of manila folders on Dennis Doyle's couch. "But I'm not talking about some teenage runaway here, and I was hoping you could reach out to somebody for me."

He knew his boss didn't like him, would have happily had him transferred out of the squad in a heartbeat if he could, but Milton couldn't think of anyone else to go to on this.

Doyle leaned back in his office chair, his head encircled by the framed portraits of his own bosses on the wall behind him.

"Who do I know there," he said, scowling into the middle distance, then picking up his phone, putting it down, picking it up again. "I got the guy. Remember that Night Watch sergeant was in here that morning I was asking you for the 494s on Cornell Harris?"

Milton slid his ass to the edge of the sofa. "Vaguely."

"Billy Graves, he spent a lot of years in the ID Squad, he's got to have a few friends in Missing Persons."

Milton got to his feet.

"Boss, you know what? Maybe I'm hitting the panic button too early on this."

"Your call." Doyle shrugged.

"I appreciate it though, thank you," he said, walking back into the squad room.

"Who is she, anyhow?" his boss called out after him.

BACK IN MARILYS'S APARTMENT, HE scoured dressers, drawers, and trash receptacles for anything that could help him find her, turning up nothing beyond those bullshit elixirs, a never-used datebook, and a set of keys that didn't fit her door. It was only after overturning half the furniture and getting down on his stomach with a Maglite to peer beneath whatever he couldn't move that he discovered the three phone numbers written in pencil on the wall above her mini-fridge.

The first was to a local deli, the second to a Chinese restaurant that delivered, but the third, with an outer-borough area code, was to an older female Hispanic with good English.

"Good afternoon, this is Detective Milton Ramos from the New York Police Department Missing Persons Unit. I'm looking for a Ms. Marilys Irrizary?"

"Not here."

"Who am I talking to?"

"Who am *I* talking to?"

Milton took a breath. "Detective Milton Ramos, NYPD, your turn."

"Anna Goury," then: "Josepha Suarez."

"Which."

"Both."

"Do you know Ms. Irrizary?"

"*Ms.?*" Sardonically dragging out the *z* sound. "Yeah, she's my sister, what's going on?"

And when Milton, overwhelmed by the question, was unable to answer, she asked, "Are you really a cop?"

ANNA GOURY/JOSEPHA SUAREZ LIVED WITH her husband, three kids, and what Milton thought might be a wolf in a federally funded prefab ranch house on Charlotte Street in the former anus mundi section of the Bronx, all six rooms of her home spotless to the point of parboiled. She looked a lot like Marilys, but then again all Indio women of a certain age seemed to him born of the same womb.

The three small cups of rocket-fuel Bustelo she served him at the kitchen table both helped and hindered his getting the full story out, breaking down his inbred reticence but making him stammer.

"I don't understand," she said after he finished. "Why would she be going to Guatemala?"

"Why? I told you, to bring back . . ."

"Our mother? Our mother's dead fifteen years," she said. "Besides, we're from El Salvador."

"Hold on, hang on," the sweat caught in his mustache suddenly reeking of coffee.

"Well, all I can say is," Goury/Suarez delicately rotating her demitasse cup on the smooth tabletop, "I hope you didn't give her any money."

Rolling onto his own street after a four-thirty a.m. police shooting in Herald Square had extended his tour nearly until noon, Billy was so jacked from all the liquid speed he had ingested that he clipped a neighbor's garbage can and then just kept on driving, his house at the end of the curved block shimmering like a mirage. Oddly enough, the sight of Pavlicek's Lexus parked in his driveway settled him down rather than sending him over the edge, artificial adrenaline, in the end, no friend to genuine alertness.

They were having coffee in the kitchen, Carmen in her nursing whites, Pavlicek in dry-cleaned jeans and a sport jacket.

"I didn't know Carmen went to Monroe," Pavlicek said as if Billy had been sitting with them all along. "Did you know that?"

"Well, yeah, she's my wife," he said carefully, looking to her for a read on the situation.

"My parents went there in the sixties, they met in tenth-grade journalism class," looking past Billy into the living room. "How's that for staying power."

"Must have been a whole different school in those days," Billy said, still trying to catch Carmen's eye.

"No, they told me it was crap back then too."

"He was asking me if I remembered any of the teachers," Carmen said. "I told him I didn't even remember going there."

"Yeah, you never talk about it," Billy too tense to take a seat in his own kitchen. "So, John, to what do we owe the honor?"

"Hey, look at this guy," Pavlicek beaming as Declan wandered into the kitchen, then pulling the boy close. "How old are you, now?"

"Eight." Always a sucker for adult attention, Declan didn't resist, standing there between Pavlicek's legs, an expectant half-smile on his face.

Billy finally caught his wife's eye: What gives? Carmen, thrown by the query, just shrugged.

"You got a girlfriend yet?" Pavlicek asked.

"I hate girls," Declan said, stating a fact.

"Yeah? What's your favorite team?"

"The Rangers."

"Baseball Rangers or hockey Rangers."

"Hockey. I hate the baseball Rangers."

"My boy's sport was football."

"I like football. I'm on a team," Declan said, then walked out of the room.

"What a guy you have there," Pavlicek said to the space between the parents.

"Well, yours is no slouch," Carmen said.

"Yeah," Pavlicek said faintly, smiling down at his coffee.

Billy finally took a seat. "So, John, what's up?"

Pavlicek took a breath, then folded his hands on the table. "Do you remember that Memory Keepers national convention Ray Rivera was talking about that time on City Island?"

"I know that group," Carmen said. "We give them a conference room for their meetings. So sad, you know?"

"Well, I went there as a guest of the Bronx-Westchester chapter, the one that meets at St. Ann's," nodding to Carmen. "It was in a Marriott outside of St. Louis and the first night they had a ceremony in this huge banquet hall, fifty, sixty tables, maybe five hundred parents from all the local chapters coast to coast. And, once everyone got settled, they passed out these cheap see-through plastic roses attached to batteries, one to a family, then they turned out all the lights in the hall and started to project a slide show onto a movie screen up front, sort of a death carousel. Each slide was a photo of someone's murdered child, could be anywheres from an infant to a forty-year-old, with name, birth date, then the 'murdered' date, printed below. 'Murdered,' not died, not killed. They'd hold the photo for twenty seconds or so, and when you saw your son's or daughter's face up there, your grandchild's, you turned on your battery-powered rose. One by one, those roses going on in the dark, here, over there, in the corner, in the back, and all the while they're playing this sappy theme music over the sound system, Michael Bolton, Celine Dion, the Carpenters, Whitney Houston, roses clicking on for infants, gangbangers, little girls, teenage boys, grown women, black, white, Chinese, "You Light Up My Life," murder date, rose, "Memories," murder date, rose, "Close to You," murder date, rose, "I Will Always Love You," murder date, rose, murder date, rose . . . And people for the most part were pretty composed, but every once in a while a face would come up on the screen and you'd hear somebody gasping in the dark or moaning, then race-walking out of the room. I think they had an understanding, if you're going to lose it, you need to leave, because it could create a chain reaction . . . So, the ceremony is going on and on, more and more roses lighting up this huge grief cave, and by the end of the slide show the whole room was, like, blazing with roses, I mean that fucking slide show went on for something like an hour and a half—twenty seconds a life, you do the math."

A silence came down, everyone staring at the table until Billy couldn't take it anymore.

"John, what's wrong with you."

"I lost you," Pavlicek blinking at him.

"I'm right here."

"Then be more specific."

"The hematologist."

Carmen looked from one to the other.

"I know you're seeing him."

"Me? No."

"John Pavlicek," Billy said. "I'm sorry, but I have the records."

"Junior."

"What?"

"That would be John Pavlicek Jr.," Pavlicek said. "It's called T-cell prolymphocytic leukemia, no one beats it, and it's fast. Six months at the outside."

"No!" Carmen's voice fluty with shock.

"Are you sure?"

"I come back from a two-week business trip four months ago, December sixteenth, I hear him in his bedroom, I walk in there," looking directly at Billy now. "I thought he had got stomped by a gang. Rings around his eyes, lumps and bruises all over his body, he can barely move, raise his eyes to me."

"Wait," Billy's hand out like a stop sign, "hold on, you told me . . ."

"I know what I told you," he said flatly.

Carmen started to cry, the sight of a weeping nurse bringing home the death sentence for Billy.

"So," Pavlicek sighed, "you ask around to Yasmeen, to Whelan, to Redman, do you know what happened to this animal, to that animal, do you think Pavlicek caught some kind of disease and lost his mind, do you think . . ."

"John, you have to understand . . ."

"Who the fuck cares, Billy. I mean, where's the scales, where's the justice in it?"

Billy closed his eyes, dreamed of sleep. "Are you telling me something?"

"I'm *asking* you something." Pavlicek leaned across the table and touched the back of his hand. "Because from where I'm sitting? If God or whoever else could just point a finger at a kid like John Junior, then all bets are off, because no one's minding the store. So, someone like me, what you do is, you take care of all your unfinished business, you do what you have to do to balance the books, so that maybe, just maybe, when the time comes, you might manage not to jump in the grave with him."

"Sometimes with that kind of leukemia . . ." Carmen began, then faded.

"My boy will be rotting in the earth while Jeffrey Bannion is getting laid? I don't think so. While Eric Cortez is going to a Yankees game? While Sweetpea Harris is becoming a father?"

"What are you telling me," Billy repeated numbly.

"You're a detective," Pavlicek said. "You figure it out."

Billy went away again, came back. "John, I swear to God, you know how much I love you, and I'm devastated for your son, but if you killed any of those . . ."

"You'll what, you'll lock me up?" Pavlicek finished his coffee and got to his feet. "You want to hear the worst, the very worst about this fucking type of leukemia he's got?" Looking around the kitchen as if trying to decide what to smash first. "The median age at onset is sixty-five. Imagine that."

THEY SAT IN SILENCE LONG after the Lexus had disappeared.

"You're not going after him, are you?" Carmen finally asked.

Billy didn't answer.

"*Are* you?"

"Can you give me a goddamn minute?"

Carmen punched him so hard his arm went dead.

"*Jesus,* Billy!" she wailed, shoving back her chair and leaving the room.

LATER THAT DAY, UNABLE TO sleep, Billy returned to Columbia Presbyterian, headed over to the information desk, and asked for John Junior's room. He dreaded seeing the kid in the state his father had described, but after Pavlicek's visit he had no choice.

The clerk sent him up to the oncology ward, where a nurse—once Billy had said that he was Junior's uncle and showed her his ID—told him that Junior had been checked out a few days ago. For a fleeting moment Billy thought that meant he was on the mend.

"He's home?"

"Transferred to Valhalla."

"To *where*?" Billy thinking she had chosen a sick way of telling him that Junior had died.

"The Westchester County Medical Center in Valhalla."

"Is that good or bad?"

"It's just closer to his family," she said breezily enough, but he'd been around nurses for the last twenty years of his life: John Junior was never going home again.

On his way back down the corridor, Billy noticed, through open suite doors, that some of the patients' rooms had second beds that sat lower to the floor and on collapsible legs for easier storage. On one, an older woman in street clothes was sleeping next to her daughter's sickbed. In another suite, a man was unpacking a suitcase as his wife watched him with near-lifeless eyes. He had slept on one of those beds himself for two nights at Lenox Hill after Carmen had given birth to Declan.

Billy returned to the nurses' station. "Family can sleep over?"

"If they want," the nurse said.

"How about the Pavlicek boy?"

"Johnnie? When we had him, his dad just about moved in. Very nice man, given the circumstances."

"Slept here every night?"

"I think that's why he moved his son. The commute was too hard on him."

"Did he need to sign in?"

"Only if he was coming in after visitors' hours."

Without too much cajoling, Billy got her to find the guest log for March 17, the night of Bannion's murder. Pavlicek had signed in at nine p.m.

"Do they sign out when they leave?"

"No need."

"So if, say, a visitor wants to go home at midnight, two in the morning . . ."

"Then they go."

Which left him with nothing.

"All right, then," offering his hand.

"Tell the Pavliceks I'm still praying for them," she said, her responding grip startlingly strong.

BACK HOME, BILLY HEADED UPSTAIRS to take another shot at sleep, passed his father's open bedroom door, and wandered in. Billy Senior lay on his bed, fully dressed for a change but snoring, flayed sections of the *New York Times* scattered around him on the bedspread.

Taking a seat at the small desk his father had brought with him from his last home, Billy scanned the spines of the books that lined the top shelf. Beside the old man's poets were luridly written original guides to nineteenth-century New York City; a first-person account of the Civil War draft riots of 1863; a hardback reissue of *1866 Professional Criminals of America;* and three fat novels about Ireland written by Thomas Flanagan, two of which Billy had actually read and somewhat enjoyed.

"Which is catching your eye?" Billy Senior murmured from the bed.

"Dad, you know me." Billy blushed.

"The dummy act doesn't become you," Senior said. "I've been telling you that since you were a kid."

"You know me," Billy unthinkingly repeated. Then, catching himself: "Must be an echo in here."

"What's on your mind?"

"Why does something have to be on my mind for me to come visit?"

Billy Senior quietly waited him out, his eyes unwavering, reducing his son, as in the old days, to a bucket of tells.

"Dad, let me give you a hypothetical situation," he began, then faltered. "If you knew that a certain friend crossed the line . . ."

"Which line?"

"The legal line . . . And you were having a real problem looking the other way . . ."

Flat on his back, his father frowned at the ceiling. "Is this friend on the Job?"

Billy didn't answer, which was answer enough.

"How good a friend is he?"

"Like a brother."

"Then first off, you have to ask yourself what would happen to him."

Billy felt his heart lurch, but he wasn't sure in which direction. "No matter what he did?"

"It's that bad?"

Again, Billy didn't answer.

"What are we talking about, mass murder?"

"Just some nonsense," he said, getting to his feet. "I should sleep."

"That was fast," his father said.

"No, I'm just . . ."

"Are you all right?"

"Yeah, no, I'm great." Billy patted his father's arm, turned, and was halfway out of the room when the old man began talking to him as if he were still seated.

"Back in June of sixty-four, there was a cop in Harlem, I won't say his name, he's passed anyhow, and this individual, he killed someone pretty much in front of his partner."

Billy sat back down.

"A pimp, had some Indian moniker, Cochise, Cheyenne, Geronimo, maybe. They had him in the back of the patrol car, and he starts mouthing off, just wouldn't stop. So this cop, let's call him Johnson, it was at night, he drives over to Morningside Park, drags him out, busts him up bad, and leaves him there to die, which he did."

"Because the guy was mouthing off?"

"Well, that and because there wasn't a girl in this man's stable over sixteen, because he had a habit of slashing Achilles tendons when any of them tried to run away from him, because he was so arrogant that he threatened Johnson's family. And yeah, because he wouldn't shut the hell up back there."

"What happened to him?"

"What happened to who."

"Johnson."

"Nothing."

"Walked away clean?"

His father propped himself up with a second pillow. "You have to understand, my son, the summer of sixty-four was red hot uptown, and this Cochise individual had more enemies than a Roman emperor. The squad pretty much went through the motions of looking into it for a few days, but nobody really gave a damn, and then a lieutenant from the One-nine, Tom Gilligan, shot and killed a fifteen-year-old black kid in the street, and we had almost a week of rioting on our hands, so the pimp was totally forgotten."

"Johnson's partner didn't say anything?"

"I can't say what it's like now, but back then? You looked the other way. Always."

"How about the partner, what happened to him?"

The old man was so long in answering that Billy almost repeated the question.

"Looking back after all those years?" his father finally said. "He could've been a better father to his kids, maybe, a better husband to his wife, but other than that?" Looking Billy in the eye now. "He sleeps like a rock."

WALKING INTO HARLEM HOSPITAL AT three a.m. in order to follow up on an agg assault that had come into the office an hour earlier, Billy wandered the halls until he found his point man, Emmett Butter, standing outside one of the ORs, notebook in hand, watching as a trauma team worked on his victim.

"What do you got."

"Bekim Ismaeli," Butter reading off his notes, "nineteen, stabbed twice in the chest."

"Is he likely?"

"Wobblin'."

"Where'd it happen."

"They're not sure, they said they were walking on either St. Nicholas or Amsterdam, all of a sudden five or six black guys jumped out of a car, stabbed Ismaeli, snatched his chain, then took off."

"Who's they."

"What?"

"'*They* were walking.' Who was walking."

"The other Albanians, his buddies. They brought him in."

"Can any of them ID the car?"

"I don't think so."

"Make, color, nothing?"

"Apparently not."

"Guys are walking down a street, middle of the night, five, six other guys jump out of a car, stab their friend twice, steal his chain, then jump back into the car and take off."

"Apparently."

"And these friends who brought him here, not one of them knows what street they were on, and nobody can even say what color car it was. Do I have that right?"

"Apparently," Butter looking away now.

"What does that sound like to you."

"Like they're selling a story."

"I agree. So where are these Albanian friends?"

"They left."

"They left. Did you interview any of them?"

"Just as far as I told you. Then I went to check with the doctor and when I came back out they were kind of gone."

"Kind of gone. You got their names though, right?"

"I was about to," Butter said, blushing with humiliation, then: "I'll put it all in the report."

"How about you don't."

"What?"

"Do everybody a favor and say you got here after they left."

"Yeah?" Butter looking at him now with dog's eyes.

"But we're clear about what happened in here, yes?"

"Yeah, yes."

"My people get to screw up once."

"I understand," Butter said, then again: "I understand."

"All right," Billy said, turning away, "stay with Ismaeli, see if he comes around."

"Hey, boss," Butter called out. "Thank you."

■ ■ ■

THINKING THAT THERE WAS A good chance the kid would screw the pooch on this, his first run, Billy had made sure to wait until something came in north of Ninety-sixth Street before sending Butter out, knowing that grievously fucking up anywhere south of that, where the press began to give a shit, would have resulted in him being transferred to Missing Persons or worse. But if Butter was ever going to be of any use to him or any other squad boss, he had to start cutting his teeth somewhere.

His wife would never admit it to him, but Billy's guess was that interns killed patients all the time, and their supervisors, with an eye for the long-term healer to come, mainly looked the other way. Well, it was the same with him. In order to get the greater job done, to mold your people as you saw fit and prepare them to effectively do the job in the years to come, you tolerated error, you turned a not-quite-blind eye to the actions of others and to your own actions. You created secrets and you kept secrets.

Out on the streets, same thing: depending on the individual and the situation, sometimes you threw the Thor hammer at a misdemeanor, other times you let an individual walk who had no right to sleep in his own bed that night. You did all these things and more because as a boss, if you weren't willing to play fast and loose when required, if you weren't willing to make a discreet hash of the rule book now and then, on this job you might as well call in sick.

That's just the way it was.

CARMEN CALLED AS HE WAS walking to his car. "Hey."

"Hey," Billy bracing himself.

"Look," she said, "I don't want you to do anything or not do anything because I pressured you. You'll resent me forever."

"I appreciate that."

"That being said, you know how I feel."

"Right."

"Just come to it on your own."

MILTON RAMOS

Marilys Irrizary Ramos.

Even her pregnancy was probably bullshit.

Another family taken away from him. And for what: fifteen hundred for the bogus plane tickets, eighty-five hundred for the bogus bribe.

A lousy 10K.

Fuck her.

It was time to get back in the game.

HERE'S WHAT HE DIDN'T LIKE about giving his daughter away to Anita:

1. Her two-story clapboard was only a curb's width distant from the city-bound service road of the Staten Island Expressway, cars flying by as if the first to reach the Verrazano Bridge was entitled to free head.
2. She was a smoker.
3. She drank. As far as could tell, nothing harder than white wine, but still . . .

And here's what he did:

1. Her husband, Raymond, was a nice enough guy who owned a gas station and made decent money.
2. She was a thirty-five-year-old teacher's aide who worked at a K-4 public school but who couldn't have children of her own, and her eyes always had that slightly tense quivery thing going on, which hopefully meant that she desperately wanted a kid before her time ran out.
3. The house was not just neat but clean, the velour couch and matching chairs in her living room sheathed in vinyl, the wall-to-wall carpet as pristine as a putting green.
4. And lastly, she was slender, at least by his standards, and the most fattening things in her refrigerator, which he opened on the pretense of getting a soda, were a still-sealed log of Cracker Barrel cheddar cheese and a small bubble pack of Genoa salami.

"WHAT DO YOU MEAN YOU'RE being targeted, what does that mean?" Anita asked him.

They were sitting at her dinette table, Sofia watching cartoons in the dustless living room, a small overstuffed suitcase at her feet.

"Some big-time banger I put away sent down orders from upstate for his crew to take me out. Gang Intel found out about it from a CI."

"But what does that mean?" Anita nervously playing with the cellophane on a new pack of Merit Lights.

"Probably nothing. I spoke to the NYPD Threat Assessment Team, they already had TARU put up surveillance cameras around the house, plus a directed patrol unit rolls by once an hour twenty-four/seven. I'm not really worried about it? But that doesn't mean nothing's going to happen."

"Milton, Jesus."

"It comes with the territory." He shrugged. "The thing is . . ." looking to Sofia, who was quietly eating mozzarella strips, eyes on the screen. "The thing is, if something does happen to me? Sofia . . ."

"Of course."

"So I was thinking . . ."

"Of course."

"Or if I'm unable to take care of her for whatever reason . . ."

"Of course of course of course."

Milton felt relieved but also freaked, his cousin going for it way too fast. "Don't you want to talk to Ray first?"

"Why. We've being trying to have a child for the last five years."

"Still . . ."

"He'd be doing handstands, trust me."

"And you like her, right?"

"Do I like Sofia?" she whispered. "The bigger question is does she like me."

Good question. Sofia hardly knew her.

"Don't be ridiculous, you're her favorite aunt."

"I'm her second cousin, if you want to get technical about it," Anita said, still whispering.

"Whatever," Milton said, "blood is blood."

"Wow," Anita said.

"It would be a simple matter of writing you into my will as Sofia's guardian."

"We have that second bedroom, I mean Ray's just using it as an office, you know?"

"Good," Milton said tightly.

"I mean what does he need it for?"

Too fast, too fast, Anita just going with the excitement without a moment's reflection, as if Milton were offering her a puppy. And she didn't seem too worried about his own dangerous situation, horseshit story that it was.

"And I have to say, the schools around here?"

"Terrific."

"Plus I've been around kids Sofia's age five days a week for the last five years, so it's not like I don't . . ."

"There you go."

This was a life-changing commitment, how could she not hesitate?

"I mean I would really love her up, Milton, you know I would,"

Anita's hands trembling a little as she finally opened the pack of cigarettes. Then, catching him staring, she tossed the whole thing in the sink.

"No more of these, I can promise you that."

"Relax, I'm still alive."

But she was a good person and he had to believe that if things went south for him—*when* things went south for him—Sofia would have a soft landing here.

"Wow." Anita shivered. "This is almost enough to make me want to bump you off myself, you know?"

THE IMPACT, A HEARTBEAT AFTER he blindly backed out of her driveway into the expressway service road, spun his rear end a full ninety degrees so that he was suddenly facing the oncoming traffic and the smashed front grille of the Ram 1500 that had T-boned him. The driver, big enough to star in TV ads for his own ride, was out of the truck so fast that at first Milton thought he had been ejected. It was all he could do to stow his weapon under the seat before Bigfoot reached his car.

"The fuck!" the guy shouted, pounding on Milton's hood.

Like she was some goddamn rescue dog . . .

Milton got out of his car. Behind the damaged truck, the nonstop honking of the city-bound cars now trapped in the one-lane road was like the sound track for his fury.

"It was my fault," Milton said. He took out his wallet, but the guy slapped it out of his hands before he could even start to fish for his insurance card.

"I feel like stomping your ass."

"You can try," Milton said.

Like she was a puppy in a cardboard box . . .

Thrown by Milton's matter-of-fact invitation, the big man hesitated.

"I think you should try."

Anita was nuts, was a child herself. She was just jumping on this without a thought in her head.

"You're crazy."

"And you're a fucking cunt," Milton said.

Red-faced with throttled violence, the guy started to tilt forward from the hips like a dipping bird, his breath puffing Milton's hair. Praying for the punch to come, Milton stood his ground and waited for it, even though he pretty much knew he had already cut off the guy's balls and that nothing would happen. And nothing did, Ram Tough man settling for a string of low face-saving curses as he returned to his front-mangled ride and took off, leaving Milton feeling so thwarted he thought his heart would break.

MILTON STOOD IN SOFIA'S BEDROOM, surveying the scatter of dolls and books and games. She would need things, obviously, but he could only send over a little of her previous life at a time in order to allow everyone, his daughter and her new parents, to gradually become accustomed to their roles. He didn't want anyone to panic.

But what did she need right away. Clothes. What kind of clothes. What did an eight-year-old girl wear. Even when she was a toddler he had never dressed her, barely took notice of what she had on unless it was something too tight for her frame.

Socks. They didn't take up much space, so he figured he could get away with three pairs without raising eyebrows. Underwear, T-shirts. Again, three of each, everything tossed into a large Hefty bag. Her floral corduroy jeans, into the bag. How about a dress, a skirt. No, two skirts; no, one, but where did Marilys keep them? This should be Marilys's job, Milton at first mildly annoyed about that, and then the irony kicked in, making him sit down before he fell down.

A moment later, once again galled to the edge of his teeth by the divide between the grief givers and the grief takers, the fuckers and the fucked, by the eternal inevitable of his violently miserable life, Milton walked out of the room dragging the half-full garbage bag behind him and headed for the basement.

A few minutes later he was out on the street, the bag, much heavier now, spackling the sidewalk red from his front door to the trunk of his car.

CHAPTER

14

It was turning out to be another nothing of a tour, the only job so far a four a.m. outdoor scene in the West Village, where a home owner had been shot by his lawn mower while cutting the backyard. The live .357 shell, previously asleep in the grass, had been sucked up into the rotary blades, ignited, then fired itself out the back end of the machine into his nuts.

By the time Billy and Stupak made it to the scene—shots fired was shots fired—Emergency Services was already combing the yard for any other stray ordnance and some joker had handcuffed the high-end mower to a lamppost.

"Who the fuck mows their lawn at four in the morning," the patrol sergeant said.

"Myself, I'd be kind of interested in finding out how the bullet got to be in his backyard in the first place." Billy yawned. "Any ideas?"

"We had a problem last month with some subhumanoids coming over the PATH from Jersey City, but nothing with guns."

"There's that indoor rifle club on MacDougal," a uniform said. "That's only a block over."

"A, it's indoor; B, the house rifle's a .22," the patrol sergeant said.

"Just the one so far?" Billy asked one of the ESUs scouring the grass.

"Found a quarter and a roach clip," the cop said. "That's about it."

Billy sent Stupak over to Beth Israel on the off chance that the victim would be able to talk between now and eight a.m., then, after deciding not to canvass the neighbors at this hour, headed for his car with the intention of going back to the office and grabbing a nap.

But the e-mail that came in over his phone a few minutes later as he was pulling out of his space knocked any notion of sleep into the next week.

There was no message, only an attached JPEG, Billy opening it to see a flash-lit snap of Curtis Taft lying cuffed and gagged on a wooden floor, his red-dot eyes buzzing from above the fat strip of electrical tape that had been slapped across his mouth. The photo had been sent from Taft's own phone, but Billy had to be an idiot not to guess who the shutterbug was.

After reversing back into his spot, he threw the car into park and immediately started to dial.

"What did you do."

"Come and see," Pavlicek said.

"Is he dead?"

"Come and see."

"Where are you."

"Fifteen twenty-two Vyse."

In the heart of their old precinct, in a building Pavlicek owned.

"Fuck you. Don't move."

"I wouldn't dream of it."

THIRTY MINUTES LATER, FLYING DOWN Vyse Avenue the wrong way, Billy sideswiped the length of Pavlicek's Lexus, continued until he was a few feet past the taillights, jumped out, and came racing back on foot.

Pavlicek was out of the car waiting for his charge, but all he did when Billy threw a sloppy haymaker was deflect the blow, then pull him into a bear hug. When it came to hand-to-hand, Billy never could fight for shit.

"What did you do," he hissed, his arms pinned to his sides, Pavlicek's bristle like sandpaper along his jaw.

"Calm down."

"What did you *do*."

Pavlicek thrust him backward, Billy tottering nearly the length of the SUV before regaining his balance and charging him again. This time Pavlicek whipped him chest-first into the Lexus's side-view mirror, the pain like a punch.

"You want to keep going with this?"

"Are you trying to jam me up?" Billy barked, ripping the side mirror off its mount and throwing it at Pavlicek's head. "You think that'll do it?"

The mirror had glanced off Pavlicek's temple, drawing a little blood. Bracing for a brawl, Billy set his feet, but instead of warring back, Pavlicek simply stanched the thin flow with the heel of his hand, then looked off down the street. At first Billy was thrown—Pavlicek had been erratically explosive for weeks—but now it was as if anger over his son's impending death had somehow gone beyond expressible fury to a higher, finer level, making Billy's rage in comparison seem so pedestrian that it hardly merited a reaction.

Three silent but alert white men in jeans and sweatshirts came out of 1522 into the predawn stillness and headed toward the Lexus, Billy recognizing one: Hal Gurwitz, carrying a Yankees bat bag, a defrocked cop who had done some time for putting a handcuffed prisoner in the hospital with a ruptured spleen. He guessed that the other two, younger and a little more tense, might still be cops.

They eyed the long scrape on the SUV's body and then Billy's sedan, slant-parked in the wrong direction.

"Everything OK up there?" Pavlicek asked.

"Yeah," Gurwitz said, taking the question as an all-clear sign. "I believe the moving van should be coming somewheres around midmorning."

"Everything OK down here?" the youngest of the three asked, looking directly at Billy.

"Absolutely." Pavlicek pulled out a wad of cash as thick as a rolled washcloth and distributed what looked like a few hundred dollars to each of them. "I'll be in touch."

The men walked off as a group, each in turn casting an eye back toward Billy and the cars, until they all piled into a minivan in front of an elementary school at the far end of the block.

"Some of my tenants on the fifth floor were confusing their apartment with a dopeteria," Pavlicek said, stooping to pick up his side mirror, then tossing it into the backseat. "You'd think everyone around here would know the score by now."

The van slow-rolled past them on its way to wherever, the three cops inside throwing deep shade Billy's way one last time.

"Do they know?"

"Know what." Then: "What do *you* know?"

"Just . . ." Billy felt his adrenaline abandon him in a reverse rush. "Where is he."

Pavlicek took a breath, tracked the last of the moon as it slipped between two dead walk-ups at the end of the street.

"You know, when I heard Bannion bought it at the train station that night? I wept with happiness. To go to Thomas Rivera's parents and bring them news like that: Somebody sliced up your boy's murderer, he died in his own blood on a filthy subway platform . . ."

"Did you tell them you killed him?"

"I didn't kill him."

"Right, that's right, you were sleeping at the hospital that night. I saw your name on the sign-in."

Pavlicek threw Billy a look that had him taking a step back.

"I didn't kill him, and that's a fact. But justice, real justice, Billy, it's like the getting of grace. The closest thing to peace on earth."

"Where is he."

Pavlicek crossed the narrow street to 1522, then waited at the entrance until Billy understood to follow.

CUFFED HAND AND FOOT LIKE a bagged deer, Curtis Taft lay curled on his side in the smaller bedroom of a ground-floor vacant, his eyes widening then narrowing at a rapid tic-like pace, the tape across his mouth tugging redly at the trapped curls of his beard. A second strip, half the size of the gag, was pasted across his forehead.

"Jesus!" Billy hissed, backing up until he hit a wall.

At the sound of Billy's voice, Taft's eyes slowed and then focused on a section of baseboard inches from his face.

Billy knew he should leave and call it in, but he didn't. He knew he should cut Taft loose, but he didn't do that either.

Taft twisted his head so he could look at Billy directly, the oh-shit sight of his five-year hunter making his chest begin to rise and fall—but not so intensely that anyone could describe it exactly as *heaving*—and despite everything Billy found himself nakedly wanting some kind of more—a tape-muffled plea, a widening eye, a stream of uncontrolled piss—and he found it enraging that his White wasn't giving it to him.

"Cut him loose," he said faintly.

Pavlicek dropped into a squat alongside Taft, peeled the smaller strip of tape off his forehead, and held it between his fingers.

"I heard that the only family member who showed up for Shakira Barker's arraignment last week was her grandmother," Pavlicek said, his eyes never leaving Taft's face. "The same for the funeral of the kid she killed. No one but Grandma. Thank God for the grannies, huh?"

"Get him up."

Pavlicek removed the tape from between his fingers and placed it across Taft's nostrils, Billy's already gagged White immediately beginning to writhe, his eyes bulging like eggs.

Billy finally started across the room, but Pavlicek removed the tape before he could get there.

"It's not my place," he said, extending the strip to Billy on a fingertip.

Billy returned to his spot on the wall.

"It's nothing," Pavlicek said, still offering the tape. "It's like applying a band-aid."

"Get him up, John," Billy said, looking away.

"Peace on earth," Pavlicek said, rising to his feet, crossing to Billy, and pressing the tape into his bruised chest on his way out of the room. "Nothing like it in the world."

A moment later the apartment door slammed shut, Pavlicek leaving Billy and Taft staring at each other from opposite corners of the empty room.

Helplessly trussed though he was, Taft sensed that Billy wasn't going to take the bait. His eyes began to recede back into their sockets, then droop with supreme contempt, the same contempt that had allowed him to kill those girls and then go back to bed, the same contempt he'd displayed whenever Billy's efforts to bring him to justice invariably came to nothing.

Billy plucked the strip of tape from his chest, stepped forward, and then, as Pavlicek had, hunkered down above his prisoner.

Taft began to look bored, his eyes dimming in his head. Billy affixed the tape to his nostrils. Taft's expression remained the same.

Like he had Billy's number. Had it since day one.

Billy got up and left the room to explore the rest of the apartment, the smell of the freshly painted walls reminding him of the day he had moved into his first home with his first wife.

When he returned to the bedroom, he saw that Taft no longer looked so bored, and that a pinkish mist had begun to seep into the whites of his eyes. Billy left again, this time to splash cold water over his face in the kitchen, wiping away the excess on the sleeves of his jacket, then drying his hands on the back of his slacks.

When he settled over Taft this time, the pink of his eyes had turned poppy and completely flooded the scleras. A few seconds after that, his hog-tied body began to repeatedly jackknife, then arch in pure animal spasm.

Billy stood up and returned to his original position against the far wall. "If you even think of flagging down a patrol car," he said evenly, "or walking into a police station? Or picking up a phone and calling 911?"

The room abruptly blossomed with the stench of involuntary evacuation.

"You see how easy he found you? You see how easy that was?"

■ ■ ■

STANDING NEXT TO THE LEXUS, they watched in silence as Curtis Taft, mustering as much dignity as possible given the circumstances, walked toward the intersection of Vyse and East 172nd Street, his stride a little off-kilter.

He was smart enough not to look back.

"I didn't really expect you to go through with it," Pavlicek said after Taft finally turned the corner. "But you got a taste of how it would feel, right?"

Billy didn't answer.

"Oh yes you did."

Billy started walking to his car.

"Looking at me like you did when I came to your house . . ." Pavlicek called out after him, sounding both imperious and resentful. "Fucking saint that you are."

Billy came back. "This shit is what heals your grief, John?"

Turning away, he noticed, for the first time, the Westchester Community College decal on Pavlicek's rear window. "This is how you honor your son?"

He had no idea how he came to be lying on his back. His jaw felt as if it was now located behind his left ear. When he managed to find his feet, he was immediately thrown belly-down onto the hood of the Lexus, his kidneys being pounded from behind. By the time he rallied enough to defend himself, twisting his hips and whipping a high and ineffective elbow to the side of Pavlicek's head, the deep one-note whoop of a patrol car brought it all to an end.

"Go ahead, tell them what's the what," Pavlicek wheezed. "Now's your chance. Go on."

Billy, gasping himself, intercepted the young cops, both Asian, as soon as they stepped out onto the street. Holding out his gold shield, he slurred, "Family feud, it's under control."

After the uniforms reluctantly rolled off, Billy tottered back to his sedan and drove away, Pavlicek watching him go with the scowling concentration of someone trying to memorize a license plate.

■ ■ ■

COMING HOME DIRECTLY FROM THE Bronx, his exploded jaw pulsing like a drum, Billy saw the red carnage on his front porch and flew into the house to check on his family, racing bedroom to bedroom, the animal priority of who he loved most coming in the order of rooms entered— Carmen before his kids, his kids before his father.

All sleeping, all breathing.

Back in the kitchen, Billy chugged down a glass of tap water, then stepped outside to verify what he thought he'd seen.

The front of the house looked like a slaughter pit, the cedar planks on the south side of the porch, the exterior wall directly behind it, and Carmen's pink-and-blue Easter banner all peppered with blossoms of gore. A split trash bag, its guts still puddled with paint, lay between the front legs of his father's rocking chair, looking, to anyone driving by, like a sleeping dog. But it was the scatter of children's clothes that froze his heart: a top, a pair of jeans, another top, another pair of pants, and a slurry of underpants and socks, all so red-drenched and twisted that he had no idea whether they were for a boy or a girl.

He went into the garage, gathered up two lawn bags, a wire-whisk brush, an aerosol bottle of Strip-All, and a joint-compound bucket filled with hot water. Checking the time—six-fifteen—he quickly set to work.

It was only later, while carefully going through the paint-stiffened clothes, looking for shop labels or laundry marks and finding nothing more than the ubiquitous Gap Kids tag, that it came to him that his family's tormentor had chosen red twice now, the porch and the children's clothes bathed in the same arterial shade as the handprint on the back of Carlos's jacket.

It made him think about the Jews in Egypt smearing their doors with lamb's blood to fend off the Angel of Death—except in this case, the message seemed to be the opposite.

AFTER DUTIFULLY DRIVING HIS KIDS to school—*Carmen before his kids*— Billy sat in the kitchen on a straight-backed chair watching his wife wrap her thumbs in heavy layers of gauze, which she then secured with surgical tape.

He had told her that his dislocated jaw had come from a roll-around with a five a.m. Dusthead in the course of making an arrest, but doubted that she believed him.

"Tilt your head back and open your mouth as wide as you can."

"This is going to hurt, right?"

"Like a bitch, but only for a second."

When she put her thumbs in his mouth, each one settling on a back molar, and then rose up on her toes in order to put her whole body into it, he thought he would puke.

"Billy, relax."

"I am."

"No you're not. I tell you what . . ." she said, lowering herself, then quickly rising up again and bringing her thumbs down so hard on his back teeth that he screamed.

"Fucking hurts, right?" Carmen said a moment later as she unspooled the tooth-shredded gauze from around her thumbs. He thought he had bitten them off.

"Guy wasn't even that big," he said, the red-hot throbbing of the last few hours miraculously down to a run-of-the-mill soreness.

"No, huh?" Avoiding his eyes.

He didn't understand why she wasn't pressing him for the truth, which made him even more edgy than he already was.

"I must've had three inches and forty pounds on him," Billy doubling down on the story. "They should have called animal control."

"We had a guy brought in last week?" she said, staying in the game. "He was so cranked on PCP he shattered both of his femurs just by tensing his legs. We go to lift him off his gurney, he jumps up and starts running down the hall like a track star. Didn't feel a thing."

Billy bent over and started to retch.

Carmen offered him an unwashed cereal bowl from the sink.

"I'm good," he said, accepting it.

"So where are you at?" she asked.

"With what." Billy blinked, hoping to duck the subject.

Choosing to let it be, at least for now, Carmen handed him three Advils and a glass of water.

"I want you to go over to Saint Joseph's for an X-ray."

"Right now I need to sleep," he said. Then, gingerly probing his jaw: "Thank you."

While Carmen was upstairs changing into her work whites, Redman called.

"I need to come by," he said.

"What for?" As if he couldn't guess.

"I need to talk to you. I'll drive up."

"Hang on," Billy said, putting the receiver to his chest. He'd had enough of visitors, announced and unannounced, coming to sit or stand in his kitchen and dump all kinds of dark drama on his head.

"I tell you what," raising a hand to Carmen as she walked out of the house, "I need to take care of something, then I'll come down to you, how's that sound."

"All right," Redman said reluctantly. "Just, until you get here? Don't do anything."

Billy walked out the front door a few minutes later, intending to take the paint-stiffened clothes over to the Yonkers precinct that was overseeing the directed patrols. At first he was startled to see Carmen still on the porch, then not, given her missing banner.

"I saw that when I came in," he said as offhandedly as he could. "Some kids must've taken it last night."

But rather than raise hell about it, she seemed distracted, barely acknowledging that he had said anything at all. Then he saw what she was focused on: a rivulet of red paint that he'd missed earlier had settled into the seam between house and porch, looking like a boundary line on a map.

She walked to her car, unlocked the driver's door, then spoke to him without looking his way. "I don't want Millie picking up the kids from school this afternoon," she said numbly. "You do it."

■ ■ ■

THE NIGHT-VISION SURVEILLANCE FOOTAGE FROM the previous evening, both chalky and luminous, was eerie enough to pass for para-
normal activity. Billy watched the tape three times, the mysteriously
launched garbage bag sailing as clumsily as an overweight turkey through
the fuzzy air before erupting on his porch and spewing out its contents.

"Those patrols are bullshit. I want a twenty-four-hour posting in front
of the house," Billy said, regretting the "I want" as soon as it came out
of his mouth.

"Not happening." The detective, Evan Lefkowitz, shrugged.

"What do you mean, not happening."

"We're undermanned as it is."

Billy reached into the bag of clothes lying on an unoccupied desk,
pulled out the pair of girls' corduroy pants, and held it in his fist.

"Let me tell you what that guy did. He sat on his ass until he saw your
doughnut eaters roll by, knew he had a good fifty-five minutes, ate a sandwich, did the crossword, bloodied up my porch, took a piss, washed his
car, and went home. I want, I need, *my family* needs, a twenty-four-hour
fixed post."

"Doughnut eaters?"

Billy took a breath. "Look, I'm sorry about that, I swear to you I'm
not one of those NYPD assholes who thinks every cop outside the five
boroughs is some eeba-geeba related by blood to Barney Fife."

Without excusing himself, Lefkowitz stepped off to talk to another
detective about a different issue, Billy taking it to mean that maybe his
Mayberry riff had been a little too lovingly delivered.

"Hey, this is my town too," he said when Lefkowitz returned. "I'm
living my life here, raising my kids here, paying my taxes, and all I'm
asking you for is just a little bit more protection."

"Like I said, we're undermanned as it is."

"All due respect, but could I speak to your boss?"

"She'll just tell you the same."

"Nonetheless . . ."

"Fine by me," Lefkowitz said, walking away. "She'll be in next week."

■ ■ ■

AS BILLY CAME UP ON Brown's Family Funeral Home that night, Redman, wearing a full-body apron and latex gloves, was standing in the narrow doorway swapping cash for Chinese takeout with a delivery boy.

"You mean to tell me you're OK walking the streets like that?" Redman said without raising his eyes from the exchange.

"Like what?"

"Don't you have a mirror at home?" Redman counted out his change. "Come in here."

Once they were inside the chapel, Redman had Billy take off his shirt and lie down on a somewhat clean gurney. Then, reaching into his cluttered cosmetics cart, he found a jar of Standard Caucasian camouflage cream and went to work on the constellation of bruises that, between Pavlicek and Carmen, had erupted across Billy's face since the morning.

"You ever notice how the storefronts line up in this neighborhood?" Redman said. "Dunkin' Donuts, Popeyes, Roy Rogers, Ashley Stewart's big women shop, then a funeral parlor, all cheek to cheek like a de-evolution cartoon."

"They have fat people in Nebraska too, last I heard," Billy said, wondering when they were going to get to Pavlicek.

"My point being," Redman stepping back to assess his work, then peeling off his gloves, "I had two bodies coming in this week, a five-hundred-pounder and a four, but when I added the weight of the casket I realized that my front steps would collapse, so I had to farm them out to Carolina Home up the block because the director over there was smart enough to put in reinforced steel."

Rafer came rolling into the room, made two quick circuits around his father, then charged at an old man sporting a Masonic fez and apron, who was lying in his casket parked by the piano.

"So." Billy sat up and reached for his shirt. "Why am I here."

Redman took a limping stroll around the chapel, straightened out a few folding chairs, then slowly came back.

"Look, I'm going to save you a lot of trouble."

"How's that," Billy said, feeling the cadaver cream starting to grip.

"It's done."

"What is."

"All what you've been looking into."

Billy was quiet, waiting for more. Then: "How am I supposed to let him get away with this."

"Who, the lone gunman?"

"What?"

"You think we all sent Pavlicek out there like that?"

"What then."

"All of us."

Billy swiped at his caked jaw with a shaking hand. "Who's all of us."

"Pavlicek didn't do anything more than his part."

" 'All of us.' Including you?"

"Why not me?"

"Look at you," Billy said cruelly.

And then he was aloft, Redman holding him two feet off the ground with those harpooner's arms, the guy wheeling so fast on his cracked hips that Billy hadn't even felt the long fingers slip under his arms.

"Why not me?" Redman holding him up in the air like a baby.

"Put me down, please?"

Redman deposited him in a folding chair, Rafer immediately raising his arms to his father: My turn.

"You did Sweetpea," Billy said. "Bullshit. The wit said the doer had straight hair. Nothing about a fucking Afro."

Redman picked up his son, held him in one arm. "That wit was six floors up and off-his-ass high. You said so yourself."

Billy grabbed a rag and swiped at his face, but the makeup had turned to cement. "His girlfriend said she heard a white voice over the cell."

"Do I sound, do I *ever* sound like some mush-mouth street nigger to you?"

"You kind of did, right there," Billy said.

Rafer started to wail.

"What you cryin' for, man?" Redman hitch-limped over to the Samsung and found something on the Cartoon Network.

Billy went momentarily south, checking his watch—ten p.m.—wondering if this kid even had a bedtime.

"Why," he said.

"Because it felt right. It felt fair."

"Why."

"Pavlicek's boy. We all known him since he was wearing a diaper. First of the kids born to us."

"Redman . . ."

"It's not like playing God, because me personally? To tell you the truth, the only time I believe in God is when something shitty happens, like Little Man here and his g-tube or John Junior catching leukemia. I'm in here sending people off three, four times a week to meet Jesus or whoever, but . . . You know what I believe in? Earth. Dirt. This right here. All the rest is a story. I guess I'm in the wrong business."

"So everybody . . ."

"Was in on it."

Billy went away again, telling himself that there had always been something off about Redman. Look how he chose to make a living, look how many wives he'd had, look how many kids . . .

"Billy, we all saved each other's lives one time or another, including me yours."

And to let the kid play around dead bodies all day . . . Redman and his wife—what was the child-rearing philosophy here?

"Billy," Redman bringing him back, "I am telling you all this because it's over." He held his long basketball hands in front of his belt, gently tamping down the air like shushing a baby. "So let it be."

BILLY MADE IT BACK HOME by midnight, but unwilling to go in and risk a conversation with Carmen tonight, he parked halfway down the street, intending to sit tight until the bedroom window went dark.

An hour into the wait, he reached for his notebook and made out the chart:

> Redman—Sweetpea
> Yasmeen—Cortez
> Pavlicek—Bannion

Tomassi's death by bus kept Whelan's name off the chart, and Curtis Taft didn't make it either, though Pavlicek had served him up to Billy hoping he would complete the sweep. But as he continued to sit there and study the neat matchups, he began to wonder if Redman, in order to protect Pavlicek, had been selling him a story back at the chapel, thinking that if Billy bought the conspiracy angle and thought he'd have to bring down three friends instead of just one, he might lose heart and walk away.

The 24/7 directed patrol unit cruised past his car without noticing him in the driver's seat, slowed down in front of the house, but never came to a stop in order to allow the cops to get out and inspect the grounds. It was the third pass he had observed since parking here, each more lax than the one before.

As he reached for his cigarettes on the dash, the pack slipped through his fingers and landed between his feet. When he bent over to retrieve them, his forehead touched the steering wheel and that was that, Billy sitting up an hour later with a pink streak above his eyes as vivid as a brand.

He checked the time: two a.m. The bedroom window was dark.

STEPPING FROM THE CAR, HE discovered that the asphalt beneath his feet was dappled with dried paint—the leakage from the clothes bag before it had been thrown onto his porch. Whoever had done the deed last night had chosen the same observation point as he had, a spot far enough away to avoid detection but near enough to track the life of the house.

Using the Maglite he kept in his glove compartment, Billy tracked the drippings from his car toward his house until they came to a stop thirty yards out from the front porch. Here the spatter took on a roughly circular pattern, the elongated drops at the outer edges suggesting that the actor, having picked this place for a launching pad, had then gone into a hammer-throw spin to build up enough centrifugal force to hit his mark ninety feet away.

Billy sat in his father's rocker on the porch, imagining their stalker, their Fury, whipping that goddamn bag around and around himself before letting it fly, just sat there running and rerunning the film until he found himself suddenly flooded by a powerful halo of light, the search beam of the directed patrol car coming by for its three-thirty a.m. look-see.

When Billy raised his hand, they cut the beam and slowly rolled off, but not before the driver called out, "Here, I'm full," and then tossed something onto the lawn. Once the car was out of sight, he walked through the damp grass and found a crumpled paper bag, inside of which was a half-eaten doughnut.

When he finally entered the sleeping house, the silence was so absolute that it created its own sound, a high even hiss like static from a distant source. Walking into the kitchen, Billy decided, once he opened the freezer, that he didn't need a drink tonight—well, maybe just a pull—wiping his lips afterward, then heading for the stairs.

Soft-stepping into the bedroom, he jumped when he saw Carmen in silhouette sitting on a chair beneath the window, her hands flat on her thighs.

"What are you doing?" he whispered. "What's wrong?"

"I saw him," she said.

"Saw who?" Then: "You saw him? Where."

"In a dream."

MILTON RAMOS

The evening had started out OK enough, Anita and Ray bringing Sofia and a little friend to meet him at a diner in Staten Island so that he could hand over his care package of new clothes, DVDs, and favorite animals. His daughter seemed excited to see him, crawling into his lap to eat her low-fat mock sundae, but the whole time he feared that at the end of the meal she wouldn't ask him to take her home, not that he would have done it.

At first, Sofia's new friend had thrown him. The kid, Jen or Jan, a scrawny little thing with no more personality than a hamster, lived two houses down the street from Anita, and the girls, once introduced, had apparently become instant blood sisters and were, in fact, having a sleepover tonight. Sofia had never had a sleepover in her life, let alone a best friend. Their caged house in the Bronx had never been a home to other kids, even for a few hours after school, and this realization made him wince.

When the bill came, Ray nearly snatched it out of the waitress's hand. "No arguments," he said.

"Fine with me," Milton said.

Sofia slid off his lap and moved to the other side of the table.

"When we go home?" she said to Anita. "Can we call Marilys?" Then to her mouse of a friend: "She's my other mom."

"I *know*!" Jan or Jen said with delighted exasperation. "You tell me all the time!"

It was the third time Sofia had brought up Marilys since the waitress had taken their orders, and it would be the last.

"Listen to me," Milton said, his sleeve sliding through the dregs of his dessert as he reached across and took her wrist. "Marilys isn't your other mom. Marilys isn't anything. She doesn't love you, she doesn't even care about you, OK?"

"Hey, Milton," Ray said.

"Can you get that through your head?"

Sofia was too shocked to do anything other than stare at him in red-faced astonishment, but the other kid, after a breathless second, started to cry as if the world had come to an end.

Mortified, he got up from the table, walked out the door, and marched into the diner's parking lot. Weaving his way through an army of parked cars to an unlit spot, he seethed in the dark for a few minutes, then pulled out his phone and called Marilys's sister.

"This is Milton Ramos, you remember me?"

She said she did, but she didn't sound too happy about it.

"I'm going to call you back in a half hour. When I do, you're going give me the names, addresses, and phone numbers of everybody in your family living in New York."

Milton stepped deeper into the shadows as Ray came out of the diner, and a moment later pulled out of the lot with a carload of mutes.

"If I call back and for any reason you don't pick up? I'm coming back to your house. Do yourself a big favor and save me the trip."

AT ELEVEN THAT EVENING HE sat across the oilcloth-covered dinette table, glaring at Marilys and her so-called cousin Ottavio, a balding runt with amphibious eyes.

They were in Ottavio's one-bedroom apartment in Astoria, Milton's former fiancée and her kinsman anxiously looking everywhere but at him.

"They were going to kill him," Marilys said numbly, staring first at

Milton's hands with their paint-rimmed nails the color of blood, then at the greasy bat he had placed between them on the table.

"Who's they," he said. Then: "*You,*" making Ottavio jump. "Who's they."

"Some individuals I got steered to wrong."

"They were going to kill him," Marilys repeated, forcing herself to meet his eye.

He didn't know what angered him more, the fact that she had so heartlessly ravaged his life for money and dismissed his daughter's need for her like it was nothing or the fact that, despite his desire to slaughter her, she was treating him like a total stranger.

"You're living here now?"

"Just for a little bit," her voice down to a hush.

"You really her cousin?"

"Distant," Ottavio said, unconsciously glancing toward the sole bedroom.

"I want my money back," he said.

"It's gone," Marilys said, once again staring at his bunched hands.

Milton went off into his boiling head long enough for Marilys to add, "We can start paying you back a little each week."

We.

And the thought of having to see her, or him, every week or month to maybe collect twenty dollars here, thirty dollars there, the excuses, the no-shows, the constant, snake-headed presence of them in his life . . .

"I don't want your fucking money."

He took up his bat and slowly got to his feet, Marilys raising her eyes and then asking in a breathless monotone, "What are you going to do."

Nothing. Whether it was some perverse residual feelings he still had for her or just a failure of nerve on his part, he would do nothing.

He reached for his coat.

When it became apparent that she was in no physical danger this night, she added more softly, "Milton, I made a mistake. I'm sorry." And then a PPS as he turned toward the door: "How's Sofia?"

■ ■ ■

WHEN VICTOR ACOSTA FINALLY LEFT the Bryant Motor Lodge at four o'clock in the morning, there was a three-woman, two-man smackdown going on in a corner of the parking lot and Milton, who had already been waiting on him for two hours, maybe longer, understood that he had no choice right now but to remain in his car. Which, he figured, was probably just as well, since he'd been hitting the thermos steady and was temporarily too drunk to not fuck this up.

While Victor was busy stowing his gear in the Range Rover, Milton, in hopes of sobering up, put all four windows down and the AC on full blast and then rolled out of the lot directly onto the southbound New England Thruway, driving from the Bronx to Queens to Brooklyn. Thirty-five minutes later, freezing but still wasted, he pulled up across the street from Victor's apartment building on Palmetto Street in Bushwick and settled in, taking one last nip of the 'Treuse to chase the chill.

He didn't have to wait long, Victor's Range Rover slow-cruising right past him while he was still feeling around the floor after dropping the thermos cap. At first, it looked almost too easy, Victor parking the Ranger one block ahead, then walking back in his direction. But when Milton stepped from the car he immediately fell back against the driver's door, weakly waved his bat at the sky, then hinged forward to puke into the roadway as Victor, wide-berthing the mess, made it to his front door unmolested and disappeared into the building.

Just as well, just as well.

When his vomiting came down to a few ropy strands of saliva and his eyes began to lose their strained filminess, he slowly raised himself up and took a few raw breaths.

Just as well . . .

Then, unbidden: *I don't want your fucking money.*

Why did he say that to her? It was *his* fucking money. She might have scammed him out of it, but he had said *your money,* as if she had taken his sense of self along with the cash. Had date-raped his brain. And he had just walked out the door, don't mind the wet spot.

He slammed the bat into his own car door, was about to do it again, do anything to fend off his other memory of tonight—Sofia's shell-shocked silence, her stunned poke-hole of a face—when the magnified clack of a turned latch abruptly brought him back, Milton looking up to see Victor returning to the street with a small dog.

It was like he was asking for it.

Like he was insisting on it.

The dog, some kind of small pug, immediately squatted and pissed on the pavement, the streetlight too bright right there to risk anything. But when Victor turned the corner, Milton, keeping his distance and sticking tight to the shadowed building fronts, followed. They walked in a two-man stagger nearly the length of the street before Victor, absorbed in his dog's doings, came to a complete stop with his back to him.

The distance between them was next to nothing, but he was still too wasted to close in fast, and the broadcasted wheeze of his lungs, the sloppy scrape of his bat against the pavement had Victor fully turned around and reaching for something on his belt before Milton could make contact.

And then came the invisible jolt to his torso, a white wallop of phosphorescent pain emanating from somewhere between his left hip and armpit that lifted him like a backhand into the side of a building. But he was too drunk and too determined to let it distract him for long, and after shutting down what needed to be shut down, Milton once again began to close in. The dazzling burn in his side made it difficult for him to really bring the bat around like he wanted, and the lead-pipe impact of the heavy-booted side kick that Victor delivered to his thigh at some point didn't help, but when he was done, Carmen's brother lay curled at his feet, blood bubbling from his nostrils each time he took a breath, an ivory shard of bone that had broken through the sleeve of his shirt winking in the moonlight.

By the time Milton managed to circle around and slowly drive past the scene, a small crowd had already formed: dope fiends, joggers, dog walkers, and what have you, everyone on their cells, either calling out or making iPhone videos, the flashers of an approaching ambo lighting up the street like a midway. From the car, he spotted his bloodied bat lying up against the curb, but there was nothing he could do about that now.

It wasn't until an hour later, while standing outside the cage-gate of his house and woozily patting himself down for the keys, that he finally noticed the dual Taser darts still buried between his ribs, their attached wires dangling down his side like extruded nerves.

There were six people in the visitors' waiting room outside the OR of the Maimonides Medical Center: Billy, Carmen, Bobby Cardozo, a detective from the 8-0 Squad, and three of Victor and Richard's friends—gym rats, by the look of them—everyone waiting for Victor to come out from under the knife. The damage—a shattered left humerus, a fractured right collarbone, the left lung pierced by the lowest and smallest of his three broken ribs—was gruesome, the only good news being that the actor had stayed away from his head.

"Bobby, can you get prints off the bat?" Billy asked Cardozo, whose black eyes, goatee, and kettle-drum gut made him look like a villain in a silent movie.

"We're sending it to the lab this afternoon. So, hopefully."

Richard Kubin came into the waiting room with a vending-machine coffee, his anger making him look broader and taller than Billy had ever seen him.

"Your friend . . ." Cardozo began.

"My husband."

"He carried a Taser?"

"You would too if you saw where he worked."

"I'm just asking."

"Look, we know who did this," a short, red-bearded weight lifter said.

They didn't, but Billy did, as did Carmen, who, rather than brow-beating Cardozo and the entire hospital staff, was sitting silently on a tatty couch, staring at her hands.

"These little mutants from the Knickerbockers," the bearded guy said. "They sport-hunt us like we're their personal buffalo herd."

"What are you talking, gay bashers?" Cardozo reared back. "You sure? I pass your friend Mr. Acosta on the street, I'm not thinking gay."

"Meaning what," Richard snapped.

"I'm just saying," Cardozo retreated.

"Saying what."

Cardozo threw Billy a quick helpless look, then stepped away to regroup.

At first, Billy didn't understand why he was refraining from volunteering information about the stalker in order to help refocus the investigation. And then he did: simply put, he felt ashamed.

As far as he knew, they had all been victimized, but somehow over the course of the last few weeks, the innocence of the people living under his roof had gradually come to feel tainted, as if they all in some way deserved what had been happening to them. It was a classic reaction, he knew, the victim falling into self-loathing and self-blame, but now that the family contagion had reached out and claimed Victor, he felt as guilty as if he had swung the bat himself. And Carmen—sitting there so uncharacteristically withdrawn—had to be feeling something of the same.

"These kids . . ." Cardozo said, taking out his notepad.

"Kids?"

"These individuals. Any names? Street tags?"

"There's two," said another friend, wearing a Bucknell T-shirt. "I know them by sight."

"And the other one," the weight lifter said. "The moron with the hat."

"How about this," Cardozo said, stowing his pad. "Why don't you all come in, we'll set you up with some photo trays, then we can do a ride-by around the Knickerbockers, see if you can maybe make some IDs that way."

"You know what?" Bucknell said. "Forget it. We'll take care of it our-selves."

"How about you don't," Billy volunteered.

"Do you know how many assault complaints we filed with your pre-cinct this year?" Bucknell wheeling on Billy. "Do you know how many times I've been in that building? You people just don't give a shit."

"First I'm hearing about it," Cardozo said.

"Exactly."

Billy looked to Richard, hoping that he could help cool out his friends, and saw that the anger in his eyes was beginning to give way to exhaus-tion and sorrow. Reaching through the scrum, Billy took his arm and steered him to a second couch, directly opposite his wife.

"He'll be all right," Billy said.

"How do you know?"

"You know how I know? I'll tell you how I know." Billy hesitated, then: "The nurses' station. If Victor was in any kind of touch-and-go situa-tion, all those nurses over there, they'd of been throwing our crowd a lot of looks by now, trying to figure out how to handle us in case things turn out bad. And I'm just not picking up that vibe from them, so relax."

It was total bullshit, but it seemed to do the job, Richard faintly nod-ding, then sliding back deeper into the cushions. Nurses: Billy stole another peek at his wife, not six feet away from them but still so pulled into herself that he doubted she had heard one word of his nonsense.

"So when are the twins coming?" he asked Richard.

"What?"

"When are . . ."

"Ten days," he said, then, sitting up: "Jesus."

"I'll come over," Carmen said dully. Raising her eyes to him, she added, "Every day."

LEAVING HIS WIFE AND RICHARD behind, Billy went along with every-one else to the 8-0. Once there, unable to bear withholding information about the family nightmare any longer, he took Bobby Cardozo aside.

"I need to talk to you about something."

"About what, the gay thing?" Cardozo whispered. "I said the guy didn't look gay. What the fuck, it was a compliment."

Billy's cell rang—Carmen—Billy stepping away from Cardozo to take the call.

"Hey," her voice as flatlined as it was when he left her.

"What's going on?"

"He's out of surgery. It went OK."

"Good. Excellent."

"I'm sleeping here tonight," she said.

"OK."

"I need you to do me a favor. When you get home make up a bag with some clothes and my meds. You know which ones?"

"The Traz and the Cymbalta."

"The Traz and the Abilify."

"When did you go on Abilify?"

"Can you just do it for me? Give it to Millie, let her take your car, punch in the address on the GPS for her, and send her over."

"All right, I'll be home in about two hours."

"Thank you."

"Carmen, what's wrong?"

"What's wrong?"

"I mean besides. You've been in a trance for days."

The silence on the other end was so absolute that Billy thought she had hung up on him.

"Hello?"

"Just, not now, OK?" she said, then added, "I'm sorry," sounding like she meant it.

Billy found Cardozo pulling up mug shots on a desk monitor.

"This kid here?" he said, tapping a shave-headed teenager with a wandering eye. "He's a stone skull-cracker. Pipes, rebar, a golf club one time. Told me that he didn't like guns because they could get you in trouble."

"Just hold off on all that for a bit," Billy said, pulling up a chair. "You need to hear this."

It took close to half an hour for him to lay it all out: the accosting of his son, the abduction of his father, the red assault on his porch, the entire systematic and now expanded tormenting of his family.

"I don't see it," Cardozo said. "With all the three-legged meat eaters we got running around this precinct? I'm shopping local."

YASMEEN RANG HIM AT HOME as he was sorting through Carmen's side of the medicine chest.

"You called me yesterday?" she said.

"I did?" Then, remembering the world as it was before this morning: "Yeah, I did."

"What's going on?"

"I need to talk to you."

"Again?"

"Just . . ."

"Jesus, I talk to you more than my husband. What are you trying to do, get back with me?"

"Right."

"Just say, we'll get a room."

"Cut it out."

"With how stressed I am? No shit, let's go."

"I seriously need to talk to you."

"You don't even have to kiss me."

"Where are you going to be today," Billy said. "I'll come to you."

"REDMAN'S NUTS. *I* SHOT ERIC Cortez? Are you on drugs?"

They were sitting on a bench overlooking the playground in River-dale where Yasmeen's younger daughter, Simone, was trying to master double Dutch with some other girls.

"You know what? I don't like to talk about people, but since he's already talking about me? I think Redman's smoking his own product."

"What product," Billy shielding his eyes from the unfamiliar mid-day sun.

"Embalming fluid. Dipping his cigarettes in that shit. It's like eating your brain with an ice cream scoop."

"Redman doesn't smoke."

"Then maybe you're doing dip. What the fuck, *I* shot Eric Cortez?"

Billy sat with his arms draped along the top slat of the bench, listening to the kids behind the mesh fence shrieking as if they were about to be butchered.

"You're drinking like you want to kill yourself, Yasmeen, why is that."

"Because I already said to you I'm going through life changes and I'm depressed. I confessed to you about that. I confided in you about that. And now you're going to use it to accuse me of some bullshit like this? Who do you think you are?"

Billy slumped forward on the bench, his head in his hands. "Tell me again about your night sweats, how you wake up thinking you're all bloody, how someone's going to hurt your kids," his voice monotone with gloom.

Yasmeen sat there for a moment, her lower face flexing and bulging as if her mouth was stuffed with marbles.

"I tell you what," she said, getting to her feet, "here's what you do. You go to your good buddy in Brooklyn Narcotics and share your, your findings with him, you tell him all about me fucking up the Del Pino investigation, you tell him all about my nightmares and my drinking, you tell him how Cortez being brain-shot just about makes me wet, and then you let him come for me, how's that."

Yasmeen went to the fence, collected her protesting daughter, then walked past him on her way out of the park. "You're like some stranger to me, you know that?"

And then she was gone, Billy sitting there, thinking, So are you. Thinking, So are you all.

AFTER A BUSTED FOUR-HOUR SLEEP and a tasteless dinner Billy found himself watching a football game on NFL Classics, his sons in full pee-wee league gear, cleats to helmets, seated on either side of him. They were all strung out, Billy over everything and the kids just because they had—no, they were—exquisite antennae when it came to in-house agitation.

The game, from 2012, was a great New York Giants come-from-behind victory, 41–34 over Tampa Bay, but when watching these old games, Billy never told his boys the final score in advance; it would be like telling a joke punch line first. Tonight, unfortunately, that meant subjecting them to three Eli Manning second-quarter interceptions with no hope in sight; by the second pick, Carlos began to cry, which got Declan, also on the verge of tears, throwing a punch and hurting his hand on his younger brother's helmet, and before Billy could intervene they were both wailing like paid mourners while blindly trading shots across the bow of his gut.

"What are you hitting him for?" he squawked at Declan. Then, turning to Carlos: "What you crying for?"

Neither kid had the words or the self-control to stop belting the other, which resulted in him pushing them off to the far sides of the couch.

"Everybody stop hitting and crying, all right? Just, please, OK?"

Pausing the game, he waited for them to subside. He knew he should turn the TV off altogether before the third interception sent them completely over the edge, but he also wanted them to hang in there, so that they could experience the thrill of the fourth-quarter comeback. So they all could.

"You guys want to keep watching or do you want to go play?"

"Watch," Declan wept.

"Watch," Carlos said, aping his brother's tragic delivery.

"You sure?"

"Yes."

"You have that new game upstairs you could play."

"Watch," Dec said in a shuddery hush.

"Watch."

"OK, watch," reaching for the remote. Then: "You know what? Let's see it tomorrow instead."

No one protested.

"Tomorrow will be better."

And it would be, Billy intending to fast-forward the DVR'ed version directly to the fourth quarter for them, all joy and no pain.

JOHN MACCORMACK CALLED AN HOUR later as Billy was coming out of the kids' bedroom after having told them their favorite story, about the time when, as a rookie, he had chased down and subdued a riderless police horse in Times Square—leaving out, as he always did, the most heroic part of the adventure, the fact that he was off-his-ass drunk at the time, otherwise he'd have never been so idiotic as to bolt from his window seat at the bar and start running like a maniac down Broadway.

"Just thought you might want to know," MacCormack said, "Eric Cortez went out of the picture."

"What happened?"

"Pulmonary infection. The fucking guy survives being left outdoors overnight, brain-shot in January weather, then goes and gets pneumonia in a warm hospital three months later."

"So now it's a homicide?"

"So now it's a homicide," MacCormack said. "Just grabbing at straws here, you sure you don't have anything for me?"

"Wish I did," Billy said, surprised by a surge of protectiveness toward Yasmeen.

"All right then."

"Let me ask you, what day was he found?"

"Cortez? The fifth, why?"

"January fifth?"

"Yeah, why?"

"No reason," Billy said. "Thanks for the update."

As soon as he got off the phone with MacCormack he began putting a call through to Yasmeen, then hung up and called her husband instead, Dennis blowing up at him halfway through "Hello."

"What the hell did you say to her today? She came home half out of her mind."

"What did she say I said?"

"She didn't, but what the fuck, Billy, she's just starting to do good again."

"It was nothing, just some bullshit I was thinking I wanted to talk to somebody about, but I shouldn't have picked her. Can you apologize for me?"

"Apologize yourself."

"No, you're right, you're right, I'll call her. Everything OK otherwise?"

"Same ol'," Dennis sounding calmer.

"So, the reason I called you, she said you took your family to Florida?"

"Yeah, Boynton Beach, to spend New Year's with my parents. And people say I don't know how to party, can you imagine that?"

"I hear you . . . How long were you down there?"

"From like the thirtieth to the eighth. Why?"

"I was thinking of taking the kids, they've never been."

The thirtieth to the eighth, Billy thinking, Good news for her. Thinking, Fucking Redman. And back to thinking: All Pavlicek, all the time.

HE HAD THE OPTION OF taking the night off, but he didn't want to be alone, didn't want to think about Pavlicek, Victor, the stalker, his father, or even his wife, and so, with Millie sleeping over and the slapdash 24/7 patrols at least going through the motions, he drove into the city at midnight, hoping, for a change, that the general malice out there would keep him busy until the morning.

But in the way of these things, the night, as of three in the morning, was another dud—a home invasion on West Forty-sixth Street in which the home invader got his ass beat by the home owner, and a brawl at Complications, a pole-dance club on the West Side Highway where a few visiting Memphis Grizzlies had been throwing back Dom and stuffing hundreds, although none of them were involved in the fight.

The Wheel called as he was driving back across Twenty-third Street to the office.

"We got a stabbing homicide in the Three-five."

"Indoors or out."

"In. Fort Washington and One ninety-first."

"Fort Washington and One ninety-first?" Billy straightened up. "What address."

"I just said."

"The building number, for Christ's sake."

BY THE TIME HE SHOWED up at Esteban Appleyard's apartment, it was a party: CSU, patrol, Stupak, Butter, and Jimmy Whelan himself, his retired gold shield hanging by a bead chain over a pullover sweatshirt. Jimmy had no business being there, but Billy wasn't going to say anything, and the others bought his expired tin at first sight even though he was wearing flip-flops.

The small dining table in the living room was a tabloid tableau: two abandoned hands of cards, a knocked-over bottle of Tattoo Spiced Rum, three used glasses, and an ashtray bearing the remains of five Kool filter tips and a hollowed-out cigar wrapper that still held shreds of skunk.

The body, belly-down on the carpet in a pool of not quite dried blood, was crammed into a corner of the room as if Appleyard had tried to escape his killers by crawling through the wall. There were multiple stab wounds to his back and buttocks. Rigor had locked his mouth into a savagely wide grin.

As the two CSU techs turned him over, they all saw that he was still holding his last hand, five cards clutched tight in a frozen grip beneath his chin.

"What's he got?" Billy asked.

One of the techs carefully prized the arm away from the body. "Aces and eights. Just like Wild Bill."

"Bullshit," Whelan said.

"Take a look."

Whelan stooped over the body and squinted at the hand.

"A pair of threes," he announced. "You assholes."

"Dead man's hand, baby," the tech laughed.

"Who's Wild Bill?" Stupak said.

Moments later, as the techs started to inventory the frontal devastation, a small intact balloon of intestine began to peep shyly out of a puncture wound above Appleyard's navel, then slowly began to expand, those in the know quickly covering their noses and mouths before it could burst.

Wanting to avoid the explosion of stench, Billy retreated into the bedroom, which, like the rest of the small four-room apartment, had been utterly ransacked—plants torn out of their pots, underwear, shirts, and sweaters hanging from open dresser drawers, along with VHS porn tapes and an upended shoe box that had been filled with small serrated-edged snapshots from Appleyard's childhood in Puerto Rico.

Whelan wandered in and picked up a ripped-out peace lily, the soil that was still clinging to its roots drizzling onto the unmade bed.

"How much money you think he could've hid in this pot, thirteen dollars?"

"You sure this was about the lottery?" Billy asked.

"Of course it was. Fuckin' guy. I told him a thousand times, you heard me yourself."

Whelan picked up one of the old photos fantailed around the shoe box, a black and white of the victim as a little kid standing with his mother by a seawall.

"I swear, when God said he was passing out brains, Appleyard heard 'trains,' didn't want any, and hid under a table."

"Any thoughts on the actors?"

"Yeah," Whelan said, "but not here."

When they left the apartment, the hallway was filled with tenants.

"He's dead?" a neighbor asked Whelan.

"You bet."

"See, I told him," another one said.

Whelan clapped his hands once. "Everybody, just go back home."

"This *is* my home."

"Inside."

"You're not the boss of me."

"Got February's rent together yet, Alvin? How about March?"

"Jimmy, you disrespect me like that?"

"Whoever owes me two months' rent. Inside."

■ ■ ■

OUT ON THE STREET, THEY slipped into Whelan's cigarette-smelling Elantra.

"There's these shitheads, the Alvarez brothers, in 2015 over there," pointing to another prewar across the street, also with a deep H-block entrance. "Out of the blue they've been buddying him up all this last week like a lost cousin."

"Apartment?" Billy writing.

"Fifth floor's all I know. The youngest brother, Marcus, just got back from upstate, Tomas I once caught trying to jimmy a storage lock in my building with a gravity knife."

"So prints are on file."

"You could say that."

"Anybody else?"

"Around here?" Shrugging as he reached for the door handle. "Start with them."

Stepping from the Elantra back out onto the street, Billy wandered to the rear of the car, paused to light a cigarette, then saw the bullet holes in the trunk, moonlight brightening their jagged edges, some curling in, some curling out.

"Come here," he said.

Whelan came around, regarded the constellation of punctures, then lit a cigarette himself.

"Can you pop it, please?"

"You're kidding me."

"Jimmy."

"You think there's something in there?"

Billy stared at him.

"If you want to be a prick about it, get a warrant."

"Sweetpea wasn't even yours."

"I don't know what you're talking about."

"You did it for Redman?"

"I don't know what you're talking about." Then, again, before Billy could say anything more, "I don't know what you're talking about."

■ ■ ■

DEAF TO THE OCCASIONAL HORNS and blind to the oncoming head-
lights, Billy took a brief walk down the center of Fort Washington Avenue, his hands clasped on top of his head.

Yasmeen was in Florida when Eric Cortez was shot. Pavlicek was at
the hospital with his son when Bannion died all over Penn Station. Sweetpea ended his days in the boot of Whelan's car. He himself was at a crime
scene in Manhattan when Curtis Taft was being hog-tied in the Bronx.

Redman had been telling the truth after all, but only the partial truth.
They were all in on it, but no one was anywhere near the scene when
their own demons had gone out of the picture.

They had swapped Whites.

Two hours later, as he and Stupak were escorting Tomas and Marcus Alvarez out of their apartment house for questioning, the uncuffed
brothers shouting in each other's face not to say shit, Billy saw that Whelan
had made no effort to move his car from in front of the building, their
entire convoy having to walk past it in order to get to the waiting van.

MILTON RAMOS

The call from Anita came in as he was sitting on the side of his bed, rewrapping the Ace bandage on his empurpled thigh, Victor's boot print there still so clearly defined on his flesh that he could have accurately ordered him a pair of shoes.

"Milton, your daughter left three messages on your phone. Why aren't you calling her back?"

"I've been drowning in work," he said, reaching for the Chartreuse on his night table. "Is she OK?"

"Other than you not calling her, she's fine."

Milton threw back a shot, got up, and began looking for his car keys. "Is she mad at me for last night?"

"She hasn't said anything."

Dropping to the floor, he felt around beneath the bed. "I have to apologize for my behavior. I was upset."

"It's OK. I just figured with all the terrible stress you have on you right now."

He stopped moving. "What do you mean."

"That gang contract."

"Contract . . ." Crouching there confused, then remembering his story, rising to his knees. "I have to ask you again. Sofia, do you still want her?"

"Do I want her?" Anita sounded unsure of his meaning. "Sure, she's a delight."

"Good," returning to his search.

"Just give me an idea of when you'll be taking her back."

"It's almost over," he said, spotting the car keys in one of his tossed-off shoes.

"I just don't understand why you don't call her."

He was pretty sure he could drive.

THE CEMETERY WAS ONE OF those unending necropoli that lined the ride into the city from JFK, a crowded mouthful of gray teeth, unkempt and askew. But up close, say, if you found yourself kneeling before a loved one or two or three, it wasn't that bad. And that's where he found himself, in a catcher's squat before the stones of his mother and two brothers, desperate to get his bearings.

He was no great master planner of revenge, no fiendish calculator; he was nothing more than an increasingly violent and out-of-control wreck whose hands shook all the time now from drinking, nothing more than a raging borderline wet-brain, so constantly tired these days that he could barely get in or out of bed. And assuming they had recovered his bat from the scene, it would only be a matter of days before they matched his prints.

In high school, his English teacher didn't think anyone in class could get through *Moby-Dick* without tossing the book out a window, so she had brought in a Betamax tape of the movie, drawn the blinds, and played it on a roll-down screen. Most of the students were bored stupid by the black-and-white film, but not him. He had been riveted by the metal-eyed captain, his blazing doggedness, and in the end, when he went down into the sea strapped to the beast that he had lived to kill, it had struck Milton as the perfect outcome.

And that's how it should end between him and Carmen.

Sofia was with the right people, and this patch of earth, right here among his brothers and his mother, looked so inviting. He was so tired, all the time now. He just had to move fast before he was unable to move at all.

16

When Billy returned to the funeral home the next morning, Redman and his wife, Nola, were sitting on facing folding chairs across the aisle from each other in the darkened chapel, both staring at the carpet while Rafer flew around the room waving a cosmetic stippling brush in his hand.

"It's ten in the morning," Redman said. "I was expecting you at dawn."

Nola stood up and left.

Billy waited while Redman got to his feet, took the brush back from his son, then lifted him in his arms.

"If I could have, I would have, you better believe that," he finally said. "Fact of the matter is, I can carry a two-hundred-and-fifty-pound body across this room from the prep table to the casket, no problem, but if I go more than a block to buy a beer? I need a walker. End of the day? All I could do was disappear him."

"Could you put Rafer down, please?"

Redman gave him a look as if Billy were about to slap on cuffs.

"I can't talk about this with the kid in your arms," Billy said.

Bending stiffly from the waist, Redman complied, Rafer taking off for his grandfather's cubicle, where the old man was once again playing poker on his computer.

"What do you mean, disappear him," Billy said. "Disappear him how."

"He left here in a casket. Underneath someone else."

"Underneath who."

"That girl you had me bury."

"You did that to her?"

"I did it to him."

All he needed was an exhumation order, find out if Martha Timberwolf had any company beneath her stone. And when the forensics came back on Whelan's trunk, they were bound to find something.

"You knew what Whelan was up to before he did it?"

"I got up one morning, went out back for a smoke, and there's Sweetpea Harris laying in the yard. And that's all I'm saying about it."

"Did you ask him to do it?"

"I said that's all I'm saying about it."

"How about the others."

"Which others."

"I want to know who did who."

"Why."

"*Why?*"

Redman opened a box of cheap hand fans advertising the funeral parlor, then began depositing them on chair seats.

"I'm just curious," Billy said. "Did you embalm him?"

"Either that or let him stink up the joint."

"Jesus Christ, Redman, where's your heart?"

"Where's yours. You pursue this, you'll be taking people away from their kids, so where's yours," he said, walking off before Billy could walk out.

AT MAIMONIDES, VICTOR WAS ASLEEP in his bed, Richard lying next to him, wide-eyed but withdrawn. On a sofa at the opposite end of the room, Carmen was also asleep, hands curled under her chin, her face pressed so deeply into a cushion that he had to resist moving her head back.

Billy stood against a wall, dutifully stared at the three of them until he thought he would go crazy.

Who did who . . .

Stepping out into the hallway, he called Elvis Perez.

"Are you in?" he asked.

"For about an hour or so. What's up?"

"Do you still have the tapes from Penn Station?"

"Of course."

"I never took a look at the one under the information boards."

"That's because I told you it's a waste of time."

"I'm leaving now."

"Really, if I thought . . ."

"I'm leaving now."

"WHERE'S WALDO, RIGHT?" PEREZ SAID, standing over Billy's shoulder as they viewed the rescued tape of the scene beneath the LIRR track information board. "See what I'm saying?"

Billy had to agree: the scrum of plastic-derby-wearing revelers was so tight under the board that when he was finally able to ID his vic, Bannion was already leaving bloody shoeprints on his way to the subway, dead man jogging.

"Where's Waldo in hell," Elvis said.

When Perez left with his partner on a witness interview run, Billy remained at his desk and reran the tape. Again, nothing, just Bannion popping out of the periphery and taking off. There were others coming and going under the board besides Bannion: staggerers, stragglers, latecomers to the party, and those who just wandered away as if having lost interest in getting home. But not one of these wanderers, all leaving the crowd at the same time or just after Bannion made his stumbling dash to nowhere, exhibited any kind of suspect body language, no one running or even walking off at anything more than a dawdling pace, no one even glancing back at the crowd they had just left.

Most of the people whose faces were turned to the camera and could be identified had already been interviewed by Midtown South, including all of Bannion's friends that night. Teams of detectives had either traveled out to Long Island or caught the potential witnesses at their workstations in Manhattan, not one of these sit-downs yielding a single helpful lead.

Billy reran the tape. Then ran it again, this time in slow motion. On his sixth viewing someone caught his eye—one of the commuters, exiting the throng a moment before, not after, Bannion, which made sense given that it must have taken the stupefied vic a moment or two before he realized what had already happened to him.

The figure, its back to the camera as it briefly lingered at the bottom of the frame before leaving the scene altogether, looked like nothing so much as a small, upright bear.

"THEY FINALLY SALVAGED THE TAPE," Billy said.

"What tape?" Yasmeen asked from behind her desk in the university security office.

"From Penn Station."

"I thought they had that tape."

"The other one."

"What other one."

Tired of the dance, Billy showed her the printout of the shaggy form walking away from the crime scene before anyone there knew it was a crime scene.

Yasmeen looked at it, then—unconsciously, Billy assumed—glanced at her Tibetan coat draped over an empty chair.

"It was either you or Janis Joplin coming out of that crowd."

"Do you know how many coats like this . . ."

"Don't jerk me around," he said wearily. "Not now, all right?"

She was a long time in responding.

"You have those two little boys," she finally said. "Could you imagine me ever coming up to you like this?"

"I didn't kill anybody, Yasmeen."

"The hell you didn't. And what did we do? Closed ranks and protected your ass."

"It was a justified shoot. I didn't need you to."

"Oh yes you did, cokey boy."

One of the other retired detectives working at the school came into the office and dropped a folder on her blotter, Yasmeen getting to work on it before he even left.

Billy sat there for a while studying the photographs push-pinned into her wall: campus trespassers, a trashed dorm lounge, the facades of problematic East and West Village bars.

"Yasmeen, the story's going to come out one way or another."

"Well, one good story deserves another," she said, flicking the side of her nose.

Billy got up to leave.

"You know, Dennis, he's a good guy, a good dad, I'll give him that . . ."

Billy stood there, waiting for the punch line.

"But I could've been with you all these years, you know? I could have been your wife, Dominique and Simone could have been your daughters."

"I'll give you a week to get a lawyer," he heard himself say.

"You'd do that for me?" she said sweetly, Billy almost positive she was being sarcastic.

"SO YOU SAY," CARMEN SAID, looking down at the Penn Station printouts spread out on the kitchen table before her.

"So I know," Billy looking at her. "And you know too."

Carmen shifted her gaze from the table to the window. "Do you remember when I couldn't get out of bed for close to three months? What did she do for us."

"This has nothing to do with that."

"No? What's it have to do with?"

"Do I even have to answer that?"

Resting her brow in the heel of her palm, Carmen looked as if she'd rather be anywhere else than in this room with this man right now.

"Do I even have to answer that?" Billy pleaded.

"Why did you marry me," she said.

"Why did I what?"

"What did you see in me."

"I don't know. I saw you. Where are we going with this?"

Carmen swept the printouts to the floor. "Jesus, Billy," her voice clotted with tears, "sometimes people just need to be forgiven."

More cryptic and distance-making shit from his most intimate of intimates, Billy watching her climb the stairs to the bedroom and feeling more isolated on this than ever before.

Three bodies, and so far everyone was either defying him, threatening him, or tossing off pronouncements fit for a Sphinx. Everyone acting like they had his number.

Billy called first Redman, then Whelan, got the machine for both and left the same message: one week to lawyer up. He started to dial Pavlicek's number, then hung up in mid-dial. This one had to be face-to-face.

NOT REALLY THINKING ABOUT WHAT he would see when he walked into the private suite at the Westchester Medical Center in Valhalla, Billy took one look at the patient, then turned and retreated, hoping no one inside had noticed. Out in the hallway, he caught his breath and then reentered, having no choice but to accept that the sallow-skinned, seemingly inert stick figure lying in the bed, with its distant, unresisting eyes, was, still was, John Junior, only six months ago a bear of a young man who'd often had to sidle through doorways.

Speechless, he floated across the room and stood in a corner.

"You know, I was trying to describe to Johnnie here," Pavlicek said, his eyes never leaving his son's face, "what it was like for us back in the nineties, the bust-ass blocks, the gangs, the dope lines going right past the precinct house, that whole rodeo."

He was seated on the side of the bed, one hand on the kid's thigh, the other on his forehead, as if he was afraid his son would start to levitate.

"John," Billy whispered, "I had no idea."

"I'll never forget the day I bought my first building on Faile Street, five thousand dollars, the old guy running down the street with the check in his hand, 'You'll never make a dime!' But then the fun began, remember? All those all-nighters, me, you, Whelan, Redman, Charlie Torreano, God rest his soul . . . Stripping, sanding, uncovering that beautiful wood, the moldings, the sconces, then that morning light coming in . . ."

Billy stepped to the bed and lightly touched Junior's hand, the kid turning his head in response but too deep in his medicated drift to raise his eyes.

"Billy, I swear to you, twenty-six buildings later and nothing ever felt as good to me as rehabbing that first dump on Faile. Well, what the hell, I made my dent."

There was no way Billy could bring up what he had come to say, not here and not now.

Pavlicek let him get halfway to the door. "Redman told me that you couldn't drop the bomb on him this morning until he put his kid down," looking at Billy for the first time since he came into the room. "So I can imagine what a bitch this must be for you right now."

"That all can wait," he said.

"For what, Junior to die? You're going to make this into a death watch before you turn me in?"

"What I meant . . ."

"I know what you meant," Pavlicek cut him off. "Just let it happen."

Billy took a seat on the edge of the narrow visitor's bed wedged under the far window, dress shirts and sweaters spilling out of a Gladstone bag on the blanket.

"John, what do I do."

He had always looked up to Pavlicek for guidance; they all did.

"It looks like you're doing it."

"How can you make me carry this?"

"In all honesty? You weren't exactly on my mind at the time," Pavlicek said. "Besides, you did it to yourself. No one told you to go fucking investigate."

"You shot Cortez?"

"Do you need me to say it?"

"I do."

"I shot Cortez. I screwed it up, but that there was definitely me."

"I can't sit on three bodies," Billy said. "I can't live with it."

"Then don't."

"Are you serious?"

"Tell me you're not asking for my permission."

But he was, he had been asking for permission all along from everyone: from Carmen, from his father, from Redman and Whelan and Yasmeen, and having finally received it from Pavlicek, no less, he felt the tension go out of his body like air from a slashed tire.

"After Taft in the apartment," Pavlicek said, "you said to me, 'This is how you honor your son?'"

"John, in all fairness . . ."

"You think I don't understand what I did? You think I don't know there's a price to pay? So let me pay it."

"All right," Billy said after a while. "All right."

"Let me be done with it."

"All right," Billy said yet again. Then: "I gave the others a week to lawyer up."

"A week's fine."

John Junior whispered something indecipherable to Billy's ears but not to his father's, Pavlicek slipping a straw through the spout of a water bottle, then raising his son's head just enough for him to take a few sips without drowning. Junior then said something else Billy couldn't understand but that made his father nod in agreement.

The room descended into silence, Billy watching Pavlicek alternately minister to his son and just hang at his side, the ticking of an unseen clock underscoring the stillness.

"Yasmeen's pulling the coke card," Billy finally said. "She said she'd use my history."

"She's full of shit," Pavlicek said without looking at him.

Billy got up, walked over to the bed, then bent down to kiss John Junior's forehead. "I should go."

"What the hell," Pavlicek said. "I made my dent."

MILTON RAMOS

He had always been somewhat indifferent about what he wore to work. Usually it was one of the three sport jackets he had bought from Men's Wearhouse the week he'd been promoted to detective, a white or blue dress shirt, pleated chinos or gabardines, and, always, the black Nike lace-up boots—good for running if the need arose and sober-looking enough to pass inspection. But tonight he was going for the suit, charcoal wool and last worn when he had spoken to Sofia's third-grade class on career day—what a clown show that was—a nice blue knit tie, and a pink broadcloth button-down from his one trip to Brooks Brothers. But he would no sooner swap out the Nikes for any other footwear than he would exchange his Glock for a slingshot.

Just past midnight, after finally nailing the Windsor knot he'd been striving for, he threaded his holster through his belt, slipped his flask into his ankle holster, dropped a mini-bottle of Scope into his inside jacket pocket, and left the house.

Forty-five minutes later, he walked into the Fifteenth Precinct, headed for the desk, and presented his ID to the duty sergeant.

"It's been a while," he said. "Where's the Night Watch office again?"

17

Tonight's hell mouth seemed to be situated in Union Square, three runs to that area in less than five hours. The first, at one a.m., on Irving Place, involved the discovery of a middle-aged lawyer who had been found nude, bound, and asphyxiated facedown in his own bed, the word ABUSE with either an R or a D at the end—a mystery for the day tour—carved into his back with a scissor blade. The second run, coming in at three, was in response to the theft of a two-hundred-pound bluefin tuna worth seven thousand dollars from the kitchen of a sushi restaurant on Park Avenue South. And the third and hopefully last run of the night, coming in at four-thirty, was a nonfatal double knifing in the park proper, directly beneath the statue of Gandhi, the actor on that one a seventy-five-year-old panhandler, the victims two drunken tourists from Munich who thought it would be a real howl to hand the old piss-bum a pre-euro ten-mark German note instead of a few American dollars.

"You should have seen them, laughing at me like they was giving a cell phone to a monkey," Terence Burns said over a five a.m. Coke in the Sixth Squad interview room a few blocks from the scene. Bug-eyed and sporting a steel-colored goatee, he was nearly doubled over with arthritis but somehow still agile as a cat. "Like I wasn't gonna know what a motherfuckin' deutsche mark looks like. Hell, I seen plenty, I had plenty,

and I spent plenty when I was over there with the Fortieth Tank back in
sixty-one."

"You were there?" Billy both liking the guy and needing the distrac-
tion.

"Didn't I just say that? Had a good time too for most of it," Burns
said. "The whores used to call us hamburgers, the white boys, cheese-
burgers. They'd see a bunch of us coming to the club, they'd start throwing out all the shitkickers, 'No cheeseburger! Hamburger only!'"

"For real?"

"Oh I'm always for real."

"Another Coke?"

"Fanta if you got it," Burns said. "Grape or orange."

Billy went out of the room to hit the vending machine and returned
with a Mountain Dew.

"So what else was going on back then?" he asked.

"What else? You don't know your history? You don't know about
Checkpoint Charlie?"

"I heard of it."

"You don't know nothing about the tank standoff with the Russians?
I was a machine gunner, they had me set up outside the hatch of a M-48
staring right into the cannon of a T-55 for sixteen motherfuckin' hours,
couldn't have been more than seventy-five yards away. I swear, as scared
as I was? If I hadn't been so drunk, we'd of had World War Three right
then and there."

RETURNING TO THE PARK TO pick up a copy of the Crime Scene Unit
report, Billy noticed that the small trucks from upstate and New Jersey
had begun to arrive for the Union Square Greenmarket, the vaguely hip-
pieish farmers dragging out their folding tables and canopies in the predawn dark. He also saw one of his supplementals, Milton Ramos from
Dennis Doyle's squad in the 4-6, standing on the edge of the scene watching the techs stow their gear.

Billy had been trying to keep his distance from the guy all tour; like
a number of one-offs, there was something not quite right about him.

He seemed to be both on edge and spacey, plus Billy was pretty sure that he'd been slipping off fairly steadily to drink. Not that Ramos would have been the first detective on Night Watch to sweeten the long hours and boredom that way; Feeley's eyes often looked like two cherries floating in buttermilk, but that was Feeley.

The CSUs, both female, were hunched over the hood of their van now, sorting through their report forms.

"So how was the great tuna robbery," Billy asked Ramos. "Anything fishy about it?"

"I think it was an inside job," Ramos said flatly.

He was short and thick but too powerfully built to be called fat, his slitted features hidden beneath thick brows and a permanently impassive expression. Billy had him pegged as a complete loner, on the job and off, the type of uncommunicative humorless near blank that made everyone in his home squad uncomfortable.

"You know," Ramos said, looking around the park, "I used to work midnights my first two years, but now? I don't know if I could handle it anymore. How does your wife put up with it?"

"She's a nurse," Billy said, "she can put up with anything short of me having a second family."

"Oh yeah? What kind of nurse?"

"ER, but over the years she's done it all."

"Done it all, seen it all . . . Easygoing?"

Billy gave him a look. "Philosophical about things," he lied.

"Philosophical." Ramos nodded, still looking away. "Shit happens."

"Something like that."

Billy saw Stupak, coming from the Irving Place homicide, enter the park and head toward the tents and tables, waiting for someone to open up.

He raised his cell to call her.

"She always want to be a nurse?" Ramos asked.

"What?"

"Your wife."

"What is this, an interview?"

"No, I'm sorry, I just . . . My wife? She passed seven years ago."

"I'm sorry to hear that," Billy said, killing the call.

"Yeah. Hit-and-run."

"I'm sorry."

"We have a daughter, she's eight," he said, then: "If the mother's dead and you say 'we,' is it 'We *have* a daughter' or 'We *had* a daughter'?"

The guy was definitely sauced, but he was talking about losing his wife.

"Grammar wasn't my strong suit," Billy said.

"You have kids?"

"Two boys."

"Two boys, double the trouble."

Billy impatiently checked the time, six-fifteen in the a.m., the crime scene techs still hunched over the hood working up their reports.

"Back when we were kids?" Ramos moved closer to him. "Me and my brother, we were the terror of the neighborhood."

"Oh yeah?" Billy tried to call Stupak again. "What neighborhood was that?"

Ramos either didn't hear him or didn't want to answer.

"What are you doing," Billy asked Stupak.

"Where are you?"

"By the Gandhi statue waiting on CSU. Bring me a coffee, cream and sugar, and a buttered roll."

"You know," Ramos plowed on, "before she died, my wife was an X-ray technician at Beth Abraham for five years, so I know a little about nurses. And, the little I know is that they're not like cops, you know what I'm saying? You don't become a nurse because your mother and grandmother were nurses, so forgive me for getting personal and you can just tell me to mind my own business, but I'm curious, why do you think your wife became a nurse?"

"Now I'm supposed to say, 'Because she likes to help people'?"

"Not at all, I was just wondering if there was any one moment where she, you know, like an event or something . . ."

Billy gave him another long look.

"Like with me," Ramos said quickly, "I never thought I was going to be a cop, I was a troubled kid, a fighter. But when I was seventeen, I lost my mother and two brothers all like within a month's time, and I needed a place to hide."

"What do you mean, hide."

"Not hide, more like I needed a structure, you know, be part of something that would give me all the dos and don'ts, keep me from going over to the dark side. It took a few years, but here I am."

"Here you are," Billy said, not liking this guy at all, him and his copious tragedies.

One of the techs finally came over, peeled off a copy of the report for Billy, then headed off to the greenmarket with her partner.

"Beautiful, right?" Ramos said, as the sun began to paint the tops of the ancient office buildings at the western edge of the square.

Billy loathed sunrises; he knew them as cruel mirages, each one a false promise that a tour had come to its end when, in fact, depending on the time of year, there were anywhere from one to three hours left for that phone to ring with a fresh disaster. Sunrises, like Ramos here, made him tense.

They made him feel fucked with.

"Listen to me," Billy said abruptly. "You've had liquor on your breath all night."

Frowning, Ramos looked away.

"I'm not going to write you up, but I don't ever want to see you on my tour again. In fact, you can take off right now, I'll sign you out when I get back to the office."

At first, Ramos didn't respond, his frown deepening into a scowl, but then he began nodding his head as if having come to some kind of decision.

"I apologize," he said quietly, turning back to Billy and handing over the keys to the squad sedan, "and I appreciate the courtesy."

Ramos walked off toward the Fourteenth Street subway entrance without another word, Billy watching him all the way, wondering if he had been too hard on the guy.

Then, tired of waiting for Stupak to deliver his breakfast, he wandered over to the market himself, where he discovered that almost all the cops involved in the three wee-hour local felonies were now cruising the food stalls as intensely as if they were at a gun show.

WALKING INTO THE HOUSE WITH two biodegradable bags filled with agave-sweetened muffins, crullers, and doughnut holes, it seemed to Billy that the only one up and about was the six-year-old, Carlos sitting in the dining room and eating the breakfast he had made for himself: a teacup of orange juice and an unthawed Eggo.

"Where's your mother?" Billy asked, dropping the waffle into the toaster. "Is she still sleeping?"

"I don't know."

"Where's your brother?"

"At Theo's house. He slept there on a sleepover."

Through the kitchen window Billy saw his father sitting on a lawn chair beneath one of the TARU cameras in the backyard, the old guy, as usual, reading the *New York Times*.

"How's Grandpa today?"

"I don't know," Carlos said, then: "A teacher in my school got quit."

"What do you mean, got quit?"

"He's not a teacher anymore."

"Oh yeah? What teacher."

"Mr. Lazar."

"Mr. Lazar quit? Or got fired?"

"I don't know."

"Why?" He couldn't imagine that the school would can him for being gay.

"He hurt some guy," Carlos said.

"What do you mean, hurt. Hurt what guy?" Billy trying to remember the name of Lazar's potential blackmailer.

"He got took away," Carlos said.

"Lazar?"

"Mr. Lazar."

"Who took him away?"

"The police guys at release time. I'm going to the basement. Dec said there's a mouse."

Billy went up to his bedroom, quietly crept past his wife, her flank beneath the sheets swelling and dipping like a chain of dunes, and stowed his weapon and handcuffs in the closet. Then, intending to call the Yonkers PD to find out about Lazar, he went back down to the kitchen.

A few minutes later, while he was still on hold with the Second Precinct Detective Squad, the doorbell began to chime. Assuming the callers were either evangelists or Con Ed, and worried that a second round of chimes would wake Carmen, he stepped briskly into the hallway and swung the door wide to see Milton Ramos standing on his doorstep, stone-faced and thick as a stump, his razored eyes staring past Billy and into the house as if he weren't even there.

Thinking that he was probably stuporously drunk by now and angry about having been booted from Night Watch three hours earlier, Billy was about to try to talk him down when Ramos reached behind his back—Billy vaguely thinking for some kind of letter of complaint—and came out with a Glock.

"Where is she," Ramos said.

Billy took a step outside the house, then made a big show of holding up his hands for the TARU cameras, though he had no idea whether anyone was even monitoring them.

"Where is she," Ramos repeated, muzzle-shoving Billy back inside as far as the living room while efficiently patting him down with his free hand even though they were both still in motion.

So, not stuporously drunk.

"Ramos." He couldn't remember his first name. "What are you doing?"

"Where is she."

This time Billy heard the question. "Where's who."

"Your wife."

"My wife?"

"Your wife, your wife, your wife," he said, as if fed up with a block-head.

"Hang on, hang on, I'm the one who gave you grief."

Done with the basement, Carlos wandered into the room and without looking at either Ramos or his father, took a seat on the couch and picked up the remote.

"Hey, buddy, not now," Billy said, his voice starting to float. "Go outside."

"He stays," Ramos said, letting the kid settle in and find his show.

"Look, just say," Billy struggling not to plead, "what do you want."

"I told you already," Ramos said. Then, tilting his chin to the sound of footsteps coming from above, "She's up there? Call her down."

"SHE STILL DOESN'T RECOGNIZE ME."

Ramos was addressing Billy but his eyes were on Carmen, sitting across the room from him as stiff as a pharaoh, her own gaze fixed on the floor. "How can that be."

Carlos, absorbed in his cartoons, was sitting alongside Ramos on the couch now, the automatic hidden beneath a throw pillow between them.

"What do you need the kid for," Billy said, striving for an offhand tone. "Just let him come to me."

Ignoring Billy, Ramos leaned forward to get Carmen to look at him. She wouldn't.

"But you remember Little Man, right?" he said.

"You're Milton," Carmen whispered dully.

"Maybe I'm Edgar."

"Edgar's dead," she said in that same downcast hush.

"So you know," he said.

Billy, barely listening, finally became aware that there was a real conversation going on, neither Ramos nor his wife raising their voices.

"My whole family, in the ground, where you put them," Ramos said to her, "and all these years I never knew why."

Carlos half-stood to reach for the remote again, Ramos slowly raising a hand to grab him in case he decided to bolt, but the kid fell back into the cushions on his own.

"Milton, I'm right in front of you, I'm right here," Carmen's voice, despite the danger, still jarringly flat. "Please don't hurt my son."

"He's not going to hurt him," Billy said lightly, his heart blowing like a bellows. "He's got a daughter of his own, right?"

The sound of the back door opening had Ramos half-rising, the automatic now down at his side. But at the sight of Billy Senior standing in the doorway, ruffled sections of the weekend paper tucked under his arm, he eased himself back down, slipping the gun once again beneath the pillow.

"What are you coming so early for?" Billy Senior said, stepping into the den. "I'm on nights this week. Didn't they tell you?"

"I just came by to visit your son," Ramos said easily. "I'll be back for you later."

"Well, see you then, my friend." Billy's father gave a short wave and left the room the same way he came in.

At first Billy was baffled, but then he realized that his father had been talking to his replacement driver, and that Ramos was the one who had been torturing them for weeks.

Milton, she had called him.

There was a glass snow globe from Jiminy Peak on the windowsill, a brass candlestick on a side table, the snow globe closer but still too far away.

"Tell me why you did it," Ramos said.

Carmen tried to raise her eyes to Carlos, couldn't. "Milton, I'm scared to look at him. Please."

"Carlos, buddy, come on over to me," Billy said. "Ramos, be a good guy, just let him come."

"Tell me why you did it."

"I never meant to," she said. "You have to believe that."

"Ramos, be a good guy . . ."

"Why."

"Ramos, you do something here, how much time do you think you'll ever have to be with your daughter? She's already lost her mother, you told me yourself."

"Why."

"Because he broke my heart," Carmen said, her voice barely carrying across the room.

"He what?" Ramos cocked his head, draped an arm atop Carlos's shoulders.

"Think it through," Billy said, eyes back to roaming for weapons.

"Broke my heart."

"Broke your heart," Ramos said. "He got you pregnant?"

"No."

"But he was fucking you." More a question than a statement.

Carlos started to fidget under the weight of his arm, but Ramos was too absorbed to even notice.

"Be cool, buddy," Billy said to his son.

"He never even looked at me but once," Carmen said.

Out the window, Billy saw a fleet of patrol cars and a Yonkers ESU van rolling up to the house, their presence, prayed for earlier, now heightening his sense of danger.

"I was fifteen years old," Carmen said heavily. "They came up to me on the stoop, he had just hurt my feelings, I was mad, and I said what I said."

Astonishingly, understandably, Carlos fell asleep against Ramos's shoulder.

"You were fifteen, he had just hurt your feelings . . . And you just said what you said," Ramos recited to himself. "Hurt your *feelings*? That's it?"

"You want a better story?" Carmen softly crying now. "I don't have one."

The house phone rang; hostage negotiators for sure, Billy knew, no one making a move to answer it.

"You know something?" Ramos said to Carmen, his voice filled with wonder. "I believe you. Fifteen years old . . . I don't know what I was expecting to hear all these years."

The fax line began to ring in the den, followed by Carmen's cell phone in the hallway.

"Would it be too little for me to say that I pray for him every day of my life?" she asked listlessly.

"Yeah," Ramos getting to his feet, the Glock rising in his fist, "it would."

Before Billy could launch himself, his father reappeared in the doorway, this time with his ancient .45 double-gripped and leveled at the back of Ramos's head. When Ramos wheeled to the threat, then kept coming, Billy Senior fired, although the fucking thing might as well have had a BANG flag pop out. Billy lunged for the snow globe on the windowsill, then giant-stepped forward and cracked it against Ramos's near temple, sending him milk-eyed to the floor, the side of his face shining with viscous liquid and glitter.

For a moment, Carmen just stood there as if still lost in whatever they had been talking about; then, snapping out of it, she scooped Carlos from the couch, screamed, *"Billy, come!"* and when he wouldn't—his father was in the house too—remained in the doorway, her legs trembling like jack-hammers, until he shoved her out of the house, toward the cops.

Having no idea where the Glock had gone, Billy snatched his father's .45 out of his hands, then dropped down to straddle Ramos's broad back, the sheer breadth of it stretching the tendons in his groin.

Billy Senior headed up the stairs.

"Dad!" Billy yelled, but the old man kept climbing.

With all the phones in the house continuously ringing as if to announce a royal wedding—all the phones except, strangely, Billy's own—Ramos began to come around, his eyes slowly opening and closing like something in a terrarium. Billy pressed the .45 hard into the nape of his neck, then searched him for his cuffs. Nothing.

He had to get to a phone and give Yonkers the green light to come on in before he lost control of the situation, but he couldn't risk rising up with Ramos unsecured, couldn't risk him seeing the barrel-plugged gun full-on and recognizing it for what it was, couldn't risk him find-ing his own live piece somewhere in the room.

"There's like a fucking army out there, OK?" Billy said, trying to keep the tremble out of his voice. "So just take it easy, OK?"

Ramos winced, then slightly, effortlessly, shifted beneath Billy's weight, Billy knowing right then that he wasn't physically strong enough to keep him down if it came to that.

"Milton, right? Milton, think of your daughter, OK? Just think of your daughter and everything is going to be OK, OK?"

Ramos was fully alert now, but he made no further effort to move, just lay there with the side of his face half-buried in the high nap of the carpet, staring off as if thinking about something unrelated.

"Your daughter, what's her name," Billy chattered. "Tell me her name."

Clearly the calmer of the two, Ramos continued to stare off, Billy's bulk and the pressure of the muzzle no more distracting than pecking birds on the back of a rhino.

"Come on, Milton, tell me her name."

Ramos cleared his throat. "If somebody in your will is down as your kid's guardian," he said, his voice half-muffled by the pile, "and you go to jail instead of dying, do they still get the kid?"

"Yeah, sure," Billy said automatically, ducking then swiveling his head in a low search for the cast-off automatic.

"Or does jail throw the whole guardian arrangement out the window."

Billy thought he saw what might be the gun lying deep under the couch, but it could just as easily have been one of the kids' toys.

"She likes it out there with her aunt," Ramos continued. "I don't want her going to foster care."

"Sure," Billy babbled. "She stays wherever you decide."

"What do you know," Ramos said calmly, then threw Billy off his back as easily as doing a push-up.

The Glock, now pointed at Billy, had been under Ramos the whole time Billy had been riding him.

"Over there," Ramos said. "On the table."

Billy did as he was told, putting his father's gun on the low coffee table.

"The fucking thing's plugged anyhow," Ramos added.

If he knew that all along, Billy thought dreamily, *and his own live piece was right under his gut . . .*

"We can get out of this, no problem," Billy said. "Just let me pick up the phone. Or pick it up yourself."

"Turn to the wall, please?"

Billy did as he was told, so stupid with fear he felt high.

"Did you know?" Ramos asked him from behind.

"Did I know what."

"She never told you," Ramos marveled.

"Tell me what," Billy said, then: "So tell me now. I want to know."

"Never said a word . . ."

As fine cracks in the wall paint, inches from his face, imprinted themselves on his brain, as the hell choir of endlessly ringing phones faded to a weak, sickly carousel tune in Billy's ears, Ramos took two steps back.

"You see?" his voice tearing up blackly. "All these years, and you fucking people, you just sail on, sail on."

Billy tried to shut himself down and just let it happen, but then he heard Ramos stepping back farther. Then farther. Then heard the front door swing open, the murderously pregnant silence out there rushing into the house like a tornado.

He wasn't sure what he experienced first, the staggered report of the volley or the sight of Ramos charging the ESU cops with Billy Senior's dummy gun. Either way the outcome was the same.

Either way the phones finally stopped ringing.

AS THE HOUSE FILLED WITH footsteps and radio squawk, Billy, intent on finding his cell phone, tuned out the calming voices, shrugged off the reaching hands that were screwing with his concentration.

"Where did it go."

"Where'd what go, Billy," someone said.

"My goddamn phone, I just had it this morning."

"It's in your front pocket," the voice said. "Why don't you come sit down."

Pulling out his cell, Billy saw that there was someone on the line.

"Who's this."

"Graves, is that you?" a familiar voice said.

"I asked who this is," Billy said, finally allowing someone to guide him to a chair.

"Evan Lefkowitz, Second Squad."

"You're calling me?"

"Actually, you called me, us, about an hour ago, then left the line open," Lefkowitz said. "We've been listening in ever since."

"Hey, while I have you?" Billy said brightly, waving off the hovering EMTs. "I was talking to my son earlier . . . What's the deal with Albert Lazar?"

A new call came in while the medics were debating whether to shoot him up with three mikes of sodium nitroprusside or let his blood pressure come down on its own.

"Hey, Billy, Bobby Cardozo from the Eighty Squad. We finally got a match on the prints from the bat."

"Good," Billy said, watching the needle go in.

"Are you sitting down? Because you're not going to believe your ears."

BY THE TIME THEY FINALLY laid eyes on each other in the trauma room of Saint Joseph's, Billy was so dizzy from the Nitropress, Carmen so bombed on Ativan, that for a while all they could do was stare.

"Who's got the kids?"

"Millie," she said, then: "Billy, I'm so sorry."

In the ensuing stoned silence, fragments of her conversation with Ramos began to revisit him.

"You knew he'd be coming for you?"

"I knew something would be coming for me," she said. "I just didn't know what."

Billy nodded, then nodded some more. "So," clearing his throat, "who's Little Man?"

IT TOOK TWO DAYS OF her pretty much sleeping around the clock before she was prepared to answer the question, Carmen announcing her readiness on the third afternoon by coming downstairs in a long plain white nightgown, silently drinking two cups of coffee, then inviting him back upstairs.

Once they were inside the semi-darkened bedroom, Carmen immediately slipped back under the covers. But Billy, intuiting that she might need some breathing room for whatever was to come, opted for the lone

chair, lugging it across the room from its spot beneath the far window
to the side of the bed.

"When I was fifteen," she began, "I would've done anything, anything
to have Rudy Ramos like me, just like me. You have no idea what I thought
of myself back then. My father was so rotten, such a lousy human being,
and my mother was his dishrag. Then my father left her for another
woman and moved to Atlanta. Which was good, I thought, because
now it would get better between us, but she just, overnight, turned into
this sour old widow. I would be like, 'Mommy, be happy, you're free,' but
no, she just, 'Who'd want me now,' I mean, she was good-looking,
thirty-seven years old, but she shut herself down, started yelling at me
and Victor nonstop over nothing, anything, just never let up . . ."

Despite the marathon hours she had spent recuperating in this room,
Billy thought he had never seen her look so exhausted, her eyes like swol-
len almonds beneath half-mast lids.

"And I knew Rudy, Little Man everybody called him, from the building and from school, not 'knew him,' he was a year ahead of me, but . . .
And I didn't think about him all that much, then one day I just did and
I couldn't stop, it was like I had suffered a stroke, but I was nothing to
him, just some ghost of a girl who lived where he lived and went to Monroe . . . He was a big deal on the basketball team, and between games and
practices he'd hardly ever leave school before five o'clock, and a lot of
those days I'd find things to do in the after-school program so I could
go home when he did. I mean, I was so fucked up that I wouldn't even
walk on the same side of the street as him, but I'd always manage to enter
the building when he did so we'd go up the stairs at the same time, and
I hated that I lived one flight below him because if I lived on his floor or
the one higher then that would be one more flight I'd have to be near
him, just day after day like that, agonizing over how maybe tomorrow I should walk in front of him instead of behind him, behind him
instead of in front of him . . . And his bedroom was right above mine,
3F and 4F, and I'd hear him walking around above my head and sometimes he'd be doing himself, and the bedsprings would creak and I'd lay
down in my own bed and . . ."

"Whoa, whoa."

"Billy, please, let me tell you."

"Carmen, I can't hear this."

"Why? You're the man I love, the father of my children, and I'm telling you things about me that I never could before."

"OK, OK, Jesus."

"What, are you jealous? He's been dead more than twenty years."

"Don't be ridiculous," Billy scoffed, thinking, She's been cheating on me with this kid, walking around with him in her head since the day they met.

Then as quick as the feeling had come down on him it lifted, Billy recognizing that what was really getting to him was not jealousy but the realization that if he hung in for this right now, that baffling and invisible dragon he'd been protecting her from all these years might finally begin to take on form and he might not to be able to handle its appearance.

"Are you angry at me?" she said. "Do you want me to stop? I'll stop, I will, just tell me to."

"Don't be ridiculous," he repeated.

"I'm serious, Billy, I will."

"I'm serious, too," he said, then forced himself to add, "I want to hear it all."

For a long moment, she looked at him like the liar he was, then carried on.

"It took me maybe two months before I had the courage to say something to him, even just bullshit, and I decided this one day, I was going to say, 'Your sweater's so fly.' I thought about saying 'so tight,' 'so dope,' 'so gangsta,' 'ill,' 'phat,' 'snap,' 'the bomb,' '*da* bomb,' but I liked 'fly' the best, and at lunch I finally went up to him in the cafeteria, but instead of saying, 'Your sweater's so fly,' I was nervous and I said, 'My sweater's so fly,' and the kids at his table heard it and they all started laughing, and he was, he said, 'Your sweater's so fly?' but looking at them not at me, 'I'm happy for you,' still looking at them, like to get their approval, and in that moment when he looked at them instead of me, with that stupid grin on his face? I saw him for what he was, a self-centered immature boy with a little bit of a cruel streak. But I had been in love, so the realization hit me like a train . . . I don't know if I felt like I actually *hated* him? But God, did he put a hole in my chest that day."

Carlos came into the room, climbed into bed, curled into Carmen's side, and quickly fell asleep. Although his son still hadn't said a word about the other day, he'd been sleeping, since then, almost as much as his mother.

"Later, after school, I saw him go into our building and I didn't want to go inside, I didn't want to walk up the stairs with him, didn't want to be in my room and hear his creaky bed over my head, so I just sat on the stoop remembering his face when he said that, 'Your sweater's so fly?' not even giving me the consideration of eye contact. And I'm just sitting there like that, feeling more and more humiliated, more and more like an invisible nothing, and then at one point I looked up and I saw these two guys coming towards our building, and the way they were carrying themselves made me nervous. Hoodies, sunglasses on a cloudy day, hands in pockets, they looked like surveillance photos of themselves, and then they stopped a few feet away, had a conversation, then one of them came up to me, says, 'Where's Eric Franco live at, what apartment,' and I knew, everybody in the building knew, Eric Franco dealt coke, but these guys didn't look like they were there to score, they looked like trouble."

Carlos started to talk in his sleep, nonsense words addressed to his brother. Billy was deaf to it, but Carmen waited until her son was finished before going on.

"But instead of giving them his apartment, 5C . . . I don't remember *consciously* thinking about what could happen if I said 4F? But that's what came out of my mouth."

Billy stood up.

"Where are you going?"

"What? Nowhere."

"You're leaving?" Carmen saying it like, leaving her.

"No, I was just stretching," he said idiotically.

"Can you sit down?"

"I'm down," he said, "I'm right here."

He began to reach for her hand, then withdrew, sensing that whatever she needed right now, physical contact was not on the list.

"I don't know if I really heard the gunshot from the fourth floor or just imagined that I did—I don't see how I could have, it was a .22 handgun going off inside a six-story building, but all of a sudden I felt this, this gripping sensation inside my chest, and a minute or two later those two came back out of the building the same way they went in, not rushed, looking around without seeming to be. And after they walked past me they stopped and had another one of those side-mouth conversations, and I knew they were discussing what to do about me, the witness . . . I was staring at the ground, I could no more run at that moment than I could fly, I was totally theirs whatever they wanted to do with me, but when I finally managed to raise my head they were gone."

"Carm . . ."

"What happened was that they rang the bell and when Rudy opened the door they shot him through the eye and the bullet went into his brain."

"Carmen . . ."

"But I killed him. Nobody could tell me different. I knew what I knew before I knew it . . . '4F,' I said."

"Carmen, listen to me, the killers were the killers."

"Billy, don't."

"They're the ones who had the guns."

"Billy, I'm begging you . . ."

"Carmen, you were a kid, fifteen, you said so yourself."

"The cops came to our door later that day, doing a canvass of the building, nobody could figure out why this basically no trouble to anyone boy was executed. And when they came to our apartment I hid in the bathroom while they talked to my mother, and when they left I told her that I saw the killers, I talked to them, and first she turned white, then, without even giving me two minutes to pack or say goodbye to my brother, she dragged me out of the apartment and into a cab for Port Authority, and put me on a bus to live with my father in Atlanta. And when I was down there I heard that Milton and Edgar killed the guys that killed their brother, then later I heard that Edgar was killed in return, and that their mother died soon after, and now, now Milton's gone."

"He's gone? He was here to kill you."

"And now you understand why."

"Carmen, how many lives have you saved in that hospital. How many people are still walking the earth because of you."

"So, whatever the law thinks of me, and it doesn't think anything of me at all about this, I know what I did."

Billy's impulse was to once again try to defend her from herself, but he finally accepted the fact that all he'd be doing was causing her more pain.

"So," she said after a long moment, "you tell me about Pavlicek, about Yasmeen, about Jimmy Whelan, what they did and why. But I've got more souls to answer for than any of them, and I live with that every day. I see the Ramos family every day, I say I'm sorry to them so many times in my head from morning to night it's like I have a chemical disorder."

Billy finally, cautiously, lay down next to her.

"I know you want to give me absolution, Billy, but you don't have that power. I wish you did." Then: "But at least now you know."

TOO EARLY THE NEXT MORNING, Billy found himself sitting alone at the kitchen table, staring out the window at the askew backboard in the driveway, his coffee as cold as a pond. Immediately after unloading to him about her part in the destruction of the Ramos family, Carmen had proceeded to pass out, was still passed out, Billy checking the wall clock, fifteen hours later. He couldn't count the times he'd seen that in murderers who'd finally owned up to what they had done—straight back to the cell and their first peaceful sleep in weeks, months, years. You couldn't wake them with grenades.

His phone rang—Redman—Billy killing it directly.

The day before, Yasmeen and Whelan had tried to call him too. If he had picked up for either of them, his guess then was, the conversation would center strictly on asking how his family was doing. For them to ask where he was at in regards to turning them in, so soon after what he'd been through, would have been a grievous error in judgment on their part and they'd know that. Nonetheless, the seven-day grace period he had given them to get ahead of their situations was more than half over, but as far as he knew not one of them had even walked into a lawyer's office yet, let alone stepped into a precinct with a story to tell. His take was that they were all banking on the trauma, hoping that in the aftermath of what had happened to him and his family he would be thrown into such a state of emotional chaos that he would no longer have the time, the brain cells, or the heart to follow through on his own ultimatum.

Hearing the thump of his father's *New York Times* landing on the porch, Billy opened the door and saw a Chevy Tahoe sitting silently at the foot of his driveway, Yasmeen staring out at him through the windshield.

At least she knew enough not to come to the door.

Billy walked down the driveway, taking his coffee with him, and settled into the passenger seat without a word.

She had barely brushed her hair and was wearing nothing more than a heavy sweater thrown over pajamas, the first time he'd seen her without the Tibetan coat in months.

"Hey, I called you so many times, you didn't answer, I just had to come by."

Billy looked at his watch: five forty-five a.m.

"I know, I'm sorry, I couldn't sleep," she said. "I just want to know how everybody's holding up."

"We'll get through."

"I can't imagine, that must have been such a nightmare for you."

"I don't want to talk about it."

"No, I understand," she said quickly. "I understand. I should go home," running her palms along the top of her steering wheel but making no move to start up the car.

She had no more driven up here to ask after his family than she had come for the latest NBA scores, the musk of her anguish growing so intense that he had to crack his window.

"Sorry," she said, "I just ran out of the house."

"This picture," Billy tapping the laminated photo of her daughters that hung from the neck of her rearview mirror, "was that always there? Or did you just put it up this morning?"

"No," she said faintly, "that's just my girls, you know."

The first oriole of the season caught his eye, a dash of bright against the early spring drab.

"Just my girls," she murmured, looking off.

He removed the photo from its bead chain, flipped it into her lap. "You see them? What the hell were you thinking?"

"It was do what I did or go kill myself. Better a mother in Bedford Hills than in a grave."

"I can't hear this shit," he said, reaching for the door handle.

Yasmeen grabbed his hand. "You don't think I know what I did?" she warbled. "You think I didn't know how I'd be after that? But at least I'm alive. It was me or him."

"Which him."

"What?"

"Cortez or Bannion."

"I didn't go near Cortez," she said.

"So, clean hands on that one, right?"

Up on the porch, Milton Ramos was leaning against the front door at an impossibly low angle, his rigid body inches from the ground, Billy taking him in and then lifting his eyes to the bedroom window, to Carmen up there desperately trying to exorcize her history via hibernation.

And all he wanted to do right now was join her.

All he wanted to do right now was to be free of himself, free of all the bodies, and tend to his family.

"What happened to your coat," he said his gaze still fixed on the window.

"What? I burned it."

"Just as well."

"What do you mean?" she said quietly.

"I mean, next time you buy a jacket, take a girlfriend."

"Billy, say what you mean," Yasmeen tilting toward him now, as taut as a bird.

Billy took a sip of the cold coffee, then opening his door, tossed the rest onto the driveway.

"You know," he said, "sometimes when I draw a slow night and I can duck out early, I'd be coming around that curve right about now, sliding for home."

"Billy, please . . ."

"Sitting out here like this?" he said. "It's like I'm waiting for myself to show up."

"Fucking Billy," Yasmeen blurted as she keyed the ignition. "Fucking Billy."

The unexpected blast of Mariah Carey coming through the car speakers made her scream.

Enough.

"You get a lawyer yet?" he said, turning off the radio.

"There's a guy," she said sullenly. "I'm going to see him today."

"Save your money," he said, finally stepping out of the car.

"What?"

But she knew what, Yasmeen clamping a hand across her mouth like a muzzle, the tears running over her knuckles.

"And do your crying at home."

CARMEN STUMBLED INTO THE KITCHEN an hour later, her face a blur.

"How long was I out for?"

"Long enough."

"Then why am I still so exhausted?" she said, wandering over to pour herself some coffee.

"I heard Victor's going home tomorrow," he said.

"He is."

"Does he know?"

"About Milton?"

"About you," he said.

"Me? No. I couldn't ever tell him."

"Well, maybe you can now."

"Now I need to."

"Just wait a little while until he settles in with the babies."

"Of course," she said. "Of course."

"Yasmeen drove up this morning."

"This morning?" Lowering herself into the chair next to his. "I didn't hear anything."

"She stayed in her car."

"Did you talk to her?"

"Yeah, I did."

"And?"

"And it's over," he said.

"Over. What do you mean, 'over.'" Then: "With just her or all of them?"

Billy shrugged.

They sat in silence for a while, Carmen joining him in looking out at the backyard.

"I'm glad," she finally said. "Thank you."

He wanted to say that he didn't do it for her, but who knew.

Milton Ramos reappeared, this time sitting on the living room couch, immobile yet full of murderous despair.

Well, Billy told himself, what did you expect.

And if Carmen hadn't seen him yet, she'd see him soon enough.

"I think I got up too early," he said.

"Me too," she said, reaching for, but missing, his hand. "Let's go back to bed."

THE CALL FROM STACEY TAYLOR came a week later.

"I need to tell you something."

"What's that."

"Have breakfast with me. It's a long story."

"Give me the headline."

"Just have breakfast with me," she said. "You'll be glad you did."

"You said that the last time."

"This time I mean it."

"I have a therapy session at two."

"Physical?"

"Family."

"Where."

"West Forties."

"Then come after."

"YOUR WHALE, CURTIS TAFT?" SHE said to him over a four p.m. breakfast in another one of her tin-can diners. "He shot his girlfriend last night."

"Girlfriend or wife?" Billy asked, thinking of Patricia Taft, big and stately, pushing a stroller that day through the atrium of the hospital.

"Girlfriend."

"You have a funny definition of good news."

"She'll live," Stacey said, fondling an unopened pack of Parliaments, "but he also clipped the first EMT coming through the door, so he's most likely going away just this side of forever."

So, yeah, good news, he guessed, but it left him flat. "He got away with a triple," he said. "Skated like Brinker."

"You catch them for what you catch them for," she said. "You told me that."

"Memori Williams, Tonya Howard, Dreena Bailey," he said loudly enough to turn heads.

And Eric Cortez, Sweetpea Harris, Jeffrey Bannion, if he was taking a true tally.

The food came, two omelets that were so oily they looked shellacked.

"So, in other news," sliding her plate to the side. "I've been hearing some wild rumors."

"About . . ."

"Bad guys getting taken out by frustrated cops."

"Frustrated, huh?" Billy thinking, Maybe the center would hold for them and maybe not, but if she had really called him here hoping he would help her out, she was dreaming. He would no more talk to her

about any of his friends than they would have talked about him eighteen years earlier.

Ignoring the food, he took a sip of coffee. "Where'd you hear that?"

"You know I can't say."

"Journalistic ethics?" he said with more of an edge than he'd intended.

The dig deflated her like a pin. "Yeah, well, we used to hear bullshit
rumors like this all the time back at the *Post*. They rarely came to anything."

He wanted to remind her that *rarely* wasn't the same as *never*, that
eighteen years ago, when she was young and mad ambitious, words like
rarely, unlikely, implausible would never have slowed her down—but what
would have been the point.

The woman sitting across from him—gray in face and grown so bony
in middle age that he could count the knobs of her spine through her
pullover—just didn't have the heart for the chase anymore; *rarely*, these
days, justification enough for her to fold her tent and go home to her wine
and her cigarettes and her death-wish drunk of a boyfriend.

"I need to tell you something," he said, before he could stop himself.

"Tell me something?" Stacey looking at him warily, not liking his suddenly breathy tone.

"It's about me and you," Billy thinking, She can get back in the game
with this. Get back in the game and redeem her good name.

"Can I go outside for a smoke first?" she nearly pleaded, her eyes
pierced with dread.

Her resistance to finally hearing the words that would vindicate the
last two punishing decades of her life at first baffled him, then sobered
him. What the hell was he thinking? The consequences for his family
and for himself . . .

"Forget it, it's nothing."

He knew she wouldn't press, and she didn't, Stacey masking her relief
by pretending that something out on the street had caught her eye. And
Billy, playing his part, started attacking his eggs as if they were edible.

"Let me ask you something," she said after a while. "Whether you
were or weren't high that day and that psycho with the pipe was still bearing down on you like that . . . Would you have done anything differently?"

"Hypothetically?" he said. "No, I don't think so." Then: "No, I wouldn't."

Stacey went back to gazing out the window, her thin features vanishing in the late afternoon sunlight that slanted through the glass.

"I mean, it's not like I never think about getting back into some kind of reporting," she said, tentatively pressing her fingertips against her throat. "But that sex advice column for men that I write? We had nine thousand hits last issue. Up from fifty-five hundred the issue before, up from three thousand the issue before that. So, I think it's safe to say that I'm onto something."

Billy nodded in gratitude.

"Can I go out and have my cigarette now?" she said.

PAVLICEK TRIED TO RING THROUGH as he was leaving the diner, the only one of them who hadn't attempted to contact him in the days after Ramos. The others had stopped calling directly after his talk with Yasmeen, Billy assuming that no one wanted to risk a conversation that, if they said the wrong thing or adopted the wrong tone, might prompt him to change his mind. Yet Pavlicek hadn't called even once, and so on the third attempted ring-through, coming forty minutes after the first, Billy yielded to his curiosity and picked up. But instead of getting Pavlicek on the other end, the voice Billy heard was Redman's.

"It's John Junior," he said. "The funeral's here on Thursday."

UNLIKE THE HOMECOMING FOR MARTHA Timberwolf, Junior's service was standing room only.

At first, when he entered the already crowded chapel with his wife and kids, Billy wondered if he had it in him to let himself go, even just for this day. But when he saw Pavlicek, lumbering wild-eyed between the casket and Redman's piano like a chained bear, he couldn't help but wade through the crowd and grab him.

"It's over now, right?" Pavlicek said too brightly, his breath rank with grief. "All over but the shoutin'."

"Sure," Billy said, wishing it were so.

"Come here," Pavlicek taking Billy by the elbow and steering him to the side of the open coffin. "Look at this, can you believe this?" Touching his son's rigid left pinkie sticking out from the folded repose of his crossed hands. "He looks like some fucking fop holding a teacup, and this here," running a finger down the left side of Junior's jaw, the skin there three shades darker than on the right, "and his hair, I don't know what Redman was thinking but this kid never had a pompadour in his life."

Pavlicek's tone was crisp and snappy and jarringly unaffected by the tears that slipped down his face in sheets. "I mean, I never thought our friend was the greatest mortician on the planet, but this is ridiculous."

"Maybe he just doesn't get to work much on white people," Billy said carefully.

"And see, I put this in," pointing to his own gold shield tucked into a corner of the casket. "And this," lifting out a framed photo of the two of them taken in Amsterdam a few years earlier. "And this," a snapshot of Junior as a toddler with his mother before she tried to drown him. "I really debated putting that one in, but . . ."

The disconnect between voice and tears continued, Billy wondering how long he could keep it up.

"You ever read that?" Pavlicek asked, pointing to a paperback copy of *Steppenwolf* near Junior's feet. "Last year he told me that it changed his life, so I tried to get through it a few times to see what he saw," the tears finally beginning to climb into his throat, "but honestly? I thought it was crap. Anyways it's all over now, right? All over but the shoutin'."

"Johnny," Billy said, stepping back from Junior's body. "I'm dying for you."

Embarrassed by his choice of words, Billy began to apologize, but he needn't have bothered, given that Pavlicek had already turned away and was now engaged in giving Ray Rivera, father of the murdered Thomas, the same manic tour of the coffin and its contents as he had given Billy.

■ ■ ■

THEY WERE ALL THERE WITH their families, those who had families: Yasmeen, Dennis, and the girls; Redman, who had prepared the body but turned the service over to his father so he could participate purely as a mourner, standing with Nola, Rafer, and two of his six or seven other sons; and Jimmy Whelan, who at least had the sense for once not to bring a date.

They all made some sort of contact with Billy, mostly sober nods, a few terse greetings, Yasmeen going so far as to hug Carmen and make a quiet fuss over the kids. But for the most part they kept their distance, which he thought was more about letting sleeping dogs lie than anything else, and he was fine with it. He preferred it.

"I believe it's time," Redman's father announced with soft authority, "for us all to be seated."

Junior apparently had been utterly indifferent to the notion of any kind of God, and so Pavlicek, no Bible beater himself, passed on having any kind of religious celebrant and instead turned the program over to his son's friends, who served up half a dozen well-spoken homages, an acoustical duet on "I'll Fly Away," and a teary solo of "Angels Among Us," sung by a young woman who had been the closest thing Junior had had to a girlfriend in the last year of his life.

When the woman returned to her seat, a retired detective from Bronx Homicide, not on the program, spontaneously got up and sang an a cappella version of Eric Clapton's "Tears in Heaven," which had half the room weeping like babies, including Carlos and Declan, hardly more than babies themselves. Billy didn't know what unnerved him more, his two sons' intuitive empathy in a room beyond their experience or the sight of Jimmy Whelan, the childless, mateless, eternally diffident ghetto harem keeper, sobbing more loudly than anyone else. As for Billy himself, the last couple of weeks had utterly tapped him out, and it would take a lot more than a sad pop tune with a painful backstory to get him weeping.

Redman Senior, seemingly singing directly to Junior's father, closed out the concert with "The Battle Is Not Yours."

And then it was his time, Pavlicek rising from the front row, giving his back to the room as he silently leaned over the coffin—Billy could hear him whispering something to his son, but too indistinctly for anyone to make out—then finally turning to the assembled, the expression on his face near homicidal.

"I don't know if anyone came here to celebrate John Junior's life, but I certainly didn't," he said, gripping the podium as if he wanted to crush it. "I am here before you, I am here among you, to rage and curse God for the arbitrarily murdering fuck that he is, not that I'm the first parent ever to feel that way, and to grant myself at least one afternoon where suicide would be logistically difficult."

Tickled by the profanity, Carlos looked up at Billy and grinned.

"You know, you read the papers after a young man dies in this city, someone's always saying, 'He was just starting to get his life together, he was just talking about going back to school, getting his GED, getting a job, talking about being a real father to his daughter, talking about getting away from the 'hood, about enlisting, about marrying his fiancée, he was just about to do this, to do that . . .' All these 'just's, whether they were true or not, because they all died young and 'just' was all they had, tomorrow was all they had. And the same could be said for my boy. He was 'just' about to finish his schooling, he was 'just' about to find his own way in the world, 'just' about to show me the man that now, now, he'll never get to be, the man that over the years would have null-and-voided every hardship, every heartache I've ever endured in my life."

Pavlicek paused, returned to the coffin as if for a quick consultation, then turned back to the seats. "You want to hear what a great kid he was? How his heart was pure gold? How he loved life, loved people, loved a challenge, all that boilerplate et cetera, et cetera? For those of you who want to hear all that, consider it said. The fact of the matter was that he was just about to be, and now he's not."

Looking around the room Billy noted that all three of the WGs were in tears, their faces in various states of contortion. Even Redman, king of the poker face and impresario of seventy-five to a hundred memorials like this every year, was swiping at his cheeks with those mile-long fingers of his.

They had all killed or been complicit in a killing, out of passion but clear-eyed and purposefully, but they had no problem giving in to their grief when it came to one another. He had nearly lost his mind trying to bring them to justice, turning on his longtime friends in order to do what was right, what he thought was right, and as a result his own eyes on this day were as dry as sand. Still, they had all been so tight over the last two decades, had gone through so much together, and for one mad minute, Billy's anger at them for excluding him from their murderous plans trumped his outrage at what they had done. But instead of passing, the anger lingered, Billy wondering if this pop-up fury he was experiencing over having been shut out from this most desperate of compacts between friends hadn't been a part of his anger at them since the beginning.

"There's some people in this room right now," Pavlicek said, "who gave twenty years or more to the Job, myself included. We've seen it all, handled it all, and when a young person dies we've all walked up the stairs, knocked on the doors, and delivered the news, between us, to an army of parents. We've caught them on their way to the floor, carried them into the bedroom or living room, then gone into their kitchens and brought them water—over the years, an ocean of water, glass by glass by glass. And so, after all that, we think we understand what it must feel like to be one of those parents, but we don't. We can't. I still can't. But I'm getting there."

Billy reflexively looked across the room at Ray Rivera, expecting him to be nodding in agreement, but instead saw a profile carved in stone.

"But so my son . . ." Pavlicek paused, looking about himself as if he had misplaced something, then seemed to give up on finding it. "I think I just want to read this," he said, pulling an envelope out of his jacket pocket and removing a single page cut from a book. "This was handed to me today by a friend, and it's as good a farewell to him as anything else."

And then, after giving it one last silent read, Pavlicek began to recite, tone-deaf to the rhythm of the words:

These hearts were woven of human joys and cares,
Washed marvellously with sorrow, swift to mirth.
The years had given them kindness. Dawn was theirs,
And sunset, and the colours of the earth.

It was Rupert Brooke's sonnet "The Dead"—"The Dead (IV)," actually, Billy knowing this because his father had read it to him, more than once, when he was a kid, and when Billy became older, more than once he had read it himself.

> ... *He leaves a white*
> *Unbroken glory, a gathered radiance,*
> *A width, a shining peace, under the night.*

At the end of the service, Pavlicek chose to stand at the head of the open coffin to once again receive mourners, the line extending from the front of the chapel to the small windowless vestibule and out into the street.

"It's over now, right?" Pavlicek chanted to Billy. "All over but the shoutin'."

"It's over," Billy said. "Everything."

Despite his state, Pavlicek picked up on his meaning right away. "Billy. I know what I did to you. What we all did to you. And I'm sorry."

"Not for today," Billy said. "Today is today, all right?"

"We just knew if you ever . . ." Pavlicek began, then cut himself off, leaving Billy to wonder how he had intended to finish that sentence.

"Another day, OK?"

"All right," Pavlicek said. "Another day."

As Billy turned to step away, Pavlicek grabbed his wrist.

"You hear about Curtis Taft?"

"I did," Billy said.

"I don't know, maybe that day we gave him PTSD, maybe we drove him to that."

"Not today, OK?"

"I mean, I sure fuckin' hope so," Pavlicek rasped with a kind of black glee, Billy looking into his eyes and absolutely knowing that if time ever folded in on itself and Pavlicek had it to do all over again, to put another bullet into the back of Eric Cortez's skull, or to re-murder any of the other Whites by gun, blade, or with his bare hands, he'd go about it with joy.

Turning back to the mourners, Billy saw that Whelan, Redman, and Yasmeen, each standing in a different part of the room, had all been quietly observing the conversation, their expressions, before they one by one turned away from him, flat-eyed and alert, Billy thinking, And so would they all.

THE CAR WAS PARKED FOUR blocks uptown from the funeral home, and as they headed north on Adam Clayton Boulevard, the boys serpentined like loons before them, racing up every stoop and making a show of high-jumping over every minuscule bit of crap on the sidewalk.

"That poem he read?" Billy said to Carmen. "It's from World War One. It made me think of my dad."

"Well, it should. He gave it to me this morning to give to John."

"My father did?"

"I was right there when he gave it to me."

"I didn't even know he knew about the funeral." Then: "Why didn't he give it to me?"

"I think he knew, he knows, what's going on with you and the others, so he gave it to me instead."

"And how the hell does he know that?"

"Don't ask me," Carmen said, "he's your father."

LATER, AS THEY UNLOADED THE kids in the driveway and then entered the house, Billy remembered that he was supposed to go in tonight, his first tour back after two weeks on medical leave.

"I'm thinking about calling in sick," he said to Carmen in the kitchen. "I don't really want to go."

"I think you should," she said.

"I don't think I'm up for it."

"I think you should," she repeated on her way to the freezer for the vodka, then to the cabinet for two juice glasses.

"Yeah? How about you?" Billy watching her pour out too much, a sure sign of a non-drinker, which, under normal circumstances, she was.

"I already called the hospital, told them to put me back on the schedule starting tomorrow."

"You sure you're up for it?"

"Keep calm and carry on," she said, raising her glass.

"What?"

"I saw it on a refrigerator magnet," Carmen taking a sip and making a face. "I mean Jesus, Billy, what else can we do?"

HIS THIRD RUN THAT NIGHT was on Madison Avenue, a four a.m. smash-and-grab of a tiny jewelry store set inside the exterior arcade of an office building in midtown, almost all of the stock snatched out of the brick-bashed window, nothing much to see now but bare earring trees and daggers of broken glass.

At this hour, the canyoned street was a ghost town, and Billy easily spotted the late-model Nissan Pathfinder slowly approaching from three blocks south. When it finally pulled to the curb, an elderly woman sporting a high helmet of frosted tangerine hair, lipsticked and dressed in a nubby plaid skirt suit as if she had been sitting up all night waiting for the phone to ring, stepped carefully out of the passenger-side door onto Madison. The driver—her husband, Billy assumed—remained behind the wheel with the engine still running, staring straight ahead as if waiting for the light to change.

She absorbed the carnage without expression. "I been here thirty-seven years and nothing ever happened," she said quietly, a soft thread of old Europe running through her words.

When Billy was a kid all of his aunts had filigreed birdcage hair like hers, and he could never figure out how they slept.

"How's your insurance?"

The woman blushed. "It only covers jewelry that's in the safe."

"How much is in the safe?"

"I have arthritis. Every little piece, in and out, in and out, morning and night, takes me two hours, I can't do it anymore." She was wiped out.

"Is that your husband?" Billy asked.

She glanced at the old guy still behind the wheel but said nothing.

"And where was he tonight?" Theodore Moretti asked.

"Do I even have to answer a question like that?" The woman addressed Billy, more amazed than insulted.

He had no idea how Moretti had gotten back on the sign-up sheet after being blackballed just the month before, but he had. "I thought you were at the Three-two," Billy snapped.

Moretti's cell rang and he walked down the block, hissing into his shoulder.

"What happens now?" she asked, Billy picking up on that near-buried refugee inflection again, thinking, This is nothing for her.

Before he could respond, a patrol car flying the wrong way down Madison came to a rocking stop in front of the store. One of the uniforms jumped out, holding a black plastic garbage bag.

"We caught the guy running on Park," he said, gesturing to the head-down, handcuffed thief in the backseat. "I feel like goddamn Santa Claus."

The woman took the bag and peered inside at her life, then up at Billy.

"Who would do such a thing?"

"I hate to say it," Billy said, "but all of this has to be vouchered as evidence."

She looked at him blankly, Billy unable to tell whether she didn't understand him or didn't care; nonetheless, he decided, it was a reasonably happy ending.

ACKNOWLEDGMENTS

My editor, John Sterling, a highly incisive and diligent master builder—and as ruthless as ever.

To all the friends and guides who have schooled me over the last few years—
First and always, John McCormack.
Irma Rivera, Barry Warhit, Richie Roberts, Rafiyq Abdellah, John McAuliffe.
And to my street-writer heroes—Michael Daly and Mark Jacobson.

ALSO AVAILABLE BY RICHARD PRICE

CLOCKERS

Veteran homicide detective Rocco Klein has had enough of life on the edge. When a warm summer night brings yet another drug-related murder, he has no sense that the case is anything special. A young black man steps forward to confess, but a little digging reveals that he's never been in any kind of trouble whereas his half-brother, Strike, runs a crew of street-corner coke dealers or 'clockers' in a nearby housing project. Rocco is soon sure that they've got the wrong man, and suddenly his appetite for the job is back. With a vengeance.

'*The Wire* wouldn't exist without *Clockers*'
DAVID SIMON, CREATOR OF THE WIRE

'The most heralded work of fiction to come out of New York since *Bonfire of the Vanities* ... timely, majestic'
TIME OUT

'Big, shocking, powerful ... resounds with vivid detail'
INDEPENDENT ON SUNDAY

BLOOMSBURY

LUSH LIFE

'So, what do you do?' Whenever people asked him, Eric Cash used to have a dozen answers. Artist, actor, screenwriter . . . But now he's thirty-five years old and he's still living on the Lower East Side, still in the restaurant business, still serving the people he wanted to be. What does Eric do? He manages. Not like Ike Marcus. Ike was young, good-looking, people liked him. Ask him what he did, he wouldn't say tending bar. He was going places – until two street kids stepped up to him and Eric one night and pulled a gun. At least, that's Eric's version.

'A visceral, heart-thumping portrait of New York City'
NEW YORK TIMES

'Richard Price is the greatest writer of dialogue, living or dead, this country has ever produced. Wry, profane, hilarious and tragic, sometimes in a single line, *Lush Life* is his masterwork. I doubt anyone will write a novel this good for a long, long time'
DENNIS LEHANE

'*Lush Life* . . . peels off the shiny top layer of New York to reveal the raw beating heart of the city post 9/11'
DAILY MAIL

BLOOMSBURY

SAMARITAN

Successful Hollywood writer Ray decides to return to the New Jersey projects of his youth in order to give something back to the community, and volunteers to teach creative writing at his old school. But one night he's savagely beaten and rushed to hospital. The only cop interested is a childhood friend, 'Tweetie' Ammons, who owes him one from long ago. It turns out that Ray knows who did it, but he's not talking. Although Tweetie is on the cusp of retirement she is determined to help Ray but finds herself being drawn into a dark and deadly drama.

'The finest writer about contemporary urban America on the planet'
DAILY MAIL

'Absolutely riveting. *Samaritan* blew my mind'
STEPHEN KING

'One of those rare writers who doesn't see why an ability to entertain and enthral should come at a cost'
EVENING STANDARD

BLOOMSBURY

FREEDOMLAND

An injured woman stumbles into an inner-city hospital with a horrifying story: she has just been carjacked by a man who was apparently unaware that her son was asleep on the back seat. As a search ensues, a shrewd detective and an ambitious young reporter smell a hoax and begin to suspect that the woman is holding back a terrible truth: could she have murdered her own child?

'A brilliant novel . . . It rips along with an incandescent heat'
DAILY EXPRESS

'A hugely ambitious, searing novel . . . *Freedomland* makes for compulsive reading'
GLASGOW HERALD

'A compelling portrait of America's flipside and a novel that obliges you to engage with it . . . Not since Toni Morrison's *Beloved* have I read a novel with such emotional force'
INDEPENDENT

ORDER YOUR COPY:

BY PHONE: +44 (0)1256 302 699; BY EMAIL: DIRECT@MACMILLAN.CO.UK

DELIVERY IS USUALLY 3–5 WORKING DAYS. FREE POSTAGE AND PACKAGING FOR ORDERS OVER £20.

ONLINE: WWW.BLOOMSBURY.COM/BOOKSHOP

PRICES AND AVAILABILITY SUBJECT TO CHANGE WITHOUT NOTICE.

WWW.BLOOMSBURY.COM/RICHARDPRICE

BLOOMSBURY